HKac

D1567734

Tales of the Magatama

Mirror Sword and Shadow Prince

Tales of the Magatama

Mirror Sword and Shadow Prince

Noriko Ogiwara

Illustrations by Miho Satake

Translated by Cathy Hirano

HAIKASORU

SAN FRANCISCO

HAKUCHO IDEN
Copyright © 1991, 1996, 2005 by Noriko OGIWARA

Original edition published in Japan in 1996 under the title
"Hakucho Iden" by Tokuma Shoten Publishing Co., Ltd.
Published in arrangement with Tokuma Shoten Publishing
Co., Ltd. through Japan Uni Agency, Inc.

Illustrations copyright © 2005, 2011 by Miho Satake

English translation © 2011 VIZ Media, LLC

HAIKASORU
Published by
VIZ Media, LLC
295 Bay Street
San Francisco, CA 94133

www.haikasoru.com

Library of Congress Cataloging-In-Publication data has been applied for.

Ogiwara, Norijo, 1959-

[Hakucho Iden. English]

Mirror sword and shadow prince/Noriko Ogiwara ; translated by Cathy
Hirano ; [illustrations by Miho Satake]

Library of Congress Control Number: 2011925637

The rights of the author of the work in this publication to be so identified
have been asserted in accordance with the Copyright, Designs and Patents
Act 1988. A CIP catalogue record for this book is available from the British
Library.

Printed in the U.S.A.
First printing, May 2011

Mirror Sword and Shadow Prince

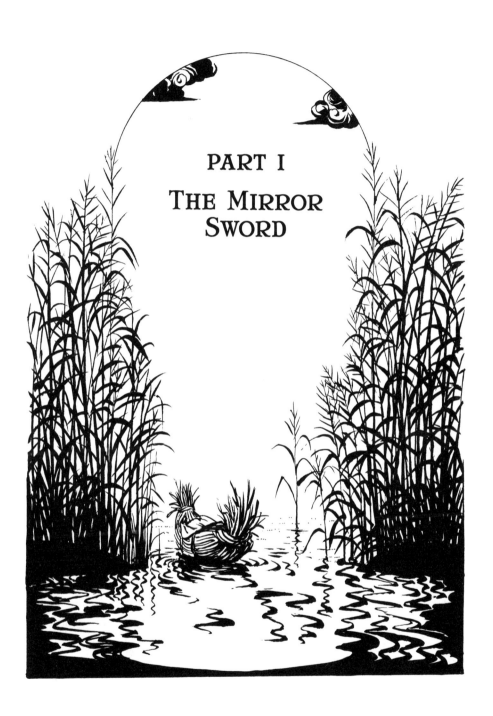

PART I
THE MIRROR SWORD

Oh, Sword that I left by my beloved's bed,
If only I had you now.

—Kojiki

chapter
one

THE
PROMISE

The Promise

Toko had mastered the perfect pout. Cheeks puffed out, mouth turned down, her face held not a trace of charm. The effect was all the more striking because she was decked out in her finest outfit, one worn only at this special time of year. It was a new crimson robe with a bright green sash and a bow of colored string tying up her hair. It was Toko's nature to laugh hard when happy and cry hard when sad, and therefore, she would never live up to the standards of her nurse, Tatame.

"Sulking won't make any difference," the exasperated Tatame said. "You're twelve years old. You should know that by now. Whether you like it or not, no means no! Oguna can't go with you to the shrine."

Toko lifted her chin defiantly. "But that's not what I'm saying. What I said was, if Oguna can't go to the shrine, then from now on I won't go either."

"Will you please listen—"

Light footsteps sounded in the corridor outside, and Toko's mother, Matono, appeared in the doorway, a long silk scarf trailing down from her shoulders. "Really, Toko! Hurry up! We're leaving. The chief and his family are almost here."

Although Toko faltered briefly at the sight of her mother, her stubborn expression did not budge. "Mother, why can't Oguna go to the shrine with us? He's part of our family too, right? That's what you and father always say, so why isn't he allowed to see the high priestess? It's not fair. It doesn't make any sense."

Matono and Tatame glanced meaningfully at each other.

"I want you to treat Oguna the same way you treat me," Toko continued.

"You've always said that he's your son, and this year I'm going to stay home to prove it."

"Toko, New Year's with the high priestess—the Keeper of the Sacred Shrine— is the most important event of the year for the Tachibana clan. You belong to the Mino chief's line, and therefore you cannot neglect this duty."

"But, Mother—"

"Toko, please sit down." Matono crossed the room and knelt purposefully in front of her daughter. It was time to make things clear, she thought. Toko was no longer a child to be humored. "Oguna is not a member of our clan. I'm sure you know that as we've made no secret of it. The blood of the Tachibana does not run in his veins."

Toko's lips began to tremble. "But, Mother, you said—"

"Oguna is part of our family. Both your father and I love him as our son. But that's not what I'm talking about. Those born into the chief's clan have a heavy responsibility—they must protect the land of Mino. The two of you are different. You're a girl and a Tachibana, born to receive and pass on the power of the high priestess. It's about time you understood that. Oguna will never bear the duty of Tachibana blood."

"What duty?"

"You'll know soon enough. When you become a woman." Matono sighed. She wanted to let her daughter enjoy the innocence of childhood for as long as possible. "Right now your duty is to go to the shrine. And I won't take no for an answer. If you understand, then hurry up and put your shoes on. Your father is already outside waiting."

When Toko's mother spoke firmly, she was even more formidable than Toko's father. Matono was, after all, the high priestess's niece. Toko had no choice but to obey. "All right," she said reluctantly. Standing up, she hurried from the room, her long sleeves fluttering.

Her mother frowned as she watched her go. The fact that Toko could not open her mouth without mentioning Oguna nor part with him for even a day did not bode well for the future.

OGUNA HAD BEEN pacing about in the darkness of a connecting passageway, afraid to enter the room where the women debated, yet unable to leave. It was late at night and torches crackled and popped loudly in the cold, clear air. He could hear the jingling of harnesses and the cheerful voices of men being served *sake* in the brightly lit front yard. It was the same every New Year's Eve.

Oguna had not expressed any desire to join the procession. He hated conflict or pushing to get his own way, and he would have done anything to avoid causing trouble, especially in this house. But Toko was his complete opposite. She was like the whirl of a storm; Oguna often felt his job was to keep her out of trouble. Whenever Toko, convinced that she must stand up for her reserved foster brother, took it upon herself to be Oguna's advocate, troubles such as this arose. By the time Toko came out of the room, Oguna was beside himself. He rushed over to greet her, immensely relieved despite the disappointment that clouded her face.

The two were identical in height and build and even in the length of their hair, resembling a pair of emperor and empress dolls made from the same mold. Only the color of their clothes distinguished them as boy and girl. No one who saw their faces, however, would mistake them for twins. Toko had the lively eyebrows and oval face characteristic of her clan, whereas nobody in this part of the country resembled Oguna.

"It's no use," Toko said, crestfallen.

Oguna peered into her face. "What did you expect? Even among your own clan, only the chief's line is allowed to go to the shrine. And besides, why would I want to go and meet someone as scary as the high priestess? I'd much rather stay behind."

"Don't be stupid!" Toko snapped so forcefully that the bow in her hair wobbled. "Grown-ups are so unfair. They say they're going to treat us equally, but they only do it when it's convenient, like when they want to punish us. If someone says they're going to do something, they should do it. Don't you think so?"

"If they were hiding the fact that I'm adopted, then I guess it would be unfair," he said, sounding indifferent. "But they aren't. I'm a foundling and that's just the way it is."

Toko frowned. "But every year on this day, you start thinking about that, right? I know you. When I'm up on the mountain with Mother and Father, you're down here wondering where your real mother is. I can't stand that."

"No, I don't. Not really," Oguna protested without conviction.

"You know what I think? I think that you'd feel much better if you just knew who your parents were. On New Year's Day, the high priestess reads our fortunes. She interprets our dreams, tells our horoscopes. Sometimes she burns bones and speaks in oracles. I'm sure if you asked her, she could even tell you about your birth. It makes me so mad that you can't go."

Oguna let out a laugh. "How could I possibly ask her? Only clansmen are allowed to meet her. Toko, you're not making any sense."

"Who cares if I'm not making sense!" she retorted with very Toko-like logic.

"It doesn't really matter anyway," Oguna said cheerfully. "Because as far as I'm concerned Matono is my one and only mother. And I'm not lying. I really mean that. After all, she's the one who nursed me as a baby. Besides, I was probably born from a bird anyway."

It was a long-standing joke in their family that Oguna had hatched from an egg found in a birds' nest that came floating down the river. Toko's expression relaxed.

"As long as you feel that way, I guess it's okay. Don't forget what you just said though."

"Off you go to the shrine. I'll go to the chief's hall and wait for you there, just like I did last year. I hear they've got some engineers up from the capital to build a dam and make a pond. It's a big project. I've been wanting to go and take a look."

Oguna was fascinated with construction of any kind, although it was still with a boy's innocent absorption. If he heard that a house was being built or any other project was under way he always went to watch. Toko, who just had to do whatever Oguna did, responded eagerly. "I want to go too. Let's go together when I come back from the shrine. Don't you dare go without me, okay?"

"All right, all right," Oguna said. It did not even occur to him to disobey. This was the affinity that always kept them together.

ONETSUHIKO, the village headman, was already mounted at the front of the procession, which stood ready to depart, torches in hand. "Aha! Here comes my little princess, all dressed in her finest," he bellowed when he saw Toko come out of the hall. "Let's see your finery. Come show your father, now. Ah, yes. Beautiful, beautiful. What do you say, Toko? How about riding with me?"

Toko haughtily ignored her father's teasing remarks and walked over to her own horse. Her father, who doted on his only daughter, was the one person still unaware that she had begun to treat him with a hint of disdain. "Well, that wasn't very friendly. Why on earth is she so huffy today?" he asked his wife.

"She was insisting that if Oguna couldn't come to the shrine, she wouldn't go either."

"I suppose that makes sense from a child's point of view. But we'd better hurry. We don't want to keep the chief waiting." He gave the order to depart, and the attendants began to lead the horses as they set off into the night. It was a moonless New Year's Eve, and torchbearers walked in front while the ranks of men sang in low voices. Matono spoke to her husband, who rode alongside her.

"Perhaps it's about time we started thinking of Oguna's future. I thought it was still a long way off, but those two, they've turned twelve already."

"Twelve? Hmm. But they're still children."

"That's true now, but children always grow up much quicker than their parents expect."

"I suppose you're right. Oguna . . . " The boy had not made much of an impression on the headman of Kamitsusato. He was like a shadow, always there whenever Toko stirred up mischief but never causing any trouble on his own. This ran contrary to the headman's expectations of what boys should be like. "I don't think he's suited to being a warrior. He's too quiet. Maybe he should study under a scholar."

"That's an idea," Matono agreed and then added with feeling, "He's a good boy. I love him as if I had given birth to him myself. Even when he was a baby, before he had ever been scolded, he never made a fuss, as if he already knew his station in life. He has such intelligent, stoic eyes . . . That's why I want him to be happy. I don't want him to end up on the bottom, always having to obey others' orders. But I can't see him escaping that fate if he stays here. I wonder if we could send him to the capital."

"There've been a lot of people from the capital in the chief's village recently. Perhaps the chief can use his influence to help Oguna. I'll ask."

Matono pictured how Toko would rant and wail if she heard that Oguna was to be sent away. The thought of it was beyond her imagination. She smiled sadly. "Yes, it hurts me to think of separating those two, but in the end it will be much better for them both. Now they're like puppies playing, but in a few years that won't be the case. When Toko learns that Tachibana women are not free to love whom they will . . . if she already loves someone, it will cut her more deeply than any knife."

She stopped abruptly and glanced furtively at her husband, wondering how he had taken this last statement. She had touched on a rather delicate subject. But Onetsuhiko was preoccupied with the political problems between the emperor in the capital and Mino, and he answered absently, the way he always did. "Yes, yes, it's just as you say."

Matono suppressed her irritation with a sigh and vowed not speak to her husband for some time.

THE TACHIBANA WERE a matrilineal clan that revolved around the high priestess, guardian of the land. So it had been since long ago, before the youngest son of the God of Light had founded the emperor's line and ruled over the land of Toyoashihara from Mahoroba. Although Chief Kamubonehiko was named ruler of Mino in the registrar in the capital, he had married into this position and it was his daughter who held the right to succession.

The true ruler of Mino was, and had always been, the high priestess who served the guardian deity enshrined on the mountain. But because she must abide with the god, listen for his voice and convey his messages, she never left the forest shrine, and few people were permitted to meet her. New Year's was the one time when she revealed herself to a large group of people. The prophecies she made at this ceremony were the most important guidelines for the coming year.

The procession from Kamitsusato joined that of the chief, forming a long line that wound up the mountain road to the northeast. Though no snow lay on the ground, it was a night to freeze even the stars in the cloudless vault above, and the pilgrims' breath rose white in the darkness as they moved slowly up the hill, the red flames of their torches floating along the road. To Toko, the black shadows of the trees looming in the torchlight and the men's ghostly faces appeared even more surreal in the taut, cold air. Praying that they would reach the shrine soon, her thoughts wandered to the high priestess.

Toko saw her only on New Year's Eve, and thus the priestess seemed imprisoned forever in the freezing winter at the edge of night, divorced from ordinary life. Though human in form, Toko was convinced she must be a frost spirit, for when the procession finally reached its destination at the end of the long journey, the shrine was not at all warm and there was barely a trace of fire to heat it.

As always, the high priestess sat on a raised platform flanked by two younger, but still middle-aged, handmaidens. Though petite, her long, shining white hair enveloped her like a robe of light so that she seemed larger than life. It was her hair that made Toko think of frost. As it had been white for at least as long as Toko could remember, the high priestess must have been extremely old. When she chanted prayers, her monotonous voice resonated like the wind in a hollow tree or a stone cavern. Watching the priestess, Toko suddenly felt chilled and uneasy.

If Oguna had been with her, they could have poked one another surreptitiously, but she had not even that for consolation. Toko looked around at her relatives as they sat listening meekly, and her eyes came to rest upon the eldest daughter of the chief's family, Lady Akaru. Her beautiful eyes were cast down, one cheek lit by the glow of a torch and her long black hair cascading over a lustrous red robe. Almost seventeen, her beauty was unparalleled even amongst her own kin, and Toko, who was usually indifferent to appearances, was irresistibly drawn to her.

She's grown even more beautiful, Toko thought. But although Akaru was the most stunning woman in Mino, it was not for her looks but for her kind and gentle nature that Toko loved her. Neither piercing nor cold, her beauty seemed to emanate from the purity of her heart, fragrant and sweet like a flower that made people smile just to look at. No matter how she tried, Toko knew she could never mimic the grace of Lady Akaru's most casual gesture.

Toko's stare was so intent that the young woman glanced up in surprise. When she realized it was Toko, she did not scowl but returned her gaze with smiling eyes that seemed to say, *Be patient. It's almost sunrise.* Toko looked down and suppressed a smile. *That's why I love her so much,* she thought.

At last, the day began to dawn. The scattered clouds above her head remained dark and the stars still glittered, but far beyond the eastern mountains the horizon began to glow, as if there lay a land of delight beyond hand's reach that she could faintly glimpse from the darkness in which she stood. She thought it must stay that way forever, but after a certain moment, the sky began to lighten and the sun pushed through the clouds, tossed into the air like a ball of molten gold, the fruit of heaven. The assembly watched reverently as the light poured over them and then looked at one another and laughed with delight.

Like every other year, drowsiness overtook Toko as soon as they welcomed the year's first sunrise. The *amazake,* a thick beverage of fermented rice served to warm them, only made it worse. By the time they were ushered into the hall to hear the high priestess's prophesies, Toko was barely conscious of what was happening and stumbled blindly after her parents. How long she remained oblivious she did not remember, but when she suddenly came to herself and sat up properly, the chief had already finished his audience and Lady Akaru was sitting by the high priestess before the bone-burning kiln. Her mother and father were both listening intently, holding their breath so as not to miss a word. *What's going on?* Toko wondered.

The high priestess spoke in her windy voice. "... And one more thing. Tell me of your dreams. Has there been anything in your dreams recently that troubled you?"

Lady Akaru was silent for a moment and then nodded. "Yes. I had a dream that was so clear it is hard to forget. I was facing west and looking at the sun when a large bird, white and shining, appeared in the middle of it and flew straight toward me. It flew down and landed on my lap. Then I woke up. What does this mean?"

Fingering the deer bones in her hand, the high priestess announced abruptly, "It is fate. You have received a sign." Startled, the chief half rose. The priestess looked at him and continued. "The emperor in Mahoroba desires to take this maiden as his wife. No doubt he will soon send his official messenger. She is fated to wed the descendant of the God of Light. You must be prepared. Do not spurn this duty, for this is destiny."

Confusion swept through the clansmen and whispers rose. Lady Akaru flushed as pink as a peach blossom but said not a word. Instead, the chief, clearly upset, exclaimed, "But she's my eldest daughter. As such, she bears a heavy responsibility. She's needed in Mino. Are you sure this is the right thing to do? Besides, if we are tied to the emperor through marriage bonds, Mahoroba would be free to intervene in the rule of Mino."

"We have a duty much greater than protecting Mino," the priestess said calmly. "The whole purpose of the Tachibana clan's existence has been and will continue to be the protection of the emperor's line, the descendants of the God of Light. We ourselves are descended from the people of Darkness, the same clan to which the Water Maiden belonged, she who married the last-born son of the God of Light so long ago. Like the Water Maiden, our task is to still the raging blood of the God of Light, the violence of the heavens that still runs in his descendants' veins, the fury which renders it impossible for their souls to set down roots."

"Set down roots? What do you mean?" the chief asked.

"Surely their actions make that obvious," the high priestess said curtly. "They can never be content no matter where they are. They build a capital only to destroy it and build another. They are constantly driven to conquer new lands, and they don't know how to stop. No matter where they go in Toyoashihara, they will never find peace, yet they remain oblivious of that fact. It's the blood of the Light. It will take centuries to still their violent nature so that they can plant their feet firmly on the ground. That is why we are here. Lady Akaru, " she said gently, "you understand, don't you? The duty you must bear is even heavier than that of the Keeper of the Shrine."

Lady Akaru had been listening with her eyes wide but she nodded her head once, slowly and deliberately.

AFTER TWO OR THREE predictions concerning the crop for the coming year, people paid their respects to the high priestess and left the shrine one by one. Though no one said so, they were all eager to leave. Their minds were still reeling from the revelation of Lady Akaru's fate, and all were impatient to go where they could talk freely.

Toko too was surprised. Although she had not understood all of it, she knew that the priestess's pronouncement had far exceeded the expectations of her parents or anyone else. Having been born in the home of the village headman, political discussions reached Toko's ears even while she played.

She had frequently heard the emperor in the capital mentioned, and while some referred to him as a ferocious hawk, she had never heard anyone say before that he was in need of protection as though he were a mere baby in diapers. Nor had she ever heard of any duty "heavier than that of the Keeper of the Shrine."

The high priestess is quite something, Toko thought, naively impressed. *Why, she must be even greater than the emperor himself, and he's descended from the God of Light. How I wish Oguna could have been there . . .* No sooner had the thought passed through her mind than she turned about-face and ran back into the shrine, in the opposite direction of everyone else. The high priestess was rising slowly with the frailty of an old woman. Leaning on her two attendants, she turned toward the inner recesses of the building.

"Keeper of the Shrine," Toko called out.

The high priestess turned to look at the crimson-robed girl with shining eyes who stood dauntlessly before her. Her eyes narrowed. "You're Matono's daughter . . . Toko, is it? The ceremony is over. What do you want?"

Toko had never spoken to the high priestess directly before. Face to face, she did indeed seem not quite human, but gathering her courage, Toko said firmly, "I have come to beg a favor. Would you please permit Oguna to come to the shrine next year? Would you please make him a member of our clan?"

"Oguna? A boy, I take it?"

"He's my brother. We were raised together. We're the same age . . . but Oguna is smarter than me. Just a little."

"I see. And how old are you?"

"Twelve."

At this point, Matono came rushing into the room. "Toko!" She pushed Toko behind her and apologized profusely. "Please pardon the child's impudence. I hope she didn't say anything to displease you."

The high priestess, however, did not seem in the least perturbed. She said slowly, "How quickly the time passes. I did not realize your daughter had already grown so much. But of whom was she speaking?"

Matono flushed slightly. "We have an adopted child. Didn't I tell you about him?"

"No, I hadn't heard. And what is his parentage? I'd be surprised to hear that any Tachibana home had so few children they needed to adopt."

Matono's blush deepened. "Actually, I don't know who his parents are. I found him floating down Yasuno River when I went there with my maidservant. It was soon after I had given birth to Toko."

"Floating down the river? A baby?"

"He was in a little vessel made of reeds. He must have been abandoned somewhere upstream. I felt so sorry for him . . ."

The high priestess looked unimpressed. "I thought you had more sense than that. You should at least have consulted me about this. Why on earth would you take in a child that you did not even know? You could have found any number of foster parents."

Matono remained silent a moment. Then, raising her head, she said, "I nursed him at my breast. It was the fifteenth day after Toko's birth and the first time I went outside. I had gone to the river to cut some grasses when I heard a baby crying, so faint that at first I thought I was hearing things. And my breasts suddenly swelled with milk . . . When I found him, I let him drink. He was so weak with hunger he looked like he would die. How could I abandon a child whom I had nursed at my own breast? I had a wet nurse for Toko, so I decided to take him home."

"He has strong luck," the high priestess said, lost in thought. "He was in a small boat made of reeds, was he?"

"I don't know who his real parents are, but I've never regretted raising him. As Toko said, he's very intelligent."

Toko stood looking from one woman to the other, waiting impatiently to see how their discussion would end. Finally, the high priestess said, "Matono, I want to see this boy's face. Next time you come, bring him with you."

Inwardly, Toko shouted, *Hooray!* concluding that the high priestess just might be human after all. When they got outside, she whispered proudly to her mother, "We did it! It shows it's worth trying to explain, doesn't it?"

"I can't believe you did that! Really!" her mother fumed.

"What have you two been up to? What took you so long?" Onetsuhiko had come looking for them, puzzled by their absence.

"That Toko! She had the nerve to ask the high priestess herself to let Oguna come to the shrine. Honestly! She put me in such an awkward position. She hasn't a clue what's going on, yet she dares to do something so rash."

"Father, guess what? The high priestess said we should bring Oguna next year!"

"Well, well."

Matono continued her lament. "Why can't you behave and stay out of trouble? Especially now when the eldest daughter of the head family has just been told her fate and the situation is so serious. Weren't you even listening?"

"Of course I was listening," Toko answered, hopping along from one foot to the other. "But Oguna is just as important, isn't he?"

"That's exactly what I meant. You don't understand a thing. If Lady Akaru doesn't stay here and become the heir to the Tachibana clan or take the place of the high priestess, then that fate must fall to Lady Akaru's younger sister or to you. You might even have to become the high priestess. And we won't know until it happens."

Toko stopped, dumbfounded. "Me . . . ?"

Matono said, "You will both have to go to the shrine to be trained. After all, the high priestess is very old. Her successor will have to come from your generation."

2

OGUNA LOOKED at the sun through the trees in the winter grove. Clouds had appeared during the afternoon and the sun shone a wintry yellow against branches that protruded like bare bones. He wandered aimlessly through the woods behind the chief's hall. Relatives already filled the hall, warming themselves by the charcoal fires and renewing old bonds while awaiting the master of the house. Among them, however, was a group of youths who were invariably nasty to Oguna when they saw him. As long as there were no witnesses, they would not hesitate to bully him. Preferring to be alone, he had gone around the back rather than enter the building.

Oguna knew what made him an easy target. He was different. He was small, he was quiet, and Toko always stood up for him. There were many reasons for Oguna's very existence to irritate those less fortunate than he, though he was at the bottom of the Tachibana social ladder. And because he understood, it did not really bother him. He accepted it as part of his situation. Oguna knew the faces of those most likely to torment him, and as long as he managed to keep out of their way, he did not suffer much.

The violence of this particular group of boys, however, had escalated over the years so that even Oguna could no longer brush it off. No matter how hard he thought about it, he could not understand why they hated him so intensely. Oguna had yet to realize that with each passing year he became increasingly conspicuous, fanning the flame of their envy.

The chief's procession would stop midway down the mountain for a rest and return to the hall before evening. Oguna tried to gauge the passage of time, and when he thought that people would be lining up outside the gate to greet the returning procession, he turned his steps in the direction of the hall. He was still among the trees, however, when he glimpsed someone's shadow. As he turned toward it, a mocking voice rang out.

"Hah! Look at the little coward hiding in the woods. Come on, guys! Let's get him!"

Oguna began to run, hoping to break out of the forest as fast as he could. But it was no use. One of the youths had run ahead and blocked his way. Oguna bit his lip. Four pimply young men confronted him; they were the same familiar faces, rebels that even the chief found hard to control. This was far worse than if they had caught him in the chieftain's hall. Here there was no one to question their behavior. Gloating, they advanced toward him like hunters who had cornered a deer. Their skin was flushed and their eyes were glazed from drinking sake all morning.

"What's your hurry now? Why are you running away? We're inviting you to spend a little time with us. What's the matter? Do you think you're too good for us? A foundling like you! Don't be such an arrogant brat!"

They jabbed at him and pushed him, surrounding him on all sides so that he could not back away. At first, Oguna was merely anxious. He knew he was in serious trouble. But when he saw how they enjoyed his predicament, his anger rose. "Are you sure you want to do this?" he said, his voice stern. "The procession will be back any minute."

"Shut up! Can you believe this squirt? He's helpless without Toko, always hiding behind her skirt. You can't tell which one's a girl!"

"Sure you can. He's the girl. Just look at his face." Their shrill laughter rang through the quiet wood. "Hey there, little girl, serve us sake. Come on now, bat those eyelashes and pour us a drink."

Oguna remained silent, and one of them grabbed him by the collar and pulled him close. "Don't underestimate us. Some who've crossed us didn't make it home in one piece."

Oguna was not afraid of being hit. At least he thought he wasn't, so he said, "If you want to hit me, go ahead. But don't blame me if you get in trouble for punching someone on New Year's Day."

"Listen to the brat!"

"We'd better teach him that there's some things a coward should never say."

Oguna's calm fanned their fury, and they let him know with their fists and feet. He felt his lip split open. That was bearable, but a hard kick in the stomach left him gasping on the ground in a pile of dead leaves, unable to rise.

"He's not even fit to be a girl," one of them jeered. It was Oshikuma, the cruelest of the four and their ringleader. "Here, I'll show you. Watch this." He put his hand in a pouch tied at his waist. Pulling out something long and black, he grabbed Oguna by the hair and shoved it in his face. Instantly, Oguna began to scream.

It was a snake. Oshikuma had gone to great lengths to dig one out of hibernation. Though small and so stiff with cold it barely moved, it was enough to make Oguna forget everything else. Swinging the snake by the tail, Oshikuma struck him repeatedly, laughing uproariously when Oguna cowered and hid his head in his hands.

"You see! Look at that! Even a girl wouldn't be so scared!"

For as long as he could remember, Oguna had been terrified of snakes. He trembled at the mere sight of one and had once even fainted at the touch, so that the nurse Tatame had mistakenly thought him ill. There was one other thing he could not stand: lightning. Snakes and lightning—for fearing these two commonplace things he was branded a coward, though he feared little else.

Now he was completely helpless. Neither pride nor appearances mattered anymore. He sobbed and begged Oshikuma to stop. "I'll do anything you want!" he cried.

Oshikuma's mouth twisted into a cruel grin as he stopped twirling the snake.

"I heard that. You said anything, right? You'd better keep your word and do what I say. I want you to . . . " What he said was so disgusting that the blood drained from Oguna's face and then flooded back again.

At that moment, a high-pitched voice, burning with rage, rang through the forest. "You there! I know your faces and your names! I'm going to tell my uncle everything. How dare you stoop so low, especially on New Year's Day!"

Toko stood on the bank looking down into the forest, her bright crimson robe vivid against the gray clump of trees. Her gaze was so fierce and her tone so forceful it was hard for the young men to believe she was just a twelve-year-old girl. Oguna's tormentors froze, rooted to the spot. "Why don't you get lost?" Toko continued. "Or do you really want me to tell my uncle? You'll be sorry then. Listen carefully. Don't ever lay a finger on Oguna again, you understand? Unless you wish to be banished from this clan forever."

They swore at her under their breath, but they could not defy Toko. While she might sound like a bossy little girl, as the high priestess's niece, her words carried weight.

"Hah! What a joke! He's such a baby he has to be rescued by a girl," Oshikuma spat as a parting shot. He smacked the snake against the ground. They sulked off looking somewhat deflated.

Toko glared after them until they were out of sight and then flew down the bank to Oguna's side. "Are you all right? Can you stand up?"

"The snake . . . could you move it?" he said faintly.

"Honestly! Where did they get this?" She picked up the snake distastefully and threw it into the bushes, then rubbed her hand against the trunk of a tree.

As soon as it was gone, Oguna perked up. "Thanks! I'm so glad you came." He stood up and began dusting the dirt from his knees.

"Your mouth, it's bleeding."

"It doesn't hurt," he said, licking the blood from his lips.

"You'd better put a cold cloth on it or it might swell up."

"Really, it's all right. Besides, I was hoping you'd get home while it was still light. Let's go to the pond and see the construction site like we planned."

"Oguna! You're unbelievable!" Toko said. "How can you get over that so easily? I'm still furious! I'll never forget how mad they made me. If I hadn't come, what would have happened to you?"

Oguna shrugged his shoulders. "Don't worry about it. Nothing really happened."

"How can I not worry about it? They were so awful, and what he said to you was disgusting. Doesn't it make you mad? It should!"

"Well, yes, it does, but . . ." he muttered doubtfully. "It's my own fault that I'm afraid of snakes . . ."

Toko stamped her foot. "Honestly! That's exactly why I can't leave you alone for a minute without worrying. But what am I to do? I won't be here forever . . ." She broke off suddenly. Oguna blinked and waited for her to go on, but she said nothing. In the sudden silence, they heard a servant calling Toko's name from the direction of the hall. Toko had rushed off in search of Oguna the instant she had dismounted from her horse.

She turned away abruptly, grabbed Oguna's hand, and began walking away from the hall. "Let's go see that pond. I just can't go back there and greet everyone cheerfully right now."

TOKO PLOWED BLINDLY into the forest, pulling Oguna along behind her. Oguna shook his head, bewildered, but followed without protest. When he noticed that her cheeks were wet with tears, however, he could not keep quiet. She had never cried silently before.

"Toko, what's wrong? You're acting strange today, very strange."

She did not answer nor did she wipe away her tears.

"Are you mad at me?"

Toko shook her head. Then, as if a dam had burst, she suddenly began to talk. "If only we didn't have to grow up. If only we could stay the way we are now forever. But you're a boy so you'll probably grow much taller than me, and one day I'll turn into a woman. At least, that's what Mother says. I don't get it. One day, just like that. Then who am I right now? I thought I was a woman. That's why I put up with all the things they said. 'You can't do this because you're a girl.' 'You shouldn't do that because you're a girl.' So what were they talking about? Was it all lies? How am I supposed to become more of a woman than I am already? Do you know, Oguna?"

Oguna answered truthfully that no, he didn't.

"And that's not all. When I become a woman I'll have to live in the shrine on the mountain and be trained. So we hardly have any time left to be together. That's what Mother told me today."

"You mean you're going to become a priestess?" Oguna looked at her incredulously and then added timidly, "You?"

"I don't want to go to the shrine. It's so cold and lonely. And if I'm not here, you'll be picked on all the time." Her tearful voice broke into sobs. Oguna did not know how to comfort her.

"Don't cry, Toko, please. It's New Year's. And besides, if you cry, you can't see where you're going and you might get hurt—" Toko almost ran into a pine tree, stumbled over a root, and finally stopped in her tracks. Oguna stopped and took her by the shoulders, turning her to face him. "I don't think that I'm picked on that much. No matter where I go, there will always be people who like to pick on someone weaker than them. There's no point in worrying about it. They don't bother me at all, those guys."

"But I don't want you to be a weakling. When people make fun of you, it's like they're making fun of me. I can't forgive someone who does that, but when I try to stop them, they use that against you too, saying that you need a girl to rescue you."

Oguna seemed uncertain. "Do you want me to hurt them back?"

"I don't care about them. I just think that if only you were strong enough, they wouldn't dare hurt you, and then I wouldn't have to worry about you."

Oguna pondered this for a moment. Then he said decisively, "If you're that worried about me, I'll find a way to become stronger. You know, I don't think I'm a coward. I'm not afraid of those guys and there aren't many other things I'm afraid of either. Just snakes and lightning."

"But there are snakes everywhere, and lightning too."

"That's true . . ."

"Oh!" Toko sighed and then blew her nose in exasperation.

WHEN THEY HAD WALKED for a while, the trees began to thin and they saw water glittering ahead. The newly finished pond was full. Toko, who was still at the fortunate age when the slightest thing could change her mood, brightened immediately. The valley they both remembered with the brook running through it was gone, having been replaced by a large expanse of water. The ripples on the pond's deep green surface, gilded by the rays of the westerly sun, shimmered like golden fish scales. The transformation was stunning, as if the engineers from the capital had bent nature to their will.

Oguna and Toko ran about the bank, crying out in wonder. As long as Toko was happy again, there was no reason for Oguna to be gloomy. "Look!" he said. "They've dammed the water downstream. Let's go see."

As they walked along the bank, the construction site came into view. A massive structure of logs and stones blocked the flow of water, and they could see a thick mud wall and the beginnings of a sluice gate on the dry side. Oguna, who had never seen a project of this scale before, was deeply impressed. It was New Year's Day and there was not a worker in sight. Taking advantage of this, the children climbed up the scaffolding and admired the dam to their heart's content.

Toko was suddenly overcome with a hunger for mischief. She pointed to the log posts that held the stones in place. "If we walked along the top of those, we could easily get to the other side," she said.

"Walk on those?" Oguna said, unenthusiastic. The posts were driven at intervals about one step apart. On one side of the dam, the surface of the water was close, but on the other side, there was a long drop down and the bottom was covered in boulders.

"I hear that the emperor has ordered a villa to be built on the other side. Really! What's to become of Mino, I wonder. Don't you want to take a look?"

If Oguna had been a dog, his ears would have pricked up. "A villa?"

"What's the matter? Are you afraid? I thought you said you weren't afraid of anything but snakes and lightning." The grin on Toko's face as she said this made it impossible for him to back down.

"Who said I was afraid? I'm just worried about you, that's all."

Toko laughed out loud. "Well, I'm even less afraid than you. Snakes and lightning don't bother me a bit."

"Let's see you prove it then!"

They were in the mood to do something reckless. The best way to forget their troubles was to take a little risk and laugh their sorrow away. Toko went first, and they began to cross, suppressing their giggles.

It was not difficult for a light-footed daredevil like Toko to walk along the tops of the posts. She had navigated much higher and narrower places before. But the rays of the sun where they pierced the clouds low in the west shone directly in her face, and she blinked repeatedly. A white bird suddenly appeared at the edge of her vision. Wanting to show Oguna how unafraid she was, she said, "Look at that big bird. Do you think it's a swan?"

"It looks like it. I wonder why it's all alone. Do you think it got separated from its flock?" Oguna said.

I was facing west and looking at the sun when a large bird, white and shining, appeared in the middle of it and flew straight toward me.

These words leapt unbidden into Toko's mind, and she started in surprise. She had heard them before, but where? Then she remembered Lady Akaru's dream and went numb with shock. *What can it mean? This is the same thing she saw. Am I caught in her dream? That can't be. But then... why do I feel so strange?* She did not understand what she saw or felt. She only knew that the white bird flying toward her filled her with dread.

It was an ill omen.

Her mind reeled, her eyes went dark, and she staggered. But she had not yet reached the other side of the dam.

"Toko! Look out!" Oguna's voice brought her back to her senses and she managed to pull herself upright. Relieved that she had not fallen onto the rocks, she fell instead into the pond with a loud splash. This, however, was not much better. The water was so cold it froze her lungs and she thought she would never breathe again. Cramped with cold, her body refused to obey her. Although she was a good swimmer, Toko knew that she was in serious trouble. Someone grabbed her collar and struggled to pull her toward the shore. It was Oguna, of course. It was nice of him to share her misery, but then who, she wondered gloomily, would pull the two of them from the pond?

But there was another helping hand after all. An arm reached out and plucked her lightly from the water, as if she weighed not a feather despite her soaked clothing. She lay curled up on the ground, racked with coughs. Between each cough she could hear someone loudly berating her.

"What the hell do you think you're doing? How dare you play on the dam we worked so hard to build! This is no place for a lover's tryst. And absolutely not for double suicide. Besides, you're ten years too young anyway. It would have served you right to drown, you little brats!"

From his accent, she knew instantly that her rescuer must be from the capital.

Pushing her clinging hair out of her eyes, she looked up and saw a tall, slim young man whose face was mostly covered by an odd-looking hood. He was now hauling Oguna out of the water, scolding him all the while.

"What are you? Stupid? What good was it to jump into the pond after her? Don't you even know what to do when someone falls in? Throw them something to grab on to and then go get help, idiot!"

Oguna tried to respond, but his teeth chattered so violently his words were unintelligible. The hooded man clucked his tongue. "I suppose you two had better come with me before you turn into icicles. I'll let you warm up by the fire, but that's all, you hear? Honestly! Who in their right mind would take a bath in the pond on a day like this? You're just lucky I happened to be here. Normally no one would bother checking the worksite on New Year's Day."

Several workers' huts stood inconspicuously in the shadow of the trees a little way from the pond. The man ushered them into one. It was a simple structure with a low ceiling and a dirt floor. The absence of any furnishings made the room quite spacious. A large hearth had been dug in the center, and the man generously heaped firewood into it so that the flames roared to life, producing a fair bit of smoke as well. He made them take off their sopping garments and wrapped them up like bagworms in clothes from the hut. Although he had said he would only let them warm themselves by the fire, he began hauling out a big pot. As she watched him move about on his long legs, Toko sensed that he was a good person at heart, despite the way he talked.

Other than the racket he was making, everything was very still and there were no other signs of life in the area. Relaxed by the warmth of the fire, Toko asked, "Isn't anyone else here?"

"It's only right to spend New Year's Day with your family, don't you think? I bet they're all at home right now enjoying a good meal," he answered.

"What about you?"

"I'm single," he said. He came over, sat down beside them, and warmed himself at the fire for a minute. Then, as if suddenly realizing he was still wearing it, the man took off his hood. His face, which they now saw clearly for the first time, was much younger than his tone of voice had led them to believe. He looked like he had only just reached manhood himself. Although he had scolded them in the lofty tones of a sensible adult, his eyes held a gleam of mischief, like someone who would be quite willing to join in their pranks. But this was not what surprised Toko most. From the moment she saw his face, she felt that she knew him. She turned to look at Oguna and then suddenly cried out excitedly.

The young man frowned. "Now what? Can't you settle down even for a minute? You'll never get married at this rate."

"But you—you look just like Oguna! I've never seen anyone like him before. Oguna! He looks like *you*!"

"No he doesn't," Oguna said in a nasal voice, his body still hunched in a ball.

But Toko was convinced. The more she looked at them, the more they resembled each other. The hairline, the eyebrows, and the shape of their chins were so similar. She could imagine Oguna looking just like this man in six or seven years when he grew up.

"Oguna, maybe you're from the capital!"

"Now wait a minute!" the young man protested. "You won't find faces like mine lying about on the street, you know. Besides, you insult me by comparing me to that snot-nosed brat." But her words must have intrigued him because he pulled back the clothes Oguna had wrapped around his head and peered at him intently.

"You see? He looks like you, doesn't he?"

After a very long pause, he said, "All right. I admit it." His voice held a note of surprise. He folded his arms across his chest. "I'd like to hear what people who knew me as a kid would say if they saw you. I have so many siblings, I've lost count, but not one of them resembles me as much as you. It's amazing. What's your name?"

"Oguna."

"Oguna? Your parents named you 'boy'? They didn't put much effort into naming you. Don't they love you?"

"How dare you say that!" Toko responded hotly. "They called him Oguna because he's the only boy in our house, and that makes him special."

"All right, all right! Don't get so mad. But you don't look like siblings. Don't you know who your parents are?"

"I'm a foundling," Oguna said.

"I see," the man said and then laughed out loud. "Very concise. I like you.

Women always babble on and on about things. But why would someone with a face like mine have been abandoned?"

"I don't know. I was found floating in a reed basket on Yasuno River. The headman of Kamitsusato took me in."

The man blinked, taken aback. "Then you're Tachibana? No wonder you were wearing such nice clothes. Well, I hope I didn't offend you earlier." But he grinned as he said this and did not appear in the least contrite.

People from the capital are so different, Toko thought. *So full of confidence.* This man seemed to do whatever he pleased without any concern for what others might think. Now he was staring at Toko, making her feel very uncomfortable, especially as he looked so much like Oguna. She had never seen Oguna scrutinize anyone so brazenly.

"Is there something wrong with my face?"

"No, no," he laughed. "It's just that Lady Akaru is rumored to be a matchless beauty. I thought perhaps you might look a little like her, seeing as you're related . . . "

"Unfortunately for you, I don't."

"Well, that's a relief. There's still some hope then."

The man actually seemed to enjoy teasing her. Incensed, Toko launched into a little tirade. "Lady Akaru is a true beauty. You only say that because you've never met her. But let's see if you dare to deny her beauty once you've seen her up close."

"I'd love to have the opportunity. But there's not much chance for an outsider to get close enough to view such a well-guarded lady."

Although Oguna had remained silent and unsmiling at first, the lively conversation between Toko and this stranger drew him in. After all, how could he ignore someone who looked like him? Hesitantly, he asked where the man was born and who his parents were.

"My father's from the capital although my mother isn't. I was born and raised in the capital."

"Does your father also build dams?"

"Not just dams. Whenever there's a big construction project, my father's in charge. I'm his heir, so I'm being given the chance to represent him. That's why I was asked to supervise construction of this dam."

"You're supervising? That's fantastic!" Oguna said, unable to conceal his awe.

The man smiled. "Do you like construction? That's good. Building is a job worth doing."

At that, Oguna smiled too. Toko realized that they looked most alike when smiling. The stranger, who seemed drawn to Oguna, said jokingly, "You really do belong in my family. Perhaps you're one of my father's illegitimate children. I wouldn't be surprised at all. He was quite popular among the ladies when he was young."

Oguna tensed and licked the cut on his lip. He had forgotten about it, but warmed by the fire, the blood circulating in his body had made his lip smart again. "You shouldn't speak about such things so lightly."

"Ah, you talk like an old sage," the young man said. Leaning forward, he took Oguna's chin in his hand and examined the cut. "You should take better care of your face if it looks like mine. I'll put some ointment on it. I've got some good stuff here."

He was just smearing a thick cream on Oguna's cut when they heard the sound of hooves galloping up to the camp. They paused, listening. Whoever it was seemed to know his way around. He walked straight toward the hut and threw the door open.

"Forgive me! I'm so sorry to be late. Were you all right? I finally—" He broke off as he entered the room, stunned to see Toko and Oguna. Even his legs froze midstride.

"Nanatsuka," the young man said with a wry smile.

"Er, who are they?"

"Some fish I hauled out of the pond a little while ago. Sorry. I'm just joking. They're Tachibana, so it won't do to treat them disrespectfully. I'm going to take them to the chieftain's hall soon. Nothing's amiss."

"Forgive me for not being here when you needed me." The man called Nanatsuka was so huge the children had to crane their necks to look up at him, and his chest was so broad it made the hood he wore appear undersized. With his tall frame stooped to avoid the low ceiling, he appeared very apologetic.

"What's this pot for?" he asked.

"Oh, I meant to heat up some sake. Would you mind doing that for me?"

"You shouldn't heat sake in this kind of pan," Nanatsuka said, as he took the pot outside.

What strange men, Toko thought. Although she had no idea what laborers were like, she did know that there was something odd about this pair.

The huge man soon returned with hot drinks made, he told them, from unrefined sake mixed with grated ginger and syrup. Toko and Oguna had never had anything that warmed them up so quickly and fiercely before. Toko's skin radiated heat so thoroughly she thought steam would start rising from it.

"Your clothes are dry now," the young man said. "It's time to take you home. I'm sure your family must be worried sick."

When they went outside, the stars were shining. The man fetched his horse, and setting both children on it, he began leading it toward the chief's hall. Although the air was cold, the children did not feel it at all. Gazing at the reflection of the stars in the pond, they chattered nonstop, their tongues loosened by the sake. When the prince mentioned that he was a good archer, Toko prattled on excitedly about the *noriyumi,* an archery tournament that would be held the next day.

"All the men in Mino who consider themselves any good with a bow practice year-round just for this event," she said. "Everyone gets involved, and it's always packed with people because of course none of the girls want to miss it either. We get to sit in a special stand with the women of the chief's household, but even that's not easy. The cheering is so loud it's enough to split your ears. Oh! And of course, the winner gets lots of gifts from the chief. Lady Akaru presents them. That's why all the archers are so set on winning."

"Ah, I see. So it's worth the effort." He laughed quietly as he led the horse by the reins.

When they reached the hall, there was some fuss, but as everyone was in the middle of New Year's celebrations and Toko and Oguna were guests as well, the only punishment they received was to be sent immediately to their room. A servant brought them their supper, and the two had no complaints about their treatment. Still, Toko would have liked to hear what the young man said to the men gathered there.

"I wonder if he told Father his name. Don't you think he's a bit strange? We talked all that time, but he never once mentioned his name."

"Maybe he didn't want to tell us." Oguna had hardly touched his food, and he now lay propped up on one elbow.

"I thought he must be your older brother, he looked so much like you. But he didn't seem to really care about that at all. I wonder if everyone in the capital is so blasé."

After a little pause, Oguna said, "You know what I think? I don't think he's an ordinary laborer at all."

"Then what is he?"

"I don't know," Oguna muttered. "I wonder why we look so much alike."

They fell silent, disturbed by a feeling for which they could find no words, a premonition that they could never return to the days that had gone before, as if some door had suddenly opened before them with the dawning of the new year. Something was going to happen. Some fate they could not avoid was drawing inexorably closer.

Unable to understand what that was, they could only wonder what made them so uneasy.

3

THE NEXT MORNING Toko and Oguna received a nasty shock. Rather than evading punishment as they had hoped, Matono ordered them to stay home all day in order to reflect on their behavior. Left behind in their room, Toko was close to tears. "It's not fair! Today's the tournament! Everyone will be there! It'll be the event of the year and we'll be completely left out of it!"

"Yeah. You're right. Everyone is bound to be there, even the servants. Everyone except us." Oguna stroked his face, something he always did when he felt a little guilty. "Which means there's no one here to make sure that we're reflecting in our room."

"Of course there isn't!" Toko snapped and then stared at him wide-eyed. "Well! I misjudged you, Oguna. You're right. Who's going to know if we happen to pop outside for just a minute while reflecting?"

"As long as we make it back without getting caught."

Toko thought it over seriously. "It's so close. I think we can manage it. But there's no way we can get out through the door downstairs. How about the roof? The ventilation hole in my aunt's house is a lot bigger than the one at home. We should be able to get through it easily."

Oguna thought for a minute and then said, "Yes. I think we can do it. But no repeats of yesterday, all right? I don't want to see you staring off into space again."

"What're you talking about?" Toko asked. After a good night's sleep, she was quite unconcerned.

"When you fell in the pond. That was really weird. What was wrong with you?"

Toko frowned. She knew there must have been some reason, but her memory of yesterday was hazy. "I can't remember. It was nothing. Don't worry, I won't make the same mistake twice."

The chief's hall was built on a plateau overlooking a large open space, so when they squeezed, soot-smudged, through the ventilation hole in the side of the roof and crawled up to the peak, they had a panoramic view of the archery field, enclosed as it was by walls of colorful fabric. Over a hundred contestants had gathered. They stood about in small groups, each man wearing a jacket in the colors of his village and grasping his favorite bow. The area roped off for spectators was jammed with people.

Originally, the noriyumi was performed by the nobility on New Year's Day, in front of the clan shrine, as a ritual prayer for a good harvest. When it became a tournament open to all, its popularity grew so that it was now the main New Year's attraction. Almost everyone in Mino attended. Though the tournament still began with a priest chanting prayers, after that it degenerated into a boisterous and unruly celebration with spectators betting on the outcome.

"Look! They've already set up the first group's target," Toko yelled, leaning forward. "There's our color! Kamitsusato green." Her tone of voice changed abruptly. "Oh! Look!"

"Don't get distracted. You'll fall," Oguna said sternly.

"I won't, so look, will you? There's the man we met yesterday."

They were too far away to distinguish the contestants' faces, but there was no mistaking the unusual hood. It was the man from the capital who had hauled them out of the pond. For some reason, he was wearing Kamitsusato green. He stood calmly, a bow in his hand. The two children lay on the roof, staring at him for a moment.

"It's him all right. But what's he doing?" Oguna said in a low voice. "He must have asked Father for permission. I bet he asked him for that jacket in return for rescuing us."

"This is going to be exciting! Let's see if he's as good an archer as he boasted. We can't miss this."

"You're right, we can't. But you'd better be careful of that one. He's got some scheme up his sleeve."

Toko looked at Oguna, slightly puzzled. "He didn't seem like a bad person to me. After all, he looks just like you."

"Personally, I wouldn't trust my face if I were you," Oguna said.

With a bit of effort they managed to slip from the roof to a nearby *keyaki* tree and down into a deserted backstreet. They reached the archery site undetected and made a large detour to avoid the chief's stand. But the public viewing ground was so packed that they could not see, even when they stood on tiptoe.

"I guess that's the only way," Toko said, pointing at the village children clinging to the branches of the surrounding trees.

Oguna shook his head. "If you climbed up there, you'd stick out like a cherry blossom in the middle of winter. We'll have to do something about our clothes if we're going to try that."

They asked some village children to switch clothes and as a result learned of a much better place for viewing the tournament: under the chief's stand. Ordinarily, this was out of bounds, but savvy children knew how to sneak underneath and stay hidden behind the banners that hung from the bottom of the stand. Toko thought this was hilarious. "So, in the end, we'll watch from the same place as always. Just a little lower down."

The tournament was still under way. The hooded man appeared to be progressing up the ranks, and more than just steadily, for he was drawing much attention in the process. Perhaps his conspicuous headgear made him stand out, but every time his arrow hit the bull's-eye, Toko noticed the roar of the crowd grow louder.

"He's good," one of the boys with them whispered excitedly. "I bet he makes it all the way to the final match. I've never seen anyone hit the mark every time like him. He's barely even aiming."

Watching him carefully, even Toko could see that he was good. Far more relaxed than any other contestant, he actually seemed to be having fun, except for the one short instant when he nocked his arrow and drew the bowstring taut. Then, his eyes were harder than ice or steel. It made her wonder what it would feel like to be the target. When the arrow found its mark, his smile was so carefree and his acceptance of the crowd's cheers so natural that he did not even seem arrogant. Toko did not take her eyes off him for an instant, and when, true to the boy's prediction, he made it to the final match, she gripped Oguna's arm impulsively.

"Do you want him to win?" Oguna asked.

"He looks so much like you, I can't help it. If you were stronger, that's what you'd be like."

The young man's opponent was about ten years older, a seasoned archer and last year's champion, yet when they stood side by side facing their targets, it was the stranger from the capital who was the more imposing. To Toko, he seemed to radiate an aura that awed everyone around him. Ignoring his opponent and the huge crowd that watched with bated breath, the man drew his bow as if he were standing alone in the forest—and won! A thunderous roar rose from the spectators.

"Now that's what you call strong, Oguna! I hope you'll be like that someday. Then no one could beat you anymore!" Toko shouted, forgetting that they were hiding under the chief's stand. But the noise from the crowd was far too loud for anyone to hear.

Then it was time for the winners to receive their prizes. When everything was ready, the best archers lined up in front of the chief's stand. No one moved to leave. They all hoped to catch a glimpse of Lady Akaru before going home. One by one the archers accepted their prizes until finally the youth, the overall winner, stepped forward, this time without his hood.

At that moment, someone in the crowd shouted, "He's got no right to the prize. He doesn't come from Mino—he's an outsider!" Toko and Oguna froze. A murmur ran through the crowd, gradually growing louder.

The young man reached the stand. Unruffled, he looked up at Lady Akaru and said cheerfully, "I am, indeed, an outsider. Therefore, let me return my prize. To stand here before you is sufficient reward."

Lady Akaru, holding the prize ready, looked slightly flustered, but with her characteristic grace she nodded and said, "Then will you tell us where you're from? I can't believe that the man who defeated the best archers in Mino could have no name. Although, now that I see your face, you remind me of a young boy I know very well."

"I too know the boy of whom you speak," he answered solemnly. "But, my lady, I do not know of anyone in Toyoashihara who resembles you. Though I have looked far and wide, I have never met any maiden as beautiful as you in all my life. I came prepared to find that rumor outshone reality, as rumors usually do, but it appears that this time, rumor failed to do justice to beauty, just as hearsay can never do justice to the fragrance of a flower or the melody of a song."

A faint blush touched her cheeks and she glanced away shyly. "I see you're skilled at flattery," she said. "And now I know where you're from. You come from the capital, don't you?"

The young man smiled and the admiration in his eyes deepened. "You're well informed. Yes, I came here all the way from the capital for one purpose only—to see you. I am Oh-usu, the firstborn son of the emperor of Mahoroba, sent to Mino on his command. He ordered me to conceal my identity and discover whether Lady Akaru lived up to her reputation. Having seen that there is no one more suited to be the emperor's wife than you, I can remove my mask and announce myself as his messenger."

"Prince Oh-usu?" Lady Akaru whispered. No one else spoke or moved.

"Let me repeat my request. I wish to take you to my father's palace in Mahoroba to be his wife. We have waited so long for someone like you."

She lowered her lashes and said, "You're a brave man. You come to Mino alone and dare to tell me this here? Are all the emperor's family so bold?"

"Depending on the time and place, yes." Then he added, "And on the person."

When the first shock had passed, pandemonium broke loose. Toko and Oguna stayed crouched under the stand, dazed, while the wave of noise broke over them.

"I'm so glad I'm not sitting up there," Oguna said. "Everyone would be staring at me."

"What a person for you to look like!"

"Yes, but at least we don't have to worry anymore. This proves that it's pure coincidence. After all, the emperor has never been to Mino."

"Yeah . . . the emperor . . . " Toko rested her chin on her knees and said gloomily, "That's disappointing. If his son is that old, the emperor must be even older than Father. And poor Akaru is going to be his bride. It's her fate, that's what the high priestess said. It doesn't pay at all to be born a woman of the Tachibana clan."

"YOU DIDN'T NEED to go to all the trouble of building an island," Lady Akaru said.

"I wanted to make a pond that was beautiful, not just useful," Prince Oh-usu responded.

"Well, it's certainly useful. I can't begin to count how many rice fields will benefit from it."

"And there'll be a beautiful view of the moon reflected on its surface from the villa we're building."

The two had left their horses and servants at one end of the pond and were strolling along the bank. Prince Oh-usu wanted to show Lady Akaru where the villa was to be built. The sun shone brightly and signs of spring were everywhere. The lilting song of the bush warblers rang like clear crystal among the trees. Butterbur plants poked their heads, green and innocent, from the soft earth.

The prince's hair was bound in loops on either side of his head and he wore his sword on his hip. The hem of Lady Akaru's pale pink silk skirt trailed along the ground, rustling the grasses along the bank. Young and beautiful, their figures provided the perfect accent to the setting, and their eyes met often with a shared delight.

"The grass is already turning green," Lady Akaru said. "And look, there's a violet."

"An early bloomer."

"No, don't pick it." She grasped his hand to stop him from plucking the flower and then drew back in confusion.

"Don't you like to receive flowers?"

"I just can't bear to see a plant carelessly plucked when it's blooming so bravely."

"Like you," the prince said with a smile. "Perhaps I should not have plucked you either. Perhaps I should have returned to the capital and told my father that you were hideously ugly, not at all like rumor claimed."

The princess raised her head. "No, you mustn't say that. It was meant to be."

"Your determination in that regard is admirable." Looking round at the pond, the prince abruptly changed the subject. "Look. That's where I plan to build the villa. It will be a palace worthy of you when visiting your homeland. I intend to build a gazebo overlooking the pond too. My father will surely honor this spot by visiting it often."

Lady Akaru smiled teasingly. "That's wonderful. But if he thinks that by picking me, Mino will fall easily into his grasp, he'll find that he's mistaken."

"Well, you certainly are surprising," the prince said. "I didn't expect to hear what even the chief hesitates to say. Perhaps you wield more power than your father. In fact, I've heard that the women of the Tachibana clan have a strange gift. Like the fragrant citrus fruit that grows in the underworld after which their clan is named, the ladies of this land reputedly have the power to grant eternal life. Is that true?"

"Where on earth did you hear such a tale? I certainly can't grant immortality," Lady Akaru said. She twirled about lightly on her feet with a laugh, setting her long skirt floating in the air. "I'm just an ordinary girl, a country maid."

"Light, wind, and water—those are the things that suit you best. This is where your beauty belongs. I should never have picked you. Not for my father."

"Please don't say that," Lady Akaru said, her eyes suddenly serious. "I knew why you'd come and that you would ask me to be the emperor's wife. I was prepared for this from the very beginning."

They looked at each other for a long moment. "Come!" the prince suddenly said. "Let's cross over to the island. The bridge isn't finished yet, but we can still get across."

The man-made isle had a small hill in the center. Yet incomplete, much of it was still bare earth and stone. The footing was precarious, and the prince took Lady Akaru by the hand. "It can't be called beautiful yet, but we'll add cherry and maple trees and other plants to enjoy in every season. It will be one of the views from the villa. Which do you like best, spring or fall?"

She did not answer his question but instead exclaimed in admiration, "You can change the scenery any way you choose. Doesn't it make you afraid?"

"What do you mean?"

"Gods inhabit the earth."

He looked at her strangely. "Really? I've never run into one myself."

"You poor thing. Have you never felt the love of the Goddess?" As she said this, she stepped on a loose stone and stumbled. The prince caught her in his arms.

"If the goddess were you, I would," he whispered and kissed her. Though brief, his kiss was fire.

There was a pause. Then Lady Akaru pushed him away, crying, "How could you! Have you forgotten your mission?"

"I won't tell my father about you. He can marry some other maiden. I can't bear to give you away to any other man. My lady, I knew from the moment I saw you that I would never find another like you. My feelings for you have only grown stronger with each passing day. Please listen to me. I'll build you a house by this pond. Let's live here together, never leaving Mino."

Tears welled in Lady Akaru's eyes. They streamed down her cheeks and spilled onto her robe. But when the prince took a step toward her, she shook her head and retreated from him. "If only we could. If only. But it's impossible. It is to the emperor's soul that I must bring peace and solace. This is my fate. You're a kind man. Even without me, the Goddess will love you and bring you happiness. Please, I beg you. Do not test me. Do not test my strength."

Turning abruptly, she ran unsteadily across the bridge and sped off along the bank without once looking back. The prince reached out his hand as she fled with her long black hair streaming behind her, but the shock was so great, he could not follow.

He sat down on the edge of a rock and buried his face in his hands. He stayed that way, motionless, for a long time. Not even the twittering of the birds reached his ears. But he could not fail to detect the presence of another human being, however faint. Putting a hand to his sword, he suddenly shouted, "Who's there? Show yourself!"

Shamefaced, Oguna stepped out reluctantly. "I'm sorry . . . " he said.

"You?" the prince said as he shoved his half-drawn sword back into its sheath. "You came again? You seem to like my pond. Where's your companion? Lady Toko?"

Oguna shook his head. "I came alone. I was on my way back from an errand to the chief's hall."

"I see. Taking a little detour, were you?" the prince teased him. "Well, if you don't tell anyone what you heard, I won't tell on you either."

Oguna nodded. He was heartily regretting having come.

The prince struck his knee with the palm of his hand and stood up. "Why don't we go together? The headman of Kamitsusato has invited me several times to come visit him. It looks like I'd be better off staying there for a while and cooling down."

"What about your attendant?"

"Don't worry. He'll take care of things for me if I'm not there."

Ignorant of the recklessness of the prince's actions, Oguna was pleased. He had never expected to have a chance to be alone with the prince like this. Even though the young man's identity was now public knowledge, the prince's attitude toward Oguna had not changed. He was still friendly and generous. They walked together toward the road through the valley that led to Kamitsusato.

Oguna was usually quiet around anyone other than Toko, but now he found himself very talkative as the prince adopted the role of confidant. When Oguna described how he and Toko had borrowed clothes from the village children and watched the tournament from under the chief's stand, however, the taciturn prince laughed out loud.

"You two certainly know how to keep people entertained. Lady Toko is quite a girl. I doubt that Lady Akaru was such a tomboy when she was little . . . or perhaps I'm wrong."

"No, she was always gentle and modest," Oguna said, and then added, "At least, on the outside."

"Yes. She looks so fragile that the wind might blow her away, but she's got a strong character," the prince said, as if to himself. Then he looked at Oguna. "You know, despite what I said the other day, Lady Toko comes from the same stock as Lady Akaru. She may be rough and unruly now, but she just might turn into a beauty one of these days."

"Toko?" Oguna looked incredulous.

"Considering that you attempted double suicide, the two of you have surprisingly little sense of romance."

"Toko likes you. She says there's no one stronger than you. Actually, most of the girls in Mino think so now."

"Well, yes," Prince Oh-usu said, not bothering to deny it.

"I've been wondering how to become stronger," Oguna continued.

"You want to be strong?"

"Yes. Toko says she can't leave me alone for a second without worrying about me."

"That's pretty pathetic."

"I think I could do it. As long as I don't run into any snakes or lightning."

The prince burst out laughing. "I'm sorry," he said. "I had no idea you'd be so entertaining. Just being with you has cheered me up."

"Do you think it's impossible?"

"I wonder. Physical force isn't where true strength comes from . . . although your fear of lightning might be a problem. To be strong means to remain unfazed no matter what. When you can stay calm and respond appropriately in any situation, you'll be strong. That's what martial arts are about. They teach you how to eliminate any wasted effort and energy during combat."

The prince remained silent for a while. Then he casually pulled a dagger from inside his robe and handed it to Oguna. "Have you ever used one of these before?" he asked.

"I've used a small knife to carve wood a little."

"This weapon is for self-defense. If you ever have to protect your life with it, point the blade forward, straight away from you, and watch your opponent calmly, following the flow of his movements. When he attacks, strike with the flow. It won't do you any good to close your eyes."

Perplexed by the prince's words, Oguna wrapped his hand around the handle of the dagger. "It looks as if you may get to try it sooner than you think," the prince continued in a low voice. "We're in for a bit of trouble. Watch out for arrows and keep your ears open."

They were standing in a natural cleft in the mountain that was roofed with pine and oak, like a tunnel leading into a tomb. It was dusky inside and no birds sang, but Oguna realized he could feel something in the air, something hard and menacing, not bighearted like the trees. "What is it?" he whispered.

"It appears that there are some in Mino who don't think so well of me."

"The chief would never allow it!"

Prince Oh-usu let out a short laugh. "Really? Even though I'm about to take Lady Akaru away?"

Straining every nerve to hear, Oguna's anxiety intensified until he felt that he was going to suffocate. His mind still doubted, but the goose bumps on his flesh affirmed what the prince had said. Besides, it was clear that while Oguna had never experienced anything like this before, the prince was used to it. Without warning, Prince Oh-usu pushed Oguna roughly to the ground. At the same moment, several arrows zipped through the air. Oguna stared wide-eyed at the white shafts quivering in the earth before his face.

"There!" the prince said, looking up at the cliff. Then he shouted, "Stop behaving like cowards! I thought the men of Mino were made of better stuff than that. If you attacked knowing that I'm the prince then at least come out and explain yourselves!"

Six or seven figures appeared from behind the trees on the cliff and swiftly descended a path known only to locals. Armed with knives and clubs, their heads were hooded so that only their eyes showed. But instead of attacking when the prince drew his sword, they formed a semicircle around him and Oguna, backing them against the face of the cliff.

The man closest to them spoke in a muffled voice. "Let me answer your question, son of the emperor beyond the mountains. As messengers of the earth gods, we've come to punish you for sauntering arrogantly into Mino. We won't let you take Lady Akaru. Go back to Mahoroba with your palanquin empty."

"You seem rather a shabby lot for messengers of the gods," the prince said with a crooked smile. "Besides, don't you think you've underestimated how many men you need to teach me a lesson?"

Several men recoiled at his words, but the rest roared with anger.

One of them attacked. As the prince parried the first blow, he yelled at Oguna. "Run!"

Oguna took off at top speed. One man was tripped by the prince as he tried to intercept Oguna, but another, hatchet raised, rapidly closed in on the boy. Oguna could not stand the thought of being struck down from behind. Desperately, he leapt to one side, evading the descending hatchet, and turned to face his attacker, the dagger gripped tightly in his hand.

"Hah! Coward! You can't stop me," the masked man jeered. Once again, he raised his weapon. It gleamed dully.

Watch your opponent, following the flow of his movements. When he attacks, strike with the flow. The thought sped through Oguna's mind as he lunged forward, striking at the man's breast. Something warm and wet spurted across Oguna's arm and chest before the man lumbered past, roaring like a beast and clapping his free hand to his side. Unable to grasp that he had caused this agony, Oguna stood stunned. And thus he was unprepared when the man turned like a wounded bear, his hatchet raised once more.

He's going to kill me. This time, he thought, it would be his turn to scream. But at that moment, an arrow sank into the man's chest with a dull thud. Oguna whirled around in surprise and saw Nanatsuka. Gripping the flanks of his galloping horse with his thighs as he fit another arrow to his bow, he swept past Oguna to aid the prince. In the thunder of hoofbeats, Oguna's attacker slowly crumpled to the ground.

Oguna sat down, gasping for breath, and stared at the motionless figure. He did not need to remove the mask. He had known from the beginning who he was—Oshikuma. And without any compunction, he would have killed Oguna to silence him. Oguna wrenched his eyes away from the body and looked down at the blood that stained his hand and dagger.

By the time Nanatsuka had dismounted, the prince was the only one left standing. Three men lay prostrate on the ground at his feet and the rest had fled at the sound of hooves. The prince called out cheerfully, "Nanatsuka! How did you know?"

"When Lady Akaru returned alone to the hall, I thought something was wrong. Are you all right?"

"Sure. They weren't worth much. They couldn't even conceal an ambush properly. I think they were just a bunch of hooligans."

"I must beg you not to make your servant follow after your scent like a hound. Especially when you know your life is in danger."

"All right, all right. But what about Oguna? Is he okay?"

"Yes. I shot his attacker."

Nanatsuka walked over to Oguna and raised him gently to his feet. It was only then that the boy turned to him with a dazed expression. Glancing at the bloodstained dagger in Oguna's hand, the prince said, "It looks like you struck quite a blow. Not bad, especially considering you'd only used a knife for whittling before."

Nanatsuka had to take his hand and pry his fingers open before Oguna let go.

"I knew him. He was someone I knew," Oguna said in a strained voice, afraid that he might cry if he let his feelings out.

"I see." The prince placed his hand gently on Oguna's head. "But it's only natural to protect yourself if you're about to be killed. If you die, you're finished. You're a good kid. I'm glad you weren't killed because of me."

"We must report this to the capital," Nanatsuka said indignantly. "We can't turn a blind eye to the fact that these people tried to kill you."

"There's no need. I don't want to damage our relationship with Mino. There can't be many of these extremists. It'll settle down soon."

"But—"

The prince cut him off. "Nanatsuka, enough. I like this land and its people. I'll show you that we can win their hearts without using force. I'm very popular, you know. After all, I won the tournament."

"It appears that you've also won their envy."

"Leave it. There's no point in getting upset over a few renegades." He patted Oguna on the head once more and said, "You forget it too. You did well. And remember that these words of praise come from a prince. If you want to become strong, then you'll have to learn to let some things go." When Oguna continued to look miserable, the prince bent down and looked him in the eyes. Then, as if he had made a decision, he said, "I'll be leaving soon to take Lady Akaru to the capital. Why don't you come with me? Come and learn what I've learned. Whether it's engineering or martial arts, you'll be instructed in the best knowledge and skills available. You've got potential. In four or five years, you could become the best double I could ever have, and not just in looks either."

"Double...?"

"You'll be my shadow, one of my closest attendants, trained to take my place when needed—a secret weapon. Think about it. It's not a bad offer. After all, one day I'll succeed to my father's throne."

4

PRINCE OH-USU and Oguna arrived together at the headman's hall in Kamitsusato. Men were sent to bring back the dead and wounded. Having barely escaped with their lives, the survivors were quick to reveal the names of those who had fled, and it was not long before the headman's men caught them. By evening, they were being interrogated by the chief, who had rushed over, pale with shock, as soon as he had heard the news. The captives hung their heads and insisted that they had acted on their own.

Although it remained unclear who led the ambush, the prince did not press the matter any further. He saw no point in pursuing it, a fact that greatly impressed the chief. Although the chief ordered everyone to keep the incident quiet, the tale had already spread from one village to the next.

When Oguna returned with blood-spattered clothes, Toko had at first turned pale, but once she knew he was all right, she bombarded him with questions and then sulked when he was unresponsive. She was terribly disappointed that he and the prince had had an adventure without her, especially as she had been forced to spend that time practicing dance with the other girls, something she detested. Although she enjoyed solo dancing, she had a hard time keeping in step with others.

"Fine, then. I understand. You go out and have this great adventure with the prince but you don't want to tell me anything about it. You've become such good friends you want to leave me out, right? Well, go ahead then. See if I care. I just won't talk to you anymore."

Having said that, of course, it was Toko who suffered. Instead of coming to apologize the way he usually did, Oguna went off on his own, despondent. Toko was so worried about him that she could not concentrate on anything, yet she could not back down either. She managed to stay true to her word until bedtime. As she lay under the covers, she kept her ears pricked for his return, but no matter how long she waited, there was no sign of him. Finally, she could stand it no longer.

Stupid, stupid Oguna! Why do you make me worry like this? She was sure he must be outside somewhere. Although a rare occurrence, he had disappeared like this before. She rose and threw on her clothes. Quietly lifting the latch on the door to their sleeping quarters, Toko slipped outside. Winter had relaxed its cold grip and a hazy moon hung in the sky. The main hall to the south where the guests were being entertained was lit by brightly burning torches and guarded by eager local youths. Toko turned away from them and headed north to search a row of low-roofed sheds. She found Oguna sitting on the thatched roof of the last shed and gazing up at the Seven Northern Stars. She climbed up with practiced movements and sat down beside him wordlessly. He showed no sign of surprise, simply accepting her presence.

"I stabbed Oshikuma," he said abruptly, as if this thought had been running through his mind the whole time. "It's the same as if I killed him. The prince pulled his blows so as not to kill anyone. Oshikuma was the only one who died."

"It was his own fault," Toko said indignantly. "What he was trying to do was unforgivable."

"He wanted to kill me . . . I wonder why he hated me so much? Do you know, Toko?"

"No, but whatever the reason, you're not to blame. You know what Mother would say if she were here: 'When you hate someone, it comes right back to you.'"

Oguna hugged his knees. "I didn't mean to kill him . . . I just . . . I guess I just wanted to do a good job."

"You must've been so scared," Toko said. "I can't even bear to think of it—being attacked by someone who wants to murder you. You couldn't have had time to even think about what you were doing. You shouldn't brood about things like that, Oguna."

"But I wasn't scared," he said flatly. "That's why it bothers me. I wanted to see what would happen if I did what the prince said. So I tried it. Even though I knew what it meant. Even though I knew that it was Oshikuma. I don't understand myself."

"No one could blame you for taking revenge. Come on, Oguna. Cheer up, would you? When you brood like this, you make me feel bad too."

In the light of the moon, the grim look on his face made him seem older—a young man, more sensitive than the prince.

"What's wrong with me? Why am I afraid of lightning but not afraid of stabbing someone? It's not right. If it were the opposite, it would make more sense. I wonder who my parents were that I should be born this way."

"Don't say that, Oguna. You're you, and personally I don't see anything wrong with that at all. It's never caused us any problems, right?"

"I want to be stronger," he said. "If I were strong like the prince, I wouldn't worry about things like this. I could fight without killing the other person and I could forgive, too. When I grow up, that's the kind of person I want to be."

Toko smiled. "Now *that* I can agree with."

Oguna gave her a pleading look. "Then you'll understand what I'm planning to do, won't you, Toko? I'm going to the capital with the prince. He invited me to go, and I've decided to accept. I want to go and see what I can do, what I can become."

Toko blinked owlishly. "Wait a minute . . . What are you talking about?"

"The prince is probably talking with Father and Mother right now. He wants to take me into his service when he goes back to the capital."

Toko's bewilderment turned to fury. "What?" she shouted, making Oguna cringe. "How could you decide something like that without even asking me?" she demanded. "When I wasn't even there? Is that how little you think of me? You're so stupid! I never want to see you again! Go ahead! Go off on your own! I couldn't care less!"

"Toko!"

But she ignored him. Before he could stop her she slid hastily down from the roof, missed her footing, and fell onto a pile of barrels stacked under the eaves.

ONETSUHIKO and Matono accepted the prince's proposal without hesitation. For someone as illustrious as the prince to take Oguna into his care was beyond their wildest dreams, and tears of gratitude welled in their eyes. Onetsuhiko immediately began preparing a celebration for the whole village while Matono threw herself into gathering the things Oguna would need for the journey. She called him to her and hugged him tightly, something she rarely did anymore.

"Oguna," she said. "It's because I'm your mother that I'm sending you away. Do you understand? I'm sending you away because I can't see anything here for you in the future. But don't forget. I will always be thinking of you. And not just me—everyone in this family will. Remember that whenever you feel alone."

Toko did not speak to Oguna for two whole days. Her silence unnerved him. Having sprained her ankle when she fell from the roof, she was immobilized anyway, but whenever Oguna went to her room and attempted to talk to her, she drew the covers up over her head. By the night of the second day, after repeated rejection, Oguna was desperate.

"Toko," he said solemnly. "I'm sorry. So would you please forgive me? Won't you at least talk to me? Please. Tomorrow I have to leave for the chief's hall, and the next day the procession will leave for the capital. This is my last chance to talk with you. Please say something . . . " The hump under the covers remained silent. "I know you're angry with me, but please be reasonable. This would have happened sooner or later anyway. Just the other way around, that's all. *You* told me that, remember? You said that one day you'd have to leave me behind. It's just happening a few years earlier, that's all."

Toko still did not respond.

"You were right. I can't do anything without you," Oguna said. "What people say about me is true. So I've got to see whether I can take care of myself without someone there to protect me. Whether I like it or not, someday I'll be on my own. I need to try before that happens, right?"

Still buried under the covers, Toko burst into loud sobs. Like a small child lacking the words to protest, she wept, heartbroken, and the noise carried so far that the guests assembled at the celebration looked up in surprise. No matter what Oguna said, she did not stop crying. Not knowing what else to do, he returned to the gathering.

"Lady Toko?" the prince asked. Oguna nodded. "Don't make her cry. You aren't going about it the right way. Girls don't respond to logic."

"But Toko's special. I want to cry myself."

"Don't even consider it. This is your party."

Oguna sighed. "Next to snakes and lightning," he confessed, "the thing I fear most is making Toko cry."

"Now *that* I can understand," the prince nodded.

THE NEXT DAY when Oguna went into the stables to load up his horse, he found Toko leaning against a post and wearing only one shoe. He was surprised, for it was a long way to hop on one foot. When he went over to her, she pushed a bundle toward him. "Here." Unwrapping it, he found a brand-new white jacket. "I sewed it myself. I didn't have anything else to do. The sleeves aren't sewn on very well, but please take it," she said.

Her eyes were red, like those of the dancers who rimmed their eyes with rouge on festival days. Whether she had been sewing or crying, it was clear that she had been up all night.

"This'll be useful. Thanks." The stitches were long and loose, but Oguna was not so foolish as to mention that.

"When are you coming back?"

He shifted uncomfortably. It would have been simple to say that he'd be back soon, but he did not want to console her with lies—not Toko. Seeing that he could not answer, she said, "Make sure you come back, no matter what. I'm not going into that shrine until you do. I'll wait right here. I won't become a woman until we see each other again. I promise. I'll be waiting for you the whole time, so please come back."

Oguna, who knew that Toko hated empty promises, said solemnly, "All right. I will. I'll come back to see you." Then he relaxed and smiled. "And when I do, I bet I'll be stronger. I'll show you that you don't have to worry about me anymore."

Toko looked doubtful. "I have a feeling that I'll never be able to stop worrying about you. But, yes, I bet you will be stronger. Just remember, Oguna, if being with the prince isn't what you hoped, come back, even if you've just left. All right?"

Although this last comment was a little disappointing, he smiled and said, "I promise to come back."

LADY AKARU finished preparing for the journey and quietly left her room. She wanted to take one last look at her home, to imprint on her mind forever the look of the familiar hall where she had grown up. She was dressed in her finest, with strings of jade and agate woven through her hair and clasped around her neck and slender wrists. When she walked, the tiny beads brushed together, whispering, and the sound seemed to cut her off from this place in which she had once run barefoot. Yesterday she had gone alone to visit the high priestess in the mountain shrine and receive her final instructions as a Tachibana woman. She thought over what she had been told with a twinge of sadness at leaving her carefree childhood behind.

Lost in thought, she rounded a corner of the walkway that opened onto the garden and then stopped in surprise. Prince Oh-usu was standing there, as if he had been waiting for some time. He must have crossed through the garden to get there. A shock ran through her to the tips of her fingers and toes. She had not seen the prince this close since the day they had gone to the pond. In fact, she had carefully avoided him. But this was so sudden and unexpected that there was no way to escape.

Lady Akaru paused for an instant, shaken, but then pulled herself together. Calm and gentle by nature, she quickly regained her composure and bowed her head in acknowledgment as politeness demanded. She resumed walking and was gliding past him when he spoke.

"Won't you even talk to me?" he asked. "Once you step into that palanquin, you belong to the emperor. We'll never have the opportunity to speak like this again. This is our last chance."

At the sound of his voice, her heart leapt violently. She was finding it hard to breathe with her tightly cinched sash, and her voice trembled slightly. "What do we have to talk about? There's nothing to be said."

"Then at least give me your hand."

"No!" She jerked away as if she had been burned. "Don't do this! You must be true to your mission."

"My father already has three wives. And I can't even guess how many concubines of lower rank. You must know that by virtue of his nature and rank, he's not the type of man to love one woman. Not even my mother, who was his first wife. I can see the hurt that will befall you once you have been presented to my father. And I can't bear that."

Lady Akaru struggled to smile. "But you're just the same. One day you'll be the emperor. You too will stand in his position, and you too will take many wives to rule over even greater territory."

The prince looked offended. "But I'm still young. I've never had a woman, and having met you, I never intend to have any other. If I gave up my right to succession, would you believe that my feelings for you are sincere? Would you come with me?"

"Please don't. You mustn't say such things. Not when I've made up my mind to watch you, even if from the shadows, as you rise to become the next emperor."

He gazed at her earnestly as if searching for even a fragment of hope in her eyes. "Once you're married, you won't think that way anymore. You don't know what it's like in my father's palace. Each wife sees the other wives and their children as bitter rivals. And if . . . if you should have a child, you too will wish that I had never been born."

Lady Akaru shook her head sadly. "How can you believe that? No matter what happens, I could never forget you. Never."

"If that's true, then why—" he burst out, but she cut him off.

"A priestess can only serve one god in her lifetime," she said quickly. "Please. Think of me as that. Although I marry as a woman, I have trained for many years as a priestess. My duty to serve the emperor transcends my personal wishes. I am very glad that I met you. But from this point onward, please let me walk the path destined for me in peace."

Oh-usu's outstretched arm fell limply to his side. In all his young life, never had he hoped so greatly nor been so firmly refused. "How cruel you are," he said roughly. "If that was your intention, then it would have been better had you never smiled at me."

You have no idea how cruel this is for me as well, she thought, but she kept these words inside and stood head bowed, her hands gripping her sleeves. And as she stood there, the prince turned away, squared his shoulders, and stalked off. Although she knew it was for the better, she could not keep back her tears.

SNOW FROM A SPRING flurry a few days earlier had already melted and the earth was dark and fragrant, making the grass appear even greener. The buds on the trees were red and swollen, as if about to burst open any minute. It was almost March, the month in which the cherry trees blossomed, when the procession bore Lady Akaru away to the capital, carrying with it the grief they all felt at parting. Lining the road to bid her farewell, the people of Mino spoke of celebration, but their feelings were mixed.

The chief riding along behind the palanquin and the prince riding in front gazed ahead grimly as they swayed atop their horses. This made it hard for Oguna, who was riding beside the chief, to search the crowd for a glimpse of Toko's face. She had promised to come and see him off, but she was not there when they left the hall. Perhaps she was hiding under the covers again . . .

The procession moved ahead and the crowd, arms waving, receded behind. The road curved and Oguna turned for one last look before they passed out of sight. Looking up at the hall, he finally saw Toko. She had climbed through the ventilation hole like they had done on the day of the tournament and was sitting on the roof. The thought of how she would get down with her foot still injured made him wince.

When she saw that he was looking, she began to wave a long, thin cloth, perhaps one of their mother's scarves. It fluttered gracefully in the air, but Toko looked as if she would fall off the roof any minute. Though he could not have caught her even if she fell, he reached forward without thinking.

"Oguna—!" the chief began, but before he could finish Oguna had fallen off his horse and had to be plucked from the ground by a servant.

chapter
two

THE SHADOW
PRINCE

The Shadow Prince

"They're so alike!"

"He's adorable! He looks just like His Highness when he was younger."

"Let me see!"

No sooner had Oguna arrived at the prince's mansion than he was surrounded by women, who vied for a chance to look at him. Their sumptuous robes would have been reserved for special occasions in Mino.

It had taken the procession five days to traverse the mountains. According to the prince, five days by palanquin was not a long journey. They could have reached the capital in half the time on a swift horse. But to Oguna, who had never set foot outside Mino before and had only a vague idea of Toyoashihara's size, the distance seemed immense. The land, the buildings, the roads, the people—everything in the capital was so foreign it made home seem even farther away. The mansion the prince pointed out to him as his father's living quarters was astonishing, but even more amazing was the fact that the magnificent buildings and gardens these people called "the palace" covered an area as large as a whole village in Mino.

Prince Oh-usu entered the room, wearing clean clothes and looking refreshed. "Honestly!" he said. "These serving girls! Oguna, just ignore them."

Oguna, who had been sitting awkwardly in their midst, jumped up, relieved.

"Did you get a chance to bathe?" the prince asked.

"Yes . . . " Oguna said, remembering the bathhouse with a shudder. The women who had waited on him there had also had plenty to say when they saw him.

"Come with me," the prince said, but then stopped and laughed at the look on Oguna's face. "Relax," he said, clapping him on the shoulder. "I'm not going to expose you to any more public ridicule. I'm sick of being compared to you and laughed at myself. You can have a nice, quiet room in a separate building where you can get used to living here at your own pace. I won't let those noisy women near you. Then, when the time is right, I'll introduce you to my mother and other people. And someday, even to my father."

Oguna recalled the emperor's palatial residence with its soaring roof and gilded crosspieces. "Will Lady Akaru live in the emperor's mansion?" he asked abruptly. His clansmen had left him at the gate to follow Lady Akaru inside while he had traveled on to the prince's residence near the eastern foothills.

"For now, I guess." The prince's face remained impassive, but his voice tightened. "She'll be granted her own hall at some point, but I couldn't tell you where."

"Can I see my clansmen before they leave for Mino?"

The prince remained silent, thinking as they walked. "I'm sorry," he said finally, "but that's impossible. I want to keep your existence secret for a while. If people found out about you, your value as my shadow would decrease. I don't want anyone to know that I've brought you here from Mino."

Oguna nodded. "It's all right. I understand. I said goodbye already anyway."

The prince smiled. "You're a smart boy," he said. Then his face grew serious. "You've got a lot to learn yet, but there's one thing I want you to remember: As long as you live here, be on your guard. Death waits for the careless. My father's palace is large, bright, and gay. It's full of people, but it's still as dangerous as being alone in the forest in the dead of night. I suppose you find that hard to believe?"

"Yes," Oguna said, surprised.

"I thought so. But that's what it means to be the emperor's son, so you'd better get used to it. I didn't master the sword and the bow for fun. I learned to use weapons because I had to."

"But who . . . who would want to kill you?"

"Who are my enemies? I have many," the prince said, almost proudly. "Given a chance any of the chiefs who resent the emperor's rule would kill my father, or me, his heir. So too would my father's wives who seek to place their own sons on the throne, and any ministers who support a different prince. There's an intense power struggle behind the facade. People who live here are good at hiding what they think behind their smiles. Then there's my father who sends me off on dangerous missions to hunt down rebels or act as his envoy. He's testing me. If I succeed I gain his trust, but if I fail, it could cost me my life."

Seeing the troubled look on Oguna's face, the prince placed a hand on his head. "It's not as bad as it sounds," he said, his smile returning. "Once you get used to it, it seems normal. I've done pretty well so far, and I plan to continue doing so."

At the end of a long covered passageway, they came to a modest building overlooking a quiet, tranquil garden of rocks and moss surrounding a small pond and bordered by a grove of pines. Prince Oh-usu slid the door open and they stepped inside. The room was tidy and bare, as if it had not been used for some time. "I'll have them bring over all the things I used when I was your age," he said. "You should learn just as I did—learn to act just like me. I'll make sure you have the very best teachers. I won't be here much, but with the teachers I select, you can't go wrong."

Oguna looked up at him like a lost puppy. "You're not going to be here?"

"I spend most of my time traveling, you see. I'll have to go back to Mino several times to build the villa, for example. But I won't treat you badly. You'll have everything you need. After all, I chose you to be my shadow, which means that your future is mine. We're destined to become far more than brothers." His face brightened. "I'll tell you what. Next time I go to Mino, I'll see if I can learn anything about your parents. Perhaps I can find some clue."

Oguna looked doubtful. "But it was twelve years ago. Do you really think it's possible?"

"It's worth a try. Oh, and one other thing. Your name doesn't really suit your role as my double. Why don't I give you a new one? My name is Oh-usu, meaning 'big mortar,' so how about Ousu—'little mortar'? It will sound like you really are my younger brother."

Oguna was touched by the prince's thoughtfulness, although he still preferred his own name. He could hear Toko's indignant voice echoing in his mind: *He's the only boy in our house, and that makes him special.*

One of the "very best teachers" was none other than Nanatsuka. Oguna was surprised by how pleased this news made him. He had not realized how much he had dreaded the thought of being left without any familiar faces.

"No one in the capital can beat Nanatsuka at field combat and hunting," the prince said, as though boasting of his own prowess. "And that goes for archery too. He's the one who taught me to shoot. Stay with him night and day and learn everything you can. He'll never run out of things to teach you. He's also the best servant you could ask for and has served me faithfully for many years." Turning to Nanatsuka, he continued, "From today, you're Ousu's teacher. I want you to live here with him and train him just like you did me. All right?"

As always, Nanatsuka held himself so respectfully that his enormous frame seemed almost small. He bowed solemnly and said, "I am at your service."

"Good," the prince said cheerfully. "No one has spent longer by my side and no one knows my habits as well as you do. I'm counting on you to make sure that Ousu is fit to serve as my shadow." Then he turned and began to stride away.

"My lord," Nanatsuka called after him hesitantly. "If I may make a request . . ."

"What is it?"

"I only ask that you take Miyadohiko in my place as your servant. Though young, he is reliable and trustworthy."

The prince frowned. "The right to choose who goes with me is mine, not yours. You have no say in the matter."

"I beg your pardon." Nanatsuka bowed his head even lower.

The prince's expression relaxed and he said teasingly, "Well, whomever I take, whether Miyadohiko or someone else, no one could be such a hound as you. You stay here with Ousu and let me run like a loosed fox for a while."

"Please take care."

The prince waved his hand impatiently and left the room. Nanatsuka's shoulders fell. Watching him, Oguna did not know what to say. But there was no trace of disappointment on Nanatsuka's face when he turned toward him. Placing a large, heavy hand on Oguna's shoulder, he said, "Since we're both here because we found favor with His Highness, let's do our best to be of service to him."

"Yes, sir," Oguna said hastily.

From the next morning, Nanatsuka took Oguna hiking almost daily. They walked the fields and mountains, gazing down on the capital from every mountain ridge as Nanatsuka drilled the geography of Mahoroba into Oguna's feet and eyes. Seen from above, the palace was a wooden miniature of gray and red buildings packed into a neat little box. Oguna not only learned the layout of the capital but also developed strong legs. His aching muscles plagued him for many uncomfortable nights until he could keep up with his teacher.

Nanatsuka was strict, demanding unsparingly the same things he had demanded of the prince. And there was much to learn in the mountains: reading animal tracks, choosing a place to wait for game, trapping, covering one's tracks, finding medicinal herbs, and marking a trail without leaving clues for others. And, of course, Oguna had to learn to shoot a bow. By the end of the day, he was exhausted, often nodding off before supper.

Nanatsuka, however, was a competent teacher. He worked Oguna hard because he recognized that the boy could withstand such treatment. And Oguna, no matter how much his legs might hurt, never once complained. Nor did he give way to homesickness or lose his temper. He absorbed everything, was quick-witted, and applied what he learned. Even by Nanatsuka's standards he was a good student. Compared to the prince at that age, however, Oguna still had a long way to go, especially when it came to his fear of snakes.

It would have been unusual *not* to come across a snake when hiking through the mountains in spring. Whenever they did Oguna panicked at the mere sight, forgetting everything he had been taught. Nanatsuka struggled not to laugh when the boy leapt screaming to his feet yet again. Schooling his features into a frown, he said sternly, "If you don't stop that, I'll have to send you back to Mino. How can you expect to double for the prince if you can't even look at a snake? You'll ruin his reputation if you act like a coward."

"I really am trying . . ." Oguna mumbled.

"Well, next time you see one, don't scream. You believe they're scary and that's why they scare you. Don't give in to your fear. Look straight at it and tell yourself it's just a snake. Do you understand? Because I won't put up with this kind of behavior anymore."

Oguna shuddered and nodded. "I'll do my best," he said.

The next time a large pit viper slithered past where they crouched waiting for game, Oguna did indeed remain very quiet. "You see. You can do it if you try," Nanatsuka said, only to find that Oguna had fainted dead away.

After thinking it over, Nanatsuka decided that Oguna might conquer his phobia if he got used to snakes through daily exposure. With great effort he managed to find some snake eggs and hatch them in an earthen jar. Then he ordered Oguna to feed the hatchlings, which were no bigger than his little finger, believing that the boy wouldn't fear something he had raised.

Oguna did as he was told, catching spiders and frogs and feeding them to the snakes. But, although he showed no aversion to taking care of them, he lost his appetite. Noticing that this growing boy was barely eating and unaware of the cause, Nanatsuka scolded him severely. "Don't waste food that's put in front of you. It's not free. And besides, your body doesn't belong to you anymore. You've been placed into my care so that I can train you as the prince's shadow. It's your duty to grow up strong and healthy as soon as possible. Now eat your food."

Oguna nodded obediently and stuffed the food in his mouth. Although he was clearly forcing himself to eat without even tasting it, Nanatsuka pretended not to notice, thankful that he was at least eating.

From that day on, Oguna ate everything placed in front of him. He still looked wan and pale, but as he kept up with his training Nanatsuka was sure that the boy would soon get over his fear. Then, one day while hiking along a mountain trail Oguna fell and failed to get up. Slipping an arm beneath his shoulders to help him up, Nanatsuka stopped in astonishment. He could feel the boy's bones through his clothing. "What's going on?" he said to himself. "I thought you were eating properly!"

He had to carry the youth home on his back. When Oguna came to his senses, he confessed that he had thrown up every meal because of the snakes. Nanatsuka was dumbfounded.

"Why didn't you tell me?" he demanded. "Did you think you'd be able to walk without eating?"

"I'm sorry . . . " Oguna shrank under the covers. "I really wanted to get over my fear . . . really, I did."

What a strange child, Nanatsuka thought. It was hard to tell if he was a coward or not. Oguna must have been experiencing the agony of fear and starvation, yet Nanatsuka hadn't even noticed until he collapsed. It had never occurred to him that a boy of twelve could bear so much without showing any outward sign. Nanatsuka was forced to revise his approach. Prince Oh-usu happened to return the same day, and when he asked for a report on Oguna's progress, Nanatsuka told him what had happened.

"I seem to have erred in my judgment. Perhaps I was too full of memories of teaching you. Now that I think about it, you always told me what you were feeling. If you were tired, you said so. When you did well, you boasted proudly. He isn't like that at all. You may look alike, but you have very different temperaments."

The prince laughed. "It sounds like you're saying I lacked patience. But never mind. That's a good trait for Ousu to have. Actually, it's perfect for someone who will be my shadow, don't you think? Take good care of him for me. I'm looking forward to seeing how he turns out."

"If he could just get over his fear of snakes, I'd have no complaints about him becoming your servant."

"He told me he hates lightning as well. Don't demand the impossible. After all, we can't expect perfection. If he's still afraid even when he reaches my age, then we'll have to think about it, but there's no rush. And even if he doesn't get over it, I could always pretend to be afraid of snakes and lightning myself. It wouldn't hurt for me to become more like my shadow, would it?" The prince seemed to accept the situation cheerfully without much concern.

Nanatsuka returned to Oguna's quarters in a new frame of mind. The first thing he did was to discard the snake jar. Then he went over to where Oguna lay and said, "Don't worry about those snakes anymore. You can rest a few more days. The important thing is for you to eat."

Oguna gripped his covers and gazed wide-eyed at Nanatsuka. "You're not going to send me home?"

"No. I'm not sending you home." Suddenly he felt sorry for the boy. From the day he had arrived, Nanatsuka had seen him only as the prince's double in the making, forgetting that he was a lonely child just recently separated from his parents. Maybe that was why Oguna had kept his feelings to himself and strove to live up to Nanatsuka's expectations.

Sitting down by his pillow, Nanatsuka said, "Or would you like to go home? Come to think of it, you never say how you're feeling."

Oguna gazed up at the ceiling for a moment, then shook his head and said in a small voice, "I don't want to go home like this. I haven't gotten any stronger. I vowed I'd do my best, but everything's gone wrong . . . "

Nanatsuka looked at him. "You're doing very well," he said, praising Oguna for the first time. "But you should let me know what you're thinking. It's good to do what you're told, but you need to tell me if you can't stand something or if you're in pain. There're some things that I won't figure out unless you say so. I'm a little thickheaded, you know."

I never had to say anything before. Toko always did that for me, Oguna thought. *She always knew what I was feeling before I put it into words. But here I'm on my own. I have to speak for myself.* A wave of homesickness caught in his throat and he longed to go home. But he held it back, and gradually the pain in his heart receded. He looked up at Nanatsuka's bearded face and said tentatively, "Nanatsuka, don't you wish that I would go back to Mino?"

"Why on earth would I wish that?"

"I've wanted to apologize ever since that first day, when the prince asked you to be my teacher. Because of me, you can't be with the prince. So I thought . . . " He hesitated, then said forlornly, "Surely you didn't want to leave the prince's side, not even for a moment?"

Once again, Nanatsuka was forced to reassess the boy. Though quiet, he was keenly aware of what was going on around him. It was only now that Nanatsuka became aware of the discontent smoldering inside him, and it surprised him that Oguna had sensed it first.

"You're very perceptive," he said gently. "It's true that I wish I could be at the prince's side. But it's not your fault. Whether you had come or not, he would have sent me away. He's like that sometimes, avoiding me because my nose is too keen, as he says." He sighed. "He's dangerous when he's thinking of something that he doesn't want me to discover. No one can stop him then. I know the cause. It's the lady from Mino . . . I just hope he doesn't do anything rash. He's not one to fall in love easily, or to forget easily either. I'd be less worried if he found another worthy maiden . . . That's why I'm concerned, although worrying won't help."

Oguna, still ignorant in matters of love, was deeply impressed that Nanatsuka knew how the prince felt without having witnessed his confession at the pond.

"So don't trouble your head over such things," Nanatsuka continued.

"I'm sorry that I made you worry. How about we start fresh? You're a good student and I have great expectations of you." He smiled for the first time in many days. Oguna smiled back at him for the first time ever. The little wall of restraint between them finally dissolved.

"Nanatsuka," he said. "I think I'm hungry."

2

SUMMER CAME, and anvil-topped clouds mushroomed in the deep blue sky, bringing with them sudden downpours. The thunder and lightning accompanying these storms caused Oguna and Nanatsuka even more grief than did snakes. Nanatsuka could not chase them away. Even the faintest rumble in the distance threw Oguna into a state of agitation.

He's so extreme, Nanatsuka thought. By now he knew that Oguna was no coward, a fact evident even in the way he drew his bow, and he had the self-control and concentration that would make him as good an archer as Prince Oh-usu. Nor did he fear the dark, heights, or pain. Although careful by nature, at times he was so heedless of danger that he appeared childishly naive. Yet at the mere hint of thunder this same boy clutched Nanatsuka's arm in terror and broke into a cold sweat. Being indoors made no difference. His fear was so great that even Nanatsuka found it hard to remain calm.

"I don't like lightning either," he told Oguna one day. "It's terrifying when it hits. But your reaction seems abnormal. Did something happen to you when you were little—like a lightning strike close by?"

Oguna shook his head.

"Well, when I was young," Nanatsuka said, "a lightning bolt struck a cedar right in front of me. The tree burst into a pillar of flame, and I thought my ears would explode. It was a terrible sight, but thunder still doesn't make me jump the way it does you."

Oguna raised a frightened face and then peered out anxiously at the rain dripping from the eaves.

"Listen, Oguna, it won't strike nearby if there's a pause between the flash of light and the sound of thunder." But his words were useless. With each low grumble, Oguna grabbed his arm so tightly it hurt.

When the storm had finally passed, Oguna tried to explain. "Every time I hear that sound, I see an image in my mind . . . an enormous, fiery snake twisting in the sky . . . " He spoke in a frightened whisper though there were no longer any clouds to be seen.

"What?" Nanatsuka exclaimed. "You mean your fear of lightning comes from your fear of snakes? Snakes and lightning look the same to you?"

After careful consideration, Oguna decided that this might be true.

"I don't understand you." Nanatsuka sighed and gave up all hope of curing him.

Nanatsuka not only trained Oguna to shoot with a bow and arrow but also to fish with a harpoon and a pole. A master at hiding in the wilderness, he passed on every survival skill he knew.

One day when they were angling for catfish, Oguna hooked a large eel. The two of them danced about madly trying to hold on to its thrashing body, but it burrowed into the swamp, leaving the muddy pair behind. They looked at each other and burst out laughing, all cares forgotten as their voices rang across the water's surface. It was the first time they had ever laughed together.

The boy's happy face touched Nanatsuka's heart, perhaps because Oguna so seldom laughed aloud. His carefree laughter had a strangely translucent quality, and his smile was like clear pristine water as opposed to the brilliant radiance of the prince's.

When their laughter finally faded, Nanatsuka said, "You should laugh more often. You're still young. When the prince was your age, he laughed like that every day. His emotions run deep, so he used to laugh a lot and get mad a lot too. He can control himself when he needs to now, but until he learned to do that, he suffered and so did the rest of us. That's one point at least in which you don't seem to need any training."

"I think I learned that before I came," Oguna said casually. "Because I spent so much time with Toko."

"Ah, I see."

Looking at the bright sky reflected in the surface of the marsh, Oguna thought of his childhood companion. Toko always burst out laughing at the slightest thing, and the sound was so familiar he could hear her even now, just thinking about it.

Nanatsuka was lost in reverie too. "The prince rarely cried," he said. "But I did see him weep a few times. Once he started, there was no stopping him. Everyone fled before his tears, even me."

Nanatsuka often told Oguna stories about the prince. It was part of his training, although Oguna suspected that Nanatsuka enjoyed it too. His expression grew tender and affectionate. "I first saw him cry when his favorite horse died. He was so upset that he killed every other horse in the stable and then destroyed the building . . . It was like a howling gale passing through. That's his nature—to love passionately and grieve deeply."

"He didn't need to kill the other horses, though," Oguna said.

"Yes, you're right. He went too far. But he's like that sometimes." He paused for a moment, and then added with feeling, "Many people flock to him for that very quality. He has the charisma of a born leader. A cold, ruthless person doesn't inspire men like me. We're drawn to leaders who have feelings and care about others, like the prince."

AUTUMN CAME, dyeing the trees and mountains crimson. Nanatsuka began carrying a large pot strapped to his back on their hikes, which made him look a bit like a turtle with an undersized shell. Oguna wondered at his strange burden, but he learned its purpose on the day he shot his first deer. Nanatsuka lit a fire on the spot and began butchering the animal. Oguna watched, entranced by the swift, deft movements of his hands. Nanatsuka threw the meat into the pot along with mushrooms and herbs he had gathered along the trail before adding salt and seasonings. Soon a stew was bubbling merrily over a makeshift fireplace of stones.

"This is to celebrate shooting your first deer. You can consider yourself on your way to becoming a hunter now, although not a great one yet. So eat up." Laughing at Oguna's look of astonishment, Nanatsuka explained that his greatest skill was neither hunting nor combat but outdoor cooking. Oguna noticed that while he was cooking he had looked happier than he ever had before, grinning with satisfaction every time he added an herb or tasted the broth. "I can't produce the kind of delicacies made by the cooks in the palace kitchen, but when it comes to making a meal from what's available in the woods, I'm sure I could beat them hands down. That's one of the skills the prince treasures me for. When I'm by his side, I make sure that he doesn't go without good food."

"You're amazing!" Oguna exclaimed. Using the chopsticks they had whittled from bamboo, he picked up a chunk of tenderly stewed meat and popped it in his mouth. His eyes widened in admiration.

Nanatsuka was in a fine mood. Oguna had made remarkable progress since the beginning of autumn and, as his teacher, Nanatsuka had much to be proud of. It helped that both snakes and thunderstorms were rare during this season. They relaxed around the fire in the shade of the colored leaves and drank in the clear, peaceful mountain air.

"My native land is famous for *hishio* seasoning," Nanatsuka said. "My mother made the best in the country."

This was Oguna's first opportunity to learn about Nanatsuka's past. "Where were you born?" he asked. "Was it near here?"

"No, I come from a land called Hidakami. It's much farther east, way past Mino—it's about a month's journey over mountains and rivers."

"That *is* a long way . . . What's it like?"

"Completely different from Mahoroba. The plains spread out forever, and the marshes too. You can't begin to imagine. I learned to hunt there. The land is so flat that the antlers on a herd of deer look like a forest of tree branches in the distance."

Oguna sat with his chin propped in his hand, trying to picture a forest of antlers. "I'd love to see it."

"I haven't been back for twenty years. There are times when I wish I could see if the deer still gather like that in the reedy fields of Hidakami. If I live long enough and grow too old to serve the prince, maybe I'll go back for one last look before I die."

Watching him speak dispassionately about his homeland, Oguna noticed for the first time how different he was from people in this part of the country with his enormous size, his heavy beard, and hawklike nose. Oguna was not the only one who had left his home far behind to live in the capital of a strange land. "So you wish you could go back sometimes too," he said.

"It's not easy to forget the place where you were born and raised," Nanatsuka responded. "But I have no intention of leaving the prince. I have a debt to repay. He saved my life." He smiled at Oguna, who was listening intently.

"I was a criminal. He intervened and pleaded for my life, then brought me here. On that day, Nanatsuka of Hidakami died and was reborn a servant to the prince. Although I still dream of home, my first duty is to the prince because I belong to him."

THE WHITE WINTER DAYS of blowing on cold, aching fingers gave way to the new buds of spring. Whether or not he had given up contemplating something of which Nanatsuka would disapprove Oguna could not tell, but Prince Oh-usu seemed to have changed his mind, for he ordered Nanatsuka to accompany him once more. Nanatsuka simply bowed respectfully and resumed his former duties. Oguna alone sensed just how happy he was. Although he couldn't help feeling disappointed, there was nothing he could do about it. *After all, Nanatsuka is here to serve the prince, not me,* he reminded himself. This knowledge made him sad, for he had come to love Nanatsuka during their year together. But it was Oguna's nature to accept his fate without complaint. He was used to other people being loved more than he. In fact, as an abandoned child, he would have found it hard to believe that anyone could put him first. It was not that he didn't wish for it, but he lacked the confidence to ask this of others, even of someone as kind as his foster-mother Matono.

Only when he thought of Toko, so stubborn and single-minded, did he feel some comfort. She, at least, would probably never forget her promise. But she was a lady of the Tachibana clan, and he was smart enough to realize that someday she would be beyond his reach. She would eventually become a noblewoman like Lady Akaru, and even if she did remain true to him, she would not be allowed to put him first.

What would it be like, he wondered, *if someone devoted his entire life to me, like Nanatsuka has done for the prince?* He sighed. *I wonder how the prince feels about having so many people give their hearts to him. I suppose he has never in his life thought that no one needed him.*

Oguna helped Nanatsuka tidy the room where they had stayed. Nanatsuka was well aware of the boy's disappointment, but by now he also knew that Oguna would never mention it. He wished Oguna felt free to let his emotions show. Nanatsuka also regretted having to leave him behind, and the boy's self-control made him sad. Oguna was so like the prince and yet in some ways the complete opposite, something Nanatsuka was reminded of every time he saw the look of surprise on Oguna's face at a simple act of kindness or consideration. For this reason, his affection for Oguna differed from his feelings for the prince.

"Don't worry. When I'm gone, you won't be left on your own. You'll have new teachers," Nanatsuka said. "You have a lot to learn, and I can only teach you a small part."

"I'd be satisfied if I could just become like you," Oguna said in a small voice.

"No. That would never do. You're training to be the prince's shadow, not mine. You still have to learn numbers and how to read, which I've never mastered. You like engineering, don't you? You'll need those skills if you want to build."

"Numbers?" Oguna's face brightened. "I was trying to learn on my own a little. I want to know how to calculate, too."

"That's the spirit! You work hard at your studies while I'm gone. I'll come back to see you whenever I can."

Just as Nanatsuka had said, three new teachers were assigned to him: one for math, another for reading and writing, and the third for martial arts. He had no time to miss Nanatsuka. Plunged headlong into a full schedule, he had so much to remember for each lesson he felt his brain would melt. His teachers were fussy about manners and movement too, and they drilled palace etiquette into him mercilessly. In martial arts, his instructor trained him at sword and pike, and grappling as well. Although Nanatsuka's training had hardened Oguna's muscles, it still wasn't easy.

The prince and Nanatsuka came to see him once in a while, but because they spent most of their time traveling to distant territories, they were rarely even in the capital. Although Oguna could not hope to grow as close to his new teachers as he had been to Nanatsuka, the subjects they taught drew his interest and he devoted himself to learning everything the son of an emperor was expected to know, including astronomy, the almanac, and history. His speed in math, in particular, astonished his teachers. None of them ever guessed, however, that his enthusiasm for learning stemmed from loneliness.

The days and months flew by. Four years passed, and Oguna turned sixteen without fulfilling his promise to Toko.

3

THAT SUMMER Oguna grew like a bamboo shoot. With every new notch marking his height on the wooden post, he thought of Toko. How much had she grown under that distant sky? She would have to be a very tall woman to reach even the fourth notch on the post, yet he could not imagine her as anything but his height, her eyes level with his.

His sixteenth summer passed uneventfully. He studied as usual, finished reading several scrolls, and honed his fighting skills to the point where he occasionally even defeated his instructor. Prince Oh-usu had taken Nanatsuka off on another journey early in the year, and the hall seemed quiet and dreary. The only real change was that Oguna now tied his hair in loops on either side of his head like the prince instead of cutting it in the childish bob he had worn since he arrived. By the time the prince and Nanatsuka returned, summer was already over and red dragonflies heralded the coming of fall.

Nanatsuka, his beard thicker than before, strolled up one sunny afternoon when Oguna was washing himself after sword practice. "Have you been eating properly?" he asked as if he had not been gone for over half a year.

Turning around, Oguna's face lit up. "Nanatsuka!"

He has the same bright smile as the prince now, Nanatsuka thought. He was flattered, for he knew that Oguna still shared this unguarded side of himself with very few people.

"I haven't seen you since New Year's," Oguna said. "How was Izumo?"

"Izumo? It's a dangerous place. But the trouble's over, at least for now. The prince plans to stay in the capital for a while."

"Good!" Oguna said. "When he's gone so long, the maidservants get bored and won't leave me alone."

Nanatsuka opened his mouth wide and laughed heartily. "That's great. So you can actually double for the prince now, at least in that regard."

Oguna gave him a puzzled look. Though the boy's expression was childlike, his slim, tall figure resembled the prince more than ever, especially with his new hairstyle. After close scrutiny, Nanatsuka decided that Oguna might even pass for the prince from a distance. "You've grown again since I saw you last," he grunted.

"A whole finger's length. If I keep on like this, I'll outgrow the prince and become as tall as you."

"That will never do. The prince would have to wear heeled clogs in order to keep up."

Oguna laughed. With a graceful movement that reflected his years of training, he adopted a wrestling stance, inviting Nanatsuka to join him. This had become their ritual whenever they were reunited.

They grappled with one another on the flat grassy space beside the well until, as always, Nanatsuka threw Oguna to the ground. Although he had grown, Oguna didn't stand a chance against Nanatsuka, who was still a head taller and more than twice his girth. The ritual was purely intended to test Oguna's strength.

Oguna lay panting on the ground. "So what do you think?" he asked. "Am I stronger than a mosquito bite?"

"Hmm. Maybe. I suppose you might be as strong as a beetle bite."

"Beetles don't bite," Oguna protested, wiping his hand across his brow. "Now I'm all sweaty again, and I just finished washing."

Lying spread-eagled on his back, Oguna seemed totally at ease. *He's progressing well,* Nanatsuka thought with satisfaction. Without the ability to relax, Oguna could not have learned to focus, and while he still needed to put on more muscle, his body was already tough and powerful.

"I'm glad I can still make you sweat. Your math teacher was telling the prince that it's you who makes him sweat now."

"Oh? I guess I'm not a very good pupil these days."

"I thought you liked numbers."

"Yes, but he's so slow at calculating. And he insists on using only one method for solving problems. He's too old and set in his ways."

"Oguna, you shouldn't criticize your elders like that."

Oguna looked up at Nanatsuka, his expression contrite, much like the way he used to look when he was younger. "I'm sorry . . . Sometimes I just can't help myself. Everyone keeps telling me how the prince would behave so that sometimes I start talking like I think he would."

"Considering that you're training to be his double, I suppose that's only to be expected," Nanatsuka said, hastily concealing his consternation. Oguna had indeed sounded just like the prince at the same age. Although not a bad thing, it had caught Nanatsuka off guard. Gazing up at the blue sky, high, distant, and flecked with white tufts of cloud, he changed the subject.

"We'll be able to hunt together this autumn. Shall we take the cooking pot with us when the leaves turn color?"

Oguna took to his feet and jumped around like a grasshopper. "Let's go now," he cried. "There's no need to wait until the leaves change."

"But there won't be any mushrooms and the venison won't be as tasty."

"Let's hunt birds then. The prince likes wildfowl right? I can shoot a bird in flight now, you know."

A grin spread across Nanatsuka's face. "The game birds in Kasayama are especially good. You're right. His Highness hasn't eaten any for some time. He'll be pleased. Let's go and ask him."

When he heard their plan, the prince wanted to join them, but having just returned to the capital, he was far too busy and regretfully conceded that they should go without him. "If you catch a lot," he said, "take some to my mother for me. I haven't been able to visit her for some time." He smiled suddenly, a glint of mischief in his eye. "Oguna, you've never met my mother, Lady Inabi, have you?"

He went to the back of the room and rummaged about in a drawer, pulling out an old hood very similar to the one he had worn when Oguna first met him in Mino. "I used to wear this whenever I wanted to travel incognito. Put this on when you visit her. I'm sure she'll be astonished to see you. She'll think the past has come to life."

In the last four years, the prince had also changed, but unlike with Oguna, the changes were barely perceptible. When his eyes gleamed mischievously as they did now, he seemed not to have changed at all.

"Considering that I've grown much older, I doubt that Lady Inabi will be deceived," Nanatsuka said bluntly.

"What are you talking about?" Prince Oh-usu retorted. "You haven't changed a bit in all the years I've known you. You looked just the same when you were younger." He tied the hood on Oguna with his own hands. "There. Now go and make sure you enjoy the hunt in my stead. You'd better change first though. I've never in my life worn such a drab outfit."

Oguna looked down at his plain white clothes.

"Come to think of it, I've never seen you wear anything but white since you first got here. Are you abstaining from wearing colorful clothing as some kind of invocation?"

Oguna ducked his head, embarrassed by the prince's probing. "No. . . . I just like it, that's all. Do you really think it's boring?"

"It's all right, I guess," the prince said. He seemed surprised to hear that Oguna actually liked wearing white. "And I suppose that there will come a time when people will only be able to tell us apart by our clothes. But when you act as my double, don't wear white. It wouldn't do for people to think that the crown prince and heir to the throne can't afford to dye his clothes."

OGUNA AND NANATSUKA raced through fields dotted with delicate purple and white bush clover. The swaying grasses spoke of the cool relief that followed summer's heat, and the leaves had darkened to a deeper shade of green. The hunt went well, and it was still light when they decided they had bagged enough game: five pheasant, seven quail, and a duck. Oguna thoroughly enjoyed himself. He had not been out with Nanatsuka for a long time, and he was proud not only to demonstrate his progress to his teacher but also to confirm it for himself. Nanatsuka teased him about his past mistakes but only because Oguna had reached the stage where they could laugh about them.

Walking back along the trail with a brace of birds slung over his shoulder, Oguna suddenly thought, *Maybe now I can go back to Mino and show Toko what I've become.* He had finally changed enough to be worthy of meeting her again.

Oguna and Nanatsuka walked in companionable silence to the palace complex. As they passed through the outer gate on the east side, however, Nanatsuka glanced behind them and said, "Take a look at that. We won't be able to use this road."

A magnificent palanquin draped with purple silk curtains was approaching the gate. Although it resembled those used by the emperor's wives, the attendants accompanying it were far too many and they had clearly traveled a long way.

When Oguna stopped to stare blankly at the procession, Nanatsuka grabbed him by the arm and yanked him into the trees that lined the road. "Idiot! Hurry up and hide. That's the Itsuki no Miya, high priestess of the royal shrine in Itsuse. If anyone finds out that we defiled the road in front of her by carrying dead game across it, we'll be punished."

"The high priestess?" Oguna repeated, craning his neck to see even as he was being forced down into the bushes.

"Yes. Haven't you heard of her? She's Princess Momoso, the emperor's sister."

"Of course I have. But Itsuse is so far away. I never expected to see her here."

"Sometimes she comes in the fall for the harvest festival. She's a little early this year though."

"That's so unusual. The high priestess in Mino never leaves the shrine."

"The shrine to the God of Light was within the palace until just fifteen years ago. It was moved when Princess Momoso became the Itsuki no Miya. Rumor has it that she suffered terribly. She was obeying the omens, but still. They say that she wandered the country and slept out in the wind and rain until she finally settled in Itsuse. It must be a great hardship for a woman of royal birth to become high priestess."

From the shadow of the trees, Nanatsuka watched the palanquin pass slowly by. Oguna watched too, filled with pity for the woman inside. Knowing about her past made the palanquin's pomp and splendor seem more understandable.

The procession wended its way solemnly toward the emperor's quarters, moving at a snail's pace that strained Oguna's and Nanatsuka's patience. To make things worse, the way to Lady Inabi's residence was now blocked. The emperor's wives lived on the north side of the emperor's palace, and there was only one official entrance into the compound.

"Now what are we going to do?"

"Why don't we try going around the back?" Oguna suggested.

Nanatsuka looked doubtful. "It would tarnish the prince's reputation for us to go sneaking through the servants' quarters to meet his mother."

"But the important thing is to deliver the birds, right?"

Nanatsuka had to agree. They decided to take a narrow road that ran along the wall encircling the palace complex, a route they would normally never travel. Soon they came upon a scene invisible from the main thoroughfare. Everything absent from the clean and tidy main streets seemed to have been crammed into this space: the homes of lower-ranking servants, livestock sheds, troughs for washing, cesspools, and garbage heaps. The number of people living here amazed Oguna. Squat huts topped with mildewed thatch extended row upon row, their wooden walls touching and their doors so narrow they would have scraped his shoulders. No sunlight penetrated the dank interiors, and the air was rank with the stench of people's lives. While the palace grounds were wide and spacious, life within the servants' quarters made even the poorest villager in Mino seem blessed with space and freedom.

Nanatsuka shook his head understandingly when Oguna pointed out the contrast. "Yet many people are here by choice," he said. "After all, this is the capital."

Oguna felt a twinge of guilt when he thought about his own living quarters—a whole building with an inner garden all to himself. He found it hard to remember that the treatment he received was far above his station in life. Even in Mino, he hadn't noticed until the village bullies had picked on him.

Looking at the closely packed huts, he thought, *I must never forget. My parents abandoned me. Nothing I have is mine by right. Everything I'm doing was made possible through the kindness of others.*

They finally reached the back gate of Lady Inabi's residence. The outdoor cooking area bustled with preparations for the evening meal. Smoke rose from several wood-fired earthen ovens and servants hurried to and fro, hauling firewood, washing rice, bearing water jugs. Oguna and Nanatsuka, each carrying a brace of birds, came to a stop. They needed someone to usher them into Lady Inabi's hall, but all the servants in the yard seemed too low in rank to set foot beyond the kitchen.

"You'll have to handle this," Nanatsuka said. "I've never mastered the niceties of palace conversation."

Although nervous, Oguna had no choice. Looking around, he caught sight of a more genteel-looking young woman outside the gate. She was carrying a bamboo colander filled with leafy greens. Although her back was turned, she moved with a grace and elegance that belied her humble attire—a simple, short tunic of hemp cloth—and her hair, tied in a bun on top of her head, was much longer than an ordinary servant's. He hurried after her and called out, "Excuse me. Could you help me?"

The woman turned toward him warily. When she saw his face, she gave a small shriek and fled, dropping her colander and scattering the contents on the ground. Oguna stood stunned for a moment, but then collecting himself, he raced after her.

"Wait!" he called, gasping for breath. "Please. Don't run away. Don't you recognize me? It's me. Oguna, from Kamitsusato."

When she heard his name, the girl finally stopped running and turned, wide-eyed, gazing timidly at him as he ran up to her. "Oguna? Is that really you, Oguna? You're not the prince?"

"Yes, it's me. Lady Akaru . . . " He stared at her in disbelief. Lady Akaru, who had come bedecked in gorgeous robes and precious beads to wed the emperor, now wore rags and was worked to the bone. She had grown very thin. Her cheeks had lost their plumpness and her eyes their sparkle, and her hands and feet looked painfully chapped.

"What have they done to you, the highest lady in all of Mino?" Oguna asked, his voice strangled.

Lady Akaru slumped down to the ground as if the energy had drained from her body. Oguna knelt before her with a look of concern. She smiled faintly and raised her hand timidly to touch his cheek. "You're so like him now. I thought my heart would stop when I saw you standing there. But now that I think of it, it makes perfect sense. After all, so many years have passed since I saw you last. Even His Highness, the prince, must have changed since I first met him in Mino."

"He hasn't changed a bit."

"Really? Well, I'm glad then. But I have changed. I couldn't bear for him to see me like this. Even if I must die forgotten here, I don't ever want him to know."

Suddenly angry, Oguna demanded, "Who did this to you? You were wed to the emperor. This is no place for the emperor's wife!"

"The emperor is punishing me," she said in a voice no more than a whisper. "I failed to appease his soul and so . . . I'm paying for it. But it's my own fault. I can't blame anyone else."

"I don't understand. I can't stand by and let him do this to you," he said vehemently. "If our clansmen knew, they would be heartbroken. You weren't born to work as a lowly servant. And the prince. He didn't bring you to Mahoroba to be treated like this."

Lady Akaru looked up at him, her eyes wild and stricken like the eyes of a doe driven to the edge of a cliff, and in them he saw what she could not say out loud. But then her eyes dulled and she looked down. "I brought this upon myself. Oguna, don't tell anyone you met me. Keep this secret safe in your heart. Please don't tell the prince. And you too. Please, please don't do anything rash."

"Lady Akaru . . . " Oguna was not satisfied, but she shook her head, silencing him.

"Off you go now. If you spend too long talking to me, people will start to think something is suspicious. Especially when you look so much like the prince. I don't know if we'll ever meet again, but take care of yourself and serve the prince well." She gave him no chance to protest. While she might have been stripped of her rank, she had not been stripped of the dignity that came with noble birth. He tried to convince her, but she brushed him off, and before he knew it, she had arranged for one of Lady Inabi's maidservants to take him and Nanatsuka into the hall.

Oguna was so distracted he could barely pay attention, but Lady Inabi was delighted to see him. Soft and plump, she was not at all like Prince Oh-usu, except perhaps in her cheerful disposition. Despite being the highest-ranked wife of the emperor, she was easy to please and had a great weakness for talking about her son. Summoning Oguna to her side, she inundated him with memories of the prince, as if, indeed, the past had come to life. Nanatsuka, who seemed to have expected this, sat and listened patiently.

When she had talked to her heart's content, she turned her attention to Oguna himself. "Are you sure you're not related to the emperor?" she asked. "I can't believe that there's no connection at all. Of all the emperor's sons, Oh-usu is most like him. Which means that you are too."

"I'm sure it's purely a coincidence," Oguna answered hastily. "I was born in Mino." Furious with the emperor for what he had done to Lady Akaru, he resented being told he looked like him.

Finally, it was time to take their leave and escape at last from Lady Inabi's reminiscences. As he rose to go, Oguna summoned his courage and asked, "Do you know the young woman with the long hair who works in the kitchens? I thought that she might be from Mino."

Lady Inabi blinked and waved her fan gracefully. "Oh no, I couldn't possibly keep track of all the lowly serving wenches. Why, I can't even remember the faces of my ladies-in-waiting."

∗ ∗ ∗

THAT NIGHT Lady Akaru could not sleep. Oguna had appeared out of nowhere, looking just like Prince Oh-usu when she had first met him at the archery tournament, and now she could not banish the prince from her mind. She had struggled so hard to forget him—his eyes, his voice, the expressions that flowed across his face, but now these images spilled forth, flooding her heart. She blamed Oguna bitterly for destroying the dam she had built to hold them back.

It's not fair, not after I made it all this way without shedding any tears.

She could hear the peaceful breathing of the other kitchen girls as they slept, crammed like sardines into the small shack. Someone stirred in the heavy darkness. She couldn't cry here. Rising quietly, she crept toward the door, being careful not to step on anyone, and slipped outside.

The chill night air caressed her cheek, and a crescent moon floated in the midnight sky. But when she glanced up, she saw only a silver blur. Perhaps hunger was making it harder to hold back her tears. The spiteful kitchen chief had made her go without dinner, claiming that she had ruined the greens when she dropped them. Although resigned to her punishment, she had neither the will nor the strength left to stop lamenting her fate. She wanted to cry out loud like a little child.

In her heart, she turned toward Mino. *O Keeper of the Shrine . . . how long must I go on living? I can never atone for my mistake. Is it wrong to wish to end it all?* If only she could become a spirit and fly home—home to Mino, to those beloved mountains, valleys, and rivers . . .

She wandered aimlessly along the wall, searching vaguely for somewhere to weep in private. But when she turned the corner, she froze, startled by a figure that stepped out of the darkness. Were the guards spying on her even at this ungodly hour? She studied his face in the faint light, trying to discern his features, only to discover that it was, impossibly, Prince Oh-usu.

Just like before, she thought. *He waited for me and when I turned the corner, there he was . . . standing at the turning point in my destiny.*

Whatever it was that had kept her will strong and steady came crashing down, and spreading her arms wide, she ran toward him. Though she half believed him to be some phantom of her imagination, the arms that caught her were warm and strong—those arms that she had known but once before . . . and those lips. This time she did not push him away. Tears rolled down her cheeks, and while she wept, she realized that she was not the only one weeping.

Prince Oh-usu whispered through clenched teeth, "You're so thin. You feel as though you might break. And all this time, I knew nothing. I traveled distant lands, ignorant of your fate."

"It was better that you didn't know. Why did you come? Oguna? That naughty boy must have told you after all. I asked him not to."

"I would never have taken him into my care if I thought he would be so heartless as to ignore your fate. I came as soon as he told me. How could I not? But I didn't know where to find you. I was just about to wake up everyone in my mother's household."

"I'm so glad you didn't. There are people here who spy on me on the emperor's orders."

Prince Oh-usu drew back slightly to see her face more clearly in the light of the moon. "Tell me. Did my father do this to you because of me?"

The tears welling from her eyes gleamed in the moonlight. " . . . Yes. Because I could not forget you. I thought that I could. But it was impossible. And so my *magatama* did not shine."

"Your magatama?"

"The curved bead passed down in the Tachibana clan. It was for the talisman that the emperor brought me here—it should have stilled his violent spirit and granted him a longer life. But I failed to move the stone, something I never imagined could happen . . . " She covered her face with her hands as sobs wracked her body. "The emperor demanded to know to whom I had given my heart. He even accused me of loving you. I insisted that it wasn't true, but he banished me to the servants' quarters until I should answer him honestly . . . "

She was shaking, and the prince pulled her to him tenderly and stroked her hair as if she were a child. "How could he do that to you?" he said, gazing into the darkness. "And I, knowing nothing, actually envied him. Do you know what I was thinking on the day you rejected me—and ever since I handed you over to my father? I was thinking of killing him and taking you for myself. You told me you could serve no one but the emperor. So my only option was to kill my father and become the emperor myself. Why didn't you tell me? If you had said just one word, I would never have let him do this to you."

"I am a lady of the Tachibana clan. I was trained, above all else, to accept my fate. But now . . . I don't understand anything anymore. I have lost any power I might have had. What destiny is there for someone who is powerless? I . . . " She broke off, hesitating, and then said plaintively, "My heart is yours, against every ban and prohibition I have tried to place upon it. I can't think of any way to stop it. If you told me to kill myself, I would gladly do so."

"As for me, if I have you, I need nothing else, nothing at all."

They held each other close without stirring until finally the prince said, "If I take you away with me now, my father will surely brand me a traitor. But I have no intention of letting you out of arm's reach ever again. Will you come with me? Even if it brings dishonor to your name?"

"I have already given you my answer," Lady Akaru whispered.

"Well then, if I'm going to be called a traitor anyway, let me be one. I've seen much these last few years as I plotted my father's death. He is not a just ruler. He's selfish, cold, and cruel and thoroughly obsessed with extending his mortal life. While traveling from one land to the next, I've secretly been gathering an army. One of my bases is in Mino.

"Lady, let us go back to Mino together—and overthrow the emperor, for our own sakes."

4

THE MEN FURTIVELY summoned in the darkest hour before dawn did not seem nearly as shaken as Oguna to hear the prince speak of treason. It was clear from their expressions that they had been waiting for this day. As Oguna was the only one not informed in advance, he was the only one genuinely surprised.

The prince issued commands with a grim calmness. "The emperor's troops won't move until they have solid proof. There's still time. We must seize this chance and escape beyond Mahoroba's influence. We'll gather again at Kukuri in Mino. Send word to our allies in Owari and Izumo. Our success depends on speed. If we can get through Suzuka Pass without being stopped, our prospects are good. With reinforcements, we could even launch a counterattack. But we must hurry. The most important thing is to get as many men through to Kukuri as possible. Don't take needless risks."

Nanatsuka too appeared to have been expecting this turn of events. When they left the prince, he immediately disappeared into the armory and began counting weapons. Seeing the stunned look on Oguna's face, he grinned and slapped him on the shoulder. "This is no time for standing around. Not if you want to survive."

Oguna frowned. "I know I was the one who asked the prince to help Lady Akaru. But I had no idea it would come to this."

"Maybe *you* didn't. But Lady Akaru is, after all, the emperor's wife. How could we possibly be pardoned for stealing her away?"

"Are traitors executed? Even princes?"

"They're hanged. Even princes," Nanatsuka replied, adding with a wicked grin, "But the prince isn't the type to stand by and let that happen. Nor are we."

Keeping the lamplight as dim as possible, Oguna packed feverishly. He didn't regret telling the prince, he decided. Besides, he had no time to worry about it. Yet his heart ached with the knowledge that Prince Oh-usu was launching a war against his own father.

They slipped out of the hall before sunrise. To avoid suspicion, only a small band rode through the east gate with the prince—few enough to convince any observers that they were just going to the hot spring. With them went Lady Akaru, Nanatsuka, and Oguna. The others exited the capital separately, each heading for Kukuri by a different route. During the hurried meeting before they left, someone suggested that Oguna pose as the prince to lure away pursuers, but Prince Oh-usu had vetoed the idea, perhaps thinking him too young. Oguna felt a strange mixture of relief and disappointment at this decision.

The sun rose between the ridges ahead just as they crested the shoulder of Mount Moroyama. In the red light of dawn, a flock of crows rose startled from their roosts and began cawing raucously. Glancing up at them, the prince frowned. "They sound unlucky. Shall I shoot them?"

Lady Akaru, who had been following silently, spoke up. "Oh no! Please don't do that." Although she looked a little strange disguised as a male servant wearing *hakama,* she sat boldly astride her horse. "No one in Mino would ever think of shooting a crow. According to clan legend, one of our ancestors became one. It would be terrible to kill a relation, even if it were a bird."

The prince gave a short bark of laughter and his face brightened. "I had no idea. You're related to crows, are you? I'll have to watch that you don't sprout wings and fly away."

Lady Akaru blushed slightly and smiled. She looked so beautiful in the early morning light that Oguna gazed at her in admiration. He could see no trace of the worn and haggard woman of the previous day. Like a flower placed in water, she had regained her vitality overnight; just being with the prince and traveling with him to Mino had transformed her. *I did the right thing,* Oguna thought, relieved and comforted. Although he knew their journey was fraught with uncertainty and there was no guarantee they would even make it to the next day, his heart still leapt at the thought of returning to Mino. If he reached Kukuri alive, he would see Kamitsusato, the old familiar valleys and fields of his homeland, the hall where he was raised. And Toko. He would see Toko again. Finally, he could fulfill the promise that had weighed on his heart so long . . .

"I remember a story about that same crow," he said, joining the conversation. "Toko loved it so much she used to ask for it all the time. The story of the bird funeral."

"The bird funeral? Tell it to me," the prince asked.

"Our ancestor, the crow," Lady Akaru began, "mourned the death of a young maiden. He gathered all the birds together to hold a funeral for her. The wild geese became the vessel bearers, the herons became the broom bearers, the sparrows became the rice-pounding girls, and the pheasants became the mourners. Birds of every kind joined in, singing and dancing for eight days and eight nights until the maiden's soul turned into a white bird and flew back from the land of the dead to be reborn. The funeral bier is said to have been on Moyama, the mountain where the Tachibana clan shrine is now located."

"I know a story a little like yours," the prince said, but his face suddenly darkened. "It's about the funeral of Amano Wakahiko. He was sent as a messenger to the earth but fell in love with the daughter of the earth gods and forgot his mission. For eight years he failed to report until finally, one day, he shot the messenger of the gods. The fatal arrow he had loosed was later used to kill him, and the birds mourned his death in the same way."

"But of course he was reborn too, wasn't he?" Lady Akaru said, trying to cheer him up.

But the prince shook his head. "No. Not that I heard."

THE PRINCE'S assumption that their flight would remain undetected for at least a day or two proved wrong. They ran into the emperor's soldiers at the first ford in the river. It was only a small patrol, insufficient to block their way and quickly scattered, but the prince's men were not fully prepared and there were a few tense moments before they seized the boats.

As he poled down the river, Nanatsuka grumbled, "My lord, I beg you to control your urge to fly headlong into battle. If you behave like that, no number of lives will be enough."

"There are too few of us. I can't always be hiding behind you every time we have to fight," the prince responded.

"Look at it from our perspective. If we lose you, we're finished."

"All right, all right," he answered in his usual offhand manner, but then he gazed soberly at the opposite bank. "We may be attacked again if we disembark at the ferry dock. Let's go a little farther downstream. I'd rather not take a detour, but we have no choice. The emperor moved faster than I expected—almost too fast."

"Almost as if he were waiting for us," Nanatsuka said.

The prince looked up quickly. "Do you think it was a trap?"

Nanatsuka fell silent. Lady Akaru was watching them anxiously. The prince turned to her and said, "It makes no difference. It doesn't change what we have to do—get to Kukuri. We knew they'd come after us. I'll show you we can shake them off."

After disembarking on the opposite shore, the prince sent out scouts. These returned to report that an unusual number of troops were on the move. The prince and his company were forced to change routes several times and finally to abandon their horses. They set them off at a gallop with bags of stones tied to their saddles to divert their pursuers and then headed deeper into the mountains, slinging whatever they could carry onto their backs.

Every time they tried to return to the main road, they found soldiers on the prowl. It looked like they would have to stay clear of established routes for some time.

Nanatsuka's knowledge of the territory proved invaluable. He led them up a steep cliff and down through the next valley, where the rest of them would have been lost. But they could not remain concealed indefinitely. The longer they put off crossing the pass, the less chance they had of making it through. Each time they were forced to combat enemy patrols, their numbers dwindled, and some of the men sent ahead as scouts never returned.

Oguna watched in anguish as the prince's faithful men fell, one after the other. *It's no good. They have too many people to protect,* he thought. There were so few men, yet they had to guard the prince, Lady Akaru, and even Oguna. They treated Oguna deferentially, just like the prince, never giving him a turn as a scout and always pushing him to the back when they had to cut their way through enemy soldiers. Although it may have been partly because he was still young, Oguna knew that the main reason was his resemblance to the prince—he was the prince's shadow, and they had been trained to treat that shadow as part of the prince himself.

Even when they were hard pressed in battle, they protected Oguna faithfully, shielding him from danger. And every time, he felt miserable. He could understand their protecting the prince, who must survive even at the cost of their lives. And Lady Akaru too. But what value could he possibly have that they should protect him? What on earth could he offer in exchange for the life of any one of these skilled and hardy warriors? *Why am I here? I'm no use at all. I'm just a burden . . . .*

When he confided in Nanatsuka, however, Nanatsuka said, "Don't think about it. It's not your problem. Just wait until the prince issues you your orders."

ONCE AGAIN THEIR pursuers caught up with them. One brave man stayed behind to hold them off so that the others could escape. He never returned. When the party finally stopped and looked at one another's weary faces in the ruddy afterglow of sunset, there were only five left: Prince Oh-usu, Lady Akaru, Oguna, Nanatsuka, and the prince's attendant, Miyadohiko.

The next morning, Lady Akaru could not take another step. She had kept pace with them all this way, never uttering a word of complaint, but now she was exhausted. "Please leave me here and go on without me. I don't wish to slow you down. The most important thing is to get the prince safely to Mino. Please go on ahead."

Hearing this, the prince hurried over to her, his brow furrowed with concern. "My lady," he said sternly. "I can't let you give up when we have come this far."

But Lady Akaru was far from discouraged. Her eyes bright, she drew herself up straight and said, "I have no intention of giving up. I believe in our future together. Though I stay behind, I will survive. I will remain hidden where none can find me and wait for you to bring your army to rescue me. I'm not about to die here. If dying would have solved anything, I would have taken my own life long ago."

The prince gazed at her radiant face. "Where on earth do you get such strength?"

She reached out her hand. "From you," she said. "You give me strength. Now I fear nothing. I can bear anything at all. Because you came to save me."

The prince hesitated for a long time and then finally called Nanatsuka to him. "Forgive me," he said. "No matter how it may jeopardize our situation, I can't leave Lady Akaru behind. Without her, there is no point in any of this. I vowed that I would never let her out of arm's reach again."

Nanatsuka nodded. "I know," he said. "I'll look for a place to hide. Let's see how she does in the next day or two. If she still can't move, I'll carry her out on my back."

A little farther up the mountain slope, Nanatsuka found a cave with an entrance barely high enough for an adult to pass through standing up. Large stones ringed the entrance as if they had been placed there purposely to conceal it. As Oguna helped him pile more stones to make a rampart, Nanatsuka explained that in the past it was quite common for people to live in such caves.

The interior was much drier than Oguna had expected, and it was empty except for some dry, odorless animal droppings. They covered the floor in a thick bed of clean, dry grasses and laid a cloth over top for Lady Akaru, who was delighted even with such a simple bed. She had not slept on anything resembling a bed for several days.

What they lacked was food and water. They had all but exhausted the dried rations they had brought with them. Nanatsuka went looking for provisions while Miyadohiko, fully aware of the risk, went to spy on the movements of the emperor's troops. Taking turns with Prince Oh-usu guarding Lady Akaru, Oguna tasted the frustration and anxiety of being cornered.

Even a single step would bring them that much closer to Mino, but instead they had to hide in this unknown place, waiting to be discovered by their enemies. There was so much time to think, it was torture. Although he no longer knew what mountains they were wandering through, the trees and shrubs told him that he was still far from home. The types of plants and the smell of the air were different from those he remembered. Nanatsuka and the prince never expressed any doubt, but Oguna was beginning to wonder if they could really make it to Kukuri.

He thought it through logically as he had been trained to do. *Even if the prince does get through, not all of us can possibly make it. Of the five of us, the prince must be protected at all costs. Next to him we must protect Lady Akaru. And Nanatsuka, because he can guide them and make sure that they reach Kukuri safely.*

He looked up at the distant blue sky. That and the color of the clouds were the only things that never changed no matter where he was. Oguna longed to go home, but this was in direct opposition to the pressing duty he felt. When it came to making a choice, he knew it was his hopes and desires that he must deny. So he had been taught. So he had been trained. He could see the faces of the prince's men who had died protecting him . . . They, too, must have had people they longed to see. But they had still chosen death as if it were the most natural thing to do. If they could do it, surely he could too.

I must help them get to Kukuri. Otherwise I'll never be able to justify my being here. There will have been no point in my going to Mahoroba. I wanted to become stronger. That's why I went. Now I must stand strong and firm.

Between the clouds, he caught fleeting glimpses of Toko's face—sometimes laughing, sometimes in an angry huff—but always twelve years old, even though he knew that this Toko could no longer exist.

Nanatsuka came back with nuts and berries from the forest. He apologized for not being able to cook a meal because the smoke would give them away.

Although Lady Akaru appeared to have lost her appetite, he handed her different nuts and berries one by one, accompanying each with a detailed explanation that made her pop them into her mouth, entertained. Oguna loved Nanatsuka all the more for keeping his passion for food and for feeding others regardless of the circumstances.

Not long after, Miyadohiko returned with unexpectedly good tidings. The prince's allies had already reached Nobono on the other side of the pass. Nanatsuka took a stick and drew a map on the ground while the others gathered around and listened intently.

"We're here," he said. "If we can just cross safely over the pass, we can reach Nobono in less than a day."

The prince's spirits lifted for the first time in a long while. "Don't worry," he declared. "We'll get across. The heavens are on my side. Let's push our way through right now. And don't try to tell me you're going to stay behind, my lady."

Lady Akaru nodded. "I feel like I could walk now. I'll do my best."

They all knew that an ambush waited for them at Suzuka Pass, but the prince's enthusiasm cheered their hearts against all logic. They felt capable of anything—all they needed was to put their heart and soul into their task. At that moment, however, Nanatsuka jerked his head up and, grabbing his bow, ran to the entrance. He peered out from the shadow of the rock, then turned and said in a flat voice, "They've found us. Miyadohiko, you were followed."

Miyadohiko stood up, the color draining from his face, and went to the mouth of the cave. Now the others could hear the clamor they had all feared. Dogs howling, men shouting, branches snapping underfoot. "This was my fault," Miyadohiko said. "I'll stay here and hold them off while you make your escape." He slung his quiver across his back.

"Do you intend to face them alone?" the prince demanded, but Oguna cut in.

"I'll stay with him. Please go." Without waiting for a reply, he continued. "Tell me to act as your shadow. Command me to take your place. You once told me that I would be your secret weapon. Well, now is the time to use it. When people hear that the prince has been captured, they'll relax their watch over the pass. It's the only way."

The prince stared at him. Oguna had spoken so calmly and dispassionately that the prince wondered if he had really understood what he was saying.

"Are you sure that's what you want? Do you know what they'll do to you in the capital?"

Oguna nodded. "You brought me to Mahoroba to be your shadow. That's why I was given the chance to learn. How else can I repay you if I don't serve you now?"

Prince Oh-usu gazed into the face that looked so much like his. It was filled with so much potential, yet Oguna's eyes held no trace of hesitation, no hint of fear or regret. "This is not what I brought you to the capital for . . . but still, I thank you." Having made up his mind, the prince removed the jade necklace he always wore around his neck and gave it to Oguna. Then he slipped off his gold armband, symbol of the God of Light. Finally, he removed the blue silk headband he wore around his forehead. As he handed these to Oguna, he said, "I will never forget you, Ousu, little brother."

"Thank you," Oguna said. His chest filled with warmth at the word *brother*. But there was no time to say anything more. The enemy was closing in on them. Lady Akaru watched Oguna with anguished eyes as Nanatsuka carried her away on his back. Nanatsuka himself was speechless with anger. If looks could kill, his would have slain the entire enemy army.

Oguna and Miyadohiko fired warning shots to let the other three slip out unnoticed through a small hole that Nanatsuka had concealed with tree branches. At least twenty soldiers were approaching the cave, but not knowing how many men they were up against, they kept their distance and fired a barrage of arrows at the entrance. The rocks acted as a shield, giving Oguna and Miyadohiko the advantage—at least until they ran out of arrows. They had used them sparingly at first until they were sure the others had had enough time to get away. Then, they began shooting in rapid succession.

"Let's make them think there's a hundred of us here," Oguna said.

Miyadohiko grinned. "Raising the stakes, are you? You sound just like the prince." Miyadohiko was a skilled archer worthy of Nanatsuka's trust, and together he and Oguna did well for just two people. No one could get near them while they still had arrows left, but finally, the last arrow was gone. They looked at each other.

"Am I right in thinking that the prince wouldn't wait for them to come and get him?" Oguna asked.

Miyadohiko nodded and said, "Yes. You too?"

"No, but I want to convince as many people as possible that I really am the prince, so I'm going out there."

"In that case, I'm coming with you," Miyadohiko said lightly and drew his sword. "Let's make those cowards run. Enough playing around. It's time to break through their ranks and be on our way."

Oguna smiled. He had not had much chance to talk with Miyadohiko, but he suddenly felt a great affection for him. Perhaps it was a comradeship born from their readiness to die. They laid aside their bows and took up their swords. Leaping outside the ring of stones, they raced down the hill. Figures emerged from the trees on every side, but Oguna felt no fear. His head was clear and every movement seemed extraordinarily vivid. *Just like before,* he thought. He could do it—he could cut these men down. Together, he and Miyadohiko might even be able to break through . . .

Somewhere inside, he knew this was impossible. *But this is what it takes to fight,* he thought, *to believe to the very end that you can do it.*

His last thought before he merged with the sword he brandished was *Goodbye, Toko.*

5

PAIN WOKE Oguna. He hurt all over, which meant he must still be alive. Dazed, he wondered where Miyadohiko was. Even as he ran toward the soldiers, he had listened for Miyadohiko's footsteps, for the sound of his breathing. The savage tumult of battle still rang in his ears—shouts, the clash of swords, random phrases. "It's the prince!" "Don't let him get away!" As Oguna had raised his sword, his gold armband flashed in the sun, and the blinding glare jolted him back to his senses.

Now he was lying facedown on the floor with his hands tied behind his back in a very unnatural position. A ray of sunlight from a tiny window far above shone full in his face. Surprised, he wondered when he had been captured. Then it all came back to him.

He and Miyadohiko had charged toward the enemy line, slashing so fiercely that at first the soldiers had fallen back. In the end, however, they were snared with surprising ease by a net thrown from a tree—the ultimate humiliation when they had been ready to die in battle.

The soldiers had removed the gold band from Oguna's arm and bound him firmly with hemp ropes. Convinced that they had successfully captured Oh-usu alive, they did not loosen his bonds even once on the way back to Mahoroba for fear that the proud prince would take his own life. This made the journey so excruciating that what little Oguna remembered seemed unreal. When they had thrown him into this room, he had been relieved to think that everything would soon be over.

That was last night. Exhausted, he had actually slept despite his circumstances. *I wonder if the prince managed to escape,* he thought as he tried to move out of the light. His body was so stiff he could barely turn over. Sighing, he comforted himself with the thought that his capture was exactly what they had planned. The soldiers, thinking they had caught the prince, had returned with him to the capital, giving the others the perfect opportunity to escape. Nanatsuka wouldn't miss that chance. By now the three survivors of the company must be on the other side of the pass, surrounded by their allies. Oguna's life had not been wasted; he should be content...

After some time, he heard footsteps on the other side of the door and the bolt slid back noisily. Two soldiers bearing pikes entered. As Oguna peered up at them blankly, they grabbed him roughly and yanked him upright. Clearly, they now knew he was not the prince. He had known all along that he was too young to fool anyone who knew Oh-usu well.

"Get up. His Majesty will question you in person. If you don't walk straight, we'll beat some manners into you." With this gentle encouragement, they shoved Oguna out the door, prodding him along with the shafts of their pikes. Although Oguna tried to walk properly, he could not help staggering. A sharp blow from one of the guards, however, cleared his head a little and brought his chin up. For many years he had both feared and longed to see the face of the man who ruled Mahoroba. While he had never imagined that it would be like this, he decided it wouldn't be so bad to pay his respects to the emperor before he died. He summoned the last of his strength and kept walking.

From his surroundings, he guessed that he must already be inside the grounds of the emperor's palace. A tall wooden fence ran around the outer edge. Inside, all was silent. The fence, the walls, the pillars of the buildings towered over him, making him feel he had shrunk. The guards led him down a mazelike path that followed a narrow cleft between the buildings—the perfect route for those on confidential missions for the emperor. They finally came into a small, secluded courtyard enclosed on all sides. In front of them stood a large building with a raised wooden floor, part of which jutted out into the courtyard. It was there that the emperor sat, shaded by the eaves.

Judging by the lack of spectators, Oguna guessed that this was a private interrogation during which the prisoner of war could be killed at will. He was here only because the emperor had shown some fleeting interest in him. Oguna was curious as well. Here, at last, was the man whose very name inspired awe, the man for whom he felt such mixed emotions yet whom he had never seen.

The emperor sat impassive as a statue, a faintly cynical look on his face. The breadth of his shoulders made it clear that he was tall, and his jade robes accentuated his jet-black hair and beard. While he showed no signs of aging, his face lacked youthfulness. His eyes looked hard, even cruel, not likely to be moved by the simple joys of life or by compassion, yet at the same time, they gleamed with an unmistakable wisdom. No matter how he might strive to find fault with him, Oguna was forced to acknowledge that this was no ordinary man. He radiated such power that it made Oguna's skin prickle.

So this is Prince Oh-usu's father, he thought.

The two guards, who had forced him to his knees and then bowed deeply, suddenly realized that their prisoner, far from prostrating himself on the ground, was actually staring at the emperor. Enraged, they struck him. The emperor, however, signaled them to step back, having sensed no hostility in Oguna's behavior.

"Oh-usu appears to have trained a good shadow," he said. "I can see why those who didn't know him well could mistake you for him. I underestimated his resourcefulness." Something in the man's voice reminded Oguna of the prince. Even the way his mouth moved when he spoke was the same. They were obviously father and son, yet Oguna found it hard to believe that he too looked like this man.

"We already know that you're an impostor. The penalty for impersonating the prince is heavy, but if you answer honestly, perhaps we can lighten your sentence. Tell me. How many men has Oh-usu drawn to his side? How many bases does he have and who are his allies?"

Oguna could not answer. Even if he had wanted to, he did not know.

"Where did they go?" the emperor demanded. "To Mino? Where in Mino?"

This question Oguna would not answer, no matter what, for if he did there would have been no point in staying behind and abandoning all hope for the future. When he remained silent, however, a searing pain suddenly raced from his shoulder down his back. The guard behind him had struck him with a bamboo switch.

"Insolent fool! The emperor is asking you a question. Silence is not permissible."

Oguna was truly sorry. He could tell from the emperor's voice that he was not a man to be ignored, that to do so was unforgivably arrogant. But he had already relinquished his claim on life. A shadow exposed to the light, Oguna had no choice but to fade into silence.

When Oguna failed to respond, the guard whipped him mercilessly, and although he thought his knees were planted firmly on the ground, Oguna felt himself fall to his face. Blinking the mist from his eyes, he saw the emperor tilted at an odd angle.

"What is your name?" the emperor asked. His tone seemed almost kind. While he was unsure of the motive behind it, Oguna was thankful that he had finally been asked a question he could answer. He wanted at least to say *something*.

"The prince called me Ousu."

"Where did he find you?"

The memory of their first meeting floated through the haze in his mind, and he wanted to laugh out loud. But that was impossible; it was hard enough just to gasp out the words, "Pond . . . at the dam . . . "

Oguna suddenly realized that a woman was now standing beside the emperor, her eyes studying Oguna's face. Though not young, she was beautiful. Unadorned by jewels or gold, she could not be a royal consort, yet she shone with inner nobility. The headband tied around her forehead was white, and from her neck hung a round copper mirror, her only accessory. The sight of this sacred object told him instantly who she was—Princess Momoso, the emperor's younger sister, keeper of the royal shrine in Itsuse and high priestess of the God of Light.

So that's who was riding in the palanquin the other day . . . Oguna felt strangely content. Not only had he seen the emperor with his own eyes, but now he had also met the high priestess of Itsuse. While Toko had spoken with awe of the Keeper of the Shrine in Mino, the woman before him was far more elegant than Prince Oh-usu's mother or any woman he had ever met. Her piercing gaze struck him with extraordinary force, and when he stared back at her, it was as though he were enveloped in cold flame. Why she looked at him that way, whether out of curiosity or pity, he could not begin to guess and had no strength left to wonder. His back burned from the lashes, and sounds ebbed and flowed around him.

Dimly, he registered the fact that the guards had grabbed him once more and he was being dragged from the courtyard. Oguna was thrown back into his cell only to be hauled out again almost immediately. Unable to walk, he was carried, slung like a sack over someone's shoulders, and then shoved inside what seemed to be a palanquin. They must have been planning to take him some distance. He wondered vaguely where the execution grounds were, but he was past caring. Nausea swept over him when the men heaved the poles upward and began to lurch forward. Thinking that he would be put out of his misery soon, he fought against the nausea until he finally lost consciousness.

HE DREAMED dream after dream, fragmented and disconnected. Oguna was standing on a riverbank watching an egg in a reed basket float down the river. Then he was sobbing as he tried to flee from a huge snake whose coils covered the sky. Prince Oh-usu bent down and looked into his eyes. "Are you sure that's what you want?" he asked.

The scene shifted, and Oguna found himself drowning in boiling water. He had to save Toko, who was also drowning, but his limbs felt like lead. Nanatsuka stalked off, his eyes angry. Oguna was alone. That was what he had wanted but now he was suffocating, alone in the darkness. This was his tomb.

"But he was reborn, wasn't he?" Lady Akaru said.

"No," the prince replied.

In the sky high above, the child Toko laughed and beckoned him. He was a boy again. *She wants to play make-believe,* he thought. *She's going to be a white bird...*

Someone gently sponged the sweat from his forehead. This felt familiar. When he had come down with the measles, Matono had wiped his brow like that.

"Mother?" he asked, blinded by the dark.

"I'm right here," a warm voice answered.

I see. This must be my room in Kamitsusato, he thought. But why hadn't he met his mother before? Where could he have been all this time? And shouldn't Toko be sleeping beside him? They had both had the measles at the same time...

I remember now. I had a terrible nightmare about a snake coiled in the sky. He wanted to tell Matono but couldn't. There were some things that just could not be said. Delirium dragged him into another dream and he no longer felt her hand.

OGUNA WAS NOT in his room in Kamitsusato. He was in a small room, neat and bright, but totally unfamiliar. Now he was wide awake. This was real—he could tell because his memory had come flooding back, but that made his circumstance all the more confusing. Why had he been laid to rest on clean bedding like a patient? The basin of water by his pillow and the young woman of about twenty sitting where he remembered Matono being in his dream just increased his bewilderment.

"Who are you?" he asked, but his voice was only a hoarse whisper. The sound caught the woman's attention, however, and he tried again. "Where am I?"

"This is the outer hall, a separate building. You aren't permitted inside because you're a man." Oguna was clearly having difficulty understanding her, so she added, "I serve the Itsuki no Miya. She asked me to care for you."

Oguna almost leapt to his feet, only to be instantly reminded that his body was incapable of doing so. He struggled to a sitting position. "This isn't... the royal shrine... is it?"

"Of course it is. This is the sacred shrine of Itsuse. Don't you remember?" she said in surprise. "What a time we had bringing you here without anyone seeing. Especially when you were so delirious."

Oguna was speechless. *Itsuse!* Maybe he was still dreaming after all. The shutters had been thrown open, and through the window's wooden slats he could see outside. There was no garden, just a steep slope covered in oak and broad-leafed evergreens. The light shining through the trees and the fragrance of the breeze spoke of early autumn deep in the mountains.

"Why did you save me?" Oguna finally asked, perplexed. It didn't feel real enough to rejoice; it was all too strange.

"You'll have to ask Her Highness. She often came to see you. I'm sure she'll be delighted to hear that you're awake."

Remembering Princess Momoso's piercing gaze, Oguna was overcome with anxiety. What on earth could the princess want with an impostor and a traitor? He wasn't actually afraid of pain, but enough was enough. When the maidservant left the room, he wondered if he could escape before she came back. His wounds, however, were not fully healed and his body was very weak. It had been all he could do just to sit up. Alone in an unknown place with no friends or familiar things to cheer him, Oguna felt as lost and helpless as a baby, something he had not experienced for a long time. And he was tired of putting up a bold front. His dreams had swept away all his defenses and left him here, naked. Even the sun on his skin felt cold and distant.

The floorboards in the corridor began to creak, and Oguna heard the swish of cloth, signaling the approach of several people. The soft rustling reminded him of a snake slithering through the grass and he trembled, desperately suppressing the urge to back up, crawling, against the far wall. That would be too humiliating.

The door was flung open, and the Itsuki no Miya glided into the room. She wore a pleated scarlet skirt over a pure white robe and bore herself with the same natural dignity he had sensed when he first saw her. Although accompanied by several ladies-in-waiting, she entered the room alone. The door closed swiftly behind her.

She stood looking down at Oguna where he sat on the futon. "I was concerned that you wouldn't survive, but my prayers have been answered." Her voice, low and rich for a woman, was surprisingly soft. Not at all imperious.

"You said your name was Ousu. Did you not come from Mino? Prince Oh-usu went there once to build a pond and villa."

There was no need to hide the truth now. Oguna nodded, averting his eyes.
"And your parents, could it be you don't know who they are?"
Once again, he nodded.

And then, suddenly, she was there, kneeling right beside him. Oguna, his nerves already stretched taut, jerked back in surprise and looked up. Instead of the stern expression he had anticipated, her face was tinged with grief and tears welled in her eyes. The fine lines etched around her eyes and mouth were like those of any woman who had lived through pain and sorrow. The sight touched his heart. Thick, lustrous hair flowed over her shoulders and a gentle, feminine scent wafted from it.

"Could it be . . . could it be that you were abandoned and set afloat on the river in a reed basket?"

"How do you know that?" Oguna demanded. He could not help himself. It was too strange. Perhaps she had the gift of prophecy like the high priestess in Mino. "Surely Prince Oh-usu would never have mentioned it . . . "

"No, no one told me. And I told no one. I have kept this knowledge sealed in my heart for sixteen years. But your face, I could never mistake your face. You are my son, the child I bore sixteen years ago at the edge of Mino, the child who was torn from my arms only a few days after I gave birth." Her voice trembled and tears spilled from her eyes. Overcome with emotion, she wrapped her arms around him and pulled him toward her, pressing him against her cheek.

"How I suffered after losing you! How I longed to hold you once again! My dear, beloved child, I can scarcely believe we have been reunited. I had given you up for dead. You cannot imagine the pain I endured, unable to share this burden with anyone."

Clasped in her arms, Oguna listened, stunned. The world seemed to shatter around him in an explosion of white light. It would have been a lie to say that he had not secretly wished to hear those words from someone someday. But never in his wildest imaginings had he expected it to happen under such circumstances as these. And this woman was the emperor's sister, the Itsuki no Miya herself! What was going on?

Questions whirled in his brain, yet, at the same time, wrapped in her scent and with her tears on his face, something that had lain dormant deep within his heart was shaken. The sight of Princess Momoso, so obviously refined and noble, weeping without restraint made his heart ache. Had she ever cried like this for anyone else? Had anyone ever wept for him like this before?

"Please don't cry," he said quietly. "If I am truly your child, then, please, tell me why you abandoned me." He trembled as he asked this question, so central to his life yet one he had never expected to ask.

"You were a gift from the God of Light. The others forbade me to give birth because I am the high priestess, the Itsuki no Miya, but I knew that it was the right thing to do, that it was my duty. So I left the shrine in Mahoroba and wandered from place to place. It was a difficult and painful journey, yet you grew strong and healthy within my womb. When I reached Mino, my time was near, and I built a birthing hut on the desolate banks of an unknown river.

"How happy I was! You were like a precious jewel. But I was blind to the treachery of my maidservant, to the fact that her mind had been poisoned by preposterous lies. While I lay sleeping, she took you . . . and set you adrift in the river. At first, she lied and said that you had drowned. Mad with grief, I plunged into the water and began searching the riverbed for your body. Then, perhaps fearing that I would die, she began to cry and plead for forgiveness, saying that she had not had the heart to kill you but instead had put you in a basket and let the river take you.

"I almost died. I lost all hope and strength. But now I am so glad that I survived; so glad that I lived on, clinging to the hope that, one day, we would meet again. How I have longed to hear you call me mother. Please do. Call me Mother."

Oguna obeyed meekly. The word, unfamiliar to his tongue, felt awkward and strange, but he could no longer doubt that she was indeed his mother.

There was one more question he had to ask. Gathering his courage, he said hesitantly, "Mother . . . what about my father? Who is my father?"

Princess Momoso finally loosened her arms and pressed a sleeve against her eyes. When she had regained her composure, she said, "Your father is the God of Light. I am the priestess. He gave you to me as a gift. You need feel no shame. Rather you should be proud. For of all the people in Toyoashihara, you are closest to the gods. The blood of the youngest child of the God of Light runs through my veins as well. You are of higher and more noble birth than anyone else who walks this earth."

Oguna suddenly remembered Toko declaring so confidently, *I think that you'd feel much better if you just knew who your parents were.* In his heart, he addressed that lively girl, still dressed in red. *Toko, now I know whose child I am. But I'm even more confused than before. What should I do? My birth . . . is it something to be celebrated or cursed?*

He did not want to think about who his father was. It was like falling over the edge into darkness. His mother had told him his father was a god so that he wouldn't worry about it. *Perhaps it's better that way,* he thought.

chapter
three

TREASON

Treason

"DID YOU SEE that? Bull's-eye!" Toko shouted proudly. Three arrows quivered in the middle of the straw bag she was using as a target.

"You show great promise, my lady," said Tsunuga, a member of the headman's guard. "You're a keen markswoman. If you could just use a slightly stronger bow, you could even compete with the men."

"Isn't this bow good enough for fighting?"

"I'm afraid it wouldn't shoot far enough."

"Well, never mind. I'll just have to build up more muscle then," Toko announced, patting an arm so slender it looked like it would never show a bicep. At that moment, she heard someone call her name.

"Toko? Toko! What on earth do you think you're doing? Come here at once!"

Glancing at Tsunuga, Toko grimaced. "Oh, dear. Mother found me," she said and ran lightly over to the house. "I wasn't doing anything, Mother. I was just borrowing the target for a minute."

Matono frowned at her daughter's innocent expression. "A girl your age shouldn't be out in the yard where there are only men. Nor should you be using a bow and arrow. And what on earth were you thinking to dress like that?"

Toko looked down at the men's hakama she was wearing. "But, Mother, you were the one who told me that a big girl like me shouldn't show her knees. And I can't wear a long skirt until I'm a woman, right? So I decided to wear hakama instead. It makes perfect sense to me."

Matono pressed her hand against her forehead. "Honestly! You're sixteen already. The chief's second daughter entered the shrine ages ago to begin her training, but you—"

"Well, there's nothing I can do about it, Mother," Toko said cheerfully. "Maybe I'll never become a woman."

"Don't be ridiculous!" Matono snapped. "Just think of the shame you would bring on our household. I'd have to commit suicide. You're a Tachibana. Such a thing would be inexcusable."

Toko was about to shrug, but Matono looked so serious she decided against it. She did not want to make her mother sad, but sometimes she just could not stand it.

"Would you please at least *behave* more like a woman and a lady of our clan?" Matono said. "Mino is so unsettled right now, and everyone's been coming and going from our hall. Try not to embarrass us like this when there are so many people watching."

After her mother had left, Toko unstrung her bow and sat down with a sigh on a bench under the eaves. *Mother's always nagging me lately. Why doesn't she leave me alone? After all, I'm not a woman yet.*

The yard was filled with young men practicing their fighting skills. Over the last few years, the peaceful mountain villages of Mino had been transformed. The good-natured local men accustomed to using a bow or pike only for sport now vied with one another to hone their techniques. These changes had begun four years ago with the appearance of Prince Oh-usu. His vitality, enthusiasm, and leadership immediately captivated the young men, and they all longed to be bold and daring like him. Soon, his influence had spread to the older generations as well. Chief Kamubonehiko was an ardent admirer, as was Toko's father, who had spent much of his personal wealth to support the prince's cause.

Toko, who practically worshipped the prince, could not bear to simply stand by and watch. She longed to demonstrate her allegiance by doing something, anything at all. Her mother, Matono, however, had become stricter with each passing year. At times, Toko wanted to run away from home, but the only refuge she could think of was the shrine on the mountain. Even her mother's nagging was preferable to that. She could not imagine living in that archaic place where visitors rarely came, and she had never gotten along with Kisako, the chief's second daughter who had been training there as a shrine maiden for the last three years. The fact was that Toko did not want to become a shrine maiden. She wanted to go out in the world, not be compelled to stay shut inside reading oracles. If she could have, Toko would have become a warrior and hunted down the enemies that threatened her people.

With her chin propped in her hand, she watched the men practice. *Why shouldn't there be at least one Tachibana woman who can wield a sword and protect Mino? But they'll never let me. I want to train, but I can only do it when no one is watching. I'll never get any better at this rate. I wish the prince had taken me to the capital like he did Oguna.*

She wondered how Oguna was doing. He had been closer to her than a brother and she still worried about him, just as she had predicted when she last saw him. She knew he kept his feelings bottled up inside, unable to express them. That was why she had always stood by him—he needed someone who understood how he felt. But perhaps he didn't anymore. Four years had passed. Even Oguna must have changed a little. *Everyone changes. Everyone except me...*

She had grown and her hair was longer—much longer, in fact, because as a princess of the clan she was not allowed to cut it. It was such a nuisance that she kept it tied in a ponytail, but even so it hung down to the middle of her back. Although she chose to act like a boy, no one would have considered treating her like one. Her long hair and slender build gave her away instantly.

Yet Toko was not quite a woman either. She lacked any hint of the coyness found in young women her age, and there was nothing sensuous about her laugh. She was not shy in the least and had no compunction about telling someone to their face how she felt about them. People saw her as a tomboy, overlooking most of her quirks with a knowing smile. Although it upset Matono that the young men did not regard Toko as a lady of the hall, she had to admit that everyone liked her. All the villagers smiled when they caught sight of "Lady Tomboy" and felt comfortable talking to her.

People rarely mentioned Oguna anymore, even in the hall where he had been raised. He had never been the type of child to make a deep impression, and as they had had no news of him since he left for the capital, people who had not known Oguna well had forgotten he even existed. Toko, however, would never forget. For her, his name was as deeply rooted in her mind as her own. She remembered the promise he had made as if it were only yesterday.

Oguna must remember too . . . At least, he should. But then why haven't we had any news? Despondent, she gazed off into space.

The sound of pounding hooves suddenly echoed through the air: a lone horse at full gallop heading for the hall. Even racing uphill, it did not slacken its pace. Toko leapt to her feet. Something must have happened.

Flecked with foam, the horse shot through the open gate bearing a rider from the chief's hall. The messenger scrambled off his mount and rushed inside, followed by a crowd of people. Toko watched them go and then hurried deeper into the building to a place where she knew she would have a better chance to hear. Gently, she eased open a partition that led into the large meeting room. Through the crack she could glimpse her father's back. Her heart froze when she heard the words muttered by the crowd.

"Treason? Did he say treason?"

"So the prince has finally—"

"The emperor's men are after him—"

"And Lady Akaru too!"

Toko pressed her hand against her mouth. This was not some entertaining little episode to while away the boredom. It was a real crisis.

"There's still hope," Toko's father was saying. "The prince hasn't been captured yet. We must gather our men and go to his aid."

The messenger nodded. "That's why I'm here. The chief wants to know how many men and horses you can spare."

A seasoned leader, Toko's father was unfazed by the shocking news and immediately began discussing details. Toko, on the other hand, felt dizzy, and the word *treason* tolled like a bell in her mind. She did not care who was right or wrong. As far as Toko was concerned, if it were a choice between the prince and the emperor, then the prince was right. The shock she felt was caused solely by the fact that people she loved were in danger. This should not, just could not be happening to them—because she loved them.

She wanted to scream. *What do they mean Lady Akaru is with them? What about Oguna? What will happen to him? Who can tell me?* But the messenger did not mention Oguna even once. He only told them that the prince and his men were planning to escape through Suzuka Pass.

Her father sent the messenger on his way with the words, "Tell the chief that we will do whatever we can." The men dispersed hurriedly, and a sense of urgency gripped the hall.

BY MIDNIGHT, Toko had made up her mind. She waited until she was absolutely determined before going to her mother's room.

"Mother," she began. "I've decided to go with the men to Suzuka Pass. I'm going to help rescue the prince."

"What on earth are you talking about?" Matono said, but Toko pressed on. "I know you're going to tell me that I can't go," she said, her voice growing stronger. "But even if you order me to stay and lock me in my room, I will find a way to go. That's why I decided to ask you. I would rather go with your permission than disobey you."

Matono stared at her daughter in astonishment. Few ever got the better of her, but the look in Toko's eyes made her pause. "But why?" she asked gently. "What makes you think that you have to go?"

Toko's expression relaxed slightly. "I have a good reason. Where the prince is, Oguna will be. Had you forgotten that? Maybe Oguna is fleeing the emperor's soldiers right now, or maybe he has already been caught and killed. But I will never know if I stay here. I have to go and find out for myself."

Matono's heart skipped a beat at Oguna's name. She had not forgotten him either. "Toko. You're right. Oguna will certainly be with the prince. He was chosen to be one of his closest aides."

"I'm going with the others so that I can help rescue him," Toko said. "He promised me that he would come back to Mino, but he hasn't returned once. I'm tired of sitting here waiting for him. And now that he's in danger I just can't stay here anymore. I'm going to go and meet him. I've been wanting to do that for so long."

Matono could not conceal her consternation. "You mean you've been waiting for him all this time?"

"Yes."

"What did he promise?"

"Just that he would come back. That he would come back when he was stronger."

"I see . . . I suppose if you were both twelve, that makes sense," Matono said, with a silent sigh of relief. Now, at last, she understood why her daughter did not behave like a young lady. Tachibana women, herself included, tended to be headstrong. If Toko decided not to become a woman, she just might succeed. Suddenly Matono felt sorry for her. "And knowing you, I suppose that you promised you wouldn't enter the shrine until he came back."

Toko's eyes widened in surprise. "Mother, you're amazing! How did you know?"

Oh dear. I was right . . . Matono looked at Toko's innocent face and slender body. The thought suddenly occurred to her that her daughter's future might not lie in Mino. Perhaps she had been wrong to repress Toko's unconventional behavior . . . It was only an intuition, but the clan accepted such epiphanies whether they were logical or not. This gave Tachibana women a reputation for being impulsive, and on impulse was exactly how Matono responded now. *If Toko doesn't outgrow this stubborn conviction,* she thought, *she'll never become a woman.* She felt that this risk far outweighed any danger Toko might meet if she set off to find Oguna. "All right," she said decisively. "You're old enough to know what you want and take responsibility for it. If you promise not to do anything reckless, I'll give you permission. And I won't mention it to your father. So off you go and find Oguna."

A smile spread across Toko's face. "I love you, Mother! I knew you'd understand!"

2

"LADY MATONO insisted . . . " Kujihiko said ruefully. The chief had summoned him as the commander of his troops to explain why Toko was riding at the rear of the company, looking as though she thought this was perfectly normal. The chief had been unable to bring himself to ask Toko directly, and now the two men carried on a whispered conversation.

"There are times when I just don't understand what goes on in a woman's mind," he said. "What can Lady Matono be thinking to send Toko off to battle like this? But I'm not about to question anyone kin to the high priestess. I don't even question my own wife about this kind of thing. Perhaps it's best to just leave Toko alone."

"You're probably right."

"Well then. Just make sure that she doesn't get near any actual fighting. Once we've rescued Akaru, I suppose she might even be useful."

Unaware of this exchange, Toko triumphantly left Mino in the company of about a hundred and fifty, led by the chief. Tsunuga was among the men from Kamitsusato. He could not believe that Matono would really allow her daughter to join them and was sure that Toko would eventually let slip the truth. "No one can make you go back now that we've come this far," he said, "so tell me how you managed to sneak out unnoticed."

Toko was looking about eagerly as she rode along, but she cast an annoyed glance in his direction. "You don't believe me. Do you really think I'd be so disobedient as to leave without telling my mother?"

"But your father didn't seem to know."

"That's because my mother said not to tell him."

"Lady . . . I know I've already said this, but there's no way of knowing what will happen when we try to rescue the prince," Tsunuga said. "We may have to fight for our lives. The future of Mino depends on whether or not we can save him. This is not some pleasure trip."

"Why do you assume that I'm here for pleasure? This is a life and death matter for me too."

"Really?"

"Of course."

"You look pretty cheerful to me."

Toko wiped the smile off her face and sat up straight. "If we're traveling so far, I should observe everything carefully for future reference, right?" Just crossing the border of Kamitsusato had filled her with excitement. Even the most ordinary trees and plants appeared rare and special. "Tsunuga, if we follow this route all the way down to the river's mouth, do you think we'll see the ocean?"

"That's exactly what I meant by a pleasure trip," he responded in disgust.

THE COMPANY from Mino traveled south along the coast, keeping an eye out for enemy troops, but they met none. Turning west, they headed into the mountains. Suzuka Pass was near the top of the highest ridge that reared in front of them, and beyond that lay Mahoroba. Racing against time, they traveled all day and through the night, so that even Toko no longer had the energy to enjoy the scenery. The road was rugged, and they had to dismount and walk with increasing frequency.

Occasionally, they came across a village nestled in a valley between the mountain slopes. Each time they did, the commander urged Toko to stay there and wait for them, and each time Toko obstinately refused. The road, however, grew rougher and people's nerves tauter. When they reached Nobono, Kujihiko made it very clear that this time he would not take no for an answer. "I cannot take you any farther. Beyond this point, there are bound to be enemy soldiers. If we run into them, the arrows will fly. I'll leave Tsunuga behind with you, but, my lady, you must not go any farther."

Toko did not protest. She could tell from the way his veins stood out on his forehead and from her own fatigue that she had reached the limit. "All right. I'll wait. Where do you plan to go from here?"

"We'll avoid the main road and head for Suzuka Pass via the northern slope. Be careful. Don't let your guard down just because we've left you behind. Tsunuga, I leave the lady in your charge. Guard her well."

When the men had gone, Toko slumped onto a tree stump, exhausted. "Ooh, ouch, my feet hurt."

Tsunuga glanced back at her and laughed. "You certainly are persistent, Lady Toko. I don't think any of us believed you would make it this far."

"You're making fun of me, aren't you?"

"No. I'm admiring your spirit."

Toko looked at him. He had been left to guard her merely because he had kept her company on the journey. For a hot-blooded young man, it must have been very disappointing to be left behind at the last moment. He continued to stare at the spot where Kujihiko and his men had disappeared into the woods. She felt sorry for what she had done to him, let alone to herself.

After resting a while, she said, "Tsunuga. Why don't we go on ourselves?" She sounded as if she were inviting him to join her on a quiet stroll.

"What? Go where?"

"To Suzuka. We'll take the main road. It will be easier walking, and no soldiers are going to even notice one girl with an escort."

"You've got to be joking!" Tsunuga said. "How could you even suggest such a thing? You yourself told the commander that you'd wait here."

"You expect me to wait after coming all this way? I may as well have never left Mino. The main road will be much faster. Whoever saves the prince first wins. Aren't you brave enough?"

"But . . . what if we're stopped and captured before we can succeed? What will happen to me when I was the one who was told to protect you?"

"I've got an idea!" Toko said, clapping her hands, as if she hadn't even heard him. "We'll disguise ourselves. Let's pretend that we're local villagers gathering firewood. I'm good at disguises."

"Do you plan to carry firewood on your back after all that?"

"No, you'll carry the firewood. You can hide your weapons in the bundle. Don't you think it's a great idea?"

In the end, Tsunuga gave in. Toko was adept at convincing others to join her in mischief, and he had met his match. Besides, once the idea was in her head, Tsunuga could not have stopped her if he had tried. She was so excited that she forgot all about her sore feet.

They traded a few things at a house in the village and set off again, Tsunuga carrying what looked like a huge and unwieldy load of brushwood and Toko carrying a basket. Spirits renewed, they walked briskly, but Toko privately steeled herself to the fact that the sandals she now wore would rub her already blistered feet raw. *Honestly! Who would do this for fun? I'm only doing it because I vowed I'd rescue Oguna. He's going to get a piece of my mind if I do see him. I'll let him know that it's all his fault for not keeping his promise,* she thought, adding this to an already long list of things she wanted to say to him.

They walked on alone without seeing anyone else on the road, not even any enemy soldiers, although they had been sure they would. The mountains were quiet, clothed in autumn hues. Occasionally a single leaf fluttered down. At first, they welcomed the absence of people, but gradually the solitude began to make them nervous.

"It's strange," Tsunuga said finally. "There should be more people on this road. The others went north because they were sure it would be full of soldiers. Something's not right. I wonder if they've retreated."

"Maybe the emperor pardoned the prince and called his troops back."

"That's very unlikely."

Feeling inexplicably anxious, they walked a little farther, when suddenly they heard the tramping of feet and the echo of voices coming down the mountain path ahead of them—a company of soldiers. "So the emperor's troops are here after all," Tsunuga said, oddly relieved. "Come, we must hide. Quickly."

"But we're disguised."

"Don't be ridiculous! Even ordinary people get out of the way of soldiers."

A group of men bearing pikes and swords and covered in sweat and grime marched two abreast past the place where Toko and Tsunuga hid in a thicket of bamboo grass. Toko shuddered at the heavy tread of their footsteps and the harsh grating of metal on metal. Yet they lacked the bloodlust of men heading for battle. Their pace was a little too leisurely and they were talking amongst themselves.

"Will they be hunting down the others?" one of them asked.

"Now that the prince is captured, only a ragtag mob remains. It wouldn't be worth it," his companion answered.

"The ones who caught him alive must be pretty proud. We wasted our time thrashing around in the mountains."

"I wish we could have seen him at least."

"They said he's being taken to the capital."

Speechless, Toko and Tsunuga looked at one another, and each trembled at the despair they saw reflected in the other's face. They had not misheard. The prince had been captured. For some time after the soldiers had passed, they remained crouched in the bamboo grass. Finally Tsunuga said slowly, "We were almost there . . . How could this have happened?"

"It can't be true. It just can't be. I won't believe it." Toko's voice was unnaturally loud. She glared at Tsunuga. "Don't believe what those stupid soldiers said. They're the enemy! I for one refuse to, at least not until I've heard it from a source I can trust."

"You're right, my lady, but still—"

"Come on, let's get going. We should be able to find someone who knows the truth, if we can just get to Suzuka. And no more talking about it until we do, all right?"

Tsunuga looked at her in surprise and then nodded. "All right. Let's go."

They forded a rushing stream and had traveled for some time when they saw two people walking toward them. Although the strangers were still small in the distance, Toko's heart began to pound. They seemed like local villagers, and she was in agony wondering whether she should ask them what they had heard of the prince. Perhaps they knew what had happened, but what if they said the same thing as the soldiers? That would make it true. This was what she feared the most. Just the thought of it made her stomach feel like lead.

As they drew nearer, Toko saw that one of them was an old man with a cane. The other, a young woman, walked slowly along beside him, lending him support. They kept their eyes on the road ahead and paid no attention to Toko and Tsunuga. It was their indifference that gave Toko the courage to speak. They looked like they knew nothing about the prince, and that at least would relieve her mind.

"Good day," she said. "It's very cool, isn't it?"

The woman looked at her suspiciously.

"Have you heard anything about the prince?" Toko forged on. "Did you hear what happened?"

The elderly man mumbled something into his beard, but she couldn't catch it. The woman, however, answered clearly, "If you mean the prince who plotted treason, he was caught. Thank goodness. Now we can travel without fear."

Toko's world went dark. Without realizing it, she staggered and then wondered indignantly why Tsunuga was gripping her arm so tightly. At that moment, the woman's tone of voice changed.

"Toko? Is that you? But it can't be!"

Startled, Toko and Tsunuga stared at the woman. "But how do you know?"

"Can't you tell? It's me. Have I really changed that much?"

"Lady Akaru!" Toko shouted, hopping up and down in astonishment. It was definitely Lady Akaru's voice, but her face was so cleverly smeared with grime that she would never have guessed. "I'm so glad you're safe!" she cried as she gave Lady Akaru a fierce hug. Lady Akaru smiled and hugged her back.

"I'm the one who should be surprised, Toko. What are you doing here on your own away from Mino?"

"I came to rescue you. Everyone else went north. But Tsunuga and I heard some soldiers saying that they had caught the prince."

Lady Akaru said quietly, "They were wrong. He's quite safe. Look. He's right here in front of you."

"What?" Toko stared at her. The old man coughed deliberately.

"Actually I wouldn't say that I was safe. I've been walking like this all day and am in danger of becoming permanently bent over." Two mischievous eyes peered out at her from under a thatch of white hair. "It's been a long time, Lady Toko. You don't seem to have changed a bit."

Toko was speechless. Never again would she boast that she was good at disguises.

"Who would have guessed that you'd be walking along the main road in broad daylight dressed like that?" Tsunuga stammered. "Our men went off to Suzuka, not knowing you'd be here."

"Don't worry. I sent Nanatsuka there. He'll make sure they catch up with us. There won't be many enemy troops left at Suzuka anyway."

"Then the danger has passed?"

"For now, at least. We have a bit of breathing room. I'm going to straighten up now. If I stay like this any longer, I'll never be able to stand straight again." He grimaced as he stretched, looking a little more like the prince.

When the first shock had finally worn off and Toko found herself able to speak again, she asked the question that was forefront in her mind. "So where's Oguna? Is he with Nanatsuka?"

Their faces stiffened, making them look once again like strangers. Toko, overjoyed at this miraculous reunion and buoyed by relief, was totally unprepared for their reaction. A chill gripped her to the bone, as though the world had frozen. "Why , , , do you look like that?"

"Toko—" Lady Akaru's voice broke.

"Lady Toko," the prince said gravely, "it's thanks to Oguna that we are here now. He sacrificed himself so that we could escape. Without him, not one of us would have been able to cross that pass alive."

"Oguna's not here . . . ?" It seemed to Toko that her voice belonged to someone else.

The prince briefly explained how they had parted. She listened silently, holding her breath, until his words finally penetrated her brain. Then she asked with unnatural composure, "So the prince that they caught was Oguna, is that right?"

"Yes."

No sooner had he answered than Toko turned on her heel and began walking in the opposite direction—toward Suzuka. The others stared after her briskly receding figure; then Tsunuga dashed after her and grabbed her arm.

"Just a minute! Where do you think you're going?"

"I came all this way to see Oguna, so I'm going after him. I'm going to the capital. Let me go!"

"Don't be ridiculous! You can't do that!"

Toko raised her eyebrows and glared at him. "When I say I'm going, I'm going. My mother told me to go and find Oguna. I might still make it in time. I'm going after him. If you're that worried about me, then you can come too."

Tsunuga was a very patient man, but this was too much. Unable to conceal his anger, he barked, "This time, my lady, you are not going to get your way. Our first and foremost duty is to take the prince and Lady Akaru to Mino as quickly as possible. Whether you like it or not, you're coming with me, even if I have to carry you."

Toko stared at him in shock. She had never imagined that he would be angry with her.

"It's no use going after Oguna," the prince said in a tight voice. "If there had been even the slightest hope of saving him, I would have done it myself. I'm sorry."

Toko's gaze roved from one face to another, her eyes wide with disbelief. It was hard enough to take Tsunuga's anger, which to her seemed totally unjustified, but it hurt even more to hear the prince say it was no use, that he was sorry. Wasn't he the strongest man in the world, a man who should never need to say such things?

But it was Lady Akaru who delivered the final blow. "Toko, please," she begged. "Don't be stubborn. It's so hard for us to hear you say things like that."

Nobody understands. I can't count on any of them. Nobody puts Oguna first. Not like me. I came all this way on blistered feet just to meet him. But they don't understand that at all.

All she could do now was cry. Watching her eyes well with tears, Tsunuga said hastily, "My lady . . . please don't cry. I'm sorry I yelled at you. But I can't let you expose yourself to any more danger. Please, please don't cry."

Tears streamed down her face. "My feet hurt..."

"Of course they do. This hike was just a bit too much for you." Tsunuga threw down his bundle of firewood and knelt in front of her. "Here, climb on my back. Come on now."

In the end, he did, in fact, have to carry her, just as he had threatened he would. Having lost any shred of defiance, Toko clung to his back, sobbing.

IN A CEDAR GROVE in Nobono they rejoined the men from Mino. Everyone was overjoyed to see the prince, and the chief wept when he learned that Lady Akaru was safe. Kujihiko, who had intended to thrash Tsunuga for disobeying his orders, decided to let it pass. In the end, things had worked out for the best. After the strain of the past few days, everyone was relieved—everyone except Toko, who sat by herself, sobbing quietly. Those who knew what was wrong left her alone, but one man frowned and, leaving the others, approached her softly.

Hearing leaves crunch underfoot, Toko stopped crying for a moment and looked around. A huge, rough-hewn man with a heavy beard appeared from behind a cedar tree—Nanatsuka.

"Are you crying for Oguna?" he asked. He looked wild and ferocious with his clothes torn and tattered and his hair and beard unkempt from their desperate flight, but his eyes were kind. Although they held no tears, they were filled with a grief as deep as Toko's. "He wasn't a talker and he rarely spoke of home, but he often mentioned your name. The only thing he ever talked about of his own accord was you."

"I don't believe you," Toko said. "You don't have to try to make me feel better."

"... But it's true."

"I'm angry. I'm just so mad at everyone. And at Oguna as well. He promised me he'd come back, but then he went and broke his promise. Even though I waited for him all this time. He chose the prince instead of coming back. So how can I believe that he was thinking of me?"

Nanatsuka moved closer. When he sat down beside her, he filled the small clearing. "Lady Toko," he said gently. "In this world, certain things must take priority over what we want most. This is especially true for men. You may not like it, but what he did was very noble. He behaved like a man. You should be praising him instead of saying such things about him. It isn't fair to criticize him when he valued loyalty so highly."

"But . . . if I can't be angry . . . then I just don't know what to do . . ." she said, choking on the words. "It's not fair!" she cried. "I want Oguna. I want to see him again."

Nanatsuka reached out his hand and patted her awkwardly on the back. He knew that nothing he could say would comfort her. Toko turned and clung to him, weeping her heart out. "It's good to know that there is someone to cry for him," Nanatsuka said as he held her. "I'm glad that he has someone who cares enough to grieve for him."

THEY RETURNED to Mino. Lady Akaru inhaled the fragrance of her homeland, now in the harvest season, and smiled through her tears at the familiar shape of the hills, drinking in every little detail.

"I'm home. I'm finally home. It's almost frightening to have my wish come true like this. To wish for anything more seems like a sin."

Something in her tone disturbed the prince. Although she was in high spirits despite her fatigue, from the moment Akaru had set foot in Mino she seemed to have become quietly resigned. "What are you talking about?" he chided her. "It's what we do from now on that really matters. Why do you speak as if it's all over? I know the emperor will never leave us alone, but Mino is a natural stronghold. If we can repel his first assault, he won't be able to touch us again for some time. Our chances are good."

Lady Akaru smiled at him. "Yes. I have complete faith in your ability as a commander. You go to Kukuri and do what you have to do. But I must go to the shrine. I don't know if I can justify my actions to the Keeper of the Shrine, but I must try."

The prince's eyes widened in surprise. "But why? Why should you need to ask pardon for what you did? Anyone who knows the truth could never blame you for what happened when the emperor took you as his wife."

Lady Akaru shook her head a little. "The priestess will. I have returned to Mino. In doing so, I have ignored our laws, defied destiny, and failed in my duty as a Tachibana . . . I can't come back without facing her judgment. I am more afraid of her than of anyone else. But this is the battle that I must fight."

She raised her eyes and her gaze was firm and steady. "You chose to fight against your own father, the emperor, for my sake, so I will face the priestess, the most powerful member of our clan. I don't want to lose this battle. For your sake, and for mine."

"In that case, I'll go with you," the prince said, taking her hands in his. "We'll let everyone know that anyone who criticizes you must face me as well. Together, we are one."

"Yes, we are one. But the high priestess will only meet people of our clan. You must let me go alone," she said firmly. "I'll be all right."

3

"THAT'S WHAT she said?" the chief asked. "My daughter? She really said that?"

"Yes," Oh-usu said. "She also said there was no need to say goodbye because she'll be back soon." Lady Akaru had left with just a few servants and headed northeast.

"I see." Kamubonehiko bowed his head.

Disturbed by his bleak expression, the prince asked, "What do you think the high priestess will do?"

"I have no idea. When it comes to the priestess's purview, I'm out of my depth. After all, I'm just her son-in-law." He sighed deeply. "Let's just pray that it doesn't come to the worst."

The prince frowned. "What do you mean by 'the worst'?"

"Nothing," Kamubonehiko said hastily, shaking his head. "Don't mind me. I'm overanxious. I've been worrying about my daughter for so long. Now that we've finally won her back, let's not think about anything bad." Having said this, however, he lapsed into a glum silence.

They pressed on toward Kukuri. As he rode, the prince struggled to suppress his concern, but finally he could stand it no longer. Jerking the reins so sharply that his steed reared and whinnied in protest, he wheeled around to face the way they had just come. "I'm sorry," he said, "but I can't stop worrying. My lord, please carry on to Kukuri ahead of me. I'll join you as soon as I know that Lady Akaru is all right."

The chief did not protest and in fact seemed relieved. As leader of the clan, he could not ask the prince to aid his daughter, yet in his heart he had hoped that he would.

Nanatsuka immediately turned to follow the prince. "I'll go with you," he said.

"So will I," came a clear voice. Everyone stared in surprise as Toko rode up.

Tsunuga hurried over. "My lady, you can't. You aren't well. You must return to the hall and rest." After weeping the entire night in Nobono, Toko had come down with a fever and had had to be carried for most of the return trip.

"I'm fine," she said. Now that she was recovering her strength, she was tired of being treated so delicately. "My fever's gone, and the prince will need someone to guide him. Besides, only members of the Tachibana clan are allowed to enter the shrine."

"You know, she's right," the prince said.

"But she shouldn't go alone," Tsunuga insisted. "I'll go with her."

"No. I think the fewer the better," the prince said. "Lady Toko can ride with me. She's as light as a feather, so she won't burden my horse." That settled the matter, and the three of them set off after Lady Akaru.

Nanatsuka rode up beside Toko and peered at her anxiously. "Are you sure you're all right?" He was so large and sturdy that to him she appeared exceedingly fragile.

She smiled up at him. "I wasn't really sick. I was just . . . dreaming. The dream's gone now, so I'm better."

"You were *dreaming?*" He looked doubtful.

Toko hesitated but then decided to share her secret. "Oguna's alive! He was badly hurt, but he didn't die and he's getting better."

The prince had been listening silently, but at this he started. "What? How do you know?"

"I felt him. I kept dreaming of our childhood, and I knew that he was having the same dream. I could tell he was wounded and delirious. That's what made me feverish. When we were little we both came down with the measles at the same time. Ever since then, when one of us gets a fever, the other always does too."

The prince and Nanatsuka were speechless, unsure as to whether they should believe her or not. Oblivious, Toko chattered on. "I was worried at first, but his injuries weren't fatal. I would never have had a dream like that if he were dead. And I wouldn't have gotten a fever either. He's alive. And if he's alive, that means I'll get to see him again someday, right? In the last dream, somebody was taking care of him . . . "

Toko stopped abruptly. She now remembered sensing some strange force that had shut her out, as if a curtain had been drawn around Oguna. This troubled her. Someone radiating waves of power had been by his side from start to finish, preventing her from drawing any closer. Consequently, she had not seen Oguna's face even once.

Who was that?

But whenever she tried to understand what she had felt, it slipped through her grasp like a lizard's tail. It was not something she could put into words and explain to her companions.

After a while the prince cleared his throat. "Do you often see things like that? I mean, you know—dreams that come true?" he asked.

"No, almost never. I only dream when I have a fever."

Nanatsuka dispelled the awkward pause that followed. "Well, if what you just told us is true," he said, "that's great news. It makes me feel much better just to think that he might be alive somewhere."

"Doesn't it?" Toko beamed at him. "I'm not going to cry or sulk anymore. I'm sorry that I made so much trouble."

It was clear from her expression that she really had recovered from her grief. Nanatsuka was impressed. Although she might look slender and fragile, Toko had extraordinary resilience and tenacity.

"Isn't this Moyama? Where the bird funeral took place?" the prince said abruptly as they climbed the mountain path.

"Oh, so you've heard the story about our ancestor the crow," Toko said happily.

"Yes. Didn't the maiden's soul turn into a white bird and fly back from the land of the dead? I wonder if that story contains some clue about how to defy death. Lady Toko, have you ever heard a tale about a magatama?"

"A magatama? No, never. What kind of tale?"

"I don't know myself, but Lady Akaru mentioned a special magatama . . . I wonder where your priestess's power comes from?" he muttered absently.

"I never thought that the powers wielded by the ancient gods might still exist; after all, so much time has passed since the world was formed. But somehow they still seem a part of your lives. At least, that's what it feels like when I'm with you and Lady Akaru. Your high priestess sounds quite formidable, you know."

"Really? It's true that people say her premonitions are from the gods . . . " Toko, unsure of what he was trying to say, followed the thread of her own thoughts. "But predictions don't always come true. Take the weather for example. People often predict sunshine and get rain instead."

The prince looked up at the trees. "This forest is so thick, you can't even see the sky let alone guess the weather. Do we still have far to go? I doubt that anyone who lives shut away in a forest like this has much sense of humor."

The ancient forest, its giant trees standing row upon row, was dark and quiet even in the daytime. It showed no hint of the season or any sign of wildlife. It finally dawned on Toko that the prince found the depth and silence unsettling.

"My father," he continued, "is obsessed with the idea of defying death. During my grandfather's reign, there was some tale of a tree whose fruit gave eternal youth. My grandfather sent a man named Tajima to search for it. Decades passed. Ironically, by the time Tajima returned with a fruit, my grandfather had passed away and no longer needed it. The fruit, however, proved to have no magical powers, and Tajima, a feeble old man himself, died soon after. But the journey was not completely in vain. My father, who was already seated on the throne, gleaned one fact from Tajima—eternal youth is somehow linked to the Tachibana tree. Ever since he has been pursuing this possibility like a man possessed. He first sent me to Mino because the name of your clan is Tachibana."

"I never knew there was such a legend about the Tachibana," Toko said, surprised but pleased.

"You really don't know anything? But you were born to become a priestess too, weren't you?"

"No, I don't have to because Kisako, the chief's second daughter, is going to be the next high priestess. She's the same age as me, but she's training at the shrine right now."

The prince seemed a little too interested. "Ah, Lady Akaru's younger sister. And is she just as beautiful?"

Toko gave him a sideways glance. "Don't ask me about Kisako, please. She and I have never gotten along. When she left to train at the shrine, she called me a 'brainless kite.' So I told her she was a vain little magpie. Everyone laughed and that made her really mad. She's never forgiven me."

Toko's words shattered the solemn, oppressive atmosphere of the forest. The prince and Nanatsuka held their breath, struggling not to laugh out loud.

IN A LARGE ROOM deep within the hall, Lady Akaru knelt on the bare wooden floor facing a dais at the end of the room. She held her hands decorously in front of her and kept her head bowed low. She had been waiting like this for some time, but the shrine priestess's chair remained empty. To Akaru, the priestess's failure to appear despite her request for an audience felt like a rebuke. The hair falling across her face hid her expression as she frantically reviewed her every action to see if she had omitted some important point of etiquette and offended the priestess. True, Akaru had been in a hurry, but she had still brushed her hair carefully, washed off all the grime of the journey, and put on clean clothes. She had regained her composure, or at least she thought she had. The way her younger sister Kisako had looked at her as she had helped her wash, however, had made her feel somehow unclean. *No matter how pure the water, you can never wash away your sin*, Kisako's eyes had said.

It can't be helped, Lady Akaru told herself. *You knew what to expect.* Yet she could not ignore the pain she had felt at the contempt on her sister's face. Enduring the storm of emotions inside her, she continued to kneel quietly, both hands on the floor in front of her. She needed every ounce of strength to keep herself from regretting her decision.

Finally, the curtain behind the dais moved slightly, and the high priestess appeared, leaning on an attendant. Lady Akaru bowed her head so low it almost touched the floor. After settling herself in her seat, the white-haired priestess spoke. Her words struck Lady Akaru's ears cruelly. "So, you have nerve to come back instead of taking your life."

Lady Akaru strove desperately to keep her fingers from trembling. *Don't shake. Don't cry. You left all such weakness behind in that little hut at Mahoroba.*

She raised her head. "Yes, I have returned to Mino. And I have therefore come today to request your blessing for the bond that unites me with Prince Oh-usu."

"I never dreamed you could be so shameless! Perhaps my old eyes were too clouded to see clearly when I gave you the magatama. Where is it? What have you done with the magatama I entrusted to you when you left Mino?"

Lady Akaru's eyes fell. ". . . It lost its brightness. The emperor took the jewel from me and it never shone again. It remains in his hands."

"What have you done?!" The high priestess shouted with such vehemence that her body seemed to lift off the chair. Her attendant rose hastily and reached out a hand. "Do you intend to destroy us? You were sent to purify his heart, but instead you have entrusted to him an object of power. Once they have realized its worth, do you know what the emperor and his bloodline will do? They will reach out their hands to tear up that power from its roots. They will stop at nothing in their pursuit of it. How could you—you who I believed so rare and special among Tachibana women—how could you commit such a dreadful mistake? Who was it that dragged you down so low? Prince Oh-usu?"

"No," Lady Akaru replied clearly. "It was Prince Oh-usu who saved me. Without him, I would surely have lost my mind or taken my own life. But instead, he gave me hope. It is thanks to him that I do not wander the world, a wraith crushed by my fate."

"Silence!" The priestess glared at her. "What do you know about fate? The omens clearly showed that the emperor would love and cherish you. You were destined to marry one another. But instead you are so depraved you chose the young prince instead."

"That's not true!" Lady Akaru said. "The emperor showed not one speck of love for me. And it was not because I had given my love to someone else. It's true that when the prince came as the emperor's messenger, my heart was moved. I admit that. But I went to the capital with every intention of serving the emperor and loving him with all my heart. And with the expectation that he would love me in return. I believed it was my destiny. It never occurred to me that there could be any other way. But I will never forget what I saw in the emperor's face when I stood in his bedroom."

She gripped her arms tightly, trying to control the emotions that shook her. "He looked at me as if I were an object, something that came with the magatama. That was the only thing he was interested in. But I am human. I am a woman. Without love, how could I possibly make the magatama shine?"

"But that can't be. You were meant to love one another."

"No. We could not," Lady Akaru stated flatly. "Keeper of the Shrine, you did not see the emperor's eyes. What I saw there was certainly not love."

The high priestess paused and then said quietly, "Are you saying that my prophecy was false?"

"When he knew that my magatama was useless, the emperor banished me away to the servants' quarters without remorse. He made me work from dawn to dusk in the kitchens and saw to it that I was punished severely for any little mistake. Do you still insist that I could have loved him when he behaved so cruelly?"

"Are you saying that my prophecy was false?"

The intensity with which the high priestess repeated her question made Lady Akaru pause for a moment. She clenched her fists. "Yes," she said finally.

A taut silence settled over them. They sat motionless, glaring at one another. The quiet shrine deep in the forest was now hushed to the point where even the hum of insect wings seemed to reverberate in the room. Finally the old woman stirred and spoke. "Let us suppose then that to marry the emperor was not your destiny. Even so, your duty to your clan is not erased. What do you intend to do? Surely you must have something in mind if you have come back bearing portents of war instead of the magatama. Tell me. How do you feel about our clan, which your selfishness has brought to the brink of destruction?"

For the first time Lady Akaru's voice shook. "I have no intention of destroying our clan. The prince will be victorious. The people of Mino have welcomed him as their commander."

"The oracles all point to misfortune. Do you intend to overturn this prophecy as well?"

Lady Akaru swallowed. "Yes."

"Then can you regain the magatama from the emperor?"

"Even if it costs me my life."

At this, the priestess's eyes flashed. "You quenched the light of the magatama. Its light will never again shine for the emperor. Nor will it shine for anyone else. Because it has lost that for which it was destined. This is the fruit of your ministry as the bearer. It will take your successor, the next bearer, to win back the magatama."

Lady Akaru bit her lip. "Then choose the next bearer and let me pass it on to her."

"The magatama can be yielded to another just once in a lifetime, and only someone, such as I, who has borne it without touching its power, can pass it on while still drawing breath. As for you, you can only surrender the magatama when your own life ends."

The blood drained from Lady Akaru's lips, and her skin, already fair, grew so pale it seemed transparent. "Is that what you would have me do?"

"I am only telling you to fulfill your duty as a priestess of the Tachibana clan."

Lady Akaru had kept her chin raised defiantly all this time, but now she bowed her head. Her freshly washed hair caressed her cheek. "So," she whispered. "You will not forgive me, Keeper of the Shrine."

"It is not I who won't forgive you," the priestess answered. Her voice seemed emotionless.

"I am not afraid of death," Lady Akaru said. "I have thought of taking my life many, many times to atone for my sin. It would have been so much easier. But I just could not see why I should be to blame. The magatama lost its light. Perhaps that is a sin unworthy of a Tachibana. Yet I just can't believe that it was my fault." Her voice grew stronger and more spirited as she spoke. She raised her face once more and her eyes were shining. Reaching a hand inside her robe, she calmly drew out a small dagger and unsheathed its thin, sharp blade. "I met Prince Oh-usu and I loved him. I will never regret that. I believe our love is true. To prove my love for him, I would gladly die here. I will gladly offer you my life, not to atone for any failure to fulfill my destiny, but rather to demonstrate the truth of one who has searched for and found her own heart."

The dagger glittered, casting a silver light in the gloom. The priestess, who seemed to have been rendered speechless by the sight, finally opened her mouth to speak. But at that moment a high-pitched shriek came from outside the door. "Keeper of the Shrine!" It was Kisako. A moment later she ran into the room with tears streaming down her face, looking very unlike a shrine maiden. "Keeper of the Shrine! That Toko! Please make her pay for this!" But before she could continue, Toko appeared, and behind her stood the prince, tall and regal.

The attendant made a sound like a strangled chicken. "She's brought an outsider!"

Lady Akaru turned to look and froze with her dagger still raised.

"Keeper of the Shrine," Toko began boldly. "This is Prince Oh-usu, first son of the emperor of Mahoroba. I apologize for coming so suddenly, but I remembered that you asked my mother to show you her adopted son. I'm afraid Oguna can't come because he has gone to the capital, but fortunately the prince is here. He looks just like Oguna. Please let him enter."

"Toko," Lady Akaru gasped. "That's outrageous."

The prince, ignoring Toko's words and without even glancing at the high priestess, flew to Lady Akaru's side and grabbed the dagger from her hand. "What on earth were you planning to do with this? Honestly! I can't leave you alone for a second."

Gazing up at him, Lady Akaru's eyes filled with tears. "But I had to . . . I had to prove myself."

The prince pulled her close and then looked up at the priestess sitting on the dais. "Forgive me for barging in uninvited, but I don't care who you are—how, as ruler of this clan, can you justify ordering her suicide just because she loves someone?"

"How dare you!" the high priestess snapped. "This woman is married to the emperor. It's you who are in the wrong."

"I am sure from what this lady has told you that you must already know who is truly worthy of censure, my father or me," the prince said, struggling to keep his voice calm. "If, even knowing that, you still insist that I'm in the wrong, you can say what you please. I intend to oppose the emperor until every last person is forced to acknowledge the truth."

"Then know this: the omens show that war will only bring you misfortune."

"And what of it?"

"Enough." The high priestess sank into her seat as if something inside her had snapped. "I'm tired. I have no strength left to deal with your stubbornness in addition to Lady Akaru's. Take her and leave this shrine. Your presence is so unruly it makes it hard to breathe in this small space."

The prince looked taken aback, but before she could change her mind he bowed his head and said, "If you'll excuse us." He turned and, placing an arm around the princess, began leading her away.

"You are indeed a Takeru," the high priestess said.

The prince turned. "What did you say?"

"I said you are a Takeru, a hero that none can withstand."

The prince smiled, showing his white teeth. "Such high praise. And I thought you said the omens were against me." He left the room and so failed to hear her final words.

"None can withstand a Takeru because he burns his life away in a moment. A Takeru is fated to die young."

Toko, however, heard and stopped short, a delay that she regretted instantly.

"Toko!" the priestess called sharply. "Where do you think you're going? I don't remember giving you permission to leave."

Seizing this chance, Kisako announced triumphantly, "It's all Toko's fault, my lady. Please punish her. She pushed me out of the way when I tried to stop her and brought that stranger in."

Oh dear. This is bad. Really bad . . . Toko thought. She had meant to come and go like a whirlwind, but she had been too slow. She could not possibly leave now. As she stood despondent, the high priestess said gently, "Don't worry. I won't punish you. I'm too tired to be angry. But there's something I want to talk to you about, so stay with me a little longer."

The high priestess rose from her chair and withdrew to a small room behind the dais, commanding Toko to join her. Kisako, ordered back to her regular duties, departed with a disgusted look, leaving the two alone. For some time the high priestess sipped a hot medicinal tea, which Toko tasted but found unpleasant. Finally, however, the priestess put down her cup and began to talk.

"Well! You certainly are bold. You've become even more devil-may-care since I saw you last. Even I was taken by surprise today. Yet . . . strangely enough, it's hard to dislike you, Toko. There's something about you that's very refreshing, although I can see that you have a long, hard road ahead of you."

Toko was thrown into confusion. Already regretting her rash behavior, she said, quite meekly for her, "I'm so sorry I was rude. I just had to help Lady Akaru somehow. She loves the prince from the bottom of her heart. And he loves her. If you must punish someone, you can punish me . . . though I hope you won't punish me too harshly. Just please forgive Lady Akaru."

The high priestess nodded. "I knew that already. There was not a trace of doubt in her eyes. No matter what happens, she will live and die with the prince. I was simply testing her resolve."

"So you had already forgiven her from the start," Toko said.

"What was there to forgive? The prophecy was false. The omens no longer speak the truth. I never dreamed I'd live to see such a terrible thing. I've lived so long that now I must watch the unthinkable happen. Your generation may be the last of the Mino Tachibana clan." Her shoulders drooped and she seemed to shrink before Toko's eyes. This woman who she had once thought as changeless as a rock now appeared frailer than a withered tree.

"Keeper of the Shrine," Toko whispered.

"Some power strong enough to twist fate has come into this world—a power that directly opposes the gods we worship. It is very dangerous. Left unchecked it will affect the entire land of Toyoashihara and cause great destruction. I have sensed this threat for many years, and when the omens told me it was linked to Mino, I tried hard to identify it. Today, I finally discovered what it is. Thanks to you, Toko."

Toko tilted her head, puzzled. "Did I do something?"

The high priestess gazed at her, her eyes dark and troubled. "It was something you said. You told me that the foster child raised in your house looks just like the prince. When I heard that, everything fell into place. I should have had him brought to me much sooner. He is the cause of this evil."

"Oguna? He what?"

"He is an abomination, the source of all our misfortunes."

"Oguna?!"

4

OGUNA RECOVERED rapidly. His body had been conditioned through hard training, and by now he knew how to regain his strength. Although the servants treated him with lavish care, it was not his nature to relax and enjoy it. Some animal instinct constantly urged him to hurry and regain control of his life. He was worried about the prince and his friends, but he was even more anxious about being here in Itsuse—and about the woman who was his mother.

Oguna worked daily to build up his stamina. He ate every morsel placed in front of him. Considering that Itsuse was located deep in the mountains, a surprisingly significant fraction of his diet was seafood. Apparently the villagers who lived along the coast below climbed the mountain every day to deliver it.

Spending mealtimes with Oguna seemed to be Princess Momoso's greatest pleasure. When she took his bowl to serve him more rice, she frequently exclaimed with delight, "My, what an appetite boys have! So this is how boys grow. It's wonderful."

"Mother, you hardly eat at all," Oguna remarked one day. "Are you not hungry?"

"Oh, but I do not wish to become fat. Would it not be a disgrace if I became like Lady Inabi?"

An image of Prince Oh-usu's plump mother rose into Oguna's mind. "If I had to choose, I suppose I prefer women who are slim," he said.

"Of course you do. Who do you think is prettier? Me or Inabi?" she asked, leaning toward him.

"You, mother," Oguna responded without any intention to flatter.

"My, how happy you make me!" she exclaimed, pressing her hands against her cheeks.

She's like a little girl, Oguna thought. The way she behaved with him was endearing and without a trace of haughtiness, so the difference in her manner when she delivered orders to those around her always came as a shock. He was gradually coming to see that the stern face she showed the rest of the world was a mask. Inside she was a lonely little girl. It was easy to tell that, being the Itsuki no Miya, she had been forced to forgo interaction with other people.

Just being with Oguna made her happy. He only had to move or speak for her to look upon him proudly. Even when he was too busy exercising to talk to her, she was content to watch him. Oguna, who had never experienced such overwhelming love before, felt bewildered and did not know how to

respond. It also concerned him that she was neglecting her duties as priestess
to be with him. At last he summoned the courage to speak.

"Mother, I think it is unwise for me to stay here for very long. Only women
are allowed in this shrine and . . . " He struggled to find the words. "Not
everyone knows that I am your son . . . so they must think this is strange.
You are, after all, the Itsuki no Miya." Her faced clouded over and he added
hastily, "Besides, I'm better now. I can't just sit around and do nothing. Please
give me your permission to go."

Princess Momoso looked at him, her expression grave. "I too have been
thinking about what you should do from now on. But first, tell me what you
wish. What do you want to do?"

Oguna answered without a moment's hesitation. "I want to go to Mino. I want
to find Prince Oh-usu and, if he is still alive, join him and his followers."

Princess Momoso's eyes widened. "Goodness! Surely you are not serious.
How innocent and gullible you are. That man left you to die. Do you really
intend to serve him again? Even though you would have been tortured and
beaten to death save for me? After all the suffering he caused you, why should
you serve Oh-usu?"

Now it was Oguna's turn to be surprised. He had never thought about it
like that. Fumbling for words, he tried to explain. "But . . . I am his shadow. I
don't know what else I should do. And after all, I grew up in Mino . . . "

Princess Momoso scowled. "Forget that you were ever his shadow," she
said firmly. "The very thought of it is revolting. You, a shadow? Why, it is he
who is the shadow. Yes, he is but a shadow compared to you. Your blood is
far purer than his. You have no lowly blood like that woman Inabi's running
in your veins."

Oguna looked at her sharply. "What do you mean?"

"I mean that I, your mother, believe you are suited to inherit the throne."

The term *doting parent* flashed through Oguna's mind, but her behavior
far exceeded that description. "It's very generous of you to say so. But to be
honest, from what I learned under the prince, being heir to the throne does
not look very appealing."

A smile lit up her face. "What a charming child! Your selflessness is truly
endearing. You must never change. There is no need to worry. As your mother,

I will make sure that everything works out for the best."

She seemed somehow to have missed the point, and Oguna, disconcerted, tried again. "But, Mother, I—"

Princess Momoso grabbed his hand and stood up. "Come with me," she said. "There is something I wish to show you."

Oguna followed, his thoughts in turmoil. He was shaken by his inability to respond to her question. She had asked Oguna what he wanted to do with his life, which had miraculously been saved, but he had thought only of returning to his old life. In retrospect, Oguna now saw that he had not chosen to be the prince's shadow out of any real desire to do so. What, then, *had* he wanted?

All I wanted was to become stronger. The prince happened to come along at the right time and offer to train me in the capital. I simply went along with his plan. I never really thought about what I wanted to be. Anything would have done . . . And the reason he had wanted to grow strong was because that was what Toko had wanted. This made him even more confused. Had he ever in his life really aspired to become anything? Most people lived with some hope or aspiration, so wasn't it strange not to know what he wanted? True, he had become a little stronger. But he had never thought about how he would use that strength or for what purpose.

Princess Momoso, her eyes fixed straight ahead, strode across the bridge to the precincts of the main sanctuary. The guards, seeing her expression, said nothing, but Oguna faltered when he noticed where they were.

"Uhm . . . aren't men forbidden to enter?" he stammered.

"Yes, that is true. However, there are exceptions," Princess Momoso said without glancing back. "The emperor of Mahoroba for instance. My older brother has set foot in this shrine. You are my son, and therefore why shouldn't you?"

"But—"

"Be quiet now and follow me. The lady of the shrine bids you to enter, so what need have you to worry?"

Oguna stared at her. She conveyed the strength and nobility of one accustomed to command. Clear and sharp as a white lily in a forest of cedar, she stood resolute and alone, magnetizing all yet allowing no one near. He had yearned for so long to discover who his parents were, yet now he did not know how to respond to this woman, his mother.

I think I'm afraid to love her.

Until then Oguna had only let himself love very reluctantly. There was nothing, no idea, no possession so precious to him that he could not bear to part with it, and very few people were irreplaceably dear. Toko, Matono, even if he included Nanatsuka and the prince, in his sixteen years of life he could count them all on one hand. This was his reality—Oguna was a young man with few strong attachments. With so little to love, there had rarely been anyone or anything he had hated or been unable to forgive. But looking at Princess Momoso, Oguna sensed that this stance might be impossible to maintain.

While her illogical, passionate love filled him with dread, it moved him deeply to think that this was how a mother loved her child. Yet how, he wondered, could his limited experience ever equip him to respond adequately, by either loving or hating her? The thought disturbed him. Oguna was terrified to let anyone in through the door he had kept so firmly closed. He had no idea what would happen if he let loose all the emotions he had pent up inside. Or perhaps it was because he did have an idea that he felt so afraid. Perhaps he lacked the courage to seek closer relationships because he sensed that deep in the dark behind that door lay feelings so violent and powerful they were beyond his control.

There was not a person in sight on the white sand-covered path that wound through the wooden buildings within the shrine precincts. The main shrine was built on a steep, forested slope, and the further into the grounds they walked, the higher they went, climbing up several flights of stairs. Princess Momoso walked ahead of him, never stopping or slowing her pace. Relieved to be out of public view, Oguna took this opportunity to stare at the architecture. At last they reached a building encircled by walls three layers deep. He assumed that this must be the inner shrine. The path stopped at a gate in the outer wall.

"Come," Princess Momoso said, sliding the bolt open. "In here. This is where it is."

A shiver ran up Oguna's spine, an instinctive reaction that startled him. He felt defenseless, as if he had forgotten something important but had no idea what. Urged on by Princess Momoso's compelling eyes, he stepped hesitantly through the gate.

They passed through two more gates and finally entered a small square enclosure paved in white sand. A plain wooden building raised on stilts, about the size of a granary, stood alone in the middle of the enclosure. After performing what looked like ritual movements, Princess Momoso climbed the steps to the double doors and pulled them slowly open. Turning her back on the darkness inside, she beckoned Oguna.

"Come and look. Tell me what you see."

By now, Oguna was so nervous he could barely keep still. Although he dreaded looking inside, he forced himself to climb the stairs. With each step, it seemed as if an invisible force was trying to push him back. His body, defying his will, ached with the desire to run away.

Reaching the top of the stairs, he stood beside Princess Momoso and, gathering his courage, looked inside. To his surprise and relief, he could see nothing. The building appeared to be deeper than he had thought because the light from the door did not reach all the way inside. He was about to tell Princess Momoso that it was so dark he could not see anything, when he suddenly noticed a glittering in the blackness. At first he thought it must be the faint light reflecting off a crossbeam, but it was too distant. The more he looked, the more lights he saw, like twinkling stars.

Stars? Impossible!

But no matter how he stared, what he saw before him could only be the night sky full of stars. He could even discern the constellations. A cool wind on his face spoke of a vastness unconfined by walls or ceiling. To his surprise, he saw more stars at his feet and panicked to feel himself floating. At that moment a massive darkness rose like an enormous black cloud and obstructed the stars. Now only two stars burned, side by side, red and growing brighter. He felt the hairs on the nape of his neck rise. The blazing orbs were eyes.

Oguna, his own eyes adjusting to the dark, saw before him a serpent as large as a small hill, coiled in the sky. It stared back at him, flicking its lightning-like tongue, and began to uncoil itself. Its body was as thick around as the trunk of a huge tree . . .

Oguna screamed, but the sound did not reach his ears. Never in his life had he experienced such terror as this. He never remembered how he managed to get down the stairs—perhaps he fell down them in his haste—but when he came to his senses he was curled up in a corner of the courtyard, his back against the wall, his body drenched with sweat and his teeth chattering so violently that they did not fit together.

Princess Momoso held him in her arms. "It is all right. You are safe. It was just a vision. See, it did not hurt you." She stroked him soothingly. "Even the emperor fears it. Your fear is proof that royal blood runs in your veins. That is good. The lowly born and ignorant could not have experienced what you have felt."

She half carried him to a building outside the gates and laid him down to rest in a small room. The color gradually returned to his face, but he still felt sick.

"What . . . was that?" he finally managed to ask.

Princess Momoso looked into his face and brushed the hair from his forehead. "I do not know. What you saw can only be seen by you. But tell me. What did it look like?"

"Like a serpent in the sky—" Oguna stopped abruptly, overcome by nausea.

"The descendants of the God of Light fear it," Princess Momoso said. "I too wept at first and feared it. But women are born with the power to withstand it. That's why a woman is always chosen as priestess. You, however, are a man, and so you cannot help your defenselessness. Still, it is rare for anyone to fear it as much as you. Perhaps it is because your body resonates more strongly with the Sword than the body of anyone else in this world."

"Sword?" Oguna asked, his eyes wide.

"Its true shape is a sword. It is one of the sacred treasures guarded in this shrine. It has many names. I call it the Mirror Sword, but you called it a serpent. That too is very close to its true essence, for it is also known as the Dragon Sword."

"But I didn't see a sword. I saw a real—"

"Of course you did," Princess Momoso interrupted. "But it was just a vision. You should not fear it."

"Not fear it?" Oguna exclaimed. "That's impossible! I've been afraid of it all my life. How can I not fear it when there has never been anything in the world that terrified me more?" Now he finally understood. What he had just seen, that was what he had feared all along every time he saw a snake or a bolt of lightning. It made him feel faint to know that it actually existed, that it was so close. "It's impossible for me not to be afraid."

"Even so, you must overcome your fear. You must grasp the Sword in your hand."

Oguna shrank and tried to back away from her. "I am never, ever, going near that thing again. I won't do it."

"Do not say that," Princess Momoso said gently. "You have the power to take it. The more you fear it, the greater the power you will wield once you make it yours. You are my son. That you should be incapable of wielding the greatest power on earth is inconceivable." She leaned toward him. "Surely you do not intend to carry that fear with you for the rest of your life? Sooner or later you will have to face and overcome it. Come, I will help you. I will make you a great man."

Oguna groaned. "Let me go. Please. Let me go back to Mino. I don't want to become a great man."

"What good will it do to run away? Do you not wish to become strong? Here before you is a power that was made for you. All you need is a little courage and it will be yours."

"No, you don't understand." Oguna was practically sobbing. "I just want to leave this place. Let me go, please."

Princess Momoso's expression turned fierce. "Can you not see that I am doing this for your sake? Listen to me. Not a single mouse can pass in and out of this sacred shrine without my permission. Know this: you will never leave this shrine until you take up the Sword."

Oguna stared at her, his eyes brimming with tears. "Are you sure you're my mother?" he asked weakly. "If you were really my mother, you wouldn't force me to do something that I can't bear. You would know that I couldn't stand it . . . "

Now Princess Momoso's eyes filled with tears and her face with pain. But still she insisted. "It is precisely because I am your mother that I tell you to do this. If I were not your mother, I would give in to momentary pity. But I am the one who bore you. I know that you are capable of succeeding. Do you think that it does not hurt me to see you suffer? No matter how difficult it may be, you must conquer the source of your fear. It is even more painful for me who must watch you do it . . . I will not leave your side. I am not asking you to fight for me. Please. Fight for your own sake."

Oguna tried. But he simply could not bring himself to look upon the dragon. Many times he stood on the threshold of the shrine only to faint or be so overcome with nausea that he could not stand his ground. He had no appetite and could not even keep water down. Yet still he retched until finally he vomited only gastric fluid flecked with blood. Princess Momoso watched stolidly at first, but as Oguna became increasingly worn and haggard she could stand it no longer. "What is it that you want to expel so violently it makes you vomit? As if you could turn yourself inside out. Avoiding your fear will not help. You must face it. Look at it and ask yourself, 'What is it?'"

When Oguna's stomach had finally stopped heaving, he raised his exhausted face and looked at Princess Momoso. She was shaking with sobs. "Mother, were you able to face your fear?" he asked hoarsely.

She nodded. "Yes, I learned what my fear is. If you continue to reject it like this, you will never know what you need to know. Please. I beg of you. Do not reject it."

Reject it? What does she think I'm rejecting? he wondered hazily.

"How I wish I could give you some of my own strength. So that you could see the rightness of the power within yourself. Ousu, take the Sword. If you do then surely your father will recognize you for who you are." Princess Momoso took his hand and pressed it over her heart.

Startled by the soft touch of her breast, Oguna jerked his hand away. *My father will recognize me?*

"You told me that my father is a god," he said. "Are you saying that taking the Sword will prove me to that god?"

"You could say that. It is proof of who you are."

An idea began to take shape in his mind. Vague, half-formed thoughts were falling into place. He spoke slowly and deliberately. "You said that the only man allowed to enter this shrine is the emperor, right?"

Princess Momoso paused for a moment and then said, "Yes..."

"Has that sword been used since ancient times to test the emperor's legitimacy?"

An even longer pause ensued. "If I said 'yes,'" she finally answered, "what would you say?"

Oguna stood up abruptly. "I'm going back to the shrine." He spoke with such violence that Princess Momoso stood paralyzed as she made to follow him. Stepping outside, Oguna felt the very air begin to stir. Clouds swelled in the sky, summoned by spiraling currents. Thunderclouds. Soon they would be right overhead. But he paid no attention, for the thing he feared most was much closer at hand. He passed through the three walls enclosing the shrine to stand before the place where it lay—the true shape of his fear, the dragon. The wind began to blow, tugging at his hair and clothes. A blue-black cloud bore down upon the trees behind the shrine. Oguna stared up at the building.

So many things would make sense if I were the emperor's son, he thought. *Why Princess Momoso said my father was a god. Why her servant tried to kill me when I was a baby. Why the princess wandered homeless. Why I look like Prince Oh-usu. Why she said my blood is pure. Why I could inherit the throne...*

But Oguna did not want to know. The emperor and the princess were siblings. As ill-informed as he was, even he knew that such a union was a terrible sin. He did not want to know... But there was no turning back.

He climbed the stairs and stood at the top. Like before, he closed his eyes and wrenched the doors open. As he did so, he told himself, *Open your eyes and look upon that which you fear most.*

And there it was—a great writhing dragon with huge red eyes, an enormous jaw, and the poised head of a venomous snake rearing in rage. Oguna reeled but stood his ground—and he thought.

This is me; this revolting, repellent thing, the thing I fear most in the world, is me...

Opening its jaws wide, the snake lunged forward. Oguna saw its curved fangs above his head and its tongue beneath his feet, but he did not run. It swallowed him whole.

Curled in a ball, Oguna felt himself slide down the serpent's throat. He was the snake, and having given up trying to expel it from his own gullet, he just let himself fall as far as he could go through the black heat of its belly. Then suddenly his feet touched firm ground and there beside him lay a sword, glowing faintly even in its sheath.

Ah. There it is. For some reason, he was not surprised. He picked it up. *The dragon, the Sword and I, we are one and the same. So if I cut the dragon's belly with this Sword, will I die?*

He hesitated for a second but then decided that it was worth a try. Princess

Momoso had said that he couldn't turn himself inside out. If not, perhaps he could rip his way out instead. Pulling the Sword from its sheath, he turned toward the hot darkness around him and slashed with all his might. Light gushed from the wound that sliced the blackness.

Princess Momoso screamed and covered her head. Huge drops of rain pelted down in the purple darkness, and a thick streak of lightning hit the ground with an ear-splitting roar. The earth shook, and a rumble that made her sick with dread sounded beneath her feet. Screams rose from every side. Shocked to her senses, she jumped up and ran out into the rain and through the gates to the inner shrine. Then she froze; the building was now a blazing pillar of flame.

"Ousu . . . "

As she watched, the posts beneath the building collapsed and crumbled onto the white sand, and black smoke billowed from the tilting roof. Oguna crawled out from beneath it. He stood up, and she saw that not a single spark had charred his white robes. In his right hand he held a naked blade, glowing red in the light of the fire. He walked straight toward her but blindly, like a sleepwalker. Even the rain could not touch his hair and instead bounced and fizzled around his head.

"Ousu, you . . . " Princess Momoso reached out and placed her hands on his shoulders. An electric shock coursed through her and was gone. Oguna came to his senses and looked straight into her face.

"Mother," he said.

"You did it. You not only seized the Sword but you wielded it. The emperors of the past and even my brother failed to do this. No one has been able to wield the Sword for centuries. Ah, how noble . . . " She choked with emotion. Ignoring the pelting rain, she knelt before him and embraced him, pressing her cheek against his belt. "You have proven yourself. There is no one closer to the gods than you. My son, my son in whom the blood of the Light runs purest, you far surpass all the royal princes."

Oguna looked up at the sky. The rain now fell on his face and dripped from his hair. He looked down at his mother, at her face drenched with rain and glowing with joy.

Perhaps I should never have been born.

chapter
four

WAR
DAMAGE

War Damage

T HE EMPEROR sat on his throne, his chin resting in his hand. The frown that creased his brow had, over time, been etched there permanently, never fading even when he was relaxed. He was contemplating a small lacquered box on a side table, its lid open to display a magatama on a bed of many-layered silk. The emperor, however, did not reach out to touch the stone. Gracefully curved with a single hole through its tip, the milky white translucent gem was magnificent, but it had lost its original hue. It ought to have glowed pale pink like cherry blossoms, as it had when he first saw it.

The sight of the cold, dead stone left a bitter taste in the emperor's mouth. He had pursued the Tachibana for so long, and then, just when their secret seemed to be within his grasp, the woman had refused to divulge it—before her claim that she had been born to bring him the magatama had even dried on her lips.

None other than Prince Oh-usu had thwarted the realization of the emperor's long-cherished dream. While the emperor acknowledged that Oh-usu was the most gifted of his children, he found his heir's brazen confidence galling, especially when coupled with a charm and recklessness permitted only to youth. And now look what the prince had done.

The emperor could easily see why the young Tachibana maid would be drawn to Oh-usu's handsome face and sweet words, but that only fanned his rage. Yet he was not one to lose control. Instead, he remained so composed that even those closest to him wondered if he were upset by the incident. He appeared to be taking action only because his position as ruler demanded that he do so. In reality, however, the more the emperor buried his rage, the more it grew.

He lifted his head abruptly and called out, "Sukune? Sukune, are you there?"

"Yes, my lord." A low voice came from an alcove behind a thick curtain near the throne, a place reserved for the emperor's closest servant. The emperor sent Sukune off on so many errands that at times he could not remember where the man was.

"Judging from the fact that we've received no fresh reports," the emperor said, "Oh-usu and Akaru must have escaped to Mino."

"Unfortunately it would appear so."

"Good. That's exactly what I intended. We have forced the prince to flee in such a way that he can never show his face in the capital again. And we now have a legitimate reason to invade Mino." He paused and then continued more slowly, as though lost in thought. "It makes sense to go there anyway if we are to discover the secret of the magatama. I am sure that Mino holds some clue. I'll be sending you as leader of the troops to capture the prince, so be ready."

"I am at your command," the voice behind the curtain answered.

"You mentioned earlier that there may be more than one magatama. Did you hear this from a reliable source? Do other magatama like this really exist elsewhere, ones that still cast their light?"

"My examination of ancient legends and myths does indeed suggest that this is true, my lord, although the number differs depending on the source. Some say there are five, others say eight, but it seems that several magatama were originally strung together. The custom of stringing together the fruit of the Tachibana to ward off misfortune would appear to support this tale. The necklace was called the Misumaru, meaning 'string of beads.'"

"The Misumaru? . . . It has a nice sound," the emperor murmured with a faint smile. "I'll never know where you find such stories, but you certainly excel at ferreting out information. Keep up the good work. There is still much I need to learn about the Tachibana. All I know now is that their power can free me from death and the curse of the Sword."

"I will make every effort to discover the secret, even if it costs me my life," Sukune said quietly. "For your sake, my lord."

The emperor nodded in satisfaction. He was about to speak when the curtain veiling the doorway moved and a handmaiden appeared. Kneeling before him, she announced in a clear, musical voice, "The Lady of Itsuki requests an audience with Your Highness."

The emperor raised an eyebrow and pressed his lips together. If the visitor had been anyone but Princess Momoso, he would have refused immediately. This unexpected visit from the Itsuki no Miya, however, troubled him. Some of her recent actions had been very strange . . .

"Let her through," he said. The handmaiden retreated behind the curtain.

Oil lamps were brought into the room for the guest. The emperor was surprised to realize that it was already evening. Recalling the last time he had seen his sister after sunset so many years ago, he suddenly felt uneasy.

Princess Momoso appeared with a rustle of silk. Standing in the lamplight, she was tall and fair, as slender as a young maiden and, as always, impeccably dressed. She still retained the dazzling beauty of her youth, something the emperor found inexcusable for, as the Itsuki no Miya, she had no need of beauty.

"How unlike you to visit after dark," he said. "What do you want?"

"I just arrived from Itsuse," she said. "The moon is very beautiful tonight, but it has become quite chilly in the evening, don't you think?" She glided across the room toward him. "There is something that I wished to speak with you about in person. Before your spies told you."

The emperor gave her a sharp look. "So you've finally decided to apologize for stealing my prisoner? Your little joke has threatened my authority over my men."

"So you knew, did you? And I thought I had been so careful to cover any traces." Princess Momoso smiled without any sign of discomposure. "Ah, yes, my dear brother, you know everything. Your hand reaches out to hold all within its grasp. I am aware, you know, that even among my servants there are some who are under your sway. So I am sure you must already know what I have done with the young man I took to Itsuse."

Exasperated, the emperor began tapping the armrest with his fingers. He was fond of his sister when she was absent but whenever they met she irritated him almost instantly. It had always been this way. "I do not have time to listen to reports of you playing house, although I hear you have treated him extraordinarily well. What use have you found for that shadow?"

Princess Momoso placed a hand over her mouth and uttered a brief, triumphant laugh. "I retract what I just said, dear brother. I see that in fact you know nothing. Even though you saw him with your own eyes, you understood nothing at all."

"Is that why you came here? To make me angry?"

She looked calmly into his glowering face. "Did you not notice? Did you not see that he looks even more like you as a young man than Oh-usu? Just one glimpse and my heart was filled with tenderness. No matter how much devotion I might show him, it could never adequately express my love for him. I was overjoyed that he was wounded for it meant that I could care for him."

For the first time, apprehension flickered in the emperor's eyes. "What are you saying—"

"At long last, dear brother, the god is in my hands; I hold my love within my grasp. That child is mine. He is the son I bore, the life I was given to harbor in my body."

The emperor had risen from his seat. Without even registering his own shock, he stalked down the steps of the dais toward Princess Momoso. "Have you lost your mind? You're the Itsuki no Miya. You have no child. You cannot possibly have a child." He reached out to grab her arm, but she slipped away. Her eyes shone dangerously, and she moved so swiftly that she appeared to be some spirit creature.

"It was supposed to have been stillborn . . . " the emperor whispered through his teeth.

"No. He did not die. He was set adrift on the river, but he lived. And I will not let you kill him again." She smiled suddenly. "He wielded the Sword."

The shock of this statement was so great that for a moment the emperor could hardly breathe. "You—what have you done? Did you show him the Sword in the shrine without my leave? Even though to do so could mean death . . . "

"I do not fear death. I would gladly die for his sake. But, brother, listen. That child took the Sword and proved his legitimacy beyond all doubt. And not only that, he actually summoned its power. There is no other alive today who can wield the Sword. If you wish to live, you will need him on your side."

She paused for a moment and then added, "I know that you have been searching for the secret of the Tachibana. But don't you think that seizing control of the Sword might be a faster way to reach your goal than the fickle power of rebirth?"

The emperor stood silently. Princess Momoso, reading within his silence consent, smiled as if the future were in her hands. "We have been estranged for so long, dear brother. I admit that I too was stubborn. But now that my child has returned, the past no longer matters. Let us cease trying to outguess one another and instead work together toward a common goal. For the sake of our son. Because he is the living bond that unites us."

2

IT HAD NEVER occurred to Toko that preparing for war could be so much work. They reinforced their stronghold by building a wooden stockade around the village, set up stone bulwarks, and erected watchtowers. With that task complete, they immediately had to bring in the harvest and take supplies to the many villages scattered far away. The blacksmiths worked against the clock, and the foremen swung their mallets all night long. The women were just as busy, producing clothes, banners, and other necessities in vast quantities.

The prince had insisted that they make a fort at the foot of Moyama where women, children, and the elderly would be safe from the battle. Building it was another huge task. With labor stretched so thin, Toko and the others who were sent to Moyama had to do almost everything themselves. Social rank and physical strength no longer mattered. For the first time in her life, Toko dug holes and pounded stakes to make a fence. It was hard work, but never boring, and much more satisfying than sewing. Or at least she thought so. More than once the stakes she pounded in had fallen over by the next day.

Kisako was excused temporarily from her duties at the shrine to help. But as far as Toko could see, she only got in the way. She was a great talker, but whenever there was hard work to do, she disappeared. *I don't think I can take this much longer without teaching her a lesson,* Toko thought.

Lady Akaru was also with them, but she was very quiet, and her actions served as a model to all around her. No one rose as early as she did or worked as late, and she was always the first to volunteer for unpleasant jobs that no one else wanted to do. Even when she only had a short time to rest, she spent it diligently sewing for the prince. When Toko expressed her admiration, Lady Akaru just smiled and told her that she was used to it, having worked like this at the palace for so many years. This made Toko sad.

We're going to win this war no matter what, she told herself. *We'll win so that the prince and Lady Akaru can live happily ever after.* This thought brought her spirits up. But whenever she remembered what the high priestess had said about Oguna, she lost her natural optimism. *He is an abomination, the source of all our misfortunes.* Although Toko refused to believe this, the words still lay heavy on her heart.

One day as she was tilling the soil to make a vegetable patch inside the fort, Toko was overcome by a sudden wave of despair. *How can she say that about Oguna when he wouldn't even hurt a fly?* she thought. Leaning against her hoe, she slid to the ground. As she stared at a clump of earth, she pictured Oguna's face and tentative smile. He rarely laughed, and she had been secretly proud of the fact that she was the only person for whom he had always smiled. She could not understand how he could be the cause of misfortune. He was far too meek to cause any trouble.

The priestess said that her premonitions were no longer coming true. So maybe she's mistaken about Oguna—

A shrill voice interrupted her thoughts. "Well! Look who's slacking off. Toko, how can you be so lazy!" She glanced up and saw Kisako's gloating face. "You're always telling others what to do when you never do anything yourself. You act like such a good little girl in front of the priestess and Akaru, but you're just a loudmouth, that's all."

Annoyed, Toko leapt to her feet and said, "You're the bigmouth. Why don't you shut up for once? The day you become high priestess will be the end of Mino."

"How dare you speak to me like that! Now you're in trouble," Kisako snapped, scowling. "I knew that I was going to have to teach you a lesson."

"You've got to be joking. That's exactly what I was thinking about you."

As they stood glaring at one another, Lady Akaru suddenly ran out of the building and hurried toward them. "Toko, Kisako, come quickly!" she shouted. "A messenger has come. The emperor's troops are on the move."

Kisako and Toko looked at one another and then ran inside, putting off their fight until later. The messenger, surrounded by a wall of people, was still talking. The soldiers gathered on the border of Mino, he reported, had fallen into a state of terrible confusion. "There's a strange rumor spreading through the troops. They're saying that the commander of the emperor's forces is the true Prince Oh-usu and that the man in Mino who claims to be the prince is actually an impostor who's deceiving us. Some of our men say that they saw this commander with their own eyes and that he was indeed the prince."

Toko felt as if she had been struck by lightning. *Oguna?* she thought. Could the enemy commander be Oguna? This suspicion quickly turned to conviction. *But why . . .*

Her heart began to pound. She had to see for herself, and if it was Oguna, she had to find out why the emperor's troops had made him out to be the prince. It might have been against his will.

When the messenger rose and headed for the door, Toko hurried over to him. "I'm going with you," she said. "I have to know the truth."

"Toko!" Kisako said. "That's not fair. You're going to leave and make everyone else do your work for you. How can you be so selfish?"

Having lost all patience, Toko raised her hand to slap Kisako in the face, but Lady Akaru slipped between them. "Stop fighting, both of you. It won't do to have two of our own people quarrelling when we're on the brink of war. You should use that energy for something more constructive."

Kisako, eyes flashing, turned on her older sister. "Don't talk like you know everything. Who was it that brought this war to Mino in the first place? You! You're no longer the first princess. You have no right to criticize me."

Lady Akaru's face clouded, but she remained calm. "You're right. I have no authority whatsoever. Far from it. In fact, I should throw myself on the ground and beg for forgiveness from our entire clan. Even so, I still have the right to say this. Kisako, a novice, no matter how great her capacity, can never truly become high priestess if she can't understand another person's pain. You don't know how Toko feels. You haven't yet found anyone who is more important to you than your own self. You've never known what it's like to worry about the safety of another."

Lady Akaru knows. She knows that I believe it's Oguna. Toko had never been able to remain obstinate in the face of sympathy. Tears welled in her eyes and she blinked hastily.

Lady Akaru turned to her and smiled. "It's all right," she said. "Go and get ready. I'll take over your work for you. Don't worry. Who knows when I'll have to run off myself."

"I'm sorry. I—" Toko's voice faltered.

"You always take Toko's side," Kisako cried. "Always! Whenever we quarrel, you take her side!" She burst into tears and blindly pushed people away as she headed for the door. "I do so feel pain. But no one cares about me. No one notices how much I'm suffering inside."

This last statement bothered Toko, so before she left, she went looking for Kisako. She finally found her cousin leaning against the wooden fence behind the fort, sobbing violently.

"Kisako . . . um . . ."

At the sound of her voice, Kisako stopped crying, but she kept her face pressed against her hands where they gripped the fence. "You always loved Akaru more too," she said. "You'll never understand what it feels like to be compared to her all the time. No matter how hard I try, I can never compete. She always shows me up. Even when I succeeded her as heir to the high priestess, everyone's eyes were still fixed on Akaru. She's forgiven, though she's committed such a terrible sin. And I'm always stuck on the sidelines."

"You're blowing things out of proportion," Toko blurted out. "No one would ever deny that you're going to be the next priestess."

"Oh, just leave me alone," Kisako said as she burst into tears again. "The last thing I want is sympathy from someone as stupid as you."

Toko shrugged and left. But for the first time in her life she realized that having an older sister who was too perfect might have its own trials.

TOKO RODE alongside the messenger to Kamitsusato. With her, she carried the jacket that Lady Akaru had made for the prince. She had watched Lady Akaru painstakingly sew it by the dim lamplight, trimming the hem and ties with red stitches.

Prince Oh-usu had moved his main base to Kamitsusato, having judged that the narrow valley would serve as more strategic a stronghold than Kukuri in the event of an attack by the full imperial army. For this reason, the Kamitsusato defenses had been constructed with particular care. The prince's plan was to lure the enemy troops deep inside Mino and attack from the rear using a force concealed at Kukuri. In this way they could divide the enemy and eliminate any advantage the invading army derived from greater numbers.

When Toko reached the stockade of sharply pointed stakes surrounding Kamitsusato, she found that no one could pass through without first being challenged by archers on the watchtower above the gate. Once through, she went straight to the headman's hall, her home. Although not much had changed, it was messier than usual. The number of people it housed kept increasing, and even the meticulous Matono seemed to be struggling to keep the confusion under control. She and several other women had decided to stay behind and look after the men rather than seek refuge. Toko guessed that this courageous decision had been inspired at least partly by her mother's unwillingness to let the hall get any more cluttered.

She found Matono out in the back, wearing an apron, scarf, and the expression of an army general as she commanded a troop of women preparing food.

"Mother!" she called.

"Toko! What are you doing here?"

"I have a good reason," Toko said hurriedly. "I've got to meet the prince. I have something important to give him. Where is he?"

"He just left this morning for Kukuri."

"Oh no! You mean I've missed him?" Toko looked crestfallen. "Well, I guess it can't be helped. I'll have to go after him."

"What on earth are you talking about? Honestly, Toko. You can't possibly go to Kukuri. The emperor's forces are already near; it may be attacked at any moment."

"But that's exactly why I have to go," Toko said. "I have to talk to the prince before there's war."

Matono looked startled. "So . . . you've heard, then? The rumor about who's leading the emperor's forces?"

"Yes. Mother, what do you think?" Toko demanded. "It can't, *it just can't* be Oguna, can it? You don't think that he would calmly agree to command the enemy troops, do you? I've just got to talk to the prince. I need to hear what he thinks."

Matono remained silent, but her grim expression deepened. Finally, she took off the scarf that bound her hair, told another woman to take over for a while, and pushed Toko toward the east wing of the house. "Come this way," she said. "It's too hard to talk here."

The room her mother chose was the one that Toko and Oguna had used as children but was now a storeroom filled with supplies. The two sat facing one another, surrounded by piles of chests and wicker boxes. Although Toko was sad to see this place full of childhood memories so changed, she ignored it as best she could. This was no time to be sentimental.

"Perhaps it would be better for you if I said nothing," Matono began, "but I doubt you would accept that, so let me tell you what I know. The prince is certain that Oguna is the impostor. And he's furious."

Toko sucked in her breath. "He's angry? With Oguna?"

"It's not surprising, really. The prince is a proud man. What could be more insulting than a rumor claiming that he's an impostor? And as for Oguna, the prince has a good reason to be angry, one that makes it impossible to laugh this rumor off as groundless. The prince left in such a rage that I'm sure his only thought is revenge. The last thing he said to me was, 'I was a fool to raise a snake in my bosom.'"

"But why? He was so fond of Oguna. Why would he say such a thing? He knows that Oguna hasn't got a single drop of malice in him."

Matono pressed her fingers against her eyelids as if she were exhausted. She remained like this for some time and then said haltingly, "Toko, Oguna . . . It turns out that Oguna is also a prince. Prince Oh-usu already suspected that he was the emperor's child. He started investigating and discovered that the Itsuki no Miya visited Mino around the same time Oguna came to us. He guessed that Oguna must be her son. But it was such a terrible crime, and he's not the type to hold something like that against anyone without proof. So he kept quiet. But this latest incident has brought it all out into the open. He told me he will never forgive the emperor and the Itsuki no Miya for hatching this scheme."

"It can't be true . . . " Toko whispered hoarsely. "Oguna, a prince? It's not possible . . . "

"You know, Toko, ever since the prince told me, I've been blaming myself. I plucked that little baby out of the reed basket and nursed him at my breast without a second thought. Yet somehow I couldn't bring myself to tell the priestess. I've been thinking. Maybe what I did was wrong. Maybe I didn't tell the priestess because I sensed the truth."

Toko grabbed her mother's arms and shook her, shouting, "Don't say that! That's not fair to Oguna. And not just to Oguna; it's not fair to me, either. What would my life have been up to now without him? What's wrong with rescuing a baby? How could a baby possibly have sinned? Mother! Mother, please! You told him it doesn't matter who his parents are, he's still your child! Remember? You told him so yourself."

Matono blinked and looked at her daughter. Then at last she smiled weakly. "Yes. Yes, that's true. What a fool I was to regret what I did. I haven't had much sleep these past few nights. I suppose I'm a little overtired. You're right, but you know, I'm afraid of the high priestess. I'm afraid of what she'll say about Oguna . . . "

Abomination. Toko swallowed hard, forcing the word, which seemed unbearably heavy, back down her throat. She refused to cause her mother any more pain. "Don't worry, Mother!" she said with excessive cheerfulness. "I'll go find out."

She was already out the door when Matono scrambled up and called after her, "Toko, wait! What do you mean you'll find out?"

But Toko had dashed far ahead. "It's all right. I'm just going to see the prince. I won't do anything dangerous."

"Honestly! That girl!" Matono muttered with a sigh. Toko's feet never seemed to touch the ground. She was always off like a shot whenever an idea occurred to her. How far, her mother wondered, did she intend to carry this freedom of spirit, this quality of lightness that seemed neither male nor female but more birdlike than anything else? This thought, however, only made her more anxious about her daughter's future.

Toko threw herself onto the horse she had ridden to Kamitsusato and headed toward the opposite gate from the one she had entered. The bulwarks here were even thicker and the watchtower heavily manned. Spotting Tsunuga among the guards at the top, Toko cupped her hands around her mouth and yelled, "Tsunuga! Tsunuga! Let me through. I have to go see the prince!"

Startled, Tsunuga leaned over the railing, his bow in hand. "So it's you again, Lady Toko!"

"I've no time to waste talking. I have to deliver something important to the prince. It's from Lady Akaru and it's urgent, so hurry up!"

"If you have something for the prince, I'll take it for you. It's too dangerous for you to ride to Kukuri right now."

Toko shook her fist in the air. "Don't be foolish. Do you think that I'd let anyone but the prince touch the jacket Lady Akaru made for him? I promised to deliver it myself."

The other soldiers began poking Tsunuga and seemed to be telling him something. After a moment, he climbed down the ladder and stood in front of her looking somewhat sheepish. "Allow me to accompany you."

"You mean you'll go with me? But you don't need to do that, you know."

"I too fear for my safety, but everyone agrees that I'm the most suited to be your bodyguard."

"They think very highly of you, don't they?"

"Not really. It's just that I've set a precedent."

"You don't seem very happy about it."

"No, really, I'm overjoyed. After all, thanks to you I've made a name for myself throughout Mino."

Toko laughed, even though the joke was on her. Their escapade, she supposed, probably did make a funny story.

ONCE THEY HAD passed through the valley, the camp at Kukuri came into view. It was built simply so that the soldiers could escape quickly, and to Toko, having just come from Kamitsusato, the difference between the fortifications was particularly clear. The man who stood before her after she had yet again exchanged words with the guards was none other than Nanatsuka. There was not a trace of amusement in his expression.

"I am far from impressed by the fact that you would choose to come here. You must know that this is not the time for such antics. If you do not wish to be the cause of unnecessary deaths among our troops, you will leave immediately."

Even Toko was chastened by his words, yet still she begged him, "Please, just let me see the prince, even for a moment. I'll give him the jacket from Lady Akaru and just ask him one thing. Then I'll go, I promise. So please. I want to know that he's not angry with Oguna. I want to hear it from his own lips."

Nanatsuka's thick eyebrows twitched and he looked pained. Toko realized that he too had been shaken by this turn of events. "Please, Nanatsuka."

"Lady Toko—I wish that I could grant you your wish, but the prince is not here. He left us in charge and went alone to meet the enemy commander."

"What?" Toko exclaimed. "He went alone? To meet Oguna?"

"It was the enemy that asked for a parley before war broke out. The prince agreed and went alone. I tried to stop him, but—"

"If they've asked for a meeting then their leader must be Oguna," Toko said, relieved. "It's bound to work out all right. Once they talk about it, they'll be able to clear up any misunderstandings and things will move in a better direction."

"I'm not so sure," Nanatsuka said grimly. "I have a bad feeling about this. I'm very worried about the way things could go. Even if Oguna has no ulterior motives, the people behind him are cunning and will stop at nothing. You know how they whipped the prince into a rage, don't you? And the prince—"

"Doesn't stop once he's angry, right?" Toko finished his sentence for him. Nanatsuka did not deny it. "Where are they supposed to meet?"

"On the island. The island in the pond the prince built."

Toko felt a pang when she remembered how enamored Oguna had been with that island. "I'm going to see."

"That's impossible. No soldiers from either side are allowed within a hundred steps of it."

"But I'm not a soldier."

"It doesn't matter. If even one person moves, the agreement will have been breached and both sides will launch an attack. Please restrain yourself. If you do not want to fight, then pray." His voice was hard and it was clear that he was struggling to resist running after the prince himself.

Toko felt like weeping. *Oguna is so close,* she thought. *He's finally come back to Mino. Yet who could ever have imagined that he would come home in such a terrible way?*

3

THE EMPEROR'S TROOPS advancing from Mahoroba had assembled on the banks of the river southeast of Kukuri and set up a large camp. Within the commander's tent at the center, Oguna was arguing with Sukune, the emperor's trusted retainer.

"The emperor told me he wished to make peace with Prince Oh-usu. He said he wanted to prevent war from breaking out in Mino. That is why he chose me for this position. So why do you keep trying to stop me from fulfilling his purpose?" Oguna demanded, glaring at Sukune. He had reached the limit of his patience. By now, Oguna was painfully aware that he was being manipulated like a puppet, forced to dance from one intrigue to another. "I didn't come here to take the prince's place. I accepted command of this army only because the emperor told me he would forgive Prince Oh-usu."

"Of course you did," Sukune said, a thin smile playing about his lips. He looked at Oguna, who stood in front of him with clenched fists. "And the people in the capital and the men in this army all believe that the commander of this force is the true prince. What could be wrong with that? If you return victorious, you will be greeted with thunderous ovations."

Sukune's narrow face and slender figure were almost feminine. He looked more like a petty officer than a warrior, but in fact it was he who made all the decisions, while Oguna, who rode at the front of the troops, was merely an ornament. Oguna found this infuriating. "It was you who planted the rumor that the prince in Mino was an impostor, wasn't it? There was no need to go around telling everyone that."

"What harm could there be in increasing your status as leader? It certainly seems to have dampened the fighting spirit of the Mino forces. Don't you think that's an effective way to prevent war?"

"And just how do you think the prince felt when he heard?"

"Doubtless he must feel your actions to be unforgivable. Which is precisely why I have been advising you that it's pointless to talk with him face to face."

Oguna's lips grew taut and he shook with anger, but still he forged on. "I must speak to him in person. He knows me. I'm sure he'll understand that I only came here to stop Mino from becoming a battlefield. I need to explain why I accepted the role of commander—that I didn't come here as his enemy."

"Do you really imagine that you can come this far and still conduct yourself as though you were his underling? When the emperor himself has recognized you as his own son?"

Oguna looked away. "He doesn't recognize me . . . I am not a prince."

Oguna vividly recalled the moment he had stood once more before the emperor after returning to the capital with Princess Momoso. The emperor had ordered him to describe what had happened when he had touched the sacred sword in the shrine, but that was all. His father's dark, glittering eyes had remained totally unmoved. Then, as if Oguna had always been under his command, the emperor had appointed him as his special envoy to attempt reconciliation with Prince Oh-usu and ordered Oguna to command his forces and bring back the prince.

"If Oh-usu returns to the capital, I will pardon his crime and forget about Lady Akaru. I will look upon this rebellion as if it had never happened," the emperor had told him. That was why Oguna had accepted this post.

Oguna had sensed at the time that the distance between him and the emperor would never get any smaller. The emperor did not mention their kinship, and he would probably never do so. But Oguna did not mind. He had never wanted to be a prince anyway. He had accepted the appointment simply because it meant he could go to Mino. Oguna had wanted to return so badly that he had thought he didn't even care how.

Now, however, he realized his own naivety. The emperor must have some scheme of his own in mind. Otherwise, Sukune, who served as the emperor's hands and feet, would never have manipulated events in this way. Even Princess Momoso, who had expressed so much concern for Oguna, seemed to have some ulterior motive. Before he had left, she had given Oguna the Sword with a secretive smile and told him never to let it leave his side. What she was planning, he did not know.

Oguna placed his hand on the hilt of that sword now and suppressed a feeling of helpless frustration. From the moment he had laid hands on it in the shrine, he had been propelled in a direction that seemed directly opposed to his own intentions. Far from freeing him, the proof of his birth had only driven Oguna further into a corner.

"I've had enough," he murmured. Taking off his helmet, he threw it aside and began untying the straps of his armor.

"What are you doing?"

"I thought it was obvious. I'm going to meet the prince. I'm going to the island where we agreed to talk."

"But your armor."

"I'm not going there to fight."

Under Sukune's incredulous gaze, Oguna stripped off all the gorgeous trappings Princess Momoso had prepared for him, right down to his undergarments, and then changed into a plain white jacket and trousers. *The prince once told me never to wear white when I served as his double,* he thought. *So I will wear this and go to meet him as Oguna.*

Sukune sighed. "If you truly wish to be killed by Prince Oh-usu, then I will not stop you. For someone who served as the prince's shadow, however, you know surprisingly little about him. He knew long ago that you were the emperor's son."

Oguna's hands froze involuntarily in the middle of tying his belt.

"Prince Oh-usu most certainly investigated your origins, probably much earlier than anyone else. And he employed you in his service, even though he knew. He continued to exploit you as his shadow for his own advantage."

"That's a lie!" Oguna cried.

"It's the truth. I too was sent to investigate, and I can recognize others who do the same work as me."

"You're just saying that to alienate me from the prince," Oguna said.

Sukune shrugged. "How I wish you would see reality. The emperor does not have a monopoly on using lies and deception. Anyone who lives in his palace must be hiding something, and Prince Oh-usu is a badger from the same den."

Oguna stalked out of the tent without uttering another word. Sukune, he realized, was a dangerous man. His soft, low voice slipped insinuatingly into the ears like poison. If Oguna were not careful, he would start believing every word Sukune said.

Oguna was about to break into a run when he suddenly realized that he had thrown aside the Sword with his armor. Although he had decided to take nothing with him, he hesitated, recalling what Princess Momoso had told him. "Wear this at all times," she had insisted as she pressed the Sword into his hands. "Keep it with you night and day. It is yours and yours alone. If you do not take care of it, something evil will happen."

Just as he turned back toward the tent, he heard a muffled shriek from within. It was Sukune. Startled, Oguna rushed inside and saw Sukune staring blankly, his face pale and his right hand cradled in his left.

"Did you touch the Sword?" Oguna asked sharply. Sukune's eyes rolled back in his head and he looked as though he were unable to speak. Oguna walked over, retrieved the Sword, and thrust it in his belt. "No one but me should ever lay a hand on it. Remember that."

"Th-that . . . sword . . . it . . . it . . . can't be . . . " Sukune stammered, finally finding his voice. His eyes were filled with dread. Oguna merely looked at him, then left the tent without answering. This was the first time he had ever seen Sukune regard him with something other than contempt.

TOO LATE, Oguna realized that he was not dressed for the weather. A cold wind had begun to blow and fallen leaves floated in brown clumps at the edge of the pond. Shrikes screeched in the distance. This was the season when people yearned for the warmth of a fire. The tread of approaching winter echoed on the wind, and the dreariness of withering and death lay heavily on field and forest.

But still those fields and forests were Mino, and the sight of them brought Oguna joy. It made him happy just to know that the pond, the island, and the bridge were still there. Although they seemed somewhat smaller than he remembered, they were just as dear. From close up, he could see that the island was more carefully tended than the first time he had seen it. Across the bridge, orderly trees grew on the bank and stone steps wound up through them to an arbor at the top of the small hill. A maple branch, its leaves crimson, stretched out over an elegant roof supported on round posts. Oguna had almost forgotten why he had come. Running up the stairs, he looked around the arbor and thought that he must have arrived first. But he was wrong. Prince Oh-usu emerged soundlessly from behind one of the posts.

"Who would've guessed, Ousu, that our positions would change so drastically in such a short time," he said.

"How glad I am to see you alive," Oguna said. His expression shone with warmth, but he noticed immediately that the prince's gaze held no trace of affection.

"You too appear to have survived. How often I regretted leaving you behind, yet it seems that the arrow I loosed at the enemy was fated to return, this time aimed at me."

Oguna had never seen the prince look this way before. The man he had known had always been cheerful with dancing eyes. But Oguna was now painfully aware that the prince reserved that face only for those under his protection. When it came to his enemies, the prince sharpened tooth and claw more coldly than any beast. Oguna's heart sank. "I came to prevent war," he said. "The emperor has sent me to ask if there is not some way to reconcile. He is willing to overlook this rebellion and to ensure that no dishonor comes to your name. Think how much better it will be for Mino if we can avert this war. Please consider his offer. Tell me your conditions and I will gladly convey them to the emperor."

The prince laughed scornfully. "And you actually believed those honeyed words? How I pity you for your foolishness. Do you still not understand how the royal family works? If my father had even a drop of such feeling in his body, I would never have gone to this extreme. My father? Care about me, his heir? What a joke! All he wants is to obtain eternal youth so that he has no need of any heirs."

"But the emperor said—"

Prince Oh-usu cut him off. "Enough. I now know what you came to tell me. This, then, is my answer. No more of this convoluted scheming. Tell him I will end it here and now by killing you."

"Prince Oh-usu." The blood drained from Oguna's face.

"You should have died," the prince said bitterly. He placed his hand on the hilt of his sword. "I think I always hoped in my heart that you would die a noble death in my stead. Because if you did, I could still think of you as you, regardless of your birth or lineage. You would have continued to shine gloriously in my memory. But instead you shamelessly survived and so revealed your parentage. You, yourself, have proved to all that you are the unthinkable, obscene offspring of my father. Not only that, but you became his pawn, and as such you dare to stand before me once again."

Oguna froze. The prince's words robbed the warmth from his body more completely than the cold wind that whistled through the arbor.

"And as if that were not enough," the prince continued, "you used my name, and posing as me, led a punitive force against me. Considering your birth, you are surprisingly devoid of shame. What a laugh that it was I who taught you how to be my double. So, now you will become the heir. That's not a bad idea, is it? I can tell what my father is thinking. If you kill me, he won't need to worry about an heir because he can put you on the throne in my stead. But I will not let him."

Oguna felt himself reeling inside. "All I wanted was to stop this war!" he shouted. "That's all I care about. If that's possible then I don't care if you kill me or not. Please, please, I beg of you. Think. If you kill me now, here, the entire army of Mahoroba will sweep through Mino like an avalanche. Please, just for now, stay your hand."

"I cannot," the prince said flatly, drawing his sword from its sheath. "I was ready for war from the beginning. And I can't stand to see you alive for one more second."

As he backed away Oguna ignored the naked blade before him and instead kept his gaze fixed on the prince's face. To his sorrow the prince's eyes were like his sword—offering nothing but pale, cold death. With the last flicker of hope fading away, Oguna pleaded once more. "Is there really no possibility of reconciliation?"

"Perhaps, when the victory is ours. But it will make no difference to you."

Without even swinging his sword, the prince had sliced Oguna's heart in two. Yet Oguna's body still evaded the blade, step by step, as the two circled counterclockwise around the arbor.

"You should unsheathe your sword. I trained you to use it. It doesn't feel right to cut down a defenseless man. Come. Show me what you've learned from me."

Until then, Oguna had not thought of the Sword as a weapon. Startled, he grasped the sheath with his left hand, but there was no way he could draw that blade. "I can't."

"Even when you have such a magnificent sword as that?" The prince glanced at the jeweled hilt and said, "It looks as grand as the legendary sword they say is kept in the shrine."

"It *is* the Sword from the shrine," Oguna said, somewhat recklessly.

To Oguna's surprise, Prince Oh-usu began to laugh. But his laughter had an even crueler edge to it than before. "Ah, now I see. This is my aunt, the Itsuki no Miya's doing. Was there ever a more degraded priestess? How deeply must she sin before she's satisfied?"

Oguna felt something stir inside him and looked at the prince as if for the first time. "You don't know. You don't know what happened at Itsuse or why I was made to bear the Sword."

"Because you're her son, of course. But that in itself is astonishing, isn't it? The priestess of Itsuki is your mother even though the gods surely forbid it. She deserves to be despised as filth."

"Please don't talk about my mother like that." Oguna was surprised to hear these words coming from his own mouth, but they expressed what he was feeling. "I don't want to hear you speak of her with contempt."

"Then why don't you take that sword and strike me? Kill me and justify your existence."

The prince lunged toward Oguna and swung his sword with powerful precision, attacking without pause. Oguna dodged but he only managed to evade the first three strokes. The fourth grazed his arm and the fifth, his chest, slashing his clothes. Blood spurted onto the tattered cloth. He staggered back against one of the posts. The prince raised his sword for the final blow but then paused.

"Draw your sword! Don't you want to strike back at least once?"

Oguna raised himself up, and his right hand grasped the sword hilt. Pain and blood seemed to have transported him to another dimension. He no longer wished that he had died when the prince praised him. Oh-usu too, Oguna suddenly realized, had only cared for him because it was to his own advantage, not for Oguna's sake. What difference was there between him and the emperor or Sukune if they were all going to turn on him as soon as they saw him as a liability rather than as a useful tool?

Oguna heard a rumble of thunder inside him. He started at the sound he had always feared. Unlike lightning in the sky, it came from within. There was nowhere for him to run away or hide. Oguna looked at the prince in despair and said quietly, "Why did you not leave when I still admired you? I never wanted to be despised by you. I never wanted to hate you either."

"Then blame your mother and your father. You should never have been born," the prince said. He raised his sword. "If you will not draw your weapon, then it can't be helped. Goodbye, Ousu."

At that moment, understanding beyond doubt that the prince had rejected his very existence, something inside Oguna snapped. Because he had believed in the prince, because he had loved the prince, his emotions now surged with a violence that burst the lock and pulverized the door that had held them back. Clenching his teeth within the torrent, Oguna raised his own blade to meet the prince's blow—and saw exploding light.

*　*　*

LADY AKARU NOTICED something fall from her hair onto the freshly tilled earth. Bending down, she saw that it was a precious comb, a gift from the prince. She had thought it firmly fixed in her hair. Hastily, she picked it up and wiped off the dirt with her sleeve, but as she did so, the teeth fell out one by one. She stared at it. *Something has happened to the prince. Is he dead?*

The sky darkened as if the sun had suddenly disappeared behind a cloud, but looking up she saw that it was still the clear blue of late autumn. She thought she saw a solitary white bird flap slowly across that wide expanse. Death felt close at hand, but she was not afraid. It was as though she had known this would happen all along and had just now reached that time and place. Lady Akaru shed no tears, but her mind sank into a sorrow so deep it felt like a stone at the bottom of a lake.

So he was the Ame no Wakahiko after all. Turning his back on heaven's laws, he loved me and came down from heaven to be with me. But our happiness was short-lived. He's gone. He's gone, and nothing will ever bring him back. Even were the birds to weep for eight nights and days, he would never come back . . .

She placed the comb inside her bosom. Returning silently to her room, she tidied away all her belongings. No one noticed her leave the fort at Moyama.

By the time they missed her and began to search, the evening star was already twinkling. But Lady Akaru was nowhere to be found.

4

AN EERIE LIGHT gushed from the island, shooting into the air. Instantly, the sky above turned as black as night and a purple glow spread across the water, as if it were liquid light. Sukune, who had concealed himself on the island to observe what transpired, leapt up and fled across the bridge at this sudden otherworldly transformation. This proved to be a wise decision, for just as he reached the opposite shore the trees on the island soundlessly ignited. For one second they appeared luminous, and the next, they burst into flame. Gusts of wind rose with a wailing roar, and the raging fire stained the pond red and gold.

Sukune's knees buckled, and he knelt on the shore unable to rise, staring numbly at the flames. Never in his life had he been so dumbfounded. *What is this force? I had no idea the Sword was so strong. It's beyond human comprehension. Perhaps it was never meant to be.*

When he saw the burning arbor in the middle of the island crumble and its roof collapse inward, he began to worry. *What has happened to that boy? Does he intend to burn as well?* Although he felt no sense of obligation toward Oguna, it seemed a waste to let the wielder of the Sword die when there might never be another like him. Moreover, having witnessed the Sword in action, he guessed that the emperor would have something to say if he did not bring Oguna back alive. Resigning himself, Sukune soaked his clothes with water and then crossed back over the bridge. The trees were in flames and the smoke and heat choked him, yet still he ran up the stone steps, dodging falling branches to reach the ruins of the arbor.

He found Oguna sheltered beneath a corner of the roof, which sagged from a tilted post. Other than the wounds inflicted by the prince Oguna appeared unharmed, yet he sat listlessly on the ground looking as if he had lost his soul. His gaze was riveted on the prince facedown on the ground. There was no need to go any closer to confirm that the prince was dead. His clothes were charred black.

The fearsome Sword lay by Oguna's side where he had dropped it. Although it looked like an ordinary sword, Sukune dared not touch it. He shook Oguna and shouted, "Put that thing away. This is no time for cowardice." Oguna, however, did not respond. Sukune slapped him hard across the face several times and repeated what he had said until Oguna finally sheathed the Sword. But he only seemed able to do what he was told. Sukune hauled him unceremoniously to his feet. "We must leave this island. At once!" He half-carried Oguna down the path and across the bridge.

They were not a moment too soon, for the bridge was already smoldering. Once across, Sukune examined himself and found a few small burns. He cursed Oguna. "What use is that power if you can't even protect yourself?" he snapped. But Oguna did not hear him. He continued to stare off into space as though lost in a dream. Clucking his tongue, Sukune shoved Oguna onto his horse, mounted in front of him and took the reins. Sukune had no time to indulge in shock. He had to return to the camp as soon as possible. Regardless of the astonishing sight he had just witnessed, his full attention needed to be reserved for directing the battle ahead. Neither he nor the emperor had ever entertained the thought that this affair could end peacefully.

TOKO RAN, gasping for breath. Although the trees surrounding her hiding place had obstructed much of the pond from view, she had seen a strange light shoot into the sky followed by an orange glow. When she finally emerged from the trees, she saw the island consumed by flames so bright they dazzled her eyes.

She stopped in her tracks with a cry and stood staring in disbelief. At that moment, she noticed a dark horse galloping toward her and instinctively darted behind a tree. The stern-faced rider wore no armor and his hair streamed in the wind. As she peered out from her hiding place, Toko's heart almost stopped beating. Someone sat behind him—a young man. For an instant, she thought it was the prince, but then she recognized the pale, terrified look on his face. It was the same expression Oguna had always worn when confronted by a snake. *Oguna?* The horse, however, raced past before she could make certain. Forgetting caution, she ran out from behind the tree, but all she saw was their retreating figures. They did not stop or look behind.

"Oguna..." Although she knew it was futile, she took a few steps after them.

Suddenly an angry voice thundered behind her. "Lady Toko!" It was Tsunuga. Noticing that Toko had disappeared, he had ridden after her. "Must you *insist* on disobeying every order?"

"Oguna was there. I saw him. I've been waiting for four years, but I only got a glimpse of him. What's happened to the prince? Weren't they supposed to meet on the island? Why is it in flames?"

Without bothering to answer, Tsunuga yanked her roughly into the saddle in front of him. Then he said, "The prince was there on the island. It was a trap. He's not coming back."

"But we've got to rescue him," Toko screamed.

"Impossible. There's no way he could have lived through that."

"That's the wrong way! Where are you going?"

"To Kamitsusato. Don't you see? This means war. Even though we've lost the prince, there are still people we must fight for."

"What am I going to do?" Toko said through tears. "I promised Lady Akaru that I'd give her jacket to the prince."

Urging his horse to a gallop, Tsunuga opened his mouth to snap that this was no time to be worrying about a jacket—and accidentally bit his tongue.

THE EMPEROR'S well-equipped soldiers crushed Kukuri in no time, sweeping through it like a tsunami. The retreating Mino force was scattered, and many never made it back to Kamitsusato. Nanatsuka was among the missing. It was easy to guess that such a loyal servant as he might choose to follow the prince even in death. Still, the loss was a bitter blow. But they were given no chance to grieve. The enemy forces were already advancing toward the stronghold at Kamitsusato.

By now Toko knew too well what war really meant. Each day seemed to pass in a delirium, swinging violently between the hot adrenalin rush of excitement and the cold grip of fear. The norms of daily life had been relegated to some far corner, and the uneventful, peaceful days of the past appeared so ephemeral that she might forget them all together. Before her very eyes, life, death, hate, and joy unfolded in tangible form. Toko could reach out and touch them. The work was grueling, but no one sought any rest; they knew that their very lives depended upon how hard they worked.

On the evening of the third sleepless night, Toko, who had been carting heavy stones all day, was finally so overcome that she nodded off while leaning against her spear. Someone gently shook her and she woke with a start. At first she thought it was her mother, but when she forced herself awake she saw that the woman bending down to look into her face was someone else.

"Lady Akaru!" Toko said, but Akaru gestured for her to be quiet. The lamp beside Toko had burned low. It must have been the middle of the night. Lady Akaru's slender figure floated palely on the surface of the deep blackness behind her. She looked sad.

"Lady Akaru, the prince…" Toko felt tears burn against her eyelids.

Akaru shook her head. "It's all right," she said. "I already knew." Her voice was resigned. "Remember the jacket I gave you for the prince? I just stopped by to see what happened to it."

"I'm so sorry. I still have it. I didn't make it in time." Toko's voice caught. She still carried the parcel tied to her body.

"So you took care of it for me, did you? I'm so glad." Lady Akaru looked relieved. "Let me have it now. I'll take it to him myself."

Toko drew in her breath and fixed her frightened eyes on Akaru's face.

"I'm sorry, Toko. I know it's selfish of me. But together we were one. We can't live without each other." Her expression was serene, and her face shone with a purity that reminded Toko of moonlight, but there was no trace of the lady's former vitality.

"No! Please!" Toko said, protesting like a little child. "I can't bear to lose you too! What are we going to do without you when we've already lost the prince and Nanatsuka?"

"Poor Toko," Lady Akaru said. A shiver went down Toko's spine. Akaru's voice sounded distant, as if she were already halfway down the road to the netherworld. "You're strong, Toko. You have the strength to overcome this sorrow and carry on. Live, Toko, please. And bring the light back to the magatama. Do what I couldn't do, Toko. Save the Tachibana."

"I'm not strong at all. I haven't trained to be a priestess and I don't know how to do anything. I have no power."

"Yes, you do. I'm sure you can do it. I have no reservations about entrusting you with that task." Lady Akaru smiled. "Now, give me the jacket, please."

"No. Please don't go!" Toko knew that if she gave Akaru the jacket, she would never see Akaru again. But she also knew that she could not win this battle. The jacket belonged to the prince; it was sacred, and only the prince and Lady Akaru had the right to keep it. Although in the end she reluctantly relinquished the parcel, she still could not help pleading one more time. "Please don't go. Please don't abandon us."

Lady Akaru gazed at her sadly, but she still receded into the distance, clasping the parcel. "Farewell, Toko. And thank you."

Toko burst into tears and wept until she knew no more.

WHEN SHE WOKE, the morning light had already spread across the sky. Toko rubbed her eyes and then checked for the prince's jacket, but it was gone. If it were not for that, she would have thought it was a dream. That was not all that was strange. No matter how many people she asked, none had seen Lady Akaru.

Maybe that was her soul. She came back in spirit just to get the prince's jacket.

Toko wept alone.

5

LIKE A STONE rolling downhill, the battle grew worse. This was all too obvious to Toko and the others who were caring for the injured, although no one said anything. A steady stream of dead, dying, and wounded soldiers already overflowed the hall. They could not go on like this, yet the emperor's forces clearly had no intention of relaxing the offensive. Instead they seemed intent on finding new ways to annihilate the defenders.

When her father summoned her, Toko thought she could guess what was on his mind, so she spoke first. "It's no good, is it?"

Onetsuhiko looked at her without bothering to deny it. His face was deeply lined with fatigue. He had rallied his men well, inspiring them to carry on, but he was reaching the end of his strength.

"Toko," he said. "There's still time. You must go to Moyama. There are things that you must do."

"No!" Toko protested. "Please. I don't want to go! I can't leave now and abandon all of you here."

"You're a woman. There's no need for you to die here with us."

"Mother's a woman too. But she's going to stay here until the very end. And so will I!"

Her father sighed but appeared unmoved. "Toko, your mother and I have already discussed this. We both agree that you should go and help Kisako, the chief's second daughter. You have a duty to protect the Tachibana bloodline. As daughter of the headman's household, you can't turn your back on that."

"I'm going to talk to Mother," Toko said. She turned abruptly and so bumped right into Matono who was just entering the room. Matono caught her by the shoulders. Looking up at her, Toko pleaded, "You're not going to send me off on my own, are you, Mother? If I go, you'll come with me, right?"

Still holding her, Matono looked into her eyes. "I'm responsible to this clan for everything that is happening now," she said steadily. "It was I who brought Oguna into our house and raised him. As such, I am partially to blame for the fact that he is now destroying Mino. I can't believe that it was a sin to rescue a baby, yet neither am I so blameless that I can desert those who are giving their lives to protect our land. You understand that, don't you?"

"But, Mother, that's true for me too," Toko said. "I want to stay here. Even if we all die, at least we'll be together."

"No," her mother said, caressing Toko's cheek. "I know it seems hard to have to go on alone, but still that is what you must do. You are the daughter of a headman of the Tachibana clan. Therefore, you must willingly accept the most difficult task of all. It takes great courage to survive; it will be much harder than staying behind in this fortress. But that is what I want you to do. I want you to live."

Toko blinked. Something about her mother reminded her of Lady Akaru. For an instant, it was as if she saw the two of them standing before her, one overlapping the other.

"Even if we are killed," Matono continued, "I know that you, at least, will be able to carry on without hating Oguna. You must never blame him, Toko. Some fate far greater than any man could resist is at work here—a sad and twisted fate. I want you to go and see if there is any way to make it right as a Tachibana."

IT WAS TSUNUGA who brought her horse. Where he had been fighting she did not know, but he was covered from head to foot in mud. The mud had dried so that he looked like a walking clay figurine, but his eyes remained undefeated and even lively.

"Don't worry, Lady Toko. This fort will not fall. We'll guard it with our lives. Please don't cry."

But his words only made her sadder. Not even Tsunuga, who had always stood by her, could go with her now. He would stay and defend his homeland until the end.

"Tsunuga, I'm sorry I caused you so much trouble."

"Looking back on it, it was actually fun," he said with a laugh. He rubbed his cheek with a muddy hand. "Next time, let's go for a walk somewhere less dangerous though, shall we? When this war is over, I would be glad to escort you."

Toko smiled. "Really? But aren't you tired of me?"

"Of course not. I'll take you, and that's a promise!" Then he opened the gate and bade her farewell. Fortified by his courage, she was able to ride off and even to keep herself from looking back. But despair soon overtook her. Trying to shake it off, she spurred her horse into a reckless gallop. *The prince. Nanatsuka. Lady Akaru. Mother. Father. Tsunuga. Everyone in the hall. Everyone in this land. Will they all die? It's not fair. Why is this happening?*

Tears blurred her vision so that she could barely see ahead. When her horse stumbled over a tree root, Toko went sailing through the air. She was fortunate to land smack in a thicket of bamboo grass. Had she landed elsewhere, she might have broken her neck. Shocked and frightened, Toko burst into tears, unable to bring herself to move. It was ridiculous, she thought, to cry just because she had fallen from her horse, but she could not help it.

I'm not that strong. How can I stop from wondering whose fault this is? How can I keep myself from blaming or hating someone for this when my home, my family, all the people I love are being taken from me? I can't help but despise whoever did this. I'll hate them forever. If it's Oguna's fault, then I'll hate even Oguna.

But after crying for a while, she gradually calmed down. Feeling somewhat foolish sitting in the thicket, she stood up slowly. She had escaped with only a few minor scratches. Toko walked along calling her horse and found it not far away rummaging about for bits of grass.

"Sorry about that," she said. "Let's start over. I promise I won't cry anymore. Crying won't change anything anyway. I'm going to the fort at Moyama. That's all I'll think about for now. I'll worry about the next step when I get there."

BY THE TIME she reached Moyama, the stars had already come out. Light spilled from the doorway of the meeting hall, the largest building in the fort and the only one in which the lamps seemed to have been lit. It was unusually quiet, but as she had not eaten since leaving Kamitsusato, she was too exhausted to notice. Ducking quickly under the woven straw curtain that served as a door, she stopped in surprise. The entire fort was gathered inside, and all eyes now turned toward her. In the middle of the silent crowd sat the Keeper of the Shrine. She looked around and said, "Ah, Toko. Good. You're back."

Toko was stunned. It had never occurred to her that the priestess would leave the shrine. "What are you doing here?" she asked.

"You should know even better than I. Mino will fall. Once Kamitsusato is defeated, the rest of this land will follow. I came down from the mountain to announce that the end is near. My end as well. He has begun to exercise his power. My own power, however, is finished, and I can no longer read the signs."

"You mean Oguna?" Toko asked in a small voice.

"Yes. The abomination. Not only has he brought destruction to Mino but he will also bring disaster and misfortune everywhere he goes. He must be stopped. I do not have the strength to do that myself, but there are other Tachibana. Originally, there were five Tachibana clans. Kisako."

The chief's daughter seemed to shrink at the sound of her name. "Yes, Keeper of the Shrine."

"Remember what I taught you? Tell us where the other clans are."

Kisako licked her lips and then recited in a rush. "In the land of Hidakami, where the sun rises; in the land of Himuka, where the sun sets; in the land of Mino and the land of Izumo and the land whose name is forgotten; in these five lands lie the magatama protected by the five Tachibana clans."

The priestess closed her eyes as if contemplating the words Kisako had rattled off. Finally she spoke. "Much time has passed since the age of our forebears. Who knows if we can still influence the power of the gods in this age when the oracles no longer hold true. As for the five Tachibana clans, we have lost touch with one another and I don't know what they are like now. Still, we must try. Kisako, Izumo is the closest of those lands. Go there and seek out the Tachibana. Tell them what has happened and ask for aid. We have lost our magatama, so there is no choice but to rely on them. Tell the Keeper of the Shrine of that land that we need a warrior. We need a hero who can take the Misumaru, the string of beads, and with it oppose the power of the Sword."

Kisako gasped at these words. "Izumo? But that's so far. How can I possibly make it all the way there?"

"I'm not asking you to go alone. Even I have reservations about sending you there by yourself. Toko, you must go with her. You too are a Tachibana. You must help each other to reach Izumo."

Toko hunched her shoulders and exchanged an uncomfortable glance with Kisako, who had turned to stare at her. "Keeper of the Shrine," Toko said. "You say that we need a warrior. Do you mean a warrior to defeat Oguna?"

"Yes."

"So you want us to look for someone in Izumo who will avenge us by killing Oguna?"

"Yes. The one who wields the Sword must not be allowed to live. His is a power that was not meant to exist in this world. The mission of the Tachibana clan since ancient times has always been to subdue that power. I know how you must feel, Toko, but this is no time for mercy or compassion." She paused and then continued. "I told you that Prince Oh-usu was a Takeru. So is Oguna, for it takes one Takeru to kill another. His life will thus be brief. I don't know if this is any comfort to you, but even if the Tachibana don't kill him, he cannot survive for very long. The power of the Sword, however, is so evil that he must not be allowed to live even for that short space of time. As long as the Sword is wielded, it will continue to twist fate and destroy any harmony in Toyoashihara."

"Keeper of the Shrine!" Toko said. "There's no need to seek a warrior in another land. I'll be that warrior. I will kill Oguna."

Everyone stared at her. The high priestess held her gaze as if weighing it. Then, seeing that Toko's resolve did not waver, she said, "Your courage at least should qualify you as a warrior. But I can no longer see the future. I long to believe that this choice will bring good fortune, but it could just as easily bring the opposite. The only way to find out is to go to Izumo. When you get there, seek the one who bears the magatama. Nothing can be done until you have the Misumaru."

PRINCESS MOMOSO sat Oguna down in front of her and chanted a long prayer. Waving a *sakaki* branch in her hand, she brushed it against his shoulders several times. When she finished, the vacant expression on Oguna's face changed and he began to blink. His eyes, however, remained unfocused.

Princess Momoso gently raised his chin and asked, "Do you recognize me?"

"Mother? What are you doing here?" Oguna murmured with a puzzled look.

She smiled with relief and stroked his hair. "That's better. I flew to your side as soon as I heard. This is the villa at Awami. You've been in a stupor for days and would not eat unless food was put in your mouth. That's why you were brought here."

Oguna looked around in surprise at the unfamiliar room. He had thought that he was still in Mino.

"You were possessed by Oh-usu's death. You must be careful not to stare too long at the dying. They can seize your mind."

With a sudden, violent motion, Oguna thrust her hands aside and backed away. His face grew deathly pale. He had remembered what he had done.

"Don't touch me! Please! Don't touch me."

Princess Momoso's eyes grew round. "What's the matter?"

Shaking, he screamed, "What am I? Some kind of monster? What is this power? Why did you give me the Sword?" With trembling fingers, he undid the belt at his waist and threw the weapon on the floor. "I don't want to see that horrible thing ever again. I don't need it. I wish it would disappear."

The Sword spun off into a corner, leaving a gash on the floor, but nothing else happened. Princess Momoso watched wordlessly. Then she went over, picked it up in both hands, and held it out to him. "You are just upset. It will not help to take it out on the Sword. Even if you try to shatter the blade or melt it down, it is already a part of you, its power is one with you."

"I don't want it." Turning his back on the Sword and Princess Momoso, he crouched down on the floor. "I don't want it. I killed the prince. With that

Sword—no, not with the Sword; with my mind. How could that be possible? I loved him . . . " He broke off and then added tremulously, "He was my brother . . . "

"Oh-usu was destined to die. If you hadn't killed him, someone else surely would have," Princess Momoso said. "As that was the case, then it was more merciful for him to be killed by your hand than by the blade of someone base and vile. It was the judgment of the heavens."

"Are you saying that I was his judge?"

"Weren't you?"

Oguna leapt up. "Stop it! I'm not that kind of person, and I don't want to become like that either." But then his voice faltered. "When I said that I wanted to be strong, this was not the kind of strength I meant . . . "

"But it's what you are. You alone can wield the Sword. You are the strongest man on earth."

Confused, he turned his anger on her. "Mother, why aren't you afraid? Why don't you fear the fact that you gave birth to me? I am afraid. I'm more afraid of myself than of anything else in the world." Once he had started, he could not stop. "You ought to fear me too. You should despise me. The prince did. I would rather you hated me from the very beginning than to have you change after you have shown me kindness."

Princess Momoso's eyes were lined with worry. "Ousu, you are upset. Why do you talk such nonsense?"

"It isn't nonsense. I—"

"I do not fear you. Even if I were the last person left on this earth, why would I fear you? You do not know what it means to be a mother."

"But what if I kill you? This power is beyond my control."

"I do not care if you kill me," she answered. "Why are you worrying about such trivial things? You are my life. No matter who you kill, even if you kill me, I will love you. It is enough for me to know that you exist. I live only for your sake."

Oguna stared at her blankly for a moment. As he stood biting his lip, at a loss for words, sobs rose unbidden to his throat. "Mother," he finally managed to say. "Mother, you should not say that." The words let forth a flood of tears. "Surely you must know, my birth was a sin. The power of the Sword is proof of that. Of all of us, the person who tried to drown me in the river was doing the right thing."

Oguna, who had never in his memory cried aloud in front of anyone, realized for the first time that it could actually relieve some of the burning pain inside.

Princess Momoso held him in her arms and whispered, "There is no need for you to suffer so. No need at all. It is my sin, not yours. You did nothing wrong. You were born. That's all, so why should you be blamed? Do not blame yourself anymore. I am the only one who is at fault."

Although sobs still racked his body, lethargy gradually stole over him. Crying seemed to be the first step toward solace. *She's wrong,* he thought. *But I don't have the courage to turn her away. She may be the only person left who will accept me as I am. Because she's my mother . . .* He pictured yet again the island engulfed in flames, a scene seared in his memory. Never again could he return to Mino. Never again could he return to being Oguna of Kamitsusato.

I wonder where Toko is. I wonder if she's all right.

He had said goodbye to her once when he had been about to die. Yet he felt much farther away than he had then, even though he was alive. *I'll never see her again,* he thought, anguished. *I have no right to even think of seeing her.*

"WHAT IS THE KEEPER of the Shrine going to do?" Toko asked Kisako in a half-hearted effort to make conversation.

"She said she was going to return to the shrine. She declared that she just can't leave, though she destroyed the oracle hearth and burned the altar; even though there's nothing left."

At dawn, everyone in the fort at Moyama had gathered their few belongings, divided up the food, and departed, each going their own way. But in the end, the high priestess had decided not to seek refuge.

"Just like Mother and Father and the others," Toko whispered. Toko and Kisako, who were hardly more than children, had been left to carry the burden of the Tachibana women alone into an unforeseeable future. Toko felt the weight of responsibility keenly. She and Kisako had left the fort and stood now on the shoulder of Moyama, looking down at their homeland. The fort was tiny in the distance, half concealed by the trees on the slope below them. The fence that Toko had helped build looked small enough to flatten with her little finger. Knowing that they would never see their home again once over the pass, the two had lingered at this spot for some time.

"Let's go," Toko said. "We won't get anywhere if we stay here all day." She slung her bag over her shoulder.

Kisako wept, unable to bring herself to leave. "Not yet. Please," she said with a sob. "Just a little longer. This is the last time we'll see Mino. I want to engrave it in my mind. Oh, how could such a terrible thing be happening? My heart is breaking. I never dreamed that we would be defeated, or that I'd be forced to wander without any idea of where to go. Why do I always have to suffer?"

Toko wondered irritably why she was being forced to set off on this long journey with Kisako of all people. The future seemed very dark indeed.

Apparently, Kisako felt the same way for she now snapped, "Toko, you're so heartless! You could at least join me in my sorrow. How can you rush me like this? You're leaving your homeland behind forever too."

But Toko gave no ear to her reproaches. "We promised the high priestess that we would go to Izumo. That's all I am going to think about. If I do what *you* want, we'll be here all day."

"You're so mean! You have no compassion at all, do you? I'm not feeling well today, you know. I have stomach cramps and a headache too. I'll need to stop and rest often if I'm going to climb any mountains."

"Honestly! It's not like anyone else is bursting with energy!" Toko exclaimed. "What's wrong with you? You were fine yesterday."

"That's why people say you lack delicacy, Toko," Kisako retorted, almost spitting with anger. "Any woman would understand immediately. They'd know that there's one day a month when they don't feel well either. But no, not you. I bet you don't even know what I'm talking about."

Toko blushed, a fact that Kisako did not miss. "It's no use talking to you if you've never experienced it," she concluded. "That's what makes women unsuited for traveling. You ought to be more considerate."

Toko recovered by becoming annoyed. "If that's the case," she said, "then I hope I never experience it. Who in their right mind would want to? When we get to Izumo, I'm going to become a warrior."

"Are you still saying that?" Kisako said, exasperated. "Are you serious?"

"Why would I say that if I wasn't serious? I'm the one who will find Oguna. I'm the one who will make him pay." Toko's decision to become a warrior was the only thing that kept her going right now. Turning her back on her homeland, she began to walk.

I won't look back and I won't cry anymore. From now on, I'll think of myself as a man. I don't need a woman's weakness. Not until I see Oguna again . . . and kill him.

And when he died at her hand, she thought, the two of them would once again be Toko and Oguna. Then she would be able to love him again, just as she had when they had played and laughed so innocently as children.

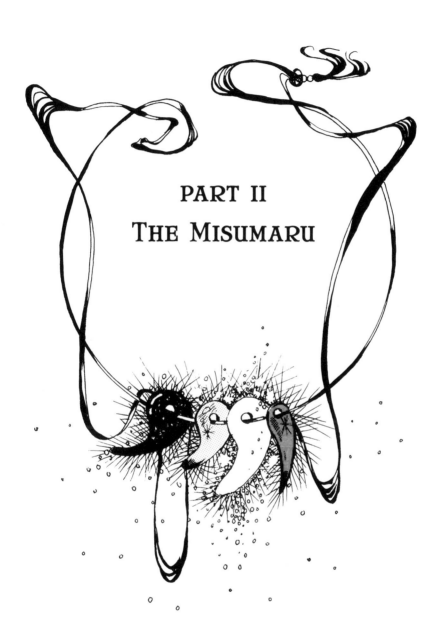

PART II
THE MISUMARU

The beautiful beads of the Misumaru,
Ah, that string of beads
that graces the neck
Of young Orihime in heaven.

—Kojiki

chapter
five

SUGARU

Sugaru

ALTHOUGH the ancient earth gods were gradually fading from the land, to travelers they were still very real. Wild and violent, gods inhabited the mountain passes and steep valleys far from the villages of men, where they randomly killed hapless travelers. Only two out of every three, and sometimes only one out of every two, made it through alive. The gods needed no reason to kill. Unpredictability and cruelty were simply part of their nature, and mortal men could only bow their heads in awe and submit to this capricious culling of their ranks.

A handful of women, however, had the ability to at least intuit what the gods felt, if not to actually converse with them. These few were the shrine maidens. Though her training was incomplete, Kisako too had learned to read their intentions, and thus she and Toko were among those who survived. Except for a moment of poor judgment on a snow-bound mountain pass, they successfully cleared the most perilous reaches, where even the strongest men feared to go.

Indeed, men were far more dangerous than gods. Of the many travelers who feared the mountain passes, more than a few fell victim to that man-made calamity known as bandits. In the face of this peril, it was Toko who displayed wits and courage. Strapped to her waist she wore a short sword she had taken when she left Mino. Too big to be a dagger, it was still small enough to fit perfectly in her hand, and she did not hesitate to use it when needed, although she used her bow more frequently.

During their long and arduous journey, the blisters on the girls' feet hardened to calluses, and their temerity and naivety gave way to determination. As two young women traveling alone through the bitter winter months, Kisako and Toko were frequently forced to rely on the compassion of others, and the warmth of unexpected kindnesses tempered the desolate loneliness of their quest.

The most memorable encounter occurred when they began climbing the mountains north of Mino at the beginning of their journey. In their haste to cross a pass, they underestimated the weather and lost their way in a blizzard. Some hunters passing by dug the half-frozen girls out of the snow and carried them to a hot spring deep in the mountains where the steaming water revived them. Toko and Kisako had heard rumors of a mountain people who shunned the settlements below, but this was the first time they had met any. Robed in bearskins and shod in thick winter boots, the men appeared wild and fierce, but of all the people the girls met on their journey, these mountain folk were the kindest.

The two girls stayed at the hot spring for about ten days. During that time, many creatures joined them under the shelter of the rocks in the steaming pools: monkeys with their young, deer, badgers, and white rabbits. Their faces looming out of the vapor made the girls laugh. It was like experiencing a different side to the violent deities of nature. Now they understood why the hunters did not want to come down to the villages below—perhaps they were even closer to the gods than the shrine maidens, for they knew what the gods protected.

When Toko and Kisako had fully recovered, they made their way slowly westward, growing a little wiser as they did, until finally they reached the land called Izumo. It had been almost three months since they had set out from Mino, and most of that journey had been through deep snow. Now winter was at last departing from the land and traveling back up the trail by which the girls had come.

The first view that Toko and Kisako saw of the town one fine spring morning was a fleet of ships gathered, like a flock of migratory birds poised for flight, in the bay.

"Izumo looks awfully big, doesn't it?" Toko said.

"It seems so much livelier than Mino," Kisako agreed.

They were visibly shocked to find the town so much grander than their own.

A bearded man belonging to a band of villagers leading packhorses laden with wares to sell overheard them and laughed. "Don't tell me you've never heard how wealthy Izumo is?" he said. "Why, her sailors travel all the way to Koshi in the north and across the seas to foreign lands in the south. They bring back things that not even the emperor in Mahoroba owns. It won't be long before the ships are ready to head off again."

Toko and Kisako followed the villagers to the marketplace and there witnessed Izumo's prosperity firsthand. The roads leading to the port converged in a large square overflowing with people. Never having seen Mahoroba, it seemed to the girls that it must be as crowded and busy as the capital.

"Well, this is where I set up shop," the bearded man said. "Have a safe journey."

Toko and Kisako bade him farewell but were reluctant to turn their backs on the marketplace so soon. The aisles were full of people, including many young women who walked among the vendors and gazed at the wares with shining eyes. Toko and Kisako had seen nothing like this on their long and difficult journey.

"It's impressive, isn't it?" Kisako said with a sigh. "The clan that rules this land must be far stronger and richer than ours. I wonder if they will even bother to meet us."

"They'll have to," Toko said. "There's no reason we should hesitate to ask them for help. We may be wearing rags, but we're still Tachibana." She spoke confidently, but inside she too was nervous.

"Wearing rags . . . " Kisako looked down at her faded hakama. "Toko, why don't we get some new clothes in the market? I still have some of the agate beads the high priestess gave me. We should be able to trade them."

"You're always so worried about appearances, Kisako."

"It's all right for you," Kisako retorted. "You can pass yourself off as a servant boy. But I must present myself to the clan ruler as the daughter of the chief of Mino. I'll bring shame to our people if I go dressed like this."

"And just what do you mean by that?" It was Toko's turn to be annoyed. True, she had pretended to be her cousin's servant boy for the entire journey, but that was not the same as having Kisako call her one. "If you're getting new clothes, then so am I."

Dividing the beads equally, they joined the throngs crowding the square. Instantly, their quarrel was forgotten and their scowls vanished. Instead, they nudged each other and pointed with cries of delight at all the fascinating goods that could only have come from across the sea—glazed pots, colorful fabrics, musical instruments they had never seen before. It was not long, however, before the girls became separated. When Toko glanced up, Kisako had disappeared in the surging crowd.

Oh dear . . .

Toko was searching anxiously when she heard someone call out in a lively voice. "Hey there, little man. That's a nice sword you've got. How about trading it for one of my magatama?"

Startled by the word *magatama,* Toko looked around to find the speaker and saw a young man sitting cross-legged at the edge of the road with his wares spread out on a cloth in front of him. Although he was just sitting there, something about him immediately drew her attention. Perhaps it was his bright red, unkempt hair. Though he grinned up at Toko in a friendly and agreeable manner, he seemed rather uncouth, and she doubted that he came from a respectable household.

Ignoring her suspicious glare, the young man continued, "I'm a bit of a connoisseur when it comes to swords. You can tell a good one by the hilt. That's not from this area, is it? It looks like a masterful piece of work. Where'd you get it?"

"Mino," Toko answered proudly. "Mino smiths are the best in Toyoashihara, and the iron is fine quality too."

"That explains it. Mino iron is famous." Then suddenly he burst out laughing. "Well, well. You're dressed like a boy, but I see you're actually a girl. All the more reason to exchange your sword for a necklace. Take a look. Which one takes your fancy?"

Necklaces of small green and red stones on colored strings were spread out on the cloth. Toko moved closer for a better look, but they were clearly just cheap beads that only young girls would wear.

"I don't see any magatama."

The young man winked at her conspiratorially. "It wouldn't do to leave a magatama lying out like this. After all, they've got magic powers, right?"

Pulling out a deerskin pouch, he shook out three stones. Green and curved, they were indeed magatama, but Toko could see that they were far too inferior to be stones of power. Even the agates she had were better quality.

"What's so special about those?" she demanded. "Stop playing games with me. I'm only interested in real magatama."

The young man looked taken aback and stared at her curiously. "I see I've picked the wrong person. You wouldn't by any chance be the daughter of a bead maker, would you?"

"No, I wouldn't." But she had barely completed her sentence when two young women butted in, blushing and giggling.

"Give us a necklace, please," one of them said. "One just right for each of us."

Immediately dropping his conversation with Toko, the young man turned his smiling face upon these new customers. "Of course. I've got just the thing for two such beautiful women as you. Take a look at these magatama. They're charmed, you know."

"What kind of charm?"

"Why, a love charm, of course."

The girls laughed.

What nonsense! Toko shrugged in disgust and left.

She had to find Kisako, but she had no idea just how hard that would be in a crowded marketplace. She went from one vendor to the next, but Kisako was nowhere to be found. Toko began to fear that something might have happened to her. The carefree faces of the people passing by seemed to mock her, and she was close to tears. Just as she stopped to look around once more, a long-legged young man raised a hand in greeting. It was the magatama seller. "Yo!" he said. "So there you are! I've been looking all over for you."

"Do you want something?" Toko asked, frowning up at him. He was a head taller than anyone else in the crowd.

"What do you mean 'Do you want something?' We were in the middle of a conversation, remember? I'll admit that my magatama are worthless. It's just a way of earning a little money on the side. But if you come back to my village, I can show you some real magatama. I come from the bead-makers' village. We use jade imported all the way from Koshi. I'm quite taken with your sword. Will you trade it for a real magatama?"

"No," Toko said without even bothering to look at him. "I need it to protect myself and my companion."

The red-haired youth snorted. "Really? You?"

"What business is it of yours?" Toko retorted. "Look. I'm trying to find my friend, so stop bothering me."

"Oh, that's why you're so preoccupied," he said, nodding. "But I bet you can't see much from down there, can you? Shall I give you a ride on my shoulders?"

"Do you want me to punch you?"

The young man laughed. "Well then, at least let me help you look. What does your friend look like?"

"She's a girl," Toko said somewhat hesitantly. "She's wearing a straw hat tied with a red ribbon and faded red hakama."

"And her face?"

"Well, she's beautiful, I guess."

"Right. Let's find her then!" he exclaimed with sudden enthusiasm.

MANY PEOPLE called out to the pair as they walked through the center of the market. The young man seemed to be very well known. Although Toko feigned disinterest, she registered the fact that most of the people who spoke to them were young women. And the looks they gave the young man made Toko feel very uncomfortable.

"Where have you been, Sugaru?"

"Did you sell your necklaces?"

"Where are you going, Sugaru?"

"Sugaru, who's the kid?"

The young man answered cheerfully and then deftly fended off any further conversation. "See you later. I'm looking for a beautiful woman wearing red hakama." But a girl from one group stopped him and said, "Really? If you're talking about a girl with a straw hat and red hakama, I saw her. She was heading for the pine grove by the sea with a group of young men from the next village."

At this, Toko's heart skipped a beat and she broke into a run. *Kisako! Honestly! She never thinks of her position.* As far as Toko could see, Kisako failed to appreciate her rank. Her naivety was understandable, for she had known only the inside of the chief's hall and the shrine before this journey.

But as the last heir of the Tachibana high priestess of Mino, she needed to realize how easily a shrine maiden could lose her purity.

Seeing Toko dash off, her face pale, Sugaru started after her, but several pairs of hands grabbed him and held him fast. "Wait a minute. You'd better explain yourself. Don't expect us to let you get away without telling us why you're looking for a beautiful woman," one of the girls said.

TOKO RACED out of the market toward the sea. She finally found Kisako at the edge of a grove of black pines that grew along the shore. Surrounded by a group of young men, she was crying, her back pressed against a tree. Grasping the situation at a glance, Toko pushed her way through and grabbed Kisako by the arm. "How could you be so stupid?" Toko whispered. "Why on earth did you come here?"

Kisako looked at her with red-rimmed eyes and burst into tears again, this time apparently from relief. "They . . . they said . . . they would show me a magatama. So I-I . . . "

Toko took a deep breath. "This country seems to be riddled with magatama. If we'd known, maybe we wouldn't have been so easily fooled."

"Hey, you," one of the young men interrupted. "Get out of the way. Our leader's talking to her. This is no place for kids."

Furious, Toko snapped, "You've got to be joking! Who in Izumo would waste his time trying to seduce a shrine maiden? You'd do better to flirt with a toad." She stared defiantly at the leader of the gang in front of her and, taking in his wide-spaced eyes and froggy expression, realized belatedly that perhaps the word *toad* had been a bad choice.

The leader's bulging eyes flashed angrily. "You'll pay for that, you little squirt!"

Kisako buried her face in her hands. *Toko! Honestly! She never thinks of her position.*

Toko was already regretting what she had said. She could not afford to get into a fight here. But there were six of them and they did not seem likely to let the two girls go easily. Reluctantly, Toko reached for the hilt of her sword. But at that moment, someone called out in an incongruously cheerful voice, "Well now, you've got some nerve, haven't you? Swaggering about my turf and picking on defenseless young women." Sugaru stood behind them, the wind playing in his hair. Pausing for a moment, he unfolded his arms and scratched the top of his nose. "What was your name, again?" he asked. "It's slipped my mind. Toad Boy, wasn't it?"

The blood rushed to the leader's face. "Don't make me laugh. You act as though you own the biggest marketplace in Izumo."

"Oh, but I do," Sugaru said. "Along with all the girls who come here. So if you want one, you'll have to ask me first."

Toko gaped in astonishment. But she was even more astounded when the girls in the crowd that had gathered to watch shouted, "You tell him, Sugaru!"

He gave them a friendly wave and then turned back to the leader, his expression serious. "I get all fired up when there's a crowd cheering me on. I like to put on a show worth watching. If you want a fight, I'd be more than happy to oblige." Casually picking up a stick from the ground, he settled into a fighting stance. He looked long, lean, and strong, like a wicked blade before the stocky Toad Boy. Toko could almost smell the flame smoldering inside him. Sugaru grinned as though he were just itching for an excuse to fight.

"Sugaru's alone. Get him!" the leader shouted.

"He may be on his own," one of the other five protested, "but he's got as many friends as there are legs on a centipede. We won't make it home alive."

They stood glaring at Sugaru for a few moments, sweat beading on their foreheads, but in the end they decided to withdraw. Gazing after the youths as they ran through the trees, Sugaru tapped the stick against his shoulder. "I'm offended. I would never have dreamed of asking for help. It would have been too good a chance to show what I can do."

Bending down to look at Kisako, her cheeks wet with tears, his eyes widened in genuine admiration. "Well, well, well. What a surprise! I only half believed it. But it's true. You really are beautiful. I never knew what beauty was until I saw you."

Kisako, who had never been praised so frankly in her life, blushed and hid her face behind her sleeve.

"It won't do to have a beauty like you wandering about on your own, much less being led on by such useless louts as that. You need to realize just how gorgeous you are."

"But I wasn't led on," Kisako protested faintly. "I'm a shrine maiden. I wouldn't flirt with anyone."

"Really? But you could have half the men in Izumo following you with just one look. I guarantee it."

"Stop talking to Kisako like that," Toko said. To her, Sugaru seemed no better than the gang leader, and she sensed that he would, in fact, be the more dangerous when it came to distracting Kisako from her objective. "You helped us by chasing away that gang, but look at you now. Have the people of Izumo forgotten how to pay reverence to a shrine maiden?"

"Of course we revere them, especially if they're as good-looking as she," Sugaru said. "To prove it, allow me to accompany you to your destination. Tell me where you're going." When he learned they wanted to meet the high priestess, Sugaru immediately went off to gather friends and horses.

Once he had gone, Kisako pressed her hands against her burning cheeks and looked at Toko. "Am I really that beautiful?"

"He told every girl we saw on the way here that she was beautiful," Toko snapped, but Kisako appeared oblivious. She smiled in the direction the young man had gone. "Sugaru . . . What a lovely name."

Just what about it is lovely? Toko thought.

WHEN SUGARU returned with a group of friends and only one horse, Toko was further incensed because he lifted Kisako onto the horse and told Toko to walk with the rest of the party. In response to her complaint that this was unfair, he replied, "I only treat women specially. After all, there's no reward to be had from flattering a child."

"But she's the same age as me!"

"Ah. But you're not a woman yet, right? I can tell."

"How?"

He looked at her gravely and said, "You aren't in love with me."

"I hate men like you who flirt shamelessly. And those who think every girl must love them are even worse."

Sugaru looked offended. "I don't *think* every girl loves me. It's simply the truth. I can't help it."

Realizing the futility of further discussion, Toko maintained a stony silence. The looks that the young women gave them as they passed were so sharp they almost pricked her skin. They also fanned her anger because she could not accuse Sugaru of lying.

Sugaru led them to the hall of the Kuni no Miyatsuko, the provincial lord of Izumo. Surrounded by a thick green hedge, the hall was just as imposing as Toko had imagined. Sugaru had bragged continually along the way that he had connections with the ruler's household, and apparently he had been telling the truth. At Sugaru's request, the servant who greeted them at the door went off to arrange a meeting with the high priestess for Toko and Kisako.

"I've been delivering beads to the Kuni no Miyatsuko ever since my grand-father got the gout," Sugaru said smugly as they waited. "You should come to my village when you're finished. I'll prove to you that we have real magatama—ones for which you'd be willing to trade that sword." Then he turned to Kisako and, switching tones completely, said, "And you must come too. From you, I will not ask for anything in exchange. It will be my gift. There's bound to be a jewel that only you could wear."

Toko suppressed a violent urge to stomp on his foot. Instead, she said, "Thank you for everything you've done, but I must remind you that it's no use flirting with Kisako. She's the last of our clan to serve the gods."

"Ah. You mean that she's beyond my reach, do you?" Sugaru flashed the same fearless grin he had shown Toad Boy's gang. "When it comes to love, I can't resist a challenge." He strode off, laughing.

"He's horrible! Oh, how I hate men like that," Toko fumed. Kisako failed to respond. Constantly having suffered in comparison to Akaru back home, Kisako had rarely been complimented on her looks. While Toko had always grudgingly thought her cousin extraordinarily pretty, she noticed with surprise that Kisako's demurely downcast face was now positively radiant. For reasons Toko could not fathom, Sugaru's attentions appeared to have transformed her into a true beauty.

2

ENTERING THE HALL, Toko and Kisako followed an elderly servant into the far reaches of the complex. People bustled about the main building and in the passageways, but once the girls had passed beyond the inner garden, everything grew silent. The only other presence seemed to be the ancient trees. Still leafless from the winter, a weeping willow drooped over a pond like a woman grieving. Here the servant finally stopped, announcing that they had reached their destination. Before them stood a solitary building surrounded by trees. A faint sound, barely audible, quivered in the air—someone was plucking a one-stringed harp.

"Her ladyship rarely accepts visitors," the servant said with a disapproving frown. "You have been granted a highly unusual privilege. She is blind and tires easily, so please speak no more than necessary and keep your voices down. She can hear even a whisper."

The two girls nodded and then exchanged glances. Apparently, high priestesses in lands other than Mino were also very particular about visitors. When they entered the building, it took a moment for their eyes to adjust to the dim light. They vaguely made out the figure of a slender woman pushing away a low harp. Kneeling and bowing low, the two girls introduced themselves nervously. The woman greeted them in a voice as faint as the beating of moth wings.

"Welcome. You are to be commended for successfully reaching Izumo. I am Toyoao, younger sister of the Kuni no Miyatsuko. Word has reached us here of the war in Mino. You must be very anxious about the fate of your homeland."

Toko looked at the woman before her and wondered how old she was. In the dusky light with only her faint whisper as a guide, she could have been fifteen or fifty. Her small pale hands and petite white face were those of someone who lived without the sun on her skin. Her eyes were closed and her expression as unreadable as if she were asleep.

Together, Toko and Kisako conveyed the words of the Keeper of the Shrine. "We fled here, to this land," Kisako concluded, "to ask you to lend us your wisdom and power, to beg you to aid us to find the warrior and the Misumaru, the string of magatama, with which we can defeat the bearer of the Sword. Please tell us what we should do."

Lady Toyoao had listened silently throughout, but now she said in a voice that sounded like a sigh, "I see . . . ." She paused for a long moment and then began to speak. "What greater joy could there be than to meet people of the Tachibana clan. I am blind, but I have been blessed with hearing far keener than others. I can learn more from people's voices than is visible to the eye.

Kisako, yours is like a bird warbling in spring. You bring joy and attract the hearts of others. I am sure you must be very pretty as well." Kisako blushed and fidgeted uncomfortably.

"Toko, you sound like a pure rushing stream. No one who comes in contact with that clarity can remain unchanged. Purity is strength. You both have a fresh, wholesome power like young buds in spring. I have always thought that that is what a Tachibana priestess must be like . . . Unfortunately, however, I must disappoint you. It grieves me to tell you this but no Tachibana blood runs in my veins. There is no longer any Tachibana blood in the line of the lord of Izumo."

"Wha—" Toko hastily clapped a hand over her mouth. In a quieter voice, she asked, "But where are the Tachibana then?"

"Nowhere. They simply died out over time," Lady Toyoao whispered. "Unlike Mino, Izumo is not protected by mountains. Many ships come and go and many wars have been fought here. There is no longer any priestess who can move Izumo. I just happened to be born to this household, and as I am blind, people believe me to be closer to the gods. I'm afraid that I cannot guide you."

Toko and Kisako sat speechless, robbed of what little strength they had left. Who could have foreseen this? They had risked their lives to get here, enduring countless hardships in the belief that once they found their people, the Tachibana, they would learn how to destroy the Sword. No one, not even the Keeper of the Shrine had considered the possibility that the Tachibana clan in Izumo had died out.

"There's no one? Not even a single Tachibana left? Did you lose the magatama of your clan too?" Toko asked.

"No," Lady Toyoao said. "No, I don't think so. But I do know one thing." Tilting her head to one side as though listening to some inner voice, she continued. "It happened long ago, when our clan replaced the Tachibana. The new lord seized the magatama from the Tachibana as proof that he was the legitimate ruler. A rumor spread that this magatama was a fake made by Kushiakahiko, a skilled Tachibana artisan. The chief interrogated him and threatened to have him drawn and quartered if he did not produce the real one. A year later, the artisan capitulated and presented another stone. It was a splendid work, a treasure. Not long after, however, the rumor spread that the second bead was also a counterfeit. Pressured by the chief, Kushiakahiko produced yet another stone, this one even finer than the last. This happened repeatedly, and each time Kushiakahiko brought a magatama that glowed even more brightly than those that came before it. Finally the chief no longer threatened him with death but instead took him into his service to make a new magatama every year. The people who live in the bead-makers' village are Kushiakahiko's descendants."

It was a strange story, one that people from Mino could never have imagined. Now Toko finally understood why fakes would be sold in the marketplace. "The bead-makers' village," she said under her breath. "So Sugaru—"

Lady Toyoao's keen ears picked up her words. "Yes, you were fortunate to meet Sugaru. He's the grandson of the village headman and the youngest descendant of Kushiakahiko."

"Can you believe it?" Toko hissed in Kisako's ear. "She's saying that that idiot has Tachibana blood."

Ignoring Toko, Kisako said to the priestess, "Really? I knew there was something special about Sugaru."

Taking advantage of the fact that the priestess could not see, Toko jabbed Kisako with her elbow and received a sharp poke back. The priestess smiled. "There's no one in Izumo who doesn't know the name Sugaru, especially not the young women. Not a day goes by that they don't mention him. It's only to be expected, I suppose. His voice is filled with sparks."

"So we may be able to find the magatama in the bead-makers' village," Kisako said. "Even to know that much is very helpful. To be honest, I've never seen a real magatama. The one from Mino was passed on to my older sister, and then it was taken from us."

"What do you know about the Misumaru, the string of beads?" Lady Toyoao asked.

Kisako shrugged. "Only that we need it to defeat the bearer of the Sword. The Keeper of the Shrine didn't tell us much, and we were expecting to learn more about it once we reached Izumo, but—"

"I see." Lady Toyoao paused for a moment. "I'm not very useful, I'm afraid. All I can do is listen to the voices of the past. But perhaps I can help by sharing the tale of how the magatama came to be. You see, it was in Izumo that the Goddess gave the Tachibana their stones. Did you know that?"

"No," Toko and Kisako said simultaneously.

"It was after the Goddess of Darkness gave birth to the fire god. Disfigured by severe burns, she was descending the hill to the netherworld to hide herself away when suddenly she stopped. 'Ah,' she thought. 'I have come to the land of the dead, leaving that evil child in the world above.' So she returned and gave birth to children in whom she invested the power to still the force of the fire god should the evil in his heart begin to rage. Those children were the ancestors of the Tachibana, and to each one she gave a sign, one of the stones from the necklace she wore around her neck. Originally, there were eight stones, each distinct: Aka, pale pink and bright. Kuro, midnight blue and dark. Ao, light blue and faint. Shiro, white and clear. Ki, yellow and full of life. Midori, green, for new birth. Kagu, light. Kura, darkness. When she broke the necklace, she took one stone for herself, saved one for her husband, the God of Light, and divided the remaining six among her children. The Water Maiden gave hers, Ao, to the Wind Child, and it became part of him. That leaves five remaining. They must still exist somewhere on this earth."

Toko and Kisako knew the story of the Water Maiden well. She and the Wind Child had founded Mahoroba and the emperor's line, which the Tachibana of Mino had protected ever since. But it seemed unbelievable that the magatama they were seeking should come from the same necklace as the stone that had once united the Water Maiden and the Child of Light. Dazed, the two girls sat in silence.

"The Misumaru," Lady Toyoao continued, "was the necklace worn by the Goddess. Therefore, if you want it, you must first gather together the five stones given to the Tachibana clans. From what I have heard, even individually these stones are imbued with power—but when brought together they have extraordinary force, as great as, or even more dangerous than, the power of the fire god's cursed Sword. Four together can bring death to all while five bring rebirth. Or, at least, so it is said."

"Four together bring death to all . . ." Toko murmured. "So that's why the Keeper of the Shrine said the warrior would need the string of beads."

Kisako thought for a while and then asked, "The Keeper of the Shrine taught me where the five Tachibana clans reside. They're spread from one end of Toyoashihara to the other. Does that mean that if we are to obtain the Misumaru, we must travel to each of those lands?"

"Yes."

"But who could possibly do that!" Kisako exclaimed. Just the journey from Mino to Izumo had seemed to her like a lifetime.

"I will," Toko said. "All I need is four magatama, right? If gathering them together will make me the warrior and the destroyer of the Sword and its wielder, then I will find them."

"Lady Toko, you sound so happy," Lady Toyoao said. "Why?"

"I grew up with that boy," Toko answered. "That's why it must be me."

"That boy? Is that what you call Prince Ousu? But I thought the prince wielded the Sword."

"Prince Ousu? I've never heard that name."

"I'm sure that's what they call the prince who killed his older brother and ravaged Mino."

Toko sighed. "He's the same person then. The bearer of the Sword."

Lady Toyoao also sighed. She appeared to be tiring. "I'm so sorry," she said in a barely audible voice. She gathered her strength and spoke more clearly. "If you wish to stop the one who bears the Sword, then you must hurry, for the destruction it wreaks is spreading. Prince Ousu is much closer than you think. Have you heard that he has left Mahoroba and is heading west?"

Toko and Kisako were shocked. "Are you sure?" Toko asked.

"Yes, he left a month later than you. But unlike you, he has been following the inland sea westward and is now farther west from here. The emperor of Mahoroba ordered him to subdue the Kumaso."

"The Kumaso?" Toko groaned. She seemed to remember tales of a people by that name who lived in the far western corner of the country.

Lady Toyoao frowned. "There were some in Izumo who, hearing that he was accompanied by only a few men, set out to take revenge. Prince Oh-usu had allies in Izumo too, you see. But not one of those who sought to avenge his death ever returned. They say that people saw a flash of light and flames, and afterwards there was nothing left but scorched fields—" She was interrupted by a fit of coughing. Toko trembled as she recalled the blue-white flash she had seen in Mino.

The elderly servant spoke from the other side of the curtain as if she could no longer restrain herself. "My lady, you must stop. If you push yourself like this, you will never recover even if you take to your bed."

"Shirame, let me be, please," Lady Toyoao reprimanded gently. Then she turned back to Toko. "I often come down with a fever, and so she worries about me. This is the first time I have ever talked at such length. But perhaps I was just waiting for this day. I may have been placed here just so that I could tell you these things." She smiled for the first time, but not for those with eyes to see her. This thought made Toko sad. Now that she knew a simple conversation was enough to give Lady Toyoao a fever, she could not linger any longer.

"We'll go to the bead-makers' village," Toko said. "Thank you so much for everything."

They were about to leave the room when the priestess, summoning the last reserves of her strength, said, "Lady Toko, you must hurry. Do you know the name of the land where the Kumaso live?"

The urgency in her voice startled Toko. "No," she answered.

"Himuka, the land where the sun sets, and home of the Tachibana and one of the stones."

3

SHIRAME was so angry with the two girls for prolonging their visit that they feared she would not follow Lady Toyoao's instructions to bring them horses and help them on their way. Well trained in the service of the ruling clan, however, Shirame made sure the girls were given strong steeds. Accepting the loan gratefully, Toko and Kisako headed for the bead-makers' village. The road, which ran south along the river toward the mountains, was wide and flat, and they sped along it with ease. They rode silently, their minds so full of what they had learned that they had no desire to talk.

What had shocked Toko most was the news that Oguna was traveling west. As the blue mountains rose before her, she envisioned him on the other side pressing his mount steadily onward. Even if his companions were few, as the commander of an imperial mission he would still be clad in armor and wrapped in an aura of dignity and power. And he would be bearing that evil sword on his hip. Yet the toil of his journey would not be much different from hers. Day after day, he would taste the loneliness of wandering, never seeing the same scenery twice, never resting with ease. The wind might blow and the rain might fall, but he would be forced to move onward.

It disturbed her to think of him experiencing the same hardships that had been drilled into her own body. She was seized by a sudden urge to spur her horse onward across the mountains in pursuit, but forced the idea from her mind as sheer stupidity. Hadn't she just heard what had happened to the men of Izumo—gone in a flash of light and flame? She could not confront Oguna yet. First she must become his equal. She must obtain the Misumaru, the only weapon that could match his power. *I must hurry!*

STILL LOST in their own thoughts, Toko and Kisako passed through several villages along the river until they reached the foot of the mountains. Here they came upon yet another settlement nestled in a valley between the steep slopes. This, Toko guessed, was the bead-makers' village, for on the bridge at the entrance stood Sugaru with a group of young men. They looked as if they had been waiting.

"Welcome," Sugaru said, stepping forward to take the reins of Kisako's horse. "You arrived much sooner than I expected."

"You knew we were coming?" Kisako asked.

"Of course. I was sure you would come. But if I had known you would be arriving today, I would have raised the ante."

Kisako and Toko stared at him, wide-eyed. One of his companions turned to the others and said in disgust, "There's no point in betting against Sugaru when it comes to women. There's not a woman alive who's immune to his charms."

The others chimed in with similar complaints. "I don't believe it. I've lost again."

"Who was the idiot who suggested we bet in the first place?"

They were betting on us? On whether we'd come or not? Toko thought.

Ignoring the disgusted expressions on Toko's and Kisako's faces, Sugaru collected his winnings from his friends, a smug look on his own face. When he finished, he said, "All right. Let's go then. My house is the one farthest upstream."

"I think you must have misunderstood," Toko said coldly. "We didn't come here to see you. We came here because we were advised to do so by Lady Toyoao."

"You came to be a guest at my house, right? It's the same thing." Ignoring her protests, he began leading Kisako's horse across the bridge, and Toko had no choice but to follow. The other young men brought up the rear, their faces alive with curiosity.

The village, dedicated as it was to the unusual craft of bead making, was very different from those the girls were used to seeing. They assumed that the grandest building must be the headman's hall, only to discover that it was the bead workshop. They were also puzzled by the many large stones, some square and some with carved patterns, scattered about the village. The houses all seemed to be the same size and shape, and even their destination, the headman's house at the very end of the village, was not particularly large. The garden behind it, however, extended into the thick forest beyond. A path led into the trees to a small wooden shrine perched on a stone column.

Kisako tugged at Toko's sleeve. "Look! There's a Tachibana tree near that shrine."

Peering at it, Toko saw that she was right. The evergreen with its dark glossy leaves looked just like the tree within the sacred grounds of the Forest Shrine in Mino. Small yellow orbs clung beneath its leaves, and Toko knew the fruit to be pungently fragrant. Just the thought brought the scent back to her. That smell belonged to Mino—a memory of her precious homeland. It had never occurred to her that she would one day miss the secluded shrine deep in the forest. Now, however, it existed only in her memory, part of the home she had lost forever.

"Hey, Grandpa, I've brought guests!" Sugaru shouted. He entered the back door but came out again almost immediately. "Ira," he said to a middle-aged woman approaching with a load of firewood. "Where's Grandpa?"

The woman stopped. "I don't know. He said there was a meeting—" She broke off and began to laugh. "There he is, right behind you."

Sugaru and the girls turned around in surprise. How he had gotten there they did not know, but an old man now stood behind them. He was thin and the hair was receding from his prominent forehead, but his bones looked sturdy and his features bore some resemblance to Sugaru. His bushy white eyebrows, however, were locked in a fierce glower, and no one would have dared to flatter him with such adjectives as gentle or kind. He raised his cane and whacked Sugaru on the head.

"Ow! That hurt!" Sugaru yelped, clutching his head.

"Imbecile! What do you mean by not showing up at the workshop for three days? Just wasting your time at the marketplace would have been enough to bring shame to the headman's house, but no, you actually had the nerve to sell your trashy beads there. Not a single day goes by without your causing some kind of trouble! Idiot!"

"Oh . . . so you heard already?" Sugaru seemed to shrink in size.

"That's all they talked about at the meeting! Put yourself in my shoes for once. I thought my face would burn with the shame of it. It's at least a decade too soon for you to be showing your work to anyone. If you go around claiming to be a bead maker while selling rubbish like that, you'll tarnish the reputation of our entire village. How can I face our ancestors when you act like that? You're a disgrace to our family name!"

Sugaru shrank even further. "But, Grandpa—"

"No buts. If you have something to say, do it when you're capable of work that is worth showing me. And now what? Are you planning to bring a bunch of women to this house? Over my dead body."

"No, no, you've got it wrong. They're shrine maidens. They've traveled all the way from Mino."

"Ha! A likely story!"

"But it's true!"

Sugaru's friends, who had hastily retreated from the line of fire, watched gleefully as Sugaru, glistening with nervous sweat, groveled in abject apology.

"Ah, it always makes me feel so much better to see him like this."

"When it comes to women, fights, or gambling, Sugaru never loses. His grandfather is the only one who can put him in his place."

"It's amazing. He gets yelled at every time."

"But just you watch. As soon as his grandfather's gone, Sugaru will forget everything."

Toko watched, and sure enough, as soon as the old man turned his back, exhausted from yelling, Sugaru's contrite expression vanished like mist in the sun. He turned to the girls. "You can stay in the east wing," he said. "I'll tell Ira to bring you some food."

"We can't stay here without first explaining ourselves properly—not when your grandfather was so angry," Kisako said.

"That's just his temper," Sugaru said. "He's quite old, you see. When he gets mad, he loses control." Then he added in his defense, "But he's still the best bead maker in Izumo. He's had a hard life. My parents died and all he has left is me."

Then why don't you do what he says and behave yourself so he doesn't have to yell at you? Toko thought.

As if he had read her mind, Sugaru laughed. "But I'm an unworthy grandson. I'm not made out to be an artisan. It doesn't suit my nature to sit around all year polishing beads."

One of the other young men piped in, "We're planning to get a boat. Not one owned by the Kuni no Miyatsuko, but our very own. We'll use it to import jade." They began talking about this project with an enthusiasm that Toko found puzzling. In her homeland, young people would never have dreamed of disobeying their elders. Here, however, it seemed to be different. Young people acted independently . . .

As they spoke animatedly among themselves, Sugaru and his friends began walking off. "Sugaru, wait!" Toko called out. "There's something we need to talk to you about."

Sugaru turned and winked at her. "Ira will take care of you," he said. "Just relax and take it easy. It wouldn't be right to talk about a subject like that in the daytime."

"Would you be serious?" Toko scowled but then suppressed her irritation and asked him a question instead. "At least tell me one thing before you go. What's inside that shrine?" She pointed toward the forest.

"You mean the shrine to the forest god? It's dedicated to my ancestor, Kushiakahiko."

"What's enshrined in it?"

"I haven't a clue. Maybe Grandpa knows. He's the one who takes care of it." And Sugaru left without having been of any use at all.

Watching the young men walk away, Kisako whispered to Toko, "I know what you're thinking. You think the magatama is kept in that shrine, right?"

"What about you, Kisako?"

"I do too."

AFTER the good-natured Ira had taken them to their room and supplied them with everything they needed, the two girls finally had a chance to talk.

"I think the Tachibana are dying out," Kisako confided to Toko. "The other clans will be destroyed too, just like we lost the shrine in Mino. Our people will vanish altogether from this earth."

"You don't know that. So far, we only know about Mino and Izumo. It's too soon to judge." But Toko spoke without much conviction. Until they had reached Izumo, both she and Kisako had seen themselves as messengers. They had believed that the burden would be lifted from their shoulders as soon as they found the Tachibana priestess in Izumo and relayed the message from the Keeper of the Shrine. Then they could simply depend on a much wiser person to guide them. Even Toko, who aimed to become a warrior, had vaguely expected that someone would appoint her to that role. But instead the high priestess of Izumo had vanished long ago, leaving only an oral tradition that had been passed down to Lady Toyoao. Toko and Kisako did not know what to do next.

"What do you expect me to do without a high priestess?" Kisako said. "There's no way to continue my training. The people of Izumo don't even know enough to respect a shrine maiden. I never imagined that we would face a situation like this after such a long journey."

"But, Kisako, you can teach them to respect you. If they knew you were a true shrine maiden, they wouldn't dare disrespect you. They're just ignorant, that's all."

"No, Toko, I can't. I'm only partway through my training and I can't become a high priestess on my own. Maybe if I had been initiated in the secret of the magatama . . . But that was my sister's role. She was the one who was supposed to become the high priestess. I'm just a substitute."

"Let's not talk about Akaru," Toko said. Thinking about Akaru made her sad.

"You just don't understand, Toko. From the time I was born, it was drilled into me that my role in life was to carry on the Tachibana line. But when my sister's destiny was revealed, our roles were suddenly reversed. I was told to become a shrine maiden instead and remain chaste for the rest of my life. So I became a shrine maiden and tried my best to train to become a priestess, but now there's no one anywhere who can teach me. I don't know what to do." Kisako sat and wrapped her arms around her knees.

Unable to refute the logic of this argument, Toko decided instead to change the subject to a more immediate problem. "Well, in any case, judging from Lady Toyoao's story, it seems quite likely that the magatama is in that shrine. Instead of sitting around wasting time, we should find out."

"What? Do you think we should ask that old man? What would we say? 'Please sir, show me what's in the shrine?'"

They looked at each other. Their first impression of the headman had been quite daunting.

"I wonder if he'll beat us with his cane . . . "

"He doesn't seem very likely to listen to our explanation, does he?" Kisako agreed. "It would be unthinkable to reveal the sacred object guarded in the shrine."

They tried to think of ways to convince him, but none of their ideas were any good. Finally Toko said, "This is impossible. I'll just have to go and take a look inside the shrine when everyone's asleep. I'm sorry, but there's just no other way."

"And if you find a magatama, will you just take it?"

Toko groaned. "I'll worry about that later. The first problem we have to solve is whether there is a real magatama here or not." She stopped suddenly, struck by a thought. "How do you tell a real magatama from a fake anyway?"

Kisako put her head in her hands. "I don't even know myself. But . . . I've heard that the magatama of the Tachibana glow from within. When they find the right person to be their bearer, they shine. And I also heard . . . " She paused, searching for words, but then gave up. "It's no use. I'll just have to come with you."

LATE AT NIGHT when the crescent moon was setting, Toko and Kisako crept outside, feeling somewhat guilty. Spring was approaching, but the nights were still chilly, and the air stabbed their lungs. Shrinking against the cold, they tiptoed under the clear, starlit sky. To their surprise, however, they ran into someone attempting to sneak through the garden gate despite the hour. It was Sugaru.

"You've got some nerve coming home this late," Toko said, forgetting her own position entirely.

"Ah, I see. You couldn't wait for me to get home, so you came looking for me. Sorry to make you go to all that trouble."

"Who on earth would bother going out in the middle of the night just to meet you?"

"I know of lots of women who do," Sugaru said. "You said you had something to talk to me about. Wasn't that what you meant?"

Fearing that Toko would start shouting, Kisako yanked her away from the young man and stepped forward. "No, that's not what we wanted to talk to you about. Your ancestors and ours shared the same destiny. That's why we wanted to talk. Would you please listen?"

Sugaru narrowed his eyes. "Under the light of the stars, you look even more beautiful. The moon tonight pales beside you."

Ignoring this comment, Kisako briefly explained about the magatama. She had doubted that he would be able to digest the content in so short a time, but he nodded. "All right," he said. "I'll go and open the shrine for you. If it's that special, then I'd like to see it myself. I always thought it fishy that Grandpa kept telling me I'd go blind if I looked inside. But that made me think there probably wasn't anything special there."

"You don't mind?" Toko asked in disbelief.

Sugaru grinned. "When Grandpa dies, it'll be my turn to guard that shrine. So I should be entitled to have a look, don't you think?"

Inside the wood, it was nearly pitch dark. Without Sugaru there to guide them, they would never have reached the shrine without a light. He warned them before every rock or tree root, as if he knew exactly where each was located. When they finally reached the shrine, Sugaru grasped the handles on the double doors and turned toward them. "If I go blind," he said, "Please take me back to the house." He did not seem to be in the least afraid.

But the doors were shut fast, and Sugaru struggled with them for some time. Stamping her feet against the damp chill in the forest air, Toko asked Kisako, "You didn't bring a flint stone, did you?"

Kisako said that she hadn't and when Toko asked Sugaru, he also said no. "Well, that was pretty stupid of us. How are we going to see what's in there if none of us has a light?"

There was a loud crack and then Sugaru said, "You may be stupid, but I'm not. I brought a light. See? The shrine's open now. Come and take a look. It's going to be hard to get this door back on again though." Something in Sugaru's hand had begun to glow, and a light shone on his face. Holding the light high, he stuck his head into the shrine and said, "Look. It *is* a magatama—and an impressive one at that. This must be the model for all the others we make."

"Sugaru, what on earth is that in your hand?" Kisako asked. Her voice shook and she had lost her usual composure.

"This? My mother gave it to me. I'm not supposed to tell anyone that it glows, but it comes in handy."

"Sugaru, that's it! That's the Tachibana magatama."

"What? No, it can't be. Grandpa never said anything about that."

"Even so, it's the Tachibana magatama," Kisako said, trembling with excitement. "I can tell."

4

THE TWO GIRLS bent forward to peer at what lay cupped inside Sugaru's long, lean fingers. Slimmer than an ordinary magatama, it resembled a fang more than a teardrop, but its light was mesmerizing. The core shone vibrant green, like sun pouring through translucent leaves in spring. The color clearly came from the light, not the stone, for not even the finest jade had such a hue.

Sugaru looked as amazed as Toko and Kisako. "Well now, that's a surprise. In my family, we just call it Midori. Are you sure it belongs to a priestess? That seems very unlikely. After all, it's supposed to be a childbearing charm. The male heir in our family always gives Midori to the woman he marries.

Then she gives it to their firstborn son. That's how Grandpa and my father inherited it. It *is* an ancient heirloom, but still . . . "

"Can I hold it?" Kisako asked. Sugaru handed it to her readily. The stone glowed briefly on her palm, but then its light faded away, and they were plunged once more into darkness. The chill in the air deepened.

"Kisako, why did it go out even though you've trained to be a priestess?" Toko said.

"I guess it doesn't respond to someone with Mino blood. Maybe the master of the stone has to be from Izumo."

Toko tried it just in case, but the vivid green light died quickly in her hand, leaving only a forlorn afterglow. "But why? Why should someone like Sugaru have more power than us?"

Returned to Sugaru, the magatama practically taunted the girls with its bright glow. Sugaru shrugged. "Don't ask me. It's no big deal anyway. It's not like I can get anything for it just because it glows."

"But it *is* important! We need that magatama," Toko protested. "We need it for the Misumaru. We've no hope of defeating the bearer of the Sword without it."

Sugaru scratched his head. "I don't see what use a childbearing charm would be in a fight. What you're really trying to say, though, is that you want my stone, right? If so, why don't you just ask me?"

"All right then, I will. I want your stone," Toko declared defiantly. "I'll give you my sword for it. I'll give you everything I've got, so please, give it to me."

"No, Toko, that won't work," Kisako said. "Magatama only have power when they glow. Even if you take it, it will be as useless as the one from Mino that's now in Mahoroba."

Toko fell silent. "There's no reason to look so gloomy," Sugaru said with a smile. "There's a very simple way to give you Midori and make it shine. All you have to do is bear me a son. Midori will glow all you want if you do that. Would you like to try it and see?"

Not surprisingly, Toko thought she had never heard anything so offensive in her life. She froze, and rage boiled up inside her. But rather than lashing out at him, she stalked off without uttering another word.

"Toko, wait!" Kisako hurried after her, stumbling in the dark. Sugaru was left on his own. In the light of the magatama, he looked a little remorseful. Now he would have to fix the door of the shrine all by himself.

SLEEPLESS, Toko lay listening to the birds chirping merrily as she stared at the ceiling in the faint dawn light. Finally, she heard movement in the main house. She opened the door a crack and saw the old man emerge and walk slowly across the frosted ground toward the forest. Glancing back into the room, she checked that Kisako was still breathing evenly, oblivious to the world. Toko dressed quietly so as not to wake her and then slipped outside.

It was not hard, she thought, to guess where Sugaru would be sleeping—in the room on the corner with the double doors closest to the gate. She was right. Peeking inside, she saw him sprawled facedown on the floor. After a moment's hesitation, she let herself into the room and closed the doors.

"Sugaru," she whispered, but he did not wake up. She shook him, but he still did not respond. Finally, she kicked him, at which point he opened his eyes to thin slits.

"Who's there?"

"It's me, Toko. I'm sorry about last night. I wanted to talk with you one more time."

"Oh, Shorty, it's you." He groaned and rolled over. "You're the only girl I know who would come to a man after daybreak. Leave me alone, will you? Why are you always in such a hurry?"

"Because there's no time! Prince Ousu is already on his way to Himuka."

"Ousu . . . I think I've heard that name before."

"He's the emperor's son who killed his own brother, Prince Oh-usu, and razed Mino to the ground."

"Ah, yes. Now I remember." He struggled earnestly to make his sleep-fogged brain think. "I once knew a supporter of Prince Oh-usu. I heard he went to take revenge but never came back. I suppose he must've died."

"It's the Sword. Prince Ousu wields the cursed power of the Sword. He's an abomination. That's why I have to kill him. But the only way to defeat the Sword is to gather all the magatama. Please, Sugaru, help me." Facing him, she knelt formally just as her mother used to do. "Only you can make your magatama shine," she said. "I want you to go with me to Himuka. Come with me and become the warrior who bears the Misumaru."

"Where did you say you were going?"

"Himuka."

"You can't be serious. You mean the land at the far western edge of Toyoashihara?"

"Yes, that one."

"Not interested," Sugaru said, closing his eyes. "I'm more worried about finding someone to take my magatama. I need to find a wife. You understand, don't you? I'm the last of the headman's line. I need to settle down and make my grandfather happy. Surely you can see that that's much more important than becoming a warrior, right?"

Toko's anger flared. Of all the times he could have chosen, why did he have to pick this one to say something so reasonable? "Why did you make all that fuss about getting your own boat then?" she demanded.

"That's different. That's a business venture. And besides, I'd be going to Koshi, which is in the opposite direction from Himuka." Sugaru raised himself up on an elbow and peered into Toko's face. Close up, she saw that his eyes, like his hair, were light in color—a clear amber. "Knock it off, squirt," he said. "Give up this silly idea of going off to fight. It doesn't suit you one bit. Why are you so wound up? I don't want to hear you talk about killing anymore. Girls should be gentle. It won't be long now before you're a pretty woman yourself—"

"Sorry, but I'm never going to be a woman—at least not the type of woman that would appeal to you. So it doesn't bother me at all to talk about killing. I'll do it as often as I like." She looked him straight in the eye. "Killing Prince Ousu is all I care about. It's more important to me than me. Every night I think about killing him so that I won't be distracted by what's happening around me. Once I've destroyed him, then I can finally be myself again. Then I'll finally have Oguna back—" Her voice caught and she bit her lip. She was surprised to feel her emotions surge so strongly inside, threatening to spill over.

"Who the heck is Oguna?" Sugaru asked. When Toko did not reply, he said, "Ah, I see. You're in love with him."

"I am not!" Toko shook her head.

"If you like someone, you should say so. You'd be surprised at how much better you'll feel," Sugaru admonished her.

But she could not tell him that Oguna was Prince Ousu; she could not say that the person she loved more than anyone in the world was also the person she hated most. Perhaps if she told him, Sugaru would agree to come with her, yet she did not have the words with which to explain. Instead, the tears Toko had held back for so long began to roll down her cheeks one by one.

"Oh, no, please, please don't cry. I'm begging you," Sugaru said, suddenly desperate. "You'll ruin my whole day. I make women cry all the time, but I just can't stand making kids cry. Please stop. Really, I'm sorry already!"

Evading the hand with which he tried to wipe away her tears, Toko asked one last time, "Won't you please come to Himuka with me?"

Sugaru's answer was gentle but firm. "No, little one. It's more important for me to find a wife."

TOKO spent the morning in a daze. She had not cried for a long time, and it made her head throb. Wanting to avoid Kisako's questioning, she decided to go for a stroll and gloomily trudged through the village. Near the bridge, she passed a group of about ten girls without really noticing them, but they immediately surrounded her. Before she knew it, they had led her behind some trees along the riverbank and begun to interrogate her.

"So what's your friend up to? The *intruder wife?*"

"Intruder wife?" The expression was not in Toko's vocabulary.

"That's right. We heard she came to the bead-makers' village chasing Sugaru. Everyone knows the two of you met him at the market, and the rumor that you're here has spread. We've come to speak for all the maidens in this area."

"Yeah. Why should we put up with outsiders like you when Sugaru belongs to us? You're not playing fair."

Four or five others chimed in simultaneously so that Toko could no longer make out what they were saying. "Hold on a minute. Stop talking all at once!" she shouted. When they had settled down, she said, "So what you're trying to tell me is this. You're worried because Sugaru is paying attention to Kisako. She's beautiful so you're afraid that he might marry her. Right? Well, in that case, you've nothing to worry about. Kisako's a shrine maiden. She'll never get married because she's dedicated her life to the gods."

"That doesn't prove anything. She could change her mind at any time. It certainly doesn't give her the right to go and live in his house, to make herself indispensable to him and trick him into marrying her!"

It's such a pain talking to people who don't know anything about shrine maidens, Toko thought. "Well then," she said in exasperation, "if you're that worried about her stealing Sugaru away from you, why doesn't one of you hurry up and marry him yourself? All he thinks about is getting married."

The first girl answered for all of them. "Sugaru has vowed to marry only the most beautiful woman in all of Toyoashihara. We know our place. None of us expects to marry him. It's enough that he's nice to us. But we will never, ever recognize your companion as the most beautiful woman in Toyoashihara. If that's her intention, then we'll do everything in our power to stop her."

Toko saw no point in arguing with them over something so ridiculous. "Personally, I think you should be talking to Sugaru, not me," she said.

"We don't need you to tell us that. That's why we're here. We came looking for Sugaru." They stomped off, raising a cloud of dust behind them. Toko shrugged and walked back to Sugaru's house, keeping an eye out for any roving bands of angry girls like them.

When she returned, she found Kisako sitting in their room looking very grumpy. "Did a group of village girls come here?" Toko asked.

"No," Kisako answered coldly. "What're you talking about?" She seemed so sensitive. Toko wondered if she was getting her period again. An uncomfortable silence ensued for some time before Kisako finally broke it.

"Toko," she said. "You've been so weird all morning, almost as if you're trying to avoid me. I really needed your advice, but how can I even talk to you when you're like that? You abandoned me at the time when I needed you most."

"I'm sorry," Toko said, feeling slightly guilty. "I just needed to clear my head. I was thinking about what happened last night."

"I was thinking about last night too. Over and over. That's what I wanted to talk to you about. Toko—" Kisako hesitated for a moment. "I've realized that I can never become the high priestess. You saw that magatama, didn't you? Izumo has its own magatama, one that is passed on in its own way. No matter how much training I might have had as a priestess, it would have been impossible for me to make it shine. When I saw you tell Princess Toyoao that you were going to find the Misumaru, I realized that I can't do this anymore. I don't want to travel any farther. Please understand. I need a place where I can have peace and quiet, a place to settle down."

Toko's mouth went dry as she struggled to digest what Kisako was saying. "But I want to settle down and live an ordinary life too."

"No, you're different, Toko. You're ready to fly off at any moment. I can't. Just getting to Izumo was hard enough for me. If I'm going to stay here, then I'll have to follow their customs. I plan to learn from them."

"You mean you're going to give up becoming a priestess? That's what you're trying to tell me?" Toko leaned in close to Kisako and asked her timidly, "You're not planning to get Sugaru to give you the magatama, are you? You're not really thinking of doing what he said?"

Kisako's cheeks flushed crimson, but she forged on. "This isn't about the magatama . . . or, actually, maybe it's the same thing. I've decided to return to the first duty that was given to me—the duty to carry on the Mino line. The blood of the Tachibana of Mino and Izumo has grown very thin, but if the two were joined together, we might be able to change the flow of fate."

Toko looked at her beautiful cousin more closely than ever before. They were the same age, yet they lived in completely different worlds. Never before had she been so aware of the huge gap between them. *What about me?* she wanted to protest, but she bit back the words, knowing they would be unfair. Kisako, she felt, was right—at least in her method of trying to obtain Sugaru's magatama. If the bearer of the magatama wanted that too, then what could be better?

"If that's really what you want to do, why don't you?" Toko said, thinking ruefully that if the girls she had met earlier could hear her now, they would rip her to pieces. But what else could she say?

Kisako's face brightened, and she beamed at Toko. "So you're not going to try to stop me? I'm so glad. I wanted to talk to you about it first. It wouldn't have felt right otherwise."

"There's nothing wrong with what you're doing. You're you. You should do what's best for you." Toko smiled, concealing the sinking feeling in her heart. But Kisako's next statement was a far harder blow from which to recover.

"So, then, you understand . . . um . . . about tonight. Let's sleep in separate rooms, all right?"

"WHAT'S UP? You seem pretty down." Toko was wandering aimlessly at dusk when someone called out to her. Turning around, she saw five or six of Sugaru's friends. Sugaru was not with them.

"Sugaru's busy trying to hide from some pretty scary women," one of his friends said. "It'll be interesting to see if he makes it home in one piece tonight. Mind you, he's reaping what he sowed."

One of the others looked at Toko with avid curiosity. "Did you really ask Sugaru to go to the western end of the country with you?" he said.

Honestly, Toko thought, *Sugaru's such a chatterbox.* But she did not have the energy left to lie. "Yes, I did," she said. "He turned me down flat though."

"Really? He was wondering what to do all morning. And after that, well, he was rather preoccupied."

"Are you serious?" Toko said in surprise. "He told me twice that finding a wife was more important."

The young man laughed. "He always says that. Don't give up. I've placed my bet on you. We've got a little fortune riding on whether or not Sugaru decides to go with you."

These guys never learn, Toko thought. "If you don't want to lose, you'd better change your bet. Sugaru's certain to do what he says this time. Kisako has decided she's willing to give up being a shrine maiden."

The young men looked at each other. "Well, that certainly changes things."

"But the other girls will put up a fight."

The only one who remained unmoved was the one who claimed to have bet on Toko. He looked at her confidently and said, "I stand by my prediction. Do you know why Sugaru is so famous in Izumo? Although there's no one stronger when it comes to fighting or women, when it comes to kids or the elderly, there's no one softer. Just you wait and see."

DESPITE THIS ENCOURAGEMENT, Toko still could not believe him. Every time she recalled that last conversation with Sugaru, her conviction that he would choose Kisako only grew. She had to admit that Kisako was the more attractive option. She had so much to offer, whereas all Toko could do was beg for help. *Pursuing Prince Ousu may be my first priority, but that doesn't mean anyone else feels the same way. Why should they? The world doesn't revolve around me.*

Although it was hard to accept defeat, doing so let Toko start thinking of an alternative solution. With her usual good grace, she channeled her despair into planning her next course of action. Regardless of what others chose, she could still go looking for the magatama. No matter how long it might take or how hard the road might be, she could still pursue the bearer of the Sword. If that was what she wanted to do, then she could go by herself. She had started this journey of her own free will, not because anyone had made her, so she could choose to carry on.

And at least I've found one of the magatama. I'll just have to be content with that instead of being upset that I can't take it with me. The first step is to get to Himuka as fast as I can. The rest will work out somehow.

Feeling better, she decided to head back and get some sleep. She had not slept the night before, and she would need all her strength to set off on this new journey.

Toko woke again in the dead of night and stepped outside. It was almost the same time as she and Kisako had gone out the night before. Though not as cold, Toko felt the darkness much more keenly. The black forms of the house and forest seemed cold and distant. Taking a step forward, she forced herself to cheer up and focus on getting to the coastal road.

"So you were planning to leave without even saying goodbye, were you?"

Toko jumped and whirled around to find Kisako standing behind her. "What are you doing here?"

Kisako walked up to her. "If you're leaving, then I'm leaving too. I don't want to stay in this house any longer," she said.

"What happened? I thought you were planning to—"

"If you mean Sugaru, I hit him. Three times. Once across each cheek and once more for good measure. He had the nerve to tell me that I'm one of five." Toko stared at her, utterly bewildered. "He meant I was one of five candidates for his bride. How humiliating! I'll never forgive him. I've decided to become a shrine maiden after all. Why should I bother marrying anyone? I was foolish to let my feelings waver." As Toko remained rooted to the spot, dumbstruck, Kisako said, "Come on. Let's go."

"Are you sure, Kisako? You said that you didn't want to travel anymore, remember? I'm going to Himuka, and after that I don't know where I'll have to go. And you haven't prepared for the journey."

"That's all right. I just want to leave this village. I'll find a place to live in Izumo. I can do that myself. I think." She looked at Toko in the starlight and smiled. "It'll be much easier than what you've decided to do—going to Himuka all by yourself. You're so strong . . . I've decided not to be dependent anymore. I'm going to take care of myself."

"Are you really sure, Kisako?"

"Yes," she said firmly.

Toko realized suddenly just how hard it would be to say goodbye to her cousin.

At that moment, a low voice spoke from the darkness. "Excuse me for interrupting, but please allow me to invite Lady Kisako to stay at the hall of the Kuni no Miyatsuko."

"Who's there?"

Peering into the darkness, the two girls finally made out the figure of a man. He was dressed all in black, which made him hard to see, but from his voice and manner he seemed both well bred and sincere.

"I am the Ear of Lady Toyoao. She asked me to discover how you fared in the bead-makers' village. I left the hall yesterday."

"Her . . . ear?" They looked at him, astonished.

"Lady Toyoao said that if you need a place to settle down, she would like to invite you to stay with her, Lady Kisako. She who listens to the wind feels that, as the last shrine maiden of Mino, there is much you can teach her."

"I would be more than honored to accept!" Kisako said. "I could not have hoped for anything better. Under Lady Toyoao, I could continue my training as a priestess. And I think I could also help serve her. After all, I spent many years serving the high priestess of Mino, who could be quite difficult to please sometimes."

"Her ladyship will be very happy."

He's a good man, Toko thought. *Kisako's going to be all right.* "I'm so glad," she said out loud. She would not have to worry about Kisako if she were staying with Lady Toyoao.

The man turned to her. "Lady Toko," he said. "Her ladyship knew that you would decide to go to Himuka. She told me to convey this message: fear no hardship. Search for the magatama in Himuka and win the bearer to your side. There is none like her in all of Toyoashihara. She is a great priestess who retains the memory of everything that has happened since the beginning of time."

BY THE TIME Toko said goodbye to Kisako and Ear at the crossroads, the sun had already risen in the sky. She walked on alone to where the pine forest dwindled and the sea, sparkling in the morning light, came into view. Small fishing boats with the wind in their sails raced toward the point at the end of the bow-shaped beach, and the port gleamed in the sun. Narrowing her eyes against the glare, Toko noticed three young men standing with their backs to the blue water. In the middle stood Sugaru. A short, wiry youth on one side laughed and waved to her. "I won," he said. "I told you so." It was the youth who had bet on her.

"Me too," said the other, a sturdy-looking young man. "We divided the winnings between us."

Toko did not know what to say. She walked up to Sugaru and looked up into his face. "You never cease to amaze me. Kisako says she'll never forgive you, you know."

Sugaru appeared unperturbed. "As far as I'm concerned, I was just telling her the truth. I can't help it if we don't see eye to eye. I've decided to go to Himuka with you."

Toko looked at him dubiously. "How can you change your mind so easily? I thought you were a man. What about making your grandfather happy and finding a wife?"

"There's bound to be good-looking women in the west too. If I'm to marry the most beautiful woman in Toyoashihara, then it makes sense to travel more. There's no need to limit myself to Izumo," he said, as if this argument were just common sense.

"How can I ever trust someone like you as a fellow traveler?"

Sugaru ran a hand through his hair. "Maybe you can't. But I can sail a boat.

How about it? If we go from port to port, we can cut the time it takes in half or maybe even down to a third. Or would you rather go ahead and cross all those mountains on your own?"

A boat! The thought had never occurred to her, and her heart raced with excitement. "You've got a boat? Really?"

"Women can't sail without bringing down the wrath of the sea god. But you, little one—"

"Of course. The god of the sea won't try to stop me," Toko said in a rush. Hope bubbled up inside her. A boat, what a fabulous idea. There would be no need to climb endless mountains like she had on the way from Mino. "Please, take me with you. If we can reach Himuka even a little quicker, I'll be forever in your debt."

"The sea is dangerous too, you know. It's going to be a gamble, and I don't want you to underestimate the risk involved. Are you still willing to try it?"

"Of course."

"You'll be fine," the wiry youth chimed in. "You've got Sugaru and us on your side. A lot of others wanted to come too, but we won the right to go. I'm Tasuki and this is Imatate. You've no need to fear rough seas with the three of us here."

"Are you sure you don't mind? Even though you aren't on a quest for beautiful women?"

"Ha! All men are looking for beautiful women. And they'll also jump at any chance to test their strength. I don't know any man who would turn down an excuse like this to set out for a foreign land."

5

THEY WERE PUSHING the boat over rollers toward the shore, when Tasuki asked, "Sugaru, is it safe to take it out in broad daylight like this? None of us are ship owners yet."

"Don't worry," Sugaru answered carelessly. "It's all set. From today, this boat is ours, whether it sinks or floats."

"That's pretty good negotiating. How did you manage it?" Imatate asked.

"Nothing to it. I paid for it with a splendid magatama that would have satisfied the emperor himself. By now, it will have reached the Kuni no Miyatsuko."

"Sugaru...you didn't," Toko said, regarding him with disbelief. "It wasn't the one from the shrine, was it?"

Sugaru grinned. "Did you look inside that shrine? You didn't, right? Well, neither did I. If nobody ever looks inside the shrine, then what difference does it make if there's something in it or not?"

Toko was at a loss for words. How Sugaru's mind worked was a complete mystery to her. She decided that he might be as much devil as human. "If your grandfather finds out, you'll be really sorry."

"I'll worry about that when it happens," Sugaru said as he pushed hard against the boat. "But, personally, I don't think I've done anything wrong. The shrine must have been a decoy to distract people's attention from the real magatama. That's why my ancestors kept a fake in it. But now, the real magatama is leaving the country, so there's no longer anything left to protect. It makes perfect sense to put the fake to good use, don't you think?"

He spoke with such confidence that Toko was almost convinced. His shirt, slightly damp with sweat, lay open across his chest and a purple string hung round his neck. He wore his mother's magatama in a pouch on the end of that string, never letting it leave his body. Gazing at it, Toko thought that perhaps it was his brazen confidence that made him fit to be the bearer of the magatama. She felt a pang of grief and loss but put the thought out of her mind, turning her attention to the boat instead.

The boat was a sturdy eight-seater made of camphor wood and built for speed. The bow arched gracefully and a red whirlpool was painted on the side as a plea to the sea god for protection. "It's a good little ship, isn't it?" Toko said as they all climbed in. She had decided that praising the ship profusely would be an auspicious way to start the journey. "It's such a nice shape and just the right size. I'm sure it can carry us safely to where we want to go. Does it have a name?"

"It's called *Oguna-maru*," Sugaru said.

Toko blinked in surprise. "Are you teasing me?"

"Why would he be teasing you?" Tasuki said. "Don't you think it's the perfect name for us?"

Toko burst out laughing. "So I'm going off to sea on *Oguna-maru*. That's very funny. When Oguna and I were small, we used to make boats out of leaves, even though we'd never seen the sea. We called our boats *Toko-maru* and *Oguna-maru* and raced them on a nearby stream. We thought that they would be carried all the way downstream to the ocean . . . Oguna was a perfectionist. His were always really sophisticated. At first mine were faster, but before I knew it his were better—more balanced and less likely to sink." She laughed again. "He figured out the best shape for a boat without anyone teaching him. But that made me mad, and I told him I didn't want to play with boats anymore."

Toko watched the waves lap against the side of the boat. *Today is part of that day. It's a continuation of the dream we dreamt as we sat on the grassy riverbank and watched our leaf boats drift away.*

"That's the first time I've ever seen you look like that," Sugaru said as he rowed. "Your expression suits you. So Oguna was a childhood friend of yours, was he?"

Startled out of her reverie, she faltered, embarrassed. " . . . Yes."

"There's nothing like the bond between childhood friends," Tasuki declared. "Like Sugaru and me. People may grow up but they don't change much inside."

"Some people do," Toko muttered and then fell silent. Holding her windswept hair out of her face, she gazed back the way they had come and watched the shore fade into the distance as *Oguna-maru* surged out to sea.

chapter
six

NEWBORN

Newborn

THOUGH TOKO and her company had embarked in high spirits, the first leg of their voyage was plagued with bad weather, as if they were being punished for their recklessness. Clear skies never lasted more than a day, and rough seas kept them landbound for a week, so that they sailed only three of the first ten days. Exasperated, Toko declared that they could have reached Himuka faster if they had walked—but she stopped complaining after facing high seas that nearly capsized *Oguna-maru*. She realized that just because her presence would not invoke the sea god's wrath did not give her license to be reckless.

They had set out a little too early in the year. Winter had not yet given way to spring, and the clash of cold and warm air currents generated storms. Once that period had passed, however, the seas quieted and they were blessed with fair weather. The boat sped over the water, and soon they were crossing a large strait. By the time the far shore came into sight, there was not a trace of winter left. Everywhere the land was covered in lush green trees that looked like they had never known the cold.

"I've heard tales that the west is a land of fire," Sugaru said lazily. "Fire burns in the mountains and in the seas. It's hot even in winter and the land groans, or at least that's what they say. As a child, it made me wonder why people would even bother to live here."

"I can understand what they mean by fire burning in a mountain, but how can fire burn in the sea?" Toko asked.

"I've heard the same story though," Tasuki said. "There're supposed to be mysterious lights on the sea, and the water burns on moonless nights."

"Impossible!"

"But it's true."

Toko fell silent, feeling uneasy, and wondered if they had come so far from home that even common sense no longer held true.

"Speaking of water, the jug's almost empty," Imatate said, peering into the water container. "We'd better stop somewhere soon." The seas might burn for all the practical Imatate cared. What really mattered was whether you could drink the water or not.

"I thought it was about time to land," Tasuki said from the prow where he served as the lookout. "Let's look for a landing spot on the other side of that point. We might find a village too."

"What do you think the 'land groaning' means?" Toko asked, but the others, absorbed in getting the boat to shore, ignored her.

The point grew larger until its cliffs towered above them. The young men edged the *Oguna-maru* toward land, watching out for reefs. They were now close enough to make out individual trees in the thick, overgrown forest, their glossy leaves glinting in the sun, and Toko's apprehension increased. *That forest looks like it would suck the life out of anything that entered it.* She shuddered at the thought.

"There're people there!" Tasuki shouted. "Just as I thought. There must be a village nearby. They've seen us. They seem to be gathering—"

Toko looked in the direction he indicated and saw men clustered on the cliff above the shore where *Oguna-maru* was headed. They were pointing and talking animatedly among themselves.

"This doesn't look good," Tasuki said. The words had no sooner left his mouth than an arrow arced toward them. Immediately, all the men on the cliff raised their bows and let loose a hail of arrows.

"What's going on?" Sugaru yelled. "Have they mistaken our innocent little ship for an invasion?"

"Maybe they're frightened by your face, Sugaru," Imatate said. "Come on. Smile at them."

"Why would I waste my time smiling at men?"

"Ah. I know. They must've figured out that you've come to take away their women."

The arrows continued to rain down. Shielding his head with his arms, Tasuki yelled, "Hard aport! Hard aport! It's no good. If we land, we'll be killed."

Sugaru turned the boat left so sharply that it tilted precariously. Toko hit her head on the gunwale. Once the men saw *Oguna-maru* pull away, they held their fire, but they remained on the cliff to make sure that the small craft did not try to come ashore.

"Well, that was a surprise," Sugaru said. "If we had come with a fleet of ships, I could understand such a welcome, but there are only four of us."

"Maybe something's happened to make them afraid."

"I bet that's it!" Toko said. "Maybe Prince Ousu has already arrived. That would certainly explain it. We've got to find out what happened."

"The first thing we need to find is water," Imatate reminded them. "Not even I can pull water out of thin air."

"No worries. I'll find us a place to land," Sugaru said, pulling hard on his oar. "They've made a big mistake if they think they can shoo us away like flies."

Rowing back the way they had come, and this time more cautiously, the party landed on the opposite side of the point. Hiding the boat under the shadow of the rocks, they all looked around carefully before crossing the beach and climbing up to the tree line. They had reached the edge of the forest when Tasuki said, "Why don't Imatate and I go ahead to check things out? If we're lucky, we may find a spring."

But Sugaru shook his head. "No, we'd better not split up. This forest gives me a bad feeling. And like Toko, I think we should find out why those men shot at us."

"Are you saying that we should go back and ask those jerks who gave us such a cold reception why they did it?"

Sugaru smiled. "To ask is to suffer a moment's humiliation. Not to ask is to be shamed for life. Or so I've been told." He had barely finished his sentence when a group of seven or eight men stepped out from behind the trees. Their eyes gleamed mercilessly and in their hands they gripped clubs and axes. Sugaru cocked his chin at them. "Would you like to start asking?"

"Mmm. I can see why you don't like this forest."

The men attacked without a word. Toko gasped and her stomach cramped into a tight knot, but her companions countered swiftly. Imatate smacked one man in the head with the water jug, shattering it against the man's skull. Sugaru and Tasuki, obviously more than used to fighting, likewise outdid their reputations. But of the three, Sugaru was by far the strongest. He had not been bragging at the marketplace. Although Toko drew her sword, she had no need to use it. The battle was over in moments.

Once he had made sure that none of their opponents were still standing, Sugaru said, "All right then. Perhaps now we can get some answers." He grasped one man's collar and pulled him close. "Tell me, what do you hold against us that you'd attack us like that? It's a pretty rude way to greet guests, don't you think?"

The man groaned. "What are you? Devils?"

"Ah, now you see what your ignorance has cost you. It's because you've never heard of Sugaru of Izumo that you met such a sorry fate."

"A-all right. I'm sorry. We thought you were the remnants of the Tachibana."

"The Tachibana?" Toko repeated, her voice a squeak.

"You mean you're hunting Tachibana?" Sugaru asked.

The man nodded vigorously. "The prince from Mahoroba slew Kumaso Takeru, the leader of the rebel Tachibana, and the rest of them scattered. We were told that we'd be rewarded if we brought the heads of the survivors to our chief. Especially women or children. The reward for them is double."

The four companions looked at one another. Or rather the three young men from Izumo looked straight at Toko. She stood, white-lipped, unable to conceal her shock. "When?" she asked. "When did the prince from Mahoroba kill the Tachibana leader?"

"About a month ago. The prince had just reached Himuka. It took everyone by surprise. We all thought Kumaso Takeru was invincible. He invited the prince into his hall, and that's where they say he died. I guess that's the power of the gods."

It takes one Takeru to kill another . . . The words of the Keeper of the Shrine echoed in Toko's mind. Pushing the voice out of her head, she addressed the man once more. "Where's the prince now? Where's Kumaso Takeru's hall?"

"I don't know where the prince is. After all, none of us were called in to fight," the man said. He did, however, tell them how to get to the hall—one day's travel southeast plus two days travel due south. Having heard all he needed to know, Sugaru let the man go. Then he walked over to Toko, who had sunk to the ground, her face stricken.

"That does it," he said. "I'm mad. Doubling the reward for killing women and children. Whoever's behind this is rotten to the core."

Toko buried her face in her hands. "We're too late. He's wiped out the Tachibana from the land where the sun sets. Why?" she whispered. "Why is he destroying the Tachibana? Why is this happening to my people? Is this what the Sword does?"

"This is no time to brood, Toko," Sugaru said. "We've come this far, but we haven't checked things out for ourselves yet. The way I see it, if they're hunting Tachibana, it means there must be some left. And if they've doubled the reward for women and children, it sounds like the most important person they're seeking must be a woman and she must still be at large."

Toko raised her face. "You're right. Lady Toyoao told us that there's a powerful priestess in Himuka. She said there's no other like her in all of Toyoashihara. The priestess must still have her magatama. It hasn't fallen into the hands of the emperor's forces yet."

"That's good news. What the priestess of Izumo hears is always right. She has the best ears in the land."

"She certainly does," Toko said, smiling as she recalled the Ear who walked on two legs.

"That settles it then," Imatate said. "Let's start looking. The priestess is bound to be at least as beautiful as the shrine maiden from Mino." All three became suddenly very anxious to head out. Toko's idea of what a high priestess looked like differed vastly from theirs, but she did not have the heart to dash their obvious enthusiasm.

REMOVING ALL that they could carry from *Oguna-maru,* they hid the small boat thoroughly and headed southeast. The way was not hard to find, for it followed the level ground between the mountains that rose on either side. Emerging from the dank forest, they crossed a meadow and entered another wood. Several times they passed houses, which they elected to avoid. They did not want any more trouble with the natives.

Outdoor living was easy in spring. There was plenty of food to be foraged in field and stream, and the ground was warm and fragrant with a thick carpet of new grasses. The stars no longer shone cold and clear, even in the dark of the moon. That night they built a campfire on a patch of dry ground at the edge of the forest and, for the first time in many days, slept enveloped in the familiar scent of the land rather than that of the sea. This was all Toko needed to feel at home. They might be at the westernmost edge of the country, but it was still Toyoashihara, and not even the vegetation differed that greatly. But she had noticed one particular difference. Although they had walked for less than a day, she had already caught the scent of the Tachibana tree several times. It seemed to be much more common in Himuka.

The young men from Izumo did not seem to care where they were. Toko thought that even if they were perched on the edge of the world they would still swagger about as though it belonged to them. They spent their first night camping in this unknown place daring each other to grill and eat a bullfrog.

"Try it. It's good medicine. It'll make you smart."

"Don't listen to him. You'll be cursed with a face like Toad Boy."

Listening to them, Toko wondered why on earth they had come. It was hard to believe they had a serious thought in their heads. Sugaru appeared to have no sense of mission whatsoever, and Tasuki and Imatate had just tagged along to keep him company. Yet she had to admit that their cheerful optimism was catching.

During their voyage, she had learned that these young men took nothing seriously, almost as if they lived just to see how much in life could be laughed at. Even when facing danger on the rough seas, they roared with laughter as if nothing could be funnier. They often poked fun at their own mistakes too. When they occasionally fought, all hard feelings were forgotten as soon as they turned the argument into a joke. As Toko became accustomed to their ways, she saw that laughter could be useful. It still made her mad sometimes, though, especially as they made fun of even the crudest subjects. She frequently stood exasperated in their midst while they rolled on the ground.

Toko no longer wondered why someone like Sugaru should bear the magatama. She still found it hard to accept, especially when she recalled the dignity of Lady Akaru or the Keeper of the Shrine, but she was forced to acknowledge that Sugaru had a certain power. Although she could not describe it in words, something about him reminded her of Prince Oh-usu. The Keeper of the Shrine had found Oh-usu's presence "unruly." Although not quite the same, Sugaru also had a certain presence. While his irresponsible attitude seemed the antithesis of the prince, people were drawn to Sugaru in the same way.

"Sugaru," Toko said suddenly, "show me the magatama again. I want to see it shine."

Sugaru scowled. "Don't talk about it in front of them. I told you it was a secret, remember?"

Tasuki and Imatate looked intrigued. "What's this? What shines?"

It was too late now. Pulling the pouch from inside his shirt, Sugaru opened it and shook the magatama into his palm. Just as when Toko had seen it in Izumo, it shone brightly in the dark—a cool, translucent green, as refreshing as mint. At Toko's request, Sugaru placed it in her palm, but no matter how hard she wished otherwise, the light faded as soon as it lay in her hand.

"You mean only Sugaru can make it shine? Well, that's quite the skill," Imatate said, impressed. "Just like a firefly. Or maybe a mushroom. You know the hikaritake mushroom glows in the dark too."

"Stop comparing me to bugs and mushrooms," Sugaru snapped. "Now you see why I didn't want anyone to know, Toko. They're too ignorant to make more intelligent comments. When my mother told me not to tell anyone about it, I knew exactly what she meant. People were bound to make fun of me if I did."

"But we already knew you were weird, whether you glow in the dark or not," Tasuki said. Sugaru leapt at his friend and wrestled him to the ground.

Toko gave up. They would just never be serious.

2

TWO AND A HALF DAYS later they reached Himuka, land of the Kumaso. Their journey had not been without incident. The further south they traveled, the more frequently they ran into soldiers, and they encountered more villages around which they had to detour. Soldiers with hounds prowled the valleys and fields, and the thought that they were not hunting deer or boar made Toko feel ill. Still, the small party of four had made surprisingly quick progress.

They were standing now in the spot where Kumaso Takeru's hall had been. It was hard to believe a building had ever stood there. Not a single post remained. Just a few charred tree trunks, blasted as if by lightning, protruded from the soil. Scorched earth, charcoal, and ashes scarred the ground. While not as thoroughly wasted as the hall, the land beyond was burned black within a radius of a hundred steps. Although the sun poured down brightly, not a blade of grass was to be seen; there was only barren earth from which all life had been torn. The stark contrast between the black silence before them and the vibrant green of the hills made the companions' blood run cold.

"He used the Sword," Toko said, her voice shaking. "So this is what it does. It's horrible. Horrible. How could he? How could he come to a land he's never seen before and do something like this? It's inhuman. How could he do this without feeling any remorse? Isn't there anyone who can make him see? Someone's got to, and right now!"

She wheeled and began walking away. Startled, Sugaru grabbed her. "Hey, where do you think you're going?"

"I'm going to find Prince Ousu. I have to see him."

"Hang on. I thought we were going to find the priestess with the magatama first."

"But I can't let him do this. He can't be allowed to get away with it." In Toko's mind, the scene before her had merged with the annihilation of Mino. She had not been there to see Kamitsusato fall. Now, however, the devastating reality was being shoved in her face. Not a single memory of those who had called this place home remained in the black death before her. All sense of life had been consumed, leaving only a cursed spot from which people shied away. It had never occurred to Toko that one's home could be erased so completely.

"I won't let him continue this destruction. I'll never be able to understand him again. Never. He's despicable."

Sugaru put his hands on her shoulders. "It never pays to lose your head in a fight," he said. "You should only throw your life away as the very last resort. You still have to find the other magatama, right?"

Toko shook her head so violently her ponytail flew around her face. "I don't care anymore! Prince Ousu's nearby. What's wrong with looking for a chance to kill him now? The sooner the Sword is stopped the better. If I go now, I'm sure—"

"Wait a minute," Sugaru said, restraining her. "You belong to the priestess's line, right? Then tell me something. What does it mean when the magatama starts jingling?"

Toko frowned up at him. "What do you mean by 'jingling'? I don't understand."

"I don't understand either, but it's like there's a bell ringing inside me even though I can't actually hear it. It started when I showed you the magatama the other night." He took the stone out of the pouch. In the light of day, its light appeared fainter, but the core still shone green. "It's getting stronger all the time. It's really annoying." Muttering to himself, he walked first one way, then another, and finally pointed his finger in one direction. "There's no mistake. It's stronger when I face this way. Do you think it means something?"

Toko stared at Sugaru in surprise. She had felt nothing. It was a voice that only the bearer could hear. She could never hope to rival him.

"What do you think? Should we check it out?"

Tasuki and Imatate came over, and their eyes grew round when Sugaru told them. "Just like a hound keen on the scent," Tasuki said.

"If you're going to compare me to a dog, go bark up some tree," Sugaru grumbled, but he led the way, following a trail that only he could find.

SUGARU LED them straight east toward the mountains. Despite the teasing of his friends, he was not a dog that could simply follow a scent, and once inside the forest, he had a much harder time guiding the party. They fought their way through briar patches and struggled halfway up a cliff only to climb back down and search for a route around it. By this time, the sun was setting, and the exhausted group made camp beside a rushing stream. When Imatate dangled a fishing line into the clear waters and caught a batch of trout, they all grinned, forgetting their fatigue.

"Don't be greedy just because there's lots, though," Imatate warned them. "We should save some for tomorrow." Several fish remained from their meal, and he wrapped them individually in large magnolia leaves. When it came to food, they all relied on him. The three young men had long ago abandoned any expectation that Toko could cook just because she was a girl. Not only had she never gutted a fish, she could not even keep the fire going properly. Although she had occasionally felt a little guilty, by now Toko had banished such thoughts as pointless and devoted herself to eating instead. It was no good pretending she could do something for which she had no aptitude.

Toko watched in admiration as Imatate deftly wrapped the fish and then turned her attention to making a place to sleep. She needed to get enough rest. If she kept her strength up, at least she would not hold everyone back. The long journey had drilled her into shape, but she still found it hard to keep up with the men. Yet she did not want them to give her special treatment just because she was a girl, and even more so because she was not acting like one. Accustomed to sleeping on the hard ground, she curled up in a ball and fell asleep instantly.

In the middle of the night, shouts shattered her dreams. She heard the sounds of a struggle and gravel scattering in the dark. For a moment, she thought they were being attacked. "What is it? What's going on?" Her voice was shrill with fear, and she regretted opening her mouth. Sugaru kicked the embers of the fire and Toko saw him grab a flaming brand as a torch.

"What happened, Imatate?" It was Tasuki's voice.

"This little . . . thieving . . . cat tried to steal the fish. Ow! Don't scratch!"

Relieved to hear that everyone was all right, Toko peered at the light cast by Sugaru's torch to see what was causing the commotion. A small, black creature struggled frantically on the ground beneath Imatate. It was not an animal but a child.

"Listen, you! Stealing is bad. If you want some fish, ask for it properly." Imatate pulled the child's face close, but the boy only fought harder, tears pouring down his cheeks. His face, hands, and feet were black with dirt and his hair was like a tangled mass of weeds.

Sugaru bent over to peer into the boy's face. "Leave him alone. He's just a kid. You won't get through to him until he stops crying anyway."

As soon as Imatate relaxed his grip, the boy leapt to his feet. But before he could dash away, Sugaru reached out a long arm and thrust a package of fish under his nose. "Take it," he said.

Snatching the parcel, the child flew off into the bushes. The rustling of his passage receded into the distance until at last there was silence.

"Are you sure it was all right to let him go?" Tasuki asked.

Sugaru nodded. "It'll be fine. Just be patient and wait. A cat wouldn't come back. But that boy will. Once he gets over the initial fear and shock and can think again. He's probably afraid of the soldiers." Sugaru sat down by the fire and began feeding it with sticks. Now that they were all wide awake, they joined him around the fire and waited. Just as Sugaru had said, after some time, the boy peeked out from the bushes looking uneasy and a little sheepish.

"Hi," Sugaru said so casually that Toko was impressed. "There's more fish. Do you want some?"

Drawn irresistibly, the boy emerged from the bushes, but he approached cautiously, ready to run at any moment. The fire burned brightly, allowing them to see him clearly. He was about five or six years old, with strong, straight eyebrows. He looked like he was starving, but there was no greed in his eyes. "Can I take one for my mother?" he asked, his voice high and clear.

"Of course."

"She's got a stomachache. She hasn't been outside since last night. That's why I . . . "

"You must be very worried. Is there no one to give her medicine?" The boy shook his head. "What about your father?" The boy shook his head again, this time angrily. "You mean it's just the two of you? That's not good," Sugaru said, passing the boy another fish. "Well, now that we know she's sick, we can't just stand by and do nothing. We brought some herbs with us. Maybe we can help. Where is she?"

The boy's guard went up instantly. "It's a secret . . . I can't tell you."

"Don't be silly. It's more important to help your mother get better, right?" Sugaru said, crouching down in front of him. "How about if I tell you our secret? We're Tachibana too, although we come from another land. You already know we're not soldiers, don't you?"

Hugging the fish to his chest, the boy stared so intently at Sugaru's face he could have bored a hole through it. Finally, he nodded, as if he had decided that Sugaru could be trusted.

"Then let's go. What's your name?"

"Abi."

They followed after him, but his secret path was no easy route for anyone larger than a small child. Most of it passed through dense brush where they could not use a torch to light their way. Without the aid of Sugaru's magatama, they would have given up in despair.

Once, when they paused to rest, Sugaru whispered to Toko, "I think the magatama was trying to lead us to Abi's mother."

Toko looked at him with a startled expression. "Really? Is it jingling?"

"Like crazy. The fact that she already has a kid is a bit disappointing—not that I mind beautiful older women."

"What on earth are you thinking?"

"The magatama of this priestess seems to be calling mine," he answered. "Just think what a tale it would be for my great-grandchildren. I followed a soundless voice to find the woman who would become my bride. Rather romantic, don't you think?"

Though taken aback, Toko had to admit that his idea was quite plausible. Each stone had power, and that power increased when they were united. It made sense that the stones would seek one another out.

They resumed their march until finally they reached the small cave in the face of the mountain where Abi and his mother had concealed themselves. The entrance was well hidden behind a camouflage of ivy, but the hole was not deep and the light of the fire inside could be seen reflected on the walls. It was not a very safe hiding place.

Pulling aside the ivy, Abi rushed inside. "Mother. Here."

They could hear his mother's frantic voice even as they stood outside. "What have you done? Where have you been? I was so worried about you. What was that noise outside?"

Toko put out a hand to stop Sugaru and the others. "It will just make her more nervous to see men right now. You wait here while I go in and explain." She pushed aside the ivy quietly and peered inside. Abi was sitting respectfully beside his mother, who was lying on her side. The roof of the cave was high enough to stand but not very wide, like the hollow in the base of a large tree. There was only enough room for one adult to lie down.

The woman raised herself up on her elbow and stared at Toko, her eyes round and her face pale. Her robe, which she had placed over herself as a sheet, slipped off to reveal full breasts glistening with sweat. Toko sighed with relief, glad that she had not let Sugaru and the others come in. "Please don't be afraid," she said. "My name's Toko. I'm a Tachibana from Mino and I've been searching the country for other Tachibana. Right now I'm traveling with Sugaru—he's a bead maker from Izumo and the bearer of a magatama—and two of his friends. I came looking for the great Tachibana priestess of Himuka. If I had known what would happen, I would have come sooner. Tonight we met Abi and he brought us here. We heard you were sick. What can I do to help?"

Abi's mother blinked several times but finally seemed to absorb what Toko had said. Her face relaxed, and she pushed back her disheveled hair, which fell in lustrous black waves upon her bed. But when she spoke, her words stunned Toko. "Ah, so it was you of whom Lady Iwa spoke just before she died. She foretold that a young woman would come from the east to ask for help. She said we must rise up to aid her. That's why Kawakamihiko mustered an army. And that's why he failed."

"For me? She knew I was coming?"

"Yes. Lady Iwa knew."

"Then..." Toko felt a cold shiver run down her spine. "Then the war was my fault? If I hadn't come, the land of the Kumaso would not have been burned—"

"No, it wasn't your fault at all. Fortune just wasn't with us. Lady Iwa passed away, and so we mistook the signs at the most important time. Kawakamihiko was shortsighted. It wasn't your fault at all."

Abi's mother appeared to be a woman of very high rank. From the way she spoke, Toko guessed that she must either be Kawakamihiko's wife or a close relative. *And Kawakamihiko must have been the one they called Kumaso Takeru,* she thought. She was humbled by the fact that this woman could remain so resolute despite her tragic circumstances. As if she guessed what Toko was thinking, the woman smiled.

"The Kumaso have been scattered, but this is by no means the end of our people. Lady Iwa will be reborn. It's very fortunate that you came tonight because..." She broke off, her face tense, and then groaned, sweat beading her brow as she fought against the pain.

"Mother! Mother!" Abi wailed, looking as though he would burst into tears.

Toko reached over to rub the woman's back, which was bent with pain, only to discover the shocking truth. She was not ill. Her abdomen was swollen with child.

"The baby's ... about to be born," the woman gasped. "Please, help my baby."

This time it was Toko who broke into a sweat. *She's going to give birth? Right now? With me as the midwife?*

Having sensed something was wrong, Sugaru and the others rushed up to the entrance. "Toko, what's going on? Is she all right?"

They were about to come in, but Toko jumped up and shoved them back so fiercely that they were astonished. "Out! Out!" she said. "You can't come in here! She's in labor. This is a birthing hut. No men are allowed in. And no peeking either."

"She's in labor? You mean, that kind of labor?" The three youths looked at each other. "What should we do?"

"I don't know," Toko wailed.

Sugaru nudged her. "That won't do, Toko. You're the only one who can help her."

"But ... " Toko tried desperately to remember what her mother and the other women had done when there was a birth in her village, but she had not been interested at the time, and now she was so shaken she could not recall a thing.

"It's all right," the woman called out. "This is my second time, so I know what to do. If you could bring some water to wash the baby when it's born, I'd really appreciate it. It would help if you could carve a small knife out of bamboo to cut the umbilical cord, too. Also, could someone take care of Abi? After all, he's a boy."

After delegating these tasks to Sugaru and the others, Toko went back into the cave to convince Abi that his mother would be all right and sent him outside. Then she turned to the woman and asked nervously, "Are you sure there's nothing else we can do?"

"Thanks, but don't worry. Everything will be fine." It was she who was comforting Toko. Between labor pains, she seemed completely composed. "I'm not worried at all about the birth. I know this child is destined to live because she's the reincarnation of Lady Iwa. She was the first child conceived after the lady's death. That's why I hid with Abi, just the two of us. I can't die until the baby is born."

"You believe in rebirth?"

The woman laughed. "What do you mean? I thought you were a Tachibana. You'll understand very soon, believe me. The baby will be born with the yellow magatama called Ki, the Stone of Life, clenched in her fist, as proof that she's Lady Iwa. The high priestess never dies, she's just reborn."

"She'll be born . . . holding a magatama?" Toko said, her voice a high squeak. It seemed unbelievable, yet it did support Sugaru's idea that the magatama were calling to one another.

"What I'm really concerned about is what will happen after the birth. The men from Mahoroba want her stone. The new clan leader, Kitsuhiko, has sided with Mahoroba, and he knows that it will reappear when she's born."

"So that's why they were looking for women and children," Toko whispered, her mind reeling from the implications. "Then Prince Ousu is looking for the magatama too? But why? What does he need it for?"

"It's the emperor's doing," the woman said. "He probably can't bear the thought of anyone having a power equal to his own." She grimaced and then moaned in pain.

The labor pains came closer and closer together. Toko felt that she could not stand it any longer. She could do nothing to ease the woman's pain and was terrified that the woman might weaken and die. When the woman's cries reached their peak, her eyes suddenly flew open and she turned her gaze on Toko. In a startlingly lucid voice, she said, "Tell me why you came to this land. What is it you wanted from the high priestess?"

Toko frowned, perplexed, but then said in a rush, "I need the Misumaru, the string of beads, to defeat the Sword. I came to ask the high priestess to help me. And to teach me. There is no one who can teach me what the magatama are or what qualities I need to become a warrior—"

The woman's expression grew stern. "You cannot bear the Misumaru if you do not believe in yourself. If you don't have the confidence to take on that task without someone telling you what to do, then I would have to advise you to abandon the whole idea."

Toko said hastily, "But I do believe. It must be me who defeats Prince Ousu. I couldn't bear it if someone else should do it."

The woman pressed her further. "Do you hate him enough?"

"Yes, I hate him. He has robbed me of so much. But none of that is really important. What I can't forgive him for is his severing of the bond between us without even stopping to think of me. When the prince first took Oguna to the capital, we still had a connection. I dreamed of him and always felt him there. It was only after he took up the Sword that my dreams ended. Now, no matter how close he is, I can no longer feel him. He's like a different person. Because of the Sword. My heart can never find peace until that Sword is destroyed."

Abi's mother said in a low voice, "Then you need to know what the Sword's power is. The Sword rejects change. Change in the world, change in life. The magatama do the opposite. They encourage change—from life to death, death to life—they urge all things toward change. Do you understand?"

"Well, no, not really," Toko answered. She only wished that someone would explain exactly how the magatama worked against the Sword.

"No, I suppose you can't understand just yet. But if you're going to pursue the Sword, you will need to know. I will share with you one thing. Once, long ago, the forces of the Sword and the magatama were joined. When the Water Maiden married the Wind Child, the magatama were reunited for the first time since they had left the neck of the Goddess. The Water Maiden wore the Misumaru at her wedding as a symbol of the felicitations of the five clans. Ever since, the powers of Light and Darkness have not been as distinctly separate as they used to be."

Toko was suddenly gripped by an icy fear. Not even Lady Toyoao had told her such things. Then to whom was she talking? It couldn't be Abi's mother if she could remember that far back in time. "Lady Iwa?" Toko said. "Is that you, Lady Iwa?"

Abi's mother gave a long, drawn-out cry that Toko thought would never end. The labor had reached the final stage. Toko could see the baby's crown. She reached out to help but there was so much blood she panicked. It seemed as though the mother's body would be torn apart. All she could do was watch as the woman struggled to give birth and the child, to be born—it was as hard as any battle. *From life to death, from death to life.* She thought the dawn would not come, not even in ten years, but come it did. With shaking hands Toko cut the umbilical cord with the bamboo knife. The newborn baby cried, her whole body shaking. She was so wrinkled she did not yet look human, but with her tiny hands and feet, she seemed to Toko like a mystery, like life itself.

"After you've bathed her, give her to me," Abi's mother said. Although exhausted with dark circles under her eyes, she appeared almost drunk with victory. The baby calmed as Toko washed her and gingerly placed her in her mother's arms. Gently prying the baby's right hand open, Abi's mother revealed the magatama. In the white morning light that shone into the cave, it gleamed with a color that reminded Toko of egg yolk.

"You see."

"Yes, but she doesn't look much like a high priestess," Toko said, looking at the baby's large almond-shaped eyes and tiny, almost invisible nose.

Abi's mother laughed. "She's just a baby, that's why. It'll be a while before she can talk, even if she is full of ancient wisdom."

"But I was just talking to her," Toko said. "That was Lady Iwa, wasn't it?"

"What do you mean?" Apparently, Abi's mother remembered nothing.

JOY WELLED UP INSIDE TOKO only after she had wrapped the baby in a cloth and taken her outside. Then it finally hit her that she had really done it. She had helped deliver a baby, and both babe and mother were safe. The first rays of the morning sun caressed the mist-draped treetops, and the air felt fresh and bracing on her face. Sugaru and Abi were sitting forlornly under a tree, but they jumped up as soon as they saw Toko.

"The baby's born? Is it a girl or a boy?" Sugaru asked. He sounded so much like an anxious father that Toko almost burst out laughing.

"How about Mother? Can I go in?" Abi asked.

"Your mother's fine, Abi," Toko said. "But she's sleeping right now. Wait just a little longer." Then she turned to Sugaru. "It's a girl, of course, and you were right. I'm sure you were destined for each other. This little baby was born with the magatama. She's the rebirth of the high priestess."

"The baby? Not the mother? It may be a girl, but it doesn't have a nose or even any hair."

"They'll grow in, don't worry. She may turn into a real beauty—in another fifteen years or so."

"Fifteen years? If I wait that long, I'll be a gray-haired old man," Sugaru groaned. "I came all this way just to see a baby? I don't believe it."

"We've found the magatama. That's what counts. The men from Mahoroba are after it too, you know."

At that moment, Tasuki and Imatate burst through the bushes into the clearing. "I think we might be in for a little trouble," Tasuki said. "The soldiers found our campfire. They've brought hounds and they're heading this way. We'd better leave quickly."

"Oh no," Toko said. "There's no way we can move Abi's mother yet."

"If she stays, she'll be killed."

Toko rushed into the cave to wake the woman, but Abi's mother showed no sign of alarm. "It's impossible for me to escape with you," she said. "Don't worry about me. As long as the baby and Abi are safe, that's all that matters. Please, take them and flee to safety. Protect the baby. Don't let them extinguish this newborn life."

"No," Toko protested. "I can't let you throw your life away. You must live too."

But the woman only smiled and shook her head firmly. "I was prepared for this. You're the ones who must live. Hurry! If you delay, it will all have been for nothing."

Furious, Toko stalked out of the cave and placed the baby in Sugaru's arms. "Protect her. Remember, she's your destiny. Don't let anyone take her or her magatama."

"Whoa! Are you crazy? How can you give me something so tiny? I might crush it in my arms," Sugaru said. The baby looked small enough to fit in the palm of his hand.

Toko knelt down in front of Abi and said, "Abi, I want you to protect your little sister. You must go with Sugaru. He's strong, and no ordinary soldiers can defeat him. But you must help your sister too, okay?"

Abi nodded solemnly.

"Please." Toko looked at all of them. "Go now. Before it's too late."

"Toko, what are you doing?"

Her eyes blazed. "I can't leave her to die. I can't leave her on her own to face those soldiers. I'm going to stay with her. But I want all of you to go. It's the baby they want."

"Then we'll stay and fight," Tasuki said. "The kids will be safe with Sugaru."

Toko shook her head. "No. I don't want anyone to die. You have better things to do than to die here." She removed her sword, sheath and all, from her belt and held it out to Sugaru. "Take this with you. I don't want it to fall into their hands." She thrust it toward him. "Hurry. Take it."

"All right, all right," Sugaru said. He reached out and took the sword. The sound of hounds baying could now be heard faintly in the distance. "Come on, you guys. Follow me."

"Sugaru, are you sure?" Tasuki started to protest, but one look at Sugaru's receding back told him it would be futile. He followed after, glancing back frequently at Toko. Imatate, unruffled as usual, gave Toko a quick wave goodbye before turning and striding after them.

When they had disappeared from sight, Toko returned to the woman's side. Abi's mother seemed surprised that Toko had stayed. "Why didn't you go? I told you I was ready for this." In her hand, she gripped a small dagger, similar to the one that Lady Akaru had had.

"You mustn't kill yourself," Toko replied in a calm voice. "Didn't you just show me how precious life is, what it means to live? You must not die—for the sake of your children as well."

"But the soldiers are coming. It would be better to die than to fall into their hands."

"No. You will live. No matter what happens, as long as you live there will be another chance. Your baby needs you. No matter how many others may give her milk, only one woman gave her life. I want you to live and hold her again. Because if you don't—" Toko felt her lips begin to quiver and struggled to keep herself steady. "You remind me of my mother," she continued. "My mother told me to flee in the middle of the battle while she stayed behind. At that time, I did not have the power to convince her or to help her. I still don't know what happened to her. But I want to do for you what I could not do for her. I want you to live. Of all people, you, who have just brought a new life into the world, must know more than anyone else just how precious life is."

The woman laid aside her dagger and then, to Toko's surprise, held out her arms. Without hesitation, Toko fell into that embrace. She was aware of what she was doing, yet at the same time, part of her saw Abi's mother as her own, for Abi's mother hugged her and stroked her hair just as she would have done for Abi. "You poor child," she said. "What terrible things you have borne. And all alone. I'm so sorry to have made you sad."

The sound of hounds and men suddenly grew louder, and Toko knew they must be very close. She let go of Abi's mother, told her to wait inside, and stepped out of the cave alone. The soldiers caught sight of her and rushed toward her, shouting.

"Over there!"

"Surround her. Don't let her get away!"

She waited for the right moment and then, taking a deep breath, shouted, "Hold! The magatama you seek is not here. There is only a woman who has just given birth in the cave. Be still. Neither she nor I will try to escape." Toko could generate an astonishingly loud and penetrating voice when she chose to. She had taken pride in this skill as a child. Just as it had once stopped bullies in their tracks, the soldiers were brought up short.

" . . . Who is that pipsqueak?"

"The woman in the cave, drag her out."

Toko turned on the soldier who tried to shove her away. "I told you, she's alone. Are you deaf? The gods will punish you for disrespecting a woman who's just given birth. Surely you know that even to enter a birthing hut is enough to bring down divine retribution."

The soldiers appeared uneasy. They all knew that men were forbidden to enter a birthing hut. One of them checked to see that the cave held only a woman and then, without touching her, turned back to Toko. "The baby's gone," he said. "Where is it?"

"I'm not telling," Toko said. The soldier hit her so hard she was flung back into the trees. Then he reached into the cave to grab Abi's mother and pull her out. Toko yelled from where she lay, "If you kill her, you will never, ever find the magatama!"

Toko noticed a man dressed all in black standing next to her. He appeared to be their commander. "So you've seen the magatama, have you, brave little one?" he said in a surprisingly gentle tone. "Ki, the Stone of Life, it was born with the baby, wasn't it?"

Toko pressed her hand against her lip, grimacing at the taste of blood. "Yes," she said. "But I won't let you lay hands on it. It's not for people who kill women and children."

"There appears to be a misunderstanding. The men of Mahoroba are not as barbaric as you seem to think. Kumaso women die by their own hands."

Toko gazed up at him. He did not seem like a warrior. His long hair was loosely bound, and his thin face seemed familiar. From her confused memories floated the image of red fire enveloping an island and a horse racing toward her, its hooves pounding. *I remember now. He was the one who held the reins. He rode off toward the enemy camp with Oguna behind him.* "You were in Mino, weren't you?" she blurted out.

He looked at her, his face expressionless. "I am a shadow. You could say that I am everywhere, and then again, nowhere."

3

AFTER ORDERING several soldiers to escort Toko and Abi's mother to Kitsuhiko's hall, the commander led the rest of his men into the forest after the fugitives, setting the hounds on the scent. Thanks to his strict orders to keep the prisoners fit for interrogation and to show particular care for Abi's mother, no further violence was committed. Abi's mother was carried on a makeshift stretcher. Though Toko's hands were bound, the soldiers did not bully her any further, and she made no attempt to escape.

They walked for a full day before they came to the village where Kitsuhiko's hall was located. The large river flowing beside it appeared to be the mother of the mountain stream where Imatate had caught the trout. Built like a fortress, the settlement was surrounded by a moat and a stockade, but Toko could see thatched roofs on the other side of the wall. It was already growing dark, and as she passed between the turrets guarding the gate, lights glowed in the windows of the houses. She had not spent time in a proper village since she had left Izumo, and her spirits rose a little, despite the fact that she was a prisoner.

Prince Ousu must be somewhere inside—he must *be if the man I saw him with in Mino is here. I might catch sight of him.*

Having given her sword to Sugaru, Toko had no means with which to carry out her plan, but it made her heart beat faster just to know that her adversary was so close. She had caught only a fleeting glimpse of him in Mino. If Toko saw him here, she wanted to engrave his image on her mind. Contrary to her hopes, however, she saw no one, for she and Abi's mother were hustled straight to a hut on the outskirts and locked inside.

Toko listened to the sound of the bolt with a sinking heart, then turned to

Abi's mother, who lay exhausted on the stretcher. "How are you?" she asked.

The woman gave her a valiant smile. "I hurt all over, but considering my condition, I'm doing very well. Thank you for standing up for me."

Her hands free now, Toko rubbed her wrists as she looked around the hut. For a dungeon, it was not as bad as it might have been. The room was small, but dry, with bundles of straw piled in one corner. She supposed that the shed had once been used to store fodder. She could smell horses, so the stables must be close by. Gathering up some straw, Toko piled it thickly and laid the ragged cloth from the stretcher over the top to make a bed for Abi's mother.

"It's far more luxurious than that cave," Abi's mother said with a chuckle as she lay down. Then she fell fast asleep. Watching the woman's chest rise and fall evenly, Toko wondered where the others were and how Sugaru would feed the baby. Knowing the three from Izumo, they had probably shaken off their pursuers with ease and found a wet nurse in some remote village. But there was no guarantee. This time the young men might not be able to laugh their difficulties away so easily. Nor were there any guarantees for Toko and Abi's mother. But Toko was too exhausted to pursue that endless train of thought. She slumped over where she was sitting and the weight of her body pulled her to the floor where she finally fell into oblivion.

THE NEXT MORNING, Toko woke starving and angry. After she had banged on the door and yelled three times, the door finally opened. A young woman, her clothes ragged and torn, passed between the spear-bearing guards and entered with an earthenware pot.

"Forgive me for being so late. So much has happened since last night and they would not let me come to you before this." Toko looked at her in surprise, for she sounded very well bred.

"Ezume?" Abi's mother called from her bed. "Ezume, is that really you?"

Dropping to her knees, the woman said in a tearful voice, "Yes, Lady Hayakitsu, it is I, Ezume. And I'm overjoyed to see that you're alive and well."

So she's a Kumaso too, Toko thought. Looking closely, Toko saw that she was quite beautiful, with dark skin and thick eyelashes, and she bore herself with dignity despite the rags she wore.

Abi's mother, or Lady Hayakitsu as Ezume had called her, said, "I never thought to see you alive again. You were living in Kawakami Hall, yet you survived. Are there any others?"

"About twenty of us are here working as servants. And there's another sixty who have been imprisoned. The chief of Kawashimo makes us take care of the prisoners. Some killed themselves rather than be imprisoned, but I decided to live, at least until I had witnessed the rebirth of Lady Iwa. I encouraged the others to do so as well. Lady Hayakitsu, judging by your condition, dare I believe that Lady Iwa has returned?"

Lady Hayakitsu nodded. "Yes, she has safely returned to this world. As long as Her Ladyship is alive, we are not defeated. Please tell the others."

"They'll be overjoyed," Ezume said, wiping her eyes with her sleeve. "I'm so glad that I didn't give up hope. Even as a slave, staying alive was worth it. Thank you."

Tears welled in Lady Hayakitsu's eyes. "It must have been so hard for you too. I'm glad that I survived to tell you this news."

"And if you're to stay alive," Toko interjected, "you must eat."

"Oh, yes, you're right," Ezume said. "Please do." She hastily removed the lid from the pot and ladled the contents into bowls—rice porridge cooked with herbs and dried shellfish. It was delicious, although anything would have tasted fabulous to Toko at that point. She ate until the pot was empty.

Ezume eyed her curiously. "Who is this?" she asked Lady Hayakitsu.

"Lady Toko from Mino. She's the one that Lady Iwa foretold would come from the east. Without her, I don't know what would have happened to me, or to Abi and the baby."

"Her? *She's* the one?" Ezume seemed almost shocked, and Toko looked at her blankly. "Forgive me," Ezume said hastily. "I didn't mean to offend you. It's just that . . . you look like a boy."

"It's all right. People often make that mistake," Toko said.

Ezume sighed. "It's no wonder the chief of Kawakami was mistaken. After all, Prince Ousu looked just like a princess."

"But Prince Ousu is a man, not a woman," Toko said, perplexed. "Who are you talking about?"

"I'm talking about the prince. He arrived at the hall of Kawakami alone, without his sword, his long hair loose and dressed in silk robes. Even to me, he looked beautiful."

Toko's mouth dropped open.

Lady Hayakitsu's expression clouded. "I haven't heard what happened yet. The messenger who came to warn us at Yamanobe Hall didn't know the details. Ezume, please tell us everything. Are you saying that my husband believed Prince Ousu was a beautiful woman? And that's why he let him into the hall?"

Ezume looked as though she was sorry she had mentioned it, but then continued. "Why would he have doubted it? Lady Iwa had told us so clearly to be ready for this before she died. If she'd been here, perhaps things would have been different. But who knows, for no one could have imagined what happened next . . . The chief led him into the inner chambers of the hall and there he was killed. How exactly I don't know for the hall was engulfed in white flames before we knew it. I escaped because I just happened to be in the garden at the time. It was so horrible I can't even describe it." Raising the hem of her robe, she revealed a burn that stretched from her calf all the way up her leg. "I was very lucky to escape with just this. Even the water in the pond boiled over. Those were no ordinary flames. It was terrifying."

Her two listeners were left speechless. After some time, Lady Hayakitsu finally whispered, "That was his one great weakness, beautiful women. And he paid for it to the bitter end. I wonder who betrayed his weakness to the men from Mahoroba."

Toko felt sick. She needed time to think. "Where's Prince Ousu now?" she asked.

Ezume shook her head. "No one's allowed near the center of the hall. I may be a woman, but even I would take the opportunity to avenge my family if they let me near him."

SEVERAL DAYS PASSED. Toko and Lady Hayakitsu remained locked in the hut, seeing no one but Ezume. No news of Sugaru and the baby reached them. Although this could only mean that they had not been caught, Toko was still anxious. Ezume told them that the troops from Mahoroba were rumored to have gone as far as the mountain of fire, but there was no way to confirm it.

The day Ezume brought this news, it was unusually hot and humid. The air felt leaden and the weight of their captivity crushing. Sleep did not come easily that night, and Toko tossed and turned. She was finally dozing off when she heard a loud rumble like thunder. It shook the ground, and the earth continued to rock beneath her even after the noise had subsided.

"What's going on?" she shouted, staggering to her feet.

"The god of the mountain has awoken," Lady Hayakitsu answered quietly.

"The god of the mountain?"

"Sometimes he dances like a shining red snake on the mountaintop. We can see him even from here. When he's very angry, he sends a hail of burning stones down upon the villages at the bottom."

"Aren't you afraid?"

"Of course I'm afraid," Lady Hayakitsu said with a low laugh. "I wonder what Kitsuhiko will make of this."

As if in answer, soldiers ordered them from the hut the next morning. They were to be taken before the chief. Hands bound, they were led through the streets under an overcast sky, yet the sight of it lifted Toko's heart. It felt so good to be outside again. Turning into the main road in front of the chief's hall, she could see the mountain of fire in the distance, its peak rearing above the lower-lying mountains. She had half expected to see a fiery red snake writhing from its mouth, but instead there was nothing but smoke pouring out. This was terrifying enough, and Toko felt the hairs prickle on the back of her neck. The thick column of smoke coiled sluggishly above the peak, then slowly oozed across the heavens, turning the sky dark and hazy. The chief's hall appeared tiny and insignificant in comparison.

When they were brought before Kitsuhiko, Toko found him to be as unimpressive as his hall. Though large and stocky with a heavy beard, he was surprisingly young. Toko looked around the courtyard hoping to see Prince Ousu but saw no one there like him. *Where is he?* The emptiness she felt inside puzzled her.

Lady Hayakitsu stared Kitsuhiko boldly in the face. She had recovered her strength. Standing straight and dignified, she looked like a queen despite the fact that she was bound. "Behold the wrath of the god," she said. "Coveting the rank of chief, you betrayed your own people and joined hands with the men from Mahoroba. This is the result."

Kitsuhiko looked slightly taken aback, but he still had enough confidence to smile. "We seem to have opposing views, Lady Hayakitsu. The god's anger is directed not at me, but at you. You entrusted the priestess and the magatama to outsiders and strangers, didn't you? These things belong in our hands, in the hands of the people of Himuka. That's why the god of the fire mountain is angry."

"Our hands? The people of Himuka? To whom are you referring?" Lady Hayakitsu laughed with disdain. "You're just a dog that sold this country to Mahoroba. You wish to have the magatama, but only so that you can present it to the emperor in tribute. And yet you have the nerve to blame me."

"That's not true. Now that I've become chief of Himuka, I realize that the stone Ki must stay here. If I vow never to give it to Mahoroba, will you work with me?"

After a long pause, Lady Hayakitsu answered. "And what are you going to do about Prince Ousu with whom you joined forces?"

"He's gone. He received orders from the emperor and left immediately to subjugate another land. The troop he left under the command of his shadow went off toward the mountain of fire and has yet to return. They were surely punished by the god. Now we no longer need to bow down to Mahoroba."

Toko felt her shoulders droop. So the prince was not here. She was disappointed, but at the same time strangely relieved. If he had been here despite the emptiness inside her, she might have lost all confidence.

Lady Hayakitsu shook her head in exasperation. "So you would turn traitor not once but twice? Kitsuhiko, you were ever the opportunist, even as a child, a shortcoming that always worried me. No, I will not join forces with you. You have no capacity for leadership. If you think you can run this country on your own, go ahead and try it."

Clenching his jaw, Kitsuhiko said in a tight voice, "Well, then, sister, if you insist, there's nothing I can do about it. As the leader, I must still the god's wrath on my own without your help. I shall give a sacrifice. I will choose ten maidens from the prisoners." He pointed at Toko. "She will be the first, and Ezume the second. I will allow you to watch the sacrifice. Then you may regret your refusal."

TOKO WAS separated from Lady Hayakitsu and thrown into a dungeon that was much more prisonlike—a hole in the ground with water seeping from the walls. Soon the soldiers brought Ezume and eight other young women. Most of them were weeping in grief and despair. Though not crying, Ezume's face was very pale. "I'm so sorry you were dragged into this," she said.

"How are people sacrificed?" Toko asked.

"I don't know. If the high priestess were here, she would never have allowed it. But when we give offerings to the god, we take them up to Yutsudana, a rock shelf facing the mountain of fire, and throw them down the cliff into the valley far below."

The sound of weeping turned to wails. Toko regretted asking. In a loud, bracing voice, she said, "No matter how great this god is, I have no intention of dying like that. My body is not an offering. Besides, I still have a job to do. There's no way I'm going to be sacrificed."

"I don't want to die either," Ezume said. "I want to see my lover again. He's now a prisoner."

"We'll be rescued. I'm sure of it. Sugaru and the others will come to save us," Toko said much more confidently than she actually felt. "Rescuing beautiful women is Sugaru's favorite pastime. He's always looking for an opportunity to do that. And here he has the chance to save ten girls at once. He won't pass that up for sure."

"But . . ." Ezume did not look convinced. "Why would someone from another land bother to help us?"

"Don't worry. When it comes to beautiful women, he'd risk his life no matter where they're from," Toko assured her.

The young women stopped crying and looked hesitantly at Toko. It was clear from their faces that they longed to cling to even the faintest hope, but they found it hard to accept her optimism. Toko kept a brave face, but she was not able to sleep that night. Lying on the damp floor of the prison, she listened to the sound of someone's muffled sobs and stared into the darkness. *I don't want to die. I can't. Not right now. I'm not going to die here in this place . . .*

As she gritted her teeth, the thought that kept coming back to her was the prince's absence. He was not here. He did not know that Toko was here. He had left to destroy some other land, without having the slightest inkling of the feelings that had driven her to Himuka. Toko felt that she might choke on her anger and despair.

Her impatience to reach Himuka had not been solely because of the magatama. She had been driven by the knowledge that Oguna was heading here. And she realized now that when she had stood by Lady Hayakitsu and allowed herself to be captured, her actions had been partly informed by the hope that it would bring her near him. Yet, Prince Ousu had left without even knowing that Toko was here at the westernmost edge of the country. No, she could not die.

4

THE YOUNG WOMEN were dragged out of the dungeon, bound together in pairs, and shoved into palanquins. Men wearing elaborate ceremonial costumes bore the palanquins on long poles and began a solemn march toward the mountain. Although the procession moved slowly, the journey inflicted a great deal of suffering on the girls, for not only were they bound back to back, their feet were also tied.

Toko was paired with Ezume, who was much taller, a combination that proved disastrous for Toko. Not a few times she was crushed against the wall and had to squirm frantically to keep from suffocating. Still, she knew she was lucky to be able to feel pain at all, for once they were thrown to the bottom of the cliff, they would feel nothing. As she was buffeted about, Toko thought about Sugaru and his friends.

Will they be able to save us? She was sure that they would come to her rescue if they knew. But how were they to find out? She had no way of knowing what had happened at the mountain of fire. Perhaps Sugaru and the others had been caught by the men from Mahoroba. Or perhaps they had escaped far away. If so, they certainly could not fly through the sky to reach her.

She closed her eyes tightly. *I won't give up. I will believe until my last breath that we will escape. It's not my fate to die here—not when I still have to defeat Prince Ousu; not when he continues to wield the Sword of destruction somewhere in Toyoashihara . . .*

The palanquin pitched violently and the two girls tumbled together, cracking heads and sliding into a corner. Once again Toko wound up on the bottom.

"Are you all right? I'm so sorry," Ezume said weakly. Just then they heard shouts of alarm and a clamoring outside. The men carrying the palanquin seemed to hesitate, and their measured tread was disrupted.

"What's happening?"

"We're under attack," Toko answered excitedly. "It sounds like quite a battle, too."

From the noise, she guessed that far from being a minor skirmish it was a violent clash with a large force. Suddenly they found themselves thrown to the ground, heads over heels, palanquin and all. Their bearers had fled, leaving them behind. The impact stunned them both. A moment later, however, someone wrenched one of the walls open, letting in the light of day.

Imatate peered inside, grinning broadly. "Are you all right?" he asked. Toko thought her heart would burst at the sight of his familiar face. Although she had believed her friends would come, that was not the same as actually experiencing it.

"You look very dashing," she said, smiling back at him.

"I thought so myself."

Freed of her bonds, Toko crawled out of her upturned palanquin and saw that all the others had been ditched along the road. The procession had been routed. While there was still some fighting going on, it was clear that the men in ceremonial dress were at a disadvantage. Their attackers were all hot-blooded young men, and there were scores of them. Toko assumed they must be Kumaso who had come out of hiding to join up with the young men from Izumo. No wonder there had been such a commotion. She saw a woman sobbing in a young man's arms and Lady Hayakitsu being helped out of her palanquin. She also caught sight of Tasuki through the trees, a spear in hand. When his opponent fled, he walked over to Toko and Imatate.

"Hey there, Toko," he called out. "When it comes to rescuing beautiful women, I'd have to say that the men of the west are just as enthusiastic as us."

"That's true." Toko laughed. Then she looked around, puzzled. "But where's Sugaru? I would have thought he'd be the first one to jump at a chance like this. Why isn't he here? What's happened?"

"There's no need to worry about him. He's fine," Tasuki said, grinning broadly. "I bet he wished he could be here to show what he can do. But it would look pretty funny if he came to the rescue with a baby strapped to his back."

Toko looked at him in surprise. "He's been taking care of the baby? Sugaru?"

"The whole time," Imatate said. "She won't have anyone but him. We tried leaving her with the wet nurse, but it was no good. And, of course, we were no good either. The only time she stops crying is when Sugaru holds her in his arms. Strangely enough." Toko was stunned.

"It's good medicine for him to be on the sidelines for once," Tasuki said. "He'll just have to be content with that. He looks pretty disgusted when Abi wakes up in the morning and mistakes him for his mother though."

Toko burst out laughing. It felt so good to be alive and capable of laughter, and although it might offend Sugaru, the thought of him and the baby was too funny. Tasuki let her laugh to her heart's content. Then he said, "But you know Sugaru. Even while he's babysitting, he's bound to be planning a big surprise." Tasuki and Imatate winked at one another. Toko realized that they were hiding something. But before she could question them further, several young men came running up to them, panting for breath.

"The chief, Kitsuhiko, has escaped. He and several men broke through our ranks and are heading back to the village."

"What should we do? He's bound to bring reinforcements."

But Tasuki shook his head. "No, there won't be any reinforcements. The shock he'll get when he sees the state of his hall will stop him in his tracks. Let's go and see Sugaru's handiwork."

"What on earth is Sugaru up to?" Toko asked, but Tasuki and Imatate merely grinned knowingly and refused to answer.

"Wait until you get there," was all they said.

IT TOOK THEM quite some time to get back down the mountain path. Unlike the chief and his men, they were not in any hurry and were escorting many young women, some of whom could only walk slowly. They finally came in sight of the plains below just as the sun was sinking in the west. From this vantage point, they could look down upon the village of Kawashimo where Kitsuhiko's hall was located. At least, they should have been able to.

The people of Kumaso cried out in disbelief. "Look! The village is gone." They strained their eyes, searching carefully, but to no avail. Not a trace remained of the walled settlement beside the river into which the sun was now setting. All they could see was water which had escaped its banks, forming a huge pond spreading like a fan from the riverbed. The murky brown flood reflected the glaring red sun. The sky was clear, undisturbed by storms, and not a drop of rain had fallen, yet the village that had been there this morning was now completely submerged.

"Impossible . . . Surely Sugaru didn't do this . . . did he?" Toko tried to laugh but her voice shook. Imatate just shrugged without denying it.

They continued walking, rendered speechless by the strange scene before them. Drawing closer, they caught sight of Sugaru on top of a small hill gazing down at the flood. In his arms, he held a baby wrapped in a blanket. By his side stood Abi. It was startling, and not just because of the incongruity of this tall, good-looking youth tenderly cradling an infant. As Sugaru stood frowning down at the water, lost in thought, his red hair blazing like flame in the setting sun, he looked so otherworldly that Toko recoiled. Yet Abi snuggled up beside him and the baby slept peacefully as if nothing was wrong. The three figures merged into one, like some sacred statue.

Toko's trepidation only lasted until Sugaru collected himself and realized he had an audience. When he turned to Toko, he was the same old Sugaru she knew.

"Ah, there you are, Toko. I'm glad to see you look so well. How kind of you to foist this baby on me. Thanks to you I'm worn to the bone. I can't even get a good night's sleep."

"Mother!" Abi cried. Lady Hayakitsu pushed her way to the front of the crowd.

"Abi!" He flew into her arms and she hugged him fiercely, tears flowing down her face. "You're safe! You're safe!"

"Here, allow me to return your baby as well," Sugaru said. "She's in good shape. And when she cries, her voice is like thunder." He passed the bundle to Lady Hayakitsu and then stretched his arms. "Ah! That's better!"

Toko doubted what she had felt but a moment earlier. *Maybe I was mistaken . . .* But from what Tasuki said next, she realized that she was not.

"You never told us you were going to flood the place," Tasuki said, nudging Sugaru. "You said you were just going to get their feet wet to teach them a lesson."

"I didn't expect the water to rise so fast." Sugaru shrugged. "To tell you the truth, I even shocked myself."

"You made sure everyone got out safely, I hope. There weren't any prisoners trapped in the dungeons, were there?"

"No, you don't need to worry about that."

Toko covered her mouth with her hands. "It was you? Sugaru, you flooded the whole village? But how?"

"With these." He held out his right hand and opened his fist. On his palm lay two magatama—his own, shining green like new leaves, and the deep gold stone that belonged to Lady Iwa.

"With the magatama?"

"The infant Lady Iwa lent me Ki. See, they're both glowing, right? Together they summon a much greater power than they have on their own. When I tried it out, this is what happened." He waved his hand toward the brimming waters and frowned. He recognized the enormity of what he had done. "They have the power to call the tides. To make them ebb and surge. I'm making the water flow out now. It wouldn't be right to leave it like this."

"But . . . how did you learn to control that power?" Toko whispered, awestruck. When she had seen the light flash from the Sword and sear the sky, she had felt the same thing—terror in the face of a power that should not be.

"Lady Iwa told me."

"The baby?"

"Well, via Abi. For some reason, Abi understands what his sister wants to say."

Toko found it hard to recover from this blow. It was not the mysterious power of the magatama that shocked her, but rather her exclusion from that power. Sugaru and Lady Iwa were both magatama bearers. As if it were the most natural thing in the world, they had made that power their own; they held the source of life and death in their hands. But Toko bore only the Tachibana name. She could not share in that mystery. *Maybe I'm not qualified to gather the Misumaru. I'm not special. Even if I try to become the warrior, just the desire to do it may not be enough . . .*

Lost in these thoughts, she nearly jumped when someone grabbed her hand. Looking down, she saw that it was Abi. He had appeared out of nowhere and was now staring up at her with round eyes.

"What is it?"

"The baby says that you should hurry up and get your own magatama. If you do that, she says, even you can bear the Misumaru."

My own *magatama?*

She turned to Abi in surprise. "What do you mean? Are you saying that I have a magatama? But the magatama of Mino was lost and is now in the hands of the emperor in Mahoroba."

The boy frowned and backed away. "I don't know. I just said that because my little sister told me to."

"Oh Abi, I'm sorry. Of course." Toko regretted drilling him with questions. Then she had an idea. Perhaps through Abi she could ask these things of Lady Iwa herself. *I just have to know if there is any hope for me. I need someone to reassure me that I have chosen the right path . . .*

"Abi," she said. "Let's go talk to your little sister. I want you to tell me what she's saying."

They found Lady Hayakitsu with Ezume and some other women sitting slightly apart beneath the shade of a tree. Lady Hayakitsu was nursing the baby, who was completely absorbed in feeding and had no eyes for either Toko or Abi. Looking at her, Toko could not imagine where the words of wisdom that Abi had conveyed could possibly have come from. She was just a baby. While she was waiting, Toko told Lady Hayakitsu what she wanted. She had already related her own story when they were imprisoned together and Lady Hayakitsu understood readily.

"I'm not able to hear Lady Iwa like Abi, but personally, I think her words mean that you should go ahead and pursue the path you've chosen. I wonder why she chose Abi as her mouthpiece. Perhaps it's because children are closer to the gods. Toko, I'm sure you can become the bearer of the Misumaru."

"But . . . " It was not comforting that Toko wanted right now, but she could not say so. She was watching the baby nurse when Abi suddenly began to speak, even though the baby was still latched to her mother's breast and Abi was twiddling Lady Hayakitsu's hair.

" . . . If you're looking for the magatama, she says you should go to the land whose name has been forgotten. What? The land whose name has been forgotten is the capital. Mother, did you know that? Doesn't the capital have a name?"

"Yes, it does. It's called Mahoroba. It was named that long ago because it's where the God of Light left his footprint," Lady Hayakitsu responded. "But she may have said that because none of us remember what that place was called before it was named Mahoroba. Lady Iwa knows what things were like long before the God of Light ever set foot in this land."

"Mahoroba is the land whose name is forgotten?" Toko exclaimed. "Does that mean there are Tachibana even in the capital, protecting a magatama in the land where the emperor rules?"

"Sacred places are unique. It wouldn't be strange for the same place to be sacred to more than one people or in more than one era." Lady Hayakitsu thought a moment and then added, "Although considering that the emperor is so determined to obtain the magatama, it does seem odd that he hasn't found and seized the one in the capital yet."

"It's often hardest to see what's right under one's nose. Still, we should hurry." Toko was suddenly overcome with the urge to leave.

As if to fuel her anxiety, Abi said, "The baby says you should hurry too. But she says you should return to Izumo first. That's where the prince from Mahoroba is heading. People will die there, just like they did here."

TOKO ALMOST FELL in her haste to get back to the others and warn them about the danger to their homeland. To her surprise, however, the three young men, who would normally respond instantly to such news, were lukewarm.

"But Lady Iwa says you must hurry," Toko said.

"Yes, but it's not like we've got nothing to do here and are free to just fly away home at a moment's notice," Sugaru said, pointing at the mud left in the wake of the receding water. "The river will be back to normal by tomorrow morning, but people's lives won't. Nothing has been solved yet. Nobody could say that we aren't responsible."

"And if the group from Mahoroba comes back, there's bound to be more trouble," Tasuki said. "We made fools of them on that mountain. And we involved the men of Kumaso. It was fun, but still."

Toko did not know what to say in the face of this argument. While they appeared to be fooling around most of the time, the three young men clearly had their own principles by which they stood. It did seem irresponsible to leave Kawashimo like this. But still.

At that moment, Lady Hayakitsu approached with the baby in her arms. She bore herself with pride and majesty. "I appreciate your feelings," she said. "But please go home. You must use your power to help your own land.

We will never forget how you helped us. But we don't intend to blame you for any of the things that happened here. It's not even Mahoroba's fault. The responsibility is ours. We brought this on ourselves with our internal bickering and weakness. The burning of Kawakami and the flooding of Kawashimo were warnings from the heavens. Now that we have lost everything, I think that we can come together as one. Under Lady Iwa. We still have Lady Iwa. I will show you that I can lead my people." It was clear that a new leader, a queen of the Kumaso, had appeared. She would surely rebuild the fortunes of her people. And she would not bow down to the might of Mahoroba.

"There's nothing more for us to do here then," Imatate said to Sugaru. "Let's go home."

AFTER THEY HAD been showered with gifts and reluctantly bid farewell, Sugaru muttered, "It's not fair. I'm finally freed from that baby and have time to spend with the women when all of a sudden I have to say goodbye. What was the point of coming to Himuka? Nothing good came out of this at all. What are you going to do to make up for that?"

"You can go home and boast, Sugaru. Tell everyone that even a newborn babe fell in love with you," Imatate answered.

"You can't call that baby a woman. There was a beautiful girl back there though."

Toko knew he was referring to Ezume. "Too bad for you, Sugaru, but she's already got a lover. It's a good thing we left before you caused an uproar."

Sugaru looked at her in surprise. "What are you so upset about?"

"Obviously the real reason you didn't want to return to Izumo was because of the girls. How stupid of me to believe that you might have even a grain of responsibility in you. Your country is in danger, but even then all you care about is picking up girls."

Sugaru shrugged and looked at Tasuki. "What's with her? Why's she in such a bad mood?"

Tasuki chuckled. "She'll do you good. Didn't you notice? Toko's the only woman you've met who's never changed her attitude toward you in all the time you've known her. She's special."

"Don't be stupid. That's because she's not a woman."

"I'm never speaking to you again," Toko snapped.

"I give her three days," Tasuki whispered to Imatate.

"I say two," Imatate responded, stifling his laughter.

AFTER PULLING *Oguna-maru* out of its hiding place behind the rocks and carefully checking the boat and their supplies, the party set to sea once again. The land at the western edge of the country gradually receded into the blue waves. Now that it was over, the time spent there seemed to have passed very quickly. *What* had *been the point of going to Himuka,* Toko thought as she let her body rock with the waves. Of course, they had accomplished their purpose. They had found Ki, the magatama borne by Lady Iwa in the land where the sun sets. Sugaru now carried it as the second stone of the Misumaru. *But it's Sugaru's, not mine. Maybe he's the chosen one after all. Not me.* She had yet to receive a clear sign that she could become the warrior capable of using the beads. The only choice left was to continue chasing after Prince Ousu, the wielder of the Sword.

5

THEY RODE THE SEA current for much of the return journey, traveling far more quickly than they had on the voyage out. Driven by favorable winds, *Oguna-maru* flew over the waves without any mishaps. Despite their speed, however, they were too late. When they docked at Izumo, they were met with the news that the prince and his men had already left.

"The prince of Mahoroba punished the Kuni no Miyatsuko," they were told. "Who knows why? Maybe the men from Mahoroba resented the fact that Izumo is so prosperous. After all, we only need one capital . . . Still, what they did was pretty drastic, especially when we thought they'd just come for an official visit." The company from Mahoroba had swept through like a typhoon, leaving massive confusion in their wake, and then vanished with the clouds. Unable to believe what they had heard, the four companions made their way to the Kuni no Miyatsuko's hall. Instead of the grand buildings and thick, green hedge, there was only a burned field with charred posts sticking out. It looked so similar to what had befallen Kawakamihiko's hall that Toko felt ill. A wave of nausea swept over her. Standing before the scorched ruins in Himuka, she had trembled with rage. This time, however, she felt as if she had been hit in the stomach with a heavy stick.

"Whoa! Toko, what's wrong?" If Sugaru had not caught her, she would have fallen. He lowered her to the ground, where she stayed, waiting for the nausea to pass. When she managed to open her eyes, she saw the three of them peering anxiously into her face. It seemed an immense effort to speak, but she felt she owed them an explanation. "Kisako was here. There's nothing left. Lady Toyoao's house is gone. Lady Toyoao and Kisako . . . "

Sugaru swore and Toko looked up in surprise. She had never seen him genuinely angry before; had never, no matter the situation or the battle, seen him look this way. "That's it. Enough." His voice rumbled like a thundercloud massing overhead. "To come here while I'm away and do as he pleases—"

His words, however, were interrupted by a quiet voice. "Lady Kisako is safe. And Lady Toyoao as well. They both escaped and are living elsewhere."

They looked around in surprise and saw a young man walking toward them. None of them recognized him, and Sugaru stared at him suspiciously. Toko vaguely felt that she should know him, but she was in such a daze that she could not place him. He looked down at her and smiled. "Have you forgotten me already, Lady Toko?"

"Ear? Is that you?"

"Yes. It's been a while."

"Who did you say he is?" Sugaru whispered, frowning.

"He's a servant of Lady Toyoao's. He can be trusted."

"We've been waiting for your return," Ear said. "Lady Toyoao is living in humble lodgings in Hikawa. She wanted to distance herself from all the speculations after the Miyatsuko died. But she wishes to see you and has asked me to guide you there."

"Can you walk?" Sugaru asked Toko.

She nodded. "Yes, I'm fine now. And I can't wait to see Kisako."

ON THEIR WAY to Hikawa, Ear told them what he could about the events that had transpired in the Miyatsuko's hall. The truth of the matter, he told them, was a riddle that not even he, Lady Toyoao's trusted informant, could unravel. " . . . We do know that there was no rift between the prince and the Miyatsuko until the very end. Rather, the Miyatsuko seemed very taken with the young prince from Mahoroba. They shared meals together and the lord took him out riding. He even took him to the bead-makers' village. The prince was apparently looking for a superb bead to present to the emperor. But it seems they did not find one, and in the end the Miyatsuko gave him one from his own treasury. Yet none of this was in response to pressure from Mahoroba or forced upon him in any way."

"Was the prince dressed like a woman?" Toko asked.

Ear looked puzzled and Sugaru and the others looked at her so incredulously that she blushed. "I'm sorry. It's nothing," she said. "You were saying?"

"Even I have no way of knowing what happened that night. But something must have caused them to fall out. The prince was planning to leave Izumo peacefully the next day, but in the middle of the night the hall was consumed in a sea of flames. It was all I could do to save Her Highness and Lady Kisako. I had no time to gather any information."

They came to a house surrounded by a wooden fence. Although deep in the mountain wood, it was neat, clean, and attractive. A young woman appeared when Ear called. As she approached, they saw that it was Kisako.

"Toko, you're back! And you've found the magatama, haven't you?" Kisako was smiling. In the short time that Toko had been gone, Kisako seemed to have acquired a poise she did not have before. She certainly did not look like someone whose home had just burned down. Wearing a pretty red skirt over a light robe, she looked positively resplendent compared to Toko, who was still covered in the grime of the journey.

"We just saw what's left of the hall," Toko said. "I'm so relieved to see that you're safe. It must have been terrible."

"Yes, a lot has happened since you left. But I'm sure not nearly as much as has happened to you. I even gained a little weight. Toko, you look thinner."

"Really?"

"Lady Toyoao wants to meet with you. She's been bedridden for the last while, but when she heard you were here she insisted on seeing you. Do you mind going to her right away? She gets tired even more easily than before."

Kisako spoke in a gentle voice without any hidden barbs. Perhaps some of Lady Toyoao's mannerisms had rubbed off on her. Though Toko was a little surprised, she nodded and rose quickly.

As soon as she had gone, Kisako's expression turned prim, for now she had to face Sugaru. "Please follow me. I am afraid that we cannot offer you much hospitality," she said in an icy voice, then stood and began to lead the way.

Unfazed by this treatment, Sugaru smiled at her and said, "I'm so glad to see that you're well. You're even more beautiful than before. I was planning to slaughter Prince Ousu if anything had happened to you."

Kisako glared at him. "You're such a smooth talker, aren't you? I doubt that you remembered me even once. I'm sure there must have been many beautiful women in the west."

"I never forgot you."

"Liar."

"I'm not lying. You're the only girl I've met who has ever hit me three times. How could I forget you? That was a pretty powerful wallop. You reminded me a little of my grandfather."

Kisako flushed bright red and her hands curled into fists. Doubtlessly she would have loved to slap Sugaru once more, but instead she turned on her heel and hurried into the adjoining room.

"Sugaru, you're terrible," Tasuki said, looking at him in disbelief.

"I just can't help thinking that she's quite beautiful. Especially when she's angry," Sugaru said.

"Thanks to you," Imatate said gloomily, "I'd be surprised if we got even a cup of water."

LADY TOYOAO'S ROOM was kept closed and just as dimly lit as her room in the Miyatsuko's hall. Sitting up in her bed with a thin shawl around her shoulders, she looked as frail as ever. Toko entered quietly and sat down, feeling a little nervous. "There are no words to adequately express my condolences. How fortunate though that we can meet again," Toko said somewhat stiffly.

Lady Toyoao went straight to the point. "Toko, I remember you called Prince Ousu 'that boy.' You told me that you were raised together. But you didn't tell me what kind of person he was, did you?" Her voice was still as quiet as a breeze, yet Toko sensed something fierce within it that had not been there before.

"Lady Toyoao," she said.

"I met the prince. He spoke with me. We didn't talk about anything important. He was courteous throughout, but, oh, did he always have that voice even when he was a child?"

Startled, Toko felt her pulse begin to race. "I don't understand what you mean."

"No, I suppose you wouldn't. You are not dependent solely on the sounds of voices like I am. But ever since I heard his voice I seem to see things differently. Even though Prince Ousu killed my brother the Kuni no Miyatsuko, even though he almost burned me to death, I don't know why, but—" She gave a long, trembling sigh. "Why is it that I want to weep for him?"

Toko was stunned. Lady Toyoao had in fact begun to weep quietly. "I cannot forget his voice. How could a prince of Mahoroba sound so forlorn? He's more pitiful than a bird separated from its flock or a leaf from its branch. What can he have lost that he should be so devoid of hope? No one can go on living like that." She wiped her eyes on her sleeve and continued. "Even if no one else might notice it, I could tell. Because we are similar in some ways. Because we both know the loneliness that comes from being different. But I do not have the power to heal him. Sympathy or pity will not reach him. All I can do for him is weep."

Toko hesitated for a moment and then said, "Lady Toyoao, what are you trying to tell me? I'm sorry to be so rude, but . . . "

"Lady Toko, can you pity Prince Ousu?" Lady Toyoao asked.

"No," Toko said flatly. "He should be destroyed. He's the enemy. You can't defeat an enemy if you feel sorry for him."

"You're quite right." Lady Toyoao sighed. "You are like a pure rushing stream. With your strength and fortitude, perhaps . . . You will not give up hope and in the end you will achieve your goal. So at least allow me to pity him."

Toko left the room feeling unsettled. Her head seemed very heavy. She went out into the garden to cool her flushed face. After standing for a while in the wind she finally realized what was bothering her. *Lady Toyoao was saying that she not only met Prince Ousu but that she liked him. And she was criticizing me indirectly. Why?* It wasn't fair. Lady Toyoao didn't realize how desperately Toko clung to this one thing. She did not even attempt to see that Toko was as forlorn and lonely as Ousu; that was why Toko had staked everything on revenge.

Kisako finally came looking for her and was surprised to see her standing all alone. "Toko, I was wondering where you were. What's wrong? Dinner's ready."

Toko turned a desperate gaze on Kisako. "I'm going to Mahoroba. I can't waste any more time. I have to find the next magatama."

"What are you talking about? You can't possibly mean right now."

"Yes, right now."

The smile faded from Kisako's lips. "Toko, you're acting very strange."

Toko shook her head. "If I don't leave as soon as possible, I won't make it in time. I won't make it. I have to get the Misumaru before I change my mind. I've got to get it."

Ignoring Toko's protests, Kisako placed a hand on her forehead and then exclaimed, "Honestly, Toko! You're such a child. You're burning with fever. You never pay attention to your own body."

"HOW'S TOKO?" Tasuki asked Sugaru, who had just returned to their room.

"Her fever's pretty bad. She drank a little gruel and now she's sleeping. Kisako's taking care of her." He looked contrite. "She collapsed this afternoon, remember? I should have realized then that something was wrong. She's been overdoing it."

"We kept up a pretty stiff pace on the way back, didn't we?" Tasuki agreed.

"Toko never complains," Imatate said. "That's why we forget to go easy on her. Even though she's a woman."

"She doesn't *act* like one. That's the problem."

"No," Sugaru said. "The problem is that she doesn't want to *be* one."

The moon, already high, threw faint shadows across the room. They were all silent for a while, thinking their own thoughts, until finally Tasuki spoke. "What are you going to do, Sugaru?"

"Toko's talking about going to Mahoroba. Even now in her delirium. There'll be no stopping her, I guess."

Imatate suddenly said, "Why don't you give her your magatama? Like Lady Iwa gave hers to you. Toko wants a magatama. That's all she thinks about. So why not give her yours?"

"Yeah, why not?" Tasuki said. "Look at the state of Izumo. Lady Hayakitsu said we should help the people in our own land. Why don't you let Toko take on the Tachibana mission, whatever it is? I bet she could do it."

Sugaru lay on his stomach, his chin resting on his folded arms. Then he finally said, "Because I don't want to. I don't want to give the magatama to Toko."

"Why? Is it that hard to give up their power once you've used them?"

"No. But I don't want to give that power to Toko. She's totally focused on defeating Prince Ousu, but she doesn't have a clue what that means. She's got guts, but she's only a kid. You saw her just now. She's pushing herself too hard."

"Are you planning to go with her then? To the very end?"

"It might come to that."

"Are you serious?"

Sugaru sat up. "Her quest has something to do with me. We weren't brought together just by chance. If Toko is going to take revenge against the bearer of the Sword, then I have to help her. And if she fails, I'll have to finish the job. Although I doubt Toko has even thought of that."

After a moment, Imatate gave a short laugh. "There you go again. You lead women on all the time, but when it comes to kids, you can't say no."

"Well, if you're going away, I think I'll try my luck with Kisako," Tasuki said, half teasing. "No complaints, all right?"

"Oh, don't worry. I won't complain," Sugaru said with a grin. "I'll just ask you later how many times she hit you."

*chapter
seven*

BANDITS

Bandits

S UMMER CLOUDS billowed white against the blue of the afternoon sky. The lush green leaves grew darker, breathing in the golden light that shone longer every day. Swallows arriving from across the seas darted to and fro. Everything pulsed with life—except Toko. Having only recently recovered, she was not quite up to form. Three days had passed since she left Izumo. But even though she was finally on her way to Mahoroba, her spirits remained low. Sensing this, Sugaru dismounted when the sun was still high. "Let's stop here for today," he said. "I'll look for a campsite."

"But we haven't traveled far at all," Toko complained. "I can go on a little farther. The days are long."

"Do what you're told, Toko. If you collapse again, I'm the one who has to look after you."

Toko pouted but swung down from her horse. Sugaru's high-handed manner irritated her, but it was just the two of them now. That was another reason she was feeling down. It was not at all like the journey to the west with Tasuki and Imatate, who had kept everyone entertained with their lighthearted banter.

Leading his horse by the reins, Sugaru said, "You don't have enough meat on your bones. That's the problem. Women should overflow with life. Look at Lady Hayakitsu. Her hips and chest are so generous it makes you want to shake them. That's why she's so attractive. You could learn from her."

"My apologies for being flat-chested," Toko snapped. "If you wanted good-looking women, you shouldn't have come with me. It's not too late. Why don't you go back to Kisako?"

"Are you kidding? I've heard the capital is full of beautiful women. How could I give up a chance like this?"

"Will you never be serious?" Toko knew it was fruitless to get upset, yet she could not help it. Kisako's feelings weighed more heavily on her mind than before, another cause of her moodiness. It was not that Kisako had said anything. In fact, she seemed to avoid even mentioning Sugaru's name. But for that very reason, Toko felt her cousin's feelings more keenly. During the four or five days Kisako had cared for her, Toko had learned a lot as she lay in bed, watching. *Kisako avoids Sugaru because she actually wants to be near him. She turns her face away whenever they meet, but her eyes follow him when no one is looking. She was thinking of him the whole time we were gone, and she's probably thinking of him still...*

Yet Toko could not help her cousin because she needed Sugaru herself— as the bearer of the magatama. He now possessed two stones—the green Midori and the yellow Ki—and without them Toko would never obtain the Misumaru. So she had pretended not to see how Kisako felt. As soon as she was able to get up, she had left Izumo, feeling Kisako's eyes follow Sugaru from the shadow of the fence until he was out of sight.

I'm sorry, Kisako. In the end, I'm the one who's selfish.

TOKO WOKE UP suddenly in the middle of the night. The memory of her dream was so vivid that for a moment she could not remember where she was. Enveloped in a cold, silent darkness, she felt like the only living thing in the world, trapped in a nightmare of hopeless despair. Unable to stand it, she burst into tears.

Oguna's gone. I can't find him anywhere...

"What's wrong?" Sugaru asked.

Only when Toko heard his voice did she remember that she was not alone; that far from being lost in complete nothingness, she was in a clearing at the edge of a forest.

"Kisako told me that you cried out in your sleep during your fever. You're not quite better yet, are you? Did you have a bad dream?"

Sugaru came over and crouched down beside her. There was not a trace of teasing in his voice, only pure concern. Toko reached out and clung to him.

Wrapping her in a blanket, he put his arms around her. This was what Toko had wanted more than anything else. She supposed that she must have seemed like Abi or the baby to Sugaru, but still she was immensely comforted. He held her like that until the chill had left her body and her sobs had ceased. Then he said, "What were you dreaming about?"

"Oguna." The word popped out so easily. She realized how grateful she was to have someone to listen. "Or I guess I should say I was dreaming about Oguna not being there. I was looking all over for him—in the back garden, the bushes, the pond, the forest. I walked everywhere in Kamitsusato. I did that so many times when we were children. Oguna would always hide somewhere and cry by himself. But in my dream, no matter how hard I looked I couldn't find him. Then I suddenly realized that he's no longer here. He's nowhere in this world. And not even Kamitsusato exists anymore." Tears ran down her cheeks again, but this time she remained calm.

"That's the boy you talked about before, right?" Sugaru said slowly, as if choosing his words with care. "The one you made leaf boats with when you were kids."

"Yes. We were always together. He was the complete opposite of me, even when he was little. He hardly ever cried, even when he broke his arm. He was so good at locking things up inside that most people thought he never shed any tears. But that wasn't true. He did cry sometimes. He just didn't show anyone. He would hide without saying anything. Like when our baby boar was killed."

As Toko talked, scenes from her childhood rose vividly to mind. The huge garden at her father's hall, the young men, the backyard where the rooster used to strut, the shed, the hill behind her home—and her friend and accomplice Oguna, sharing an innocent secret, then both of them smothering their laughter after a quick glance. "We found a baby boar that had been separated from its mother and wandered lost in the hills. We kept it in a secret place and smuggled food for it. But some young men found it. They killed and ate it. I was so upset that I burst into tears in front of everyone. The men were surprised and apologized. But then I noticed that Oguna wasn't there. He'd disappeared without telling me. I realized that he must have been even sadder than I was. He was the one who usually comforted me, but there were times when he just couldn't. When he cried, he cried alone." She sighed. "At times like that, I would go looking for him. I'd walk around checking all his hiding places. Because I was the only person he had. I was the only one who knew him, the only one who could find him. He could never ask for help when he needed it . . . "

"Is he dead?" Sugaru asked.

Toko fell silent. She was quiet for so long that Sugaru thought she was not going to answer. Finally she whispered, "I think so."

"He must have been pretty special if you still care about him that much. But it's not good to cling to someone who's dead, Toko. You need to find someone you can like as much as you did Oguna."

I'll never find anyone like him, Toko screamed inside. *Not anywhere in the world.* She could not shake the feeling that Oguna was somewhere crying. If only that were true, she would have done anything to find him. *But it's not. I can't find Oguna even in my dreams. The bond that once joined us has been broken. Oguna is gone.*

She must discard her memories and clad herself in armor.

SEVERAL DAYS LATER they came to a wide and clearly well-traveled road. It stretched on before them in the direction they were headed, due east and over the mountain pass. Sugaru cocked his chin at it. "That's the road used to carry tribute to Mahoroba."

"Right. Tribute," Toko said with contempt. "Mino paid tribute too. Lots of it. Every year, without fail. But the soldiers from Mahoroba didn't give that a thought when they invaded. That's what they're like. We were so stupid."

"The strong always win. You heard what happened to my ancestors, right?" But Sugaru's voice held no rancor and he seemed not to care. "This road will bring us to Mahoroba. Shall we take it?"

"Of course! What road could be easier to travel than this?" But then she looked at him suspiciously. "Or is there some reason we shouldn't?" Sugaru smiled. "Oh no. Just the possibility of being waylaid by bandits."

Toko recalled rumors they had heard. A band of thieves in the hills had been ambushing travelers and stealing their packhorses. She hesitated a moment but then shrugged. "We've got nothing to fear. We don't have any packhorses with us. Surely there's nothing wrong with taking this road if it will get us to Mahoroba quicker."

"True."

Toko did not like the way Sugaru laughed. When given a choice between two roads, he invariably staked his luck on the riskier one. If she was going to continue traveling with him, she needed to think more carefully, but she was not very good at that yet. *Oh well, never mind. Things will work out somehow.* Putting her anxiety firmly from her mind, she urged her horse forward.

They traveled several days without incident, meeting hardly anyone on the road. After all, it was not the time of year for carrying tribute. But just when Toko had relaxed, believing that they would make it to the capital smoothly, they ran smack into a group of bandits. She and Sugaru were riding through a meadow in a valley, the tall summer grasses brushing the tops of the horses' knees, when a group of seven or eight men suddenly rose up out of the grass, arrows flying from their bows.

Astonished, Toko reined in her horse. "But why? Can't they see that we have nothing to steal?"

"We have horses," Sugaru said, dodging an arrow. "They're the most valuable prize of all. Anyone who has the luxury of traveling on horseback should expect to be attacked."

"Then why didn't you say so sooner?" Toko said, turning her horse's head around.

"No, don't turn back. That's exactly what they want." His tone was suddenly sharp and commanding. "Listen. If you don't want to lose your horse, ride straight at them. Forget about the arrows. They're just a threat. They won't want to hurt the horses."

Toko sucked in her breath, but what Sugaru had said made sense. His eyes were dancing. For him, an attack like this was just another thrill, and his contempt for the thieves gave her courage.

"Let's go!" he said.

Following his example, Toko bent low in the saddle and spurred her horse to a gallop. They raced neck and neck, swooping down on the bandits. Toko could not help closing her eyes as they drew close, but Sugaru's tactic caught the men off guard, and she and Sugaru swept through, leaving them far behind.

"You see. I told you," Sugaru said triumphantly.

Still in a cold sweat, Toko wondered whether she could stand to travel like this much longer. "I have yet to figure out if it's good or bad that someone like you is the bearer of the magatama," she said.

"What do you mean?" Sugaru said, looking surprised. "You won't find a better man than me no matter where you look." He so clearly meant it that Toko dropped the subject.

The next day they ran into the bandits again. But this time they were mounted. After confirming they had Toko and Sugaru, they charged.

"They don't give up, do they?" Sugaru said.

"They didn't like you making fools of them, that's why."

There were more of them than on the previous day, and Toko and Sugaru had no choice but to flee. They rode as hard as they could, but the bandits' light-footed steeds gained on them quickly.

"Toko!" Sugaru yelled. "Keep going! Flee to the forest and don't stop!" Toko could see the dense trees looming up ahead. Biting her lip, she urged her steed on.

"See you later," Sugaru called out. Toko looked back in surprise to see him riding away, his red hair streaming in the wind. He planned to stop their pursuers and let her escape. *But how...*

He was clearly outnumbered—just one against ten or more. He might be strong, but there was a limit to what even he could do. She drew her horse up. *I can't leave him to fight alone.* Her mind flashed back to the day she had left the fort at Kamitsusato. Recalling the anguish that had wrung her heart then, she knew that she could not escape on her own. Turning her horse, she sped back.

The bandits, seeing Sugaru and Toko racing toward them, opened their ranks and spread out to surround them. Glancing back over his shoulder, Sugaru looked shocked to see Toko riding up behind. "Idiot!" he yelled. "Go back!" But it was too late. Several of the men had turned their mounts to let her through, then quickly crossed in front of her, cutting her off from Sugaru. Spooked, her horse reared. Ropes flew through the air, snaring Toko and her steed. *They're going to take my horse.* The men yanked the ropes tight, and before she knew it neither she nor her horse could move. Falling to the ground, Toko saw several men leap toward her. She had had no chance to even draw her sword. She closed her eyes, certain that she would be killed.

But no matter how long she waited, nothing happened. Although she could hear what sounded like a fierce battle raging, no one even touched her. She opened her eyes cautiously and then stared in astonishment. A shadow, outlined in light, was wreaking havoc like some sort of malevolent spirit. Terrified horses screamed and reared, dumping their riders on the ground as they fled in panic. The riders staggered to their feet only to be felled, one by one, like trees in a high wind. Yet no blood flew. Squinting against the glare, Toko saw that the strange apparition wielded not a real sword, but a wooden one—or rather, a stick, the stick that Sugaru had sheathed in a scabbard of woven vines just to make it look like a sword.

Recognizing the haloed creature to be none other than Sugaru, Toko calmed her racing heart. She chided herself for thinking, even for a moment, that he was some kind of demon. Even so, she was still a little afraid. When he finished off the last bandit and strode over to her, she could not help cringing.

"So you just couldn't bear to be parted from me," Sugaru teased her. "You need to practice doing what you're told."

Toko was so relieved to hear him sound like his old self that tears pricked her eyes. "I was going to help you . . . but I see that you didn't need it."

"Did I scare you?" Sugaru asked, crouching down to peer into her face. Toko nodded silently. "Are you still afraid?"

She looked up at him. "Sugaru," she said. "Did you know? From before?"

"Yeah. I found out when we routed the guys from Mahoroba at the mountain of fire." He scratched his nose, looking slightly sheepish. "I didn't want to frighten you. That's why I told you to go on ahead."

"Is that the power of the magatama?"

"Yes. Because now there are two."

Toko sighed. "I feel like I'm finally beginning to understand. Stringing the magatama together to make the Misumaru isn't that simple, is it?"

"You're not kidding. Every time you add a new one, their power increases. I can't imagine what it's going to be like when there're three or even four of them. I've just got two and already I'm not quite human."

Toko looked at him. *If it weren't Sugaru, I would have been even more afraid. Because it's him, I can handle it. Maybe that's another reason he's the bearer.*

"Are you ready to give up the quest then, Toko?" Sugaru said, flashing another of his wicked grins.

"Don't be ridiculous. That was nothing," she replied indignantly. She jumped to her feet and began brushing the grass and dirt from her clothes. "It's only natural that the Misumaru is powerful. After all, it can defeat the Sword. I'm going to get that string of beads no matter what. So—" She hesitated for a second, then continued. "Please come with me, Sugaru. I want you to be there to the very end. I need your power."

Sugaru just smiled, looking highly satisfied.

THE BANDITS STILL lay sprawled on the ground, but unfortunately, Toko's and Sugaru's horses had fled. "There'll have been no point to this if we lose our horses. Let's go find them. They're sure to be somewhere close by," Sugaru said. They had run off in the direction from which Toko and Sugaru had originally come, so the pair retraced their steps. They passed through the dim light of the wood and out into the open again. There, an unexpected sight awaited them. Row upon row of bandits, their weapons held at the ready, stood facing Toko and Sugaru. Evidently, the men Sugaru had beaten were not the only members of that band. A whole troop confronted them.

2

TOKO FELT SUGARU brace himself beside her. He was planning to fight. But now there were thirty or forty men confronting them. Even if Sugaru could beat them, Toko had had enough. She didn't want him to test his power like that. She didn't want him to see how much of that power his body could actually take.

The bandits did not attack immediately, perhaps because they had already heard of Sugaru's extraordinary strength. Both sides just stood there, glaring at each other for several moments, when suddenly a voice broke the silence.

"Lady Toko? It can't be. Is that Lady Toko from Mino?"

"Who is it?" Toko asked, searching for the speaker. From the midst of the band stepped a fearsome man, a giant in both girth and height. Keen eyes, heavy brows, and a hawklike nose. No longer young, his calm self-possession made it clear that he was their leader. Toko doubted her own eyes. She knew this man.

"Nanatsuka?" she said, her voice husky. "But I thought you died along with the prince . . . "

"So it *is* you, Lady Toko." He sighed. "To think that we should meet again like this. I'm ashamed to even look you in the face. Yes, I should have died. But for some reason, fate deemed otherwise, so here I stand before you. Although in your eyes that in itself must seem a great disgrace."

Toko stood rooted to the spot. It was his voice, not his words, that held her mesmerized; his was a voice that summoned a flood of memories, transporting her back to the world as it had once been when Nanatsuka was there in Mino with the merry Prince Oh-usu and his radiant Lady Akaru. Toko came back to the present and suddenly she was flying toward him, leaping into his arms like a little bird alighting on a huge and ancient tree.

"How can you say that? I'm so glad you're alive! Thank you for recognizing me."

Nanatsuka seemed stunned. "Lady Toko . . . you haven't changed a bit."

The band of thieves lowered their bows at this unexpected turn of events, glancing uneasily at Sugaru. But no one dared to interrupt. Sugaru was just as confused. Folding his arms, he called out irritably, "How fortunate that you've found an old friend, Toko. Why don't you tell him to return our horses so we can get out of here?"

"But first you must let us make up for our rude welcome," Nanatsuka said. "If I had known that it was Lady Toko and her companion, we would never have done this. We've never encountered anyone before who could lead us around in circles like that. How about it? Our base is nearby. Won't you allow me to offer you some hospitality to atone for what we did?"

"I'm not interested in befriending any bandits. I haven't fallen that low," Sugaru said curtly. "Toko, hurry up. Let's go."

Nanatsuka looked at Toko. "Who is that red-haired young man?" he asked. "He's as strong and fearless as a demon."

"His name's Sugaru. He's from Izumo," Toko said. She needed to do something to bridge the gap between the two men. Turning to Sugaru, she said, "I want to hear what Nanatsuka has to say. I'd like to accept his invitation. I can vouch for him. He's a good man."

"You're the one who's always in a hurry. Not me."

"I know. And I'm saying that I'd like to take a little detour. So there's even less reason for you to hurry, right?"

Sugaru looked disgruntled, but still he came and together they followed Nanatsuka to his fort.

NANATSUKA, it turned out, was the leader of a small army of thieves. When they reached his base in the mountains, Toko was surprised. Built directly into a cliff, it looked more like a rock castle than a fort.

"You were such a faithful servant to the prince. I had no idea you had this other side," she said.

"I was a bandit before the prince found me and took me into his service."

Caves had been carved into the bare rock, and rope ladders hung down to the ground and also across the cliff face, from cave entrance to cave entrance, to ensure swift passage. The fortress was equipped with a watchtower, stables, and a kitchen as well. Toko and Sugaru were led high up the cliff to a cave reserved for Nanatsuka. Although it was just a hole in the rock, the interior was luxurious, with furs covering the floor and a fire to keep the space dry.

"You certainly live in style, don't you? " Sugaru said bluntly. "Stealing from innocent travelers. You won't get away with this for long, you know."

"It's true we take tribute that's headed for the capital. But we try to limit our evil deeds to that," Nanatsuka said.

"You expect me to believe that when you tried so hard to kill us?"

"That—" Nanatsuka suddenly broke into a grin. "You were just so much stronger than us. It was a matter of pride. And besides, I thought that anyone as strong as you could only be heading to Mahoroba on a secret mission with some important message."

"And what if we had been?"

Nanatsuka paused to give Sugaru a measured look. "We don't intend to spend the rest of our days as thieves," he said finally. "We're gathering our strength so that when the time is right we can infiltrate the capital and take revenge on the emperor."

Sugaru and Toko both started in surprise. "The emperor?"

Nanatsuka looked at Toko. "There are quite a few among my men who survived the battle in Mino. They all loved the prince. They joined me because they share the same goal. Every one of them was willing to sever their attachments to their families and the world and become outcasts—we won't let it end like this."

"You're going to avenge the prince's death?" Toko asked in a small voice.

"What else can I do? Why else did I survive? I'd have no regrets about sacrificing my life for my prince."

Toko felt tears rising. "I know how you feel," she said. "Because I feel the same way. That's why I'm here. Only you said that you're going to take revenge on the emperor. But it was Prince Ousu who killed the prince."

"At first, that's what I thought too. I thought that I could never forgive him for his betrayal. I already tried to kill him once. But . . . in the end, I came to see that it's the emperor who's behind it all. That cold, hard man who sends his own flesh and blood to war and death, he's the true monster."

"But Prince Ousu is the one who wields the Sword," Toko protested. "The Sword is an abomination. It twists fate and brings death and destruction to all. And not just to Mino. The Sword has left tragedy in its wake everywhere. Terrible things will happen if it isn't stopped and the bearer destroyed."

Nanatsuka stared at Toko in disbelief. "Lady Toko, you aren't thinking of taking revenge against Prince Ousu yourself, are you?"

Toko looked surprised that he should even ask. "Didn't I mention it? We're on a quest to find the Misumaru, which is powerful enough to defeat the Sword. That's why we're going to Mahoroba."

"But, Lady Toko, you can't possibly."

"I can understand why you might think so, but you're wrong. It's my duty as a Tachibana. Since ancient times, my people have been endowed with the power to sheathe the Sword."

Nanatsuka's face remained clouded. "That's not what I meant. Lady Toko, do you seriously mean to kill him, to kill your Oguna?"

"Don't say that," Toko said sharply.

But Nanatsuka continued. "Remember the time we met in Nobono? You wept inconsolably. How can you possibly kill someone for whom you shed so many tears? It's not right. It would be like killing your own self."

"Oguna's dead." She leaned forward, her voice fierce. "It's precisely because I grieve for him, precisely because I wept for him, that I must do this. It's the only thing that I can do for him, now that he's changed beyond recognition. I have no intention of letting anyone else do it."

Realizing that it was better to change the subject, Nanatsuka called for food and drink. The meal was as rich as the furnishings. Plates piled high with grilled meats and big bowls of stew were placed on the table. Drawn by the food, Toko regained her cheerful spirits. She rarely had a proper meal while traveling. She consumed whatever was put in front of her, but the sake proved to be a little too strong. Soon her head felt fuzzy and she could no longer carry on a conversation.

"Whoops. I should have thought of that," Nanatsuka said. He quickly removed the sake cup from Toko's hand, but by this time she was already hopelessly drunk. After some commotion, she was carried to a room that housed the few women in the fort, after which she knew no more.

In stark contrast, Sugaru downed cup after cup but showed no sign of getting drunk. Impressed, Nanatsuka kept pouring more. "I know that thieving is not something I should recommend as a profession," he said, "but it's a shame to bid farewell to someone as strong and fearless as you. How do you intend to use those abilities? Would you consider joining us in overthrowing the emperor?"

Sugaru emptied his cup yet again. "I'm not interested in saving the world. I'm going to go home and get married. I have to take care of the old man."

"Then why are you here, traveling with Lady Toko?"

Sugaru paused for a moment and then blurted out, "You know, I've been wanting to ask you something. I'm a bit confused. When you and Toko were talking before, it sounded like Oguna and Prince Ousu are the same person."

"They are. Oguna is Ousu. Ousu is Oguna."

"Are you sure?"

"I've never been more sure of anything in my life. Prince Oh-usu named Oguna Ousu when he brought him from Mino."

Sugaru scowled. "That Toko . . . She didn't tell me. I might have chosen differently if I had known."

"She couldn't tell you. Or, more likely, she refuses to even let herself think of it." Nanatsuka's voice was heavy. "When I first saw them in Mino, Toko and Oguna were like two little lovebirds. When they laughed, they had exactly the same look on their faces. But everything changed so quickly once Oguna came to the capital. He took up the Sword and led the forces that invaded Mino. He robbed Toko of everything she loved—her land, her people. Hating him would not be enough."

"I can't believe it." Sugaru gazed up at the ceiling. "The only time I've ever seen Toko look like that is when she's talking about Oguna. And now you tell me that all this time she was actually talking about the man she plans to kill. What does she mean 'he's dead'? She's out of her mind."

"Lady Toko mustn't kill Oguna. It would be better for me to kill him than she." Nanatsuka spoke with such vehemence that Sugaru looked at him in surprise.

"Ousu was my pupil from the age of twelve to sixteen," Nanatsuka explained. "He was quiet, but a quick learner. We got along well. When he killed Prince Oh-usu, I felt responsible, because I had trained him. I decided that I would have to kill him with my own hands. I thought that maybe that was why I hadn't managed to die during the war. I escaped west with the remnants of our forces. There was a village in the south of Izumo that was loyal to the prince. We waited there for an opportunity."

Sugaru nodded. "I heard about that. So the band that was rumored to have attacked the prince was yours, was it?"

"Yes. Then you know what happened. It was a disaster. We were destroyed by the Sword without even a fight. It's a mystery to me that I'm still alive. All that was left was a burnt field." He rubbed a hand over his face and then continued. "But what stays seared in my memory is not the fire or the destruction. It's the expression I saw on Ousu's face a moment before that flash of light. He recognized me. He realized that I, Nanatsuka, had come to kill him. And his eyes . . . I will take that memory with me to the grave. Until that moment, I never realized how special I was to him. I never knew how few people he had trusted. But it was too late. He knew what I had come to do. And then there was that flash of light."

Nanatsuka sighed deeply and drained his cup. "I fell into a ditch. That's what saved me. I had survived yet again, and so I began to think . . . What was it that drove Ousu to that point? What victor in the world has eyes like that? That's when I realized that the emperor is the ultimate cause. You must not let Lady Toko go through with this."

Sugaru was playing absently with a chicken bone. His fingers tightened and it snapped in two. Staring at the pieces, he said, "Toko doesn't know how to be flexible. If she isn't careful, she'll break . . . like this. And even if I try to convince her, she won't listen. I may have taken on more than I can handle this time."

WHEN TOKO woke the next day, it was already past noon. She had slept off the effects of the sake and was feeling quite refreshed, but she had a vague memory of being rather noisy the night before. When she apologized to the women who brought her some food, they burst out laughing. "You sang every song you knew. That was the first time you'd ever had a drink? Well, that explains it then."

Oh dear. I hope I didn't sing in front of Nanatsuka and Sugaru.

Feeling embarrassed and contrite, she went to Nanatsuka, but he did not even broach the subject. Instead, he said, "I already told Sugaru last night, but I'd like to accompany you to Mahoroba. What do you think?" Toko looked at him in amazement. "I may have a clue to where you can find the magatama you're looking for," he continued. "After I heard your story, I remembered something. One of Prince Oh-usu's soldiers was a man named Miyadohiko. He came from a place called Kazuragi in the southwest of Mahoroba. I'm pretty sure that he belonged to an ancient line of priests that venerated a magatama. Perhaps I can help you get more information. He was killed in the war, but if we visit his family—"

Toko clapped her hands together. "I couldn't have hoped for anything better! But is it really all right for you to come with us?"

"I was thinking of establishing a stronger foothold in the capital anyway. I have a reason to go already, so I won't be going out of my way." This was very encouraging. Nanatsuka had spent many years in the capital and would know his way around, unlike Toko and Sugaru, neither of whom had ever visited there.

Thank goodness, Toko thought. *It looks like I didn't sing in front of Nanatsuka after all.* Nanatsuka knew that within her own clan Toko ranked as high as a princess; she would have felt ashamed to have behaved like that in front of him.

Just then, Sugaru walked up. Toko tried to be nonchalant, and he did not burst out laughing at her. She was just breathing a sigh of relief when he suddenly placed a hand on her head. "You poor thing," he said.

"Why?" Toko asked, startled.

"Don't you know any songs other than nursery rhymes?"

3

CLOUDS OF DUST billowed up from the main street, a broad road so well trodden that not even the most wayward weed could grow. Toko and Sugaru had at long last set foot in the capital. At a crossroads near the edge of the city was a marketplace overflowing with goods from every part of the land. This was exactly where the three of them were headed, leading packhorses hung with unglazed pots. Nanatsuka had insisted that posing as peddlers from the rural provinces was the best way to enter the capital without attracting suspicion.

Toko could not help staring about in open curiosity. They were right in the middle of the busiest place in the entire capital. To her, it seemed like a dazzling, colorful melting pot teeming with people, people, and more people—all strutting about, showing off their brilliant costumes.

"Aha, I see." Sugaru smiled. "Hmm. So eye-catching, it's hard to choose." The moment they had set foot on the main road, Sugaru had come to life like a fish returned to water. Toko, who knew why, watched him out of the corner of her eye while she listened to Nanatsuka tell them about the city.

"Far down on the left you can see the great gate. Beyond it is the emperor's palace. That roof you see over there is the chancellor's hall, and this grove of trees over here houses the royal mausoleum. And over there . . . "

Until they had entered the city, Toko had forgotten how much Sugaru stood out. It was no wonder that the place was going to his head. He wasn't just looking; he was being looked at in return. People passing by turned to stare. Even in the crowded, bustling capital, this red-haired, merry-eyed, long-legged youth effortlessly drew attention. And, to Toko's consternation, he was obviously enjoying it. Nanatsuka frowned in concern when he noticed the effect Sugaru was having.

"Sugaru," Toko said, "if you don't try to blend in a little more, we won't be able to walk with you. Why do you think we went to all the trouble of bringing packhorses?"

But her words did nothing to dampen his spirits. "No problem," he said amicably. "Let's go our separate ways then. Good thing Nanatsuka's here. I'm sure he can take care of you." Toko could only stare at him, speechless. Sugaru seized this chance to address Nanatsuka. "I'm so glad you came with us. Now I can finally get a break. I'm going to spread my wings a little bit. It's been such a long time."

"What do you mean 'get a break'?" Toko demanded.

"Give me two days—no, make that three—then let's meet again. I've come a long way without any entertainment. You can spare me for a few days, can't you?"

Toko was furious. "You worthless playboy. I overrated you. You really did come to Mahoroba just for the girls."

"No, for both." Sugaru grinned. "I haven't forgotten that we're hunting magatama. That's why I only asked for three days."

Nanatsuka nodded. "That should be enough time to find out about the priest of Kazuragi. Let's meet at the market in three days then."

"Nanatsuka!" Toko protested, but he just shrugged.

"I don't see what we can do to stop someone like him," he said.

"Exactly. You're a smart man." With a wave of his hand, Sugaru strode off laughing, leaving Toko behind to fume.

Realizing that there was no way to smooth things over, Nanatsuka did not even try to appease Toko. "He's quite the man," he said. "He can hold his drink, he's strong, and he has a way with women."

"He's a troublemaker, that's what he is. You'll be sorry you let him loose. You'll see." Toko was furious that Sugaru had dumped her on Nanatsuka as if she were so much unwanted baggage. But how could she say so? Especially when this might not have happened if Nanatsuka hadn't come.

"Follow me," Nanatsuka said. "We too can make good use of our time here. The market isn't just for trading goods. It's also where rumors congregate. We've set up a little hideout nearby so that some of my men can stay and gather information."

Making their way to the market, Toko and Nanatsuka set out just enough

wares to make it look like they were in business. Then Nanatsuka sat down
and became a friendly peddler who enjoyed a bit of gossip. He looked like he
could stay there all day just listening to others talk. Sitting beside him, Toko
saw what he meant. Many others were engaged in lively conversation instead
of buying and selling. Someone with ears to hear could trawl for information
and hook what they wanted just like a fisherman.

"Go and see all the exotic things in the market," Nanatsuka told her. "But
keep your ears open. That's the way to catch something big."

What I want most is news of Prince Ousu. I'll go see what I can find. With
this aim, Toko wove her way among the stalls. She did not have far to look.
She heard Prince Ousu's name everywhere she went. Here, so close to the
palace, he was praised as a brilliant warrior and revered almost as a god,
for the people of Mahoroba knew no better. It was only natural that they
would side with the prince, yet Toko began to feel irritated. *Try being on the
receiving end of the Sword for once,* she thought every time she heard him
called a hero. As she walked about, feeling far from tranquil, she began to
notice something else. Many people sided with the prince because they felt
he was being treated unfairly. Far from rewarding his son for his meritorious
service, the emperor, it seemed, ignored him.

The emperor, his own father, rejects him... So the glory that enveloped
Prince Ousu was not pure and untainted. Toko should have been glad, but
for some reason she did not feel like rejoicing. Why, she wondered, did his
father behave so coldly? She was even more bothered by the fact that people
talked about Prince Ousu as if he were not there. Hadn't he just returned
from the west? Then why wasn't he in Mahoroba?

Returning to Nanatsuka's stall, she found that he had already learned what
she wanted to know. "It looks like Prince Ousu has left," he said. "The emperor
didn't let him relax even for a moment before sending him off to conquer the
east. Such a convenient way to get rid of someone who's in your way."

"But why?" Toko asked.

"He did the same thing to Prince Oh-usu," Nanatsuka said, frowning. "That's
how he keeps power in Mahoroba to himself. By sending Prince Ousu off to
distant places, he excludes the prince from any meaningful role in the capital
and prevents him from gaining popular support."

TOKO'S CLAIM that Sugaru was a troublemaker proved to be prophetic. On the night of the third day, he caused an uproar that convulsed the entire city. Toko and Nanatsuka were asleep in their hideout, a hut located in a clump of trees near the market, but the clamor reached them even there. One of the men ordered by Nanatsuka to investigate returned to report. "The streets are filled with private guards bearing torches. It appears that thieves snuck into the chancellor's residence."

"Well, there're some thieves that deserve admiration here in the city too, it seems." Nanatsuka chuckled at his own remark without much concern. But as additional details reached him, it became clear that the situation was no laughing matter.

"They're saying that it was just one person, not a band of thieves. Apparently someone snuck into the chancellor's residence and abducted a concubine. I heard that he's being pursued to the west. He appears to possess extraordinary powers. The rumor is that he's not human but a demon. A demon in the guise of a young man with red hair."

Toko gasped. She could picture it vividly: Sugaru, a cocky grin on his face, caught in the light of burning torches; Sugaru, leaping boldly over a wall, the most beautiful woman in the capital under his arm.

"Is he out of his mind?" she said. "I'll never understand him."

"If it's really Sugaru, then we can't just wait around doing nothing," Nanatsuka said. "We have to help him escape." He moved to grab his gear, but Toko stopped him.

"He doesn't need our help. No, I'm not just saying that because I'm angry. I'm saying that because I know they'll never catch him. If you aren't careful, you'll give yourself away."

Nanatsuka's man agreed. "You and the lady have already been seen with him in the marketplace. I think it would be safest if you both left as soon as possible. Leave the rest to us."

It took a moment for Nanatsuka to decide, but then he nodded. "All right. Let's go on ahead to Kazuragi. Although I failed to find Miyadohiko's family in the capital, we should be able to find out more once we get there."

And so it was that Toko and Nanatsuka set out on the main road in the middle of the night, leaving Sugaru to his fate. Toko was angrier with Sugaru than she had ever been, and it did not help that she was also worried. She found it particularly hard to forgive him for using the magatama's power to serve his own selfish ends. He hadn't spared a thought for her and Nanatsuka. "What's so great about beautiful women anyway?" she grumbled. "I'll never trust him again. He's not suited to bear the magatama. I was a fool to even consider that he might be." Every time she thought of him, it made her angry all over again. Nanatsuka, on the other hand, seemed to have put all concern for Sugaru aside and to be focused solely on what they would do when they reached Kazuragi. Along the way, he shared his thoughts with Toko.

"Miyadohiko was a loyal soldier. When Prince Oh-usu rebelled, he gave up his life so that the prince could escape to Mino. But as far as Mahoroba was concerned, Miyadohiko was a traitor. This wouldn't be a problem in my case because I have no kin, but his family home was in Mahoroba. It would be very unlikely for his family to escape unpunished. According to my men, he came from an ancient line of shrine priests. His family home was destroyed and all his relations scattered. We haven't managed to find out where they went."

Toko prepared herself for the fact that finding leads would not be easy. No one willingly associated with those who fell out of favor with the emperor. She and Kisako had themselves needed to be very cautious after Mino fell.

Everywhere I go, the emperor has already been there first, persecuting those who guard the stones. I may not like it, but if he's trying to prevent us from gathering the Misumaru, he's right . . .

Just before they reached Kazuragi, Nanatsuka stopped at a small, empty hut previously selected as a base, and the next day he began cautiously probing for information.

TOKO, who had relied completely on Nanatsuka since their unexpected reunion, decided that the least she could do was cook up a meal. But what seemed like simple tasks—lighting a fire in the stove and placing the washed rice in a pot to boil—were much harder than she had thought. Her mother had once told her that a god lived in the stove, but Toko did not seem to have won his favor. She was so engrossed in blowing on the fire, fanning the flames, and peering inside, that she failed to notice there was someone behind her. She whirled around at the sound of chuckling.

"I must applaud your enthusiasm, but you're going to burn the rice with a fire that hot."

"Sugaru!" The demon that had caused chaos in the capital stood before her, looking completely at ease. Despite being three days late for their rendezvous, he showed no remorse. Toko was so indignant that at first she could not speak.

"I appear to have come at a good time. Feed me, will you? I haven't had a bite to eat since last night."

"No, I won't," Toko snapped. "Do you have any idea how much we—"

But Sugaru did not let her finish. "Please, don't be stubborn. I'm not alone."

Toko started. Outside the doorway where Sugaru stood, she could see a flash of mauve cloth—the edge of a woman's robe. "You didn't. Not . . . from the chancellor's hall . . . " Toko whispered.

With a nod, Sugaru pulled the girl inside and pushed her toward Toko. "The very one. Let me introduce you to Lady Kage. Lady, this is Toko, the Tachibana girl I was telling you about."

So here she was—the peerless belle from the capital, Toko thought, only to find that she was not. Lady Kage was certainly pretty, but to Toko's eyes she did not come even close to Kisako. She looked about eighteen, but she lacked Kisako's blossomlike blush, and her pale, sad face seemed listless. Toko could not imagine why Sugaru would have risked his life to make this woman his own. Still, Lady Kage was clearly exhausted. It seemed that Sugaru had not been lying about not having eaten since the previous night.

"I'm sorry to bother you," Lady Kage said. "But this gentleman encouraged me, and so I came . . . "

She looked as timid as a doe, and Toko could not find it in her heart to be unkind. "It's all right," she said. "Here, sit down. I'm afraid the food won't be very good."

These last words proved to be true; the rice was indeed burnt. The two fugitives, however, ate it without complaint. Toko heaved a sigh of relief. She had actually succeeded in feeding people for the first time in her life. At that moment, Nanatsuka returned. He did not seem surprised to see Sugaru, but when he looked at Sugaru's guest, his eyes widened.

"Are you by any chance related to Miyadohiko?"

"He was my elder brother. Did you know him?"

"I certainly did. You look very much like him."

They all marveled at this coincidence—all but Sugaru. "It's no coincidence," he said and looked at Toko. "As soon as we walked down that main road, I knew there was someone connected to the magatama nearby. The resonance between the stones is far stronger than before. But Lady Kage herself is not the bearer. Apparently, her family worshipped a god that now keeps the magatama."

Lady Kage nodded. "My father, Miyazukasa, intended to raise me as a shrine maiden. But he was stripped of his rank as priest after my older brother was killed, and he died disappointed, leaving my mother, several small children, and me behind. I agreed to enter the chancellor's hall in return for safe passage for my mother and siblings to Awa."

"No wonder we couldn't find any clues," Nanatsuka said. "It must have been terrible for you."

"I had given up all hope. Having been used as a concubine, I could never become a shrine maiden again. Yet out of all the women in the chancellor's hall, this gentleman found me. He told me that the magatama guided him. Thanks to him, I've regained my pride in my family heritage." Her eyes shone with gratitude as she looked at Sugaru.

Sugaru smiled and turned to Toko. "And I bet you were thinking something entirely different, weren't you? I hope you're sorry for misjudging me."

Toko shrugged. She could not think of a quick retort, but it still didn't change the fact that he had been off having fun on his own. Why else would Lady Kage look at him like that? Sugaru, she concluded, was wicked.

At their request, Lady Kage related what she knew about the shrine in Kazuragi. "There's a range of mountains behind our village. The god lives on the tallest peak. He has the body of a serpent, and he's a terrible, vengeful god. Just to put foot on the mountain brings down his wrath. Since the time of our ancestors long ago, my family has been entrusted with the task of stilling the god. There's an altar on the mountainside where we take offerings and pray for the safety of our village. It's forbidden to climb beyond that point, and those who try, whether priest or laymen, die by their own choosing. Once, an emperor climbed the mountain intending to subjugate the god. But before he had even reached the peak, he fled, barely escaping with his life, and he ordered everyone to leave the god alone. So no one has ever seen it—except the priest who was first entrusted with performing the rituals."

TOKO WANDERED away from the hut and strolled through the woods, thinking. She had plenty of time to think on her own. Sugaru and Lady Kage, who had spent the night traveling, needed rest, and Nanatsuka had rushed off to give new orders to his men. Every time Toko recalled the story Lady Kage had told them, she was more astonished. The magatama had left the hands of men and been given to a fierce and punishing god. As a Tachibana, Toko could not tell whether that action had been wise or deplorable. But there had probably been no alternative if they were to protect the magatama right here within reach of the emperor's hand.

The problem was how to wrest the stone from a god who was likely to kill anyone who came near. According to Lady Kage, not even members of her own family had ever met the god. It was unlikely that an outsider like Toko or Sugaru could enter his territory and come out safely.

If only I could ask the Keeper of the Shrine in Mino. I know nothing of the gods. I don't even understand the mission of the Tachibana or what I should do. There's so much that I don't know.

Despondent, she crouched down at the edge of a small creek. It was already close to sunset, and the shallow stream sparkled in the long rays of the sun that shone over the brow of the hill. After staring blankly at the water for some time, she reluctantly admitted to herself that Lady Kage, brought here by Sugaru, was one cause of her gloom. Toko was beginning to feel completely useless, just a burden, even to Sugaru. How could she retain any confidence when faced with this bond between Sugaru and Lady Kage, which had been forged by the magatama?

"So there you are. You made me look all over." Toko jumped and turned to see Sugaru approaching. To her surprise, dusk was already falling and the light was growing dim, even though she thought she had only paused for a moment.

"You're up already?"

"I didn't want to leave without telling you. Lady Kage and I are going to the mountain. I wanted to let you know." Toko opened her mouth, but Sugaru did not give her time to speak. "You're not coming. I told Lady Kage the same thing, but she won't listen. She says that she has a duty to pray and still the wrath of the god."

"Then how can you tell *me* not to come? Of course I'm going with you." Her voice was sharp.

"Knock it off, Toko. Can't you see how stupid that would be? Besides, why would we want a kid like you tagging along on our lover's tryst?"

"Sugaru, stop teasing me."

But Sugaru was indifferent to her anger. "All right then," he said with a faint smile, "I'll be serious. It's impossible for you to get the magatama this time. It's impossible for you or any other ordinary human being. You'll be killed. I'm the only one who can do it. Stay here and out of danger. I'm telling you this for your own sake."

"But it was *you* who came with *me,* wasn't it?" Toko cried. "Just who do you think was trying to gather the magatama in the first place? I'm the one who needs the Misumaru. I'm the one that's got to destroy the wielder of the Sword. I'm not going to back down now just because there's a little risk."

"It's about time you woke up, Toko," Sugaru said earnestly. "Stop pretending you don't know what everyone else knows. You can't become the bearer of the Misumaru. There's no way you can kill Prince Ousu. I know you're obsessed with this idea, but that's just because you can't forget Oguna. That's all. Even if he's now the wielder of the Sword, Oguna is still Oguna. And you still love him."

"That's not true!" Toko shouted. "I don't love him. I hate him. I hate him so much that if I don't kill him with my own hands I'll never get over it. Sugaru, why are you saying these things? Don't you see that I can't possibly stop now?"

"It's all right," he said, his expression lightening. "I'll kill him for you. I'll avenge you and your people. No matter how you look at it, I'm the warrior who must bear the Misumaru. I now know that we can't let Prince Ousu live. Leave it to me, Toko. And forget your obsession. It's unnatural. If you carry on like that, you'll never escape from his shadow."

Toko's voice was shaking. "No! You can't do this. Please don't take that away from me. It has to be me who goes to him."

"If you said that you loved him, I could understand your insistence. Why won't you admit what you really want?"

His words confused her and her confusion made her angrier. "Don't judge me by your standards. Don't put me in the same category as people like you who lose sight of reality because of so-called love."

Sugaru gave up. "Stubborn little squirt. Don't come, you hear me? If you do, you'll be sorry." He turned and began walking away.

"Sugaru!" Toko ran after him, but he spun around and put his finger on her nose.

"Listen. You're not the one who bears the stones. You have no right to put your life at risk. Whether he wills it or not, the bearer becomes something not quite human. Your Prince Ousu is the same. He's no longer human. But you, Toko, you're just an ordinary girl. Think about that until it sinks in." His face was stern, and Toko felt as if he had shoved her away. Not even she could follow him after that. She burst into tears. Sugaru strode off through the trees without a backward glance—toward the place where Lady Kage waited.

Stupid Sugaru! Toko wept out loud and threw herself onto the ground, crushing the grass in her fists. She could not help but feel sorry for herself. Never had she dreamed that Sugaru would betray her in this way. He had told her he didn't need her. He had told her not to come because she wasn't the bearer of the magatama. Yet even as she reeled with shock and felt all hope ebb away, a tiny flame flickered stubbornly inside her. *I know it's illogical. I know there's no proof. But even so, it still has to be me who goes to Oguna. It has to be . . . If only I had a magatama. Then I could prove it . . .* Suddenly her eyes flew open and she gazed into the darkness that was closing in on her. A crazy idea had just entered her mind.

There is a stone in Mahoroba. One besides Lady Kage's. In the palace. In the emperor's hall. Lady Akaru's magatama.

4

NANATSUKA had returned to the marketplace on the main road to contact his men. While he had been away, several incidents had occurred that required his instructions, and after discussing the situation with his followers, he had spent the night at the hideout, intending to return to Kazuragi in the morning. He was thus astounded to wake the next day and find Toko, her eyes red and swollen, standing outside the door.

"What're you doing here?" he demanded. "Where are Sugaru and Lady Kage?"

Toko smiled. "They've gone to find the god on the mountain. I walked all night to get here."

"Couldn't you stay put and wait in the hut? That was so dangerous. What if you'd been captured by bandits?" Toko burst out laughing for Nanatsuka appeared to have forgotten that he himself was a bandit. There was a hard edge to her laughter, however, and Nanatsuka quickly realized that something must have happened. "What was so pressing that you couldn't wait until morning?" he asked.

"It's quite simple. You're planning to take revenge on the emperor, right? And you have men in the market who gather information for you. So I thought you'd be the best person to tell me how to sneak into the emperor's palace."

Nanatsuka hastily grabbed Toko's arm and pulled her inside, closing the door firmly behind her. "That's not something to talk about lightly. It's a good way to shorten your life. What's going on?"

"I want to get Lady Akaru's magatama," Toko said, a fierce light in her eyes.

"You're planning to sneak inside and steal it?"

Toko nodded.

"That's crazy."

"I know it's crazy. But it's not impossible. No matter how strong the emperor may be, he's still only human. He's not a god like the one Sugaru has to face. If he's human, then even I should be able to do something about him. You can't be sure that it's impossible for me to get the stone."

Nanatsuka thought he could now understand what had happened. "So you had a fight with Sugaru, did you?"

"That's not the problem." Her gaze was so resolute that Nanatsuka was taken aback. "Sugaru is doing what he needs to do to get the magatama. I can't blame him for doing that. And when I think about it rationally, the reason he pushed me away was out of consideration for me. He didn't come to destroy the wielder of the Sword by choice, you know. Nanatsuka, the bearer of the

Misumaru must be me. I can't keep taking advantage of Sugaru's kindness. If I don't lay my own life on the line, then I'll never know if I have what it takes to be the bearer."

Nanatsuka sighed. "You're willing to go that far to get to Prince Ousu?"

"It's a gamble," Toko replied. She remembered how she had viewed Sugaru and his friends' love of gambling with contempt. Now, however, it was her turn to gamble, her turn to stake everything on the greatest, most desperate chance of all.

"I can see in your eyes that you've already made up your mind. You're ready to give up everything and still laugh," Nanatsuka said. "You remind me of Lady Akaru. When she fled with the prince, her eyes were just like yours. She was dazzling. I would have been justified in hating her for causing the prince's downfall, yet I couldn't find it in myself to hate her. It made me glad to see them together." He paused for a long time, lost in thought. Toko was silent too, following her own memories. Finally, Nanatsuka said, "So you say that the emperor has something that belonged to her, a memento, right? It would be unjust to leave it with the man who treated her so cruelly. I'm sure the prince would be very angry."

Toko's heart began to pound. "You mean . . . you'll help me? You'll tell me how to sneak into the palace?"

"I will be your guide. I walked the palace from one end to the other many times with the prince. I know it well." He flashed her a quick grin. "It's a matter of my honor as a thief. Let's find it and get it back."

NANATSUKA set his men to work and by evening everything was ready. Calling Toko to him, he quickly explained. "We managed some time ago to infiltrate strategic points in the palace. We have only a handful of men inside, mind you, but they'll help us once we're in. As for Lady Akaru's magatama, there are three possible places where it might be kept—the treasury behind the emperor's hall where he keeps almost all his gems, his dressing chamber where the court ladies wait and where he keeps oft-used accessories, and, finally, his own room. We won't know where it is until we actually see it, but there's a record of all his treasures that I'm having checked secretly right now."

"When are we going?"

"Tonight," Nanatsuka answered, as if he had guessed that Toko couldn't wait.

"Really?"

"We got word that there's a huge banquet planned. People will be distracted by all the entertainment. How could we pass up an opportunity like that?"

"But won't it be easier for people to see us? They'll light more torches and there'll be more people everywhere."

"No problem. We'll dress as if we belong there too. You'll go as a court lady and I'll go as an officer. The palace is so crowded that it's quite common to run into people you've never seen before."

One of Nanatsuka's men prepared clothes for them. Toko stared at her outfit in admiration. How he had managed to procure it she didn't know, but it was made of real silk. The top robe was a beautiful jade green tied with red ribbons, and the long skirt with embroidered hem was as light as cicada wings. The costume came complete with a crimson comb and a hair ornament decorated with artificial flowers. Even when Toko had lived in Mino, she had never worn anything as luxurious as this. Of course, she had refused to wear skirts or anything feminine in the first place, but that was beside the point.

Well, it can't be helped. It's a disguise after all, she told herself, though she couldn't help feeling a flutter of excitement. The skirt, the first she had ever worn, was so light and soft it made her feel like she was floating. She could not take long strides in her usual manner without stepping on the hem, but she'd adjust to that somehow. The problem was the hair ornament in her hand. She had always worn her hair in a simple ponytail and had never put it up by herself. She was still struggling when Nanatsuka came to see how she was faring.

With a laugh, he said, "Here. Give me that, will you?" Despite his huge, knobby fingers, he deftly fixed her hair. He brushed it until it shone, then wound it up into a bun and fixed it in place with the comb. Into this he slid the hair ornament.

"Nanatsuka, you can do anything!" Toko said in awe.

"I've tried my hand at a lot of different things since I left home, you know."

"Where are you from?"

"A land so far away that no one here has ever heard of it. Hidakami."

The name seemed familiar to Toko. "The land of Hidakami . . . where the sun rises?" she exclaimed.

"Yes, it's a remote place at the far eastern edge of this country."

"Nanatsuka, there are Tachibana there too, guarding a magatama." Excited, Toko told him what little she knew, but it did not seem to spark any memories.

Nanatsuka shook his head. "It's unfortunate, but I never heard any tale like that where I was born. It's a land of great open spaces, nothing like here. Just wide meadows and soaring mountains. So perhaps the people you speak of do live there somewhere. I come from a place where the Emishi, another race, mingle with the people of Toyoashihara. Someday I would love to show you Hidakami. The wind sweeps through the reeds that stretch as far as the eye can see; deer and wild horses race through the morning mist. That's what my home is like."

The homesickness in his voice touched Toko's heart. *The fact that he never showed it must make his yearning for his homeland all the stronger,* she thought. He remained silent for some time and then said, "Once I told Prince Ousu about the herds of deer in the reeds. That was when Prince Oh-usu was alive and I was still planning to retire to Hidakami someday."

Toko suddenly remembered that Prince Ousu was now heading east. Did he recall the tale Nanatsuka had told him?

Toko was ready. Nanatsuka held out his hand and helped her rise to her feet where he carefully inspected her. Seeing the admiration in his face, she waited, expecting a compliment. "You can have confidence, Toko," he said, nodding. "You definitely look like a woman."

SUGARU and Lady Kage stopped and looked up at the crosspiece over a dilapidated shrine gate. They had wound their way up the mountainside and were now standing before the altar. Behind it, the slope rose steeply upward, but the peak was hidden beneath a menacing cloudbank that had become lower and denser as they climbed. By now, the clouds were dark and glowering, pressing down upon their heads.

"This altar is the boundary," Lady Kage said. "Beyond this point is the god's territory, the place from which those who enter can never return."

Sugaru looked up at the cloud. "All right. You stay here and pray that the god of the mountain peak doesn't get too upset. I suppose it would be asking too much to pray that he won't get mad at all."

He seemed about to leave without saying goodbye. Lady Kage called after him. "Do you have to go? Even though it means you'll be punished by the god? Do you really have to get that magatama?"

"Don't worry. I'll be fine. I'll come back with the stone."

Lady Kage shook her head. "How can I not worry about you? The god at the top of this mountain is terrible. If you don't come back, I'll never be able to forgive myself."

"I wouldn't bother going if the odds weren't good. I'm not an ordinary man." He smiled at her. "You should know that."

Lady Kage looked at him sadly. "When I first saw you in the chancellor's hall, I thought you were a god, not a man—a god materializing out of a whirlwind right in front of me. I thought the same thing when you grabbed me and ran. As long as I live, I will never forget how a god descended to the earth to save me. But . . . " She cast her eyes down. "Your hand is warm. You laugh and you feel pain. I do not think that I can merely worship you as a shrine maiden worships a god. I am afraid for you, afraid of this battle with the merciless god of the mountain peak. I'm so worried I can't bear it."

"I'm glad you care. But I'm not going to lose," Sugaru said cheerfully. "I've never lost a fight yet. And I'm not going to this time either."

Lady Kage handed him a dagger with a red hilt and scabbard. "In that case, at least take this. It's a protective charm that has been passed down from priest to priest in my family. If you should provoke the god's wrath, throw this on the ground and you'll be aided, but only once. Or at least, so it's said."

"Thank you. I'll take it."

Lady Kage knew that it was futile to try and stop him. She said sadly, "If I were a true shrine maiden, I'd go with you. I'd go with you to the end no matter what happened. If only I hadn't been defiled. If only my virtue hadn't been violated in the chancellor's service."

"You shouldn't dwell on such things," Sugaru said, comforting her in his own unique style. "You're not defiled. Being a shrine maiden means being strong-willed. You'll only bring yourself down if you go around thinking you're unclean. You didn't do those things by choice. Your heart is still pure.

If you believe in yourself, then the god will have to respect you. But don't worry. I'll be fine on my own. I'll come back, I promise. You wait here."

He waved the bright red sheath and then strode up the mountain, smiling. Lady Kage stood beside the altar and watched him go. She continued to stare long after he had vanished from sight, as if she could still see him in the distance.

5

THE BANQUET WAS in honor of fireflies. On the south side of the emperor's hall was a garden with a pond and stream large enough for boating. Thousands of fireflies had been brought in from outlying regions to be released: an extravagant entertainment perfect for a summer's night. Packhorses and carts laden with food for the feast, as well as firefly cages, passed through the large gate into the palace grounds.

"We couldn't have asked for anything better," Nanatsuka said, taking in the situation. "To enjoy the light of the fireflies, they'll have to use fewer torches, and once everyone is in the garden, the number of guards in the palace will decrease." Toko nodded. The night seemed to have been planned just for them. Surely the gods were on their side.

They waited until the sun had set, and then walked around behind the palace where one of Nanatsuka's spies, employed as a servant, led them safely inside. Tall fences enclosed the palace grounds, and guards with spears and whistles seemed to be stationed everywhere. Toko and Nanatsuka followed their guide as he carefully bypassed each one. Without his help, Toko realized, they would never have made it into the inner reaches of the palace.

"Remember, don't do anything rash," Nanatsuka warned Toko. "Tonight we only need to find out where the magatama is. As you can see, we can enter anytime we want. There'll be other opportunities to actually steal it." Toko nodded solemnly. She was so nervous she could think of nothing but carrying out the task assigned to her. They were planning to split up and explore the treasury, the dressing chamber, and the emperor's room. Toko would go to the latter, which was why she was dressed as a court lady. Only the emperor's wives and the court ladies who served closest to him were allowed free access to his quarters.

As they drew closer to the garden, the stir of voices and instruments being tuned drifted toward them on the evening breeze. A host of musicians must have been invited to perform. The sound of their flutes and stringed instruments warming up was an overture to the spectacular event to follow. Even Toko, who certainly did not have time to spare, felt her heart beat faster in anticipation. She took a deep breath, and the scent of summer—green leaves and water—filled her. *How lucky are those who can stop to appreciate the season,* she thought. But she felt no envy. For her, time was still something through which she raced rather than something she regretted passing her by. There would be time enough to enjoy the seasons later.

Up ahead, she saw a covered walkway that must have run all the way to the emperor's quarters. Nanatsuka had already separated from them, heading for the treasury. Toko looked at the other man and nodded. From here she was on her own. She left the shadows of the bushes and, making sure no one was in sight, pulled herself onto the edge of the platform and hoisted herself over the railing and onto the walkway. Light and quick, a moment later she was on the other side smoothing her robes.

All right. Let's get on with it. With a glance back at the shrubs, she saw that the third man in their party had already disappeared and so turned her attention to the walkway. It made a sharp turn up ahead and continued on, passing under the large overhanging eaves of a building on the left. *That must be the emperor's quarters.* She had only taken a few steps, however, when she stopped short. Three women exited the building and began gliding along the corridor toward her. The light was already dim but still Toko shrank back.

Turning the corner, the women saw her. "Who are you?" one of them asked. "His Highness has already gone. If you're new here, you should already be lined up outside."

To say nothing at all would arouse their suspicions. Toko was desperately trying to formulate a reply when one of the others said, "Oh, never mind the slowpoke. If we don't hurry up ourselves, we'll be late. They'll have extinguished the torches by the time we get there, and then we won't get to ride in the boats."

Toko was fortunate that they were in such a hurry. Without pressing her any further, the court ladies moved away with a rustle of silk. Toko took a deep breath and calmed her pounding heart. By the time she reached the emperor's quarters, it was much darker. She could hear cheers from the garden. *They must have put out the torches and freed the fireflies.* Peering inside the building, Toko saw that one lamp remained lit in the inner chamber, its light diffused through a thin curtain. She held her breath and waited a long time, but she did not sense anyone else nearby. Gathering her courage, she pulled the curtain aside.

No one was there. Contrary to Toko's expectations, the emperor's room was amazingly bare. It was just a big empty room, its walls draped with pleated purple cloth. A black chair inlaid with mother of pearl sat on a dais against the far wall. *That must be the emperor's throne,* Toko thought. Beside it stood a small side table with a pitcher of water on it. That, however, was the only furniture.

Could this really be the room of the man who rules over Mahoroba? It was a cold place. Surely Akaru's magatama could not be here. It seemed unlikely that this emperor would keep anything at all close to hand. Toko passed in front of the throne and was about to enter the chamber beyond when she stopped, startled. At first she did not know why. She had not seen or heard anything nor had she sensed any danger. Deciding it was nothing, she moved forward, but there it was again. It felt like a tiny golden bell ringing beside her. She listened intently in the direction she thought it came from. And then she remembered. *Sugaru talked about something like this . . . He said the magatama jingle like a bell when they call. Could this be it?*

Her heart racing, Toko looked carefully around the throne room one more time. On the side table near the throne she noticed a small box that had been concealed by a fold in the curtain. The instant she saw it, she knew with a certainty that surprised even her. *The magatama is calling me. If not, this could not possibly have happened.* Joy surged through her. The magatama of Mino, Lady Akaru's stone, and Toko's as well. The stone wanted her, just as she had longed for it. Stepping up onto the dais, she reached out to pick up the box—then froze.

Without any warning at all, a man spoke from behind her, there, where no one should have been.

"What are you doing?"

Toko felt her blood sink to her feet as she turned to look.

"What are you doing here? In the middle of the banquet?" The man repeated. He had a sword on his hip and appeared to be an officer.

Toko hastily covered her face with her sleeve. "I was late going out and there were no lights . . . "

"A new lady-in-waiting, are you?" he said. Toko's relief, however, was short-lived. He strode toward her and grabbed her by the wrist. She had no time to even cry out. Yanking her toward him, he dragged her toward the lamp. Then, taking her chin, he forced her face into the light.

"Ah, I thought as much. I've seen you before," he said in a low voice. Toko stopped struggling and looked up at him in surprise. She could see him clearly now. His long hair was tied back, and his face... Toko remembered it very well. She had met him once in Mino and once again in Himuka. The worst possible person had discovered her. She had no hope of passing herself off as a court lady now.

"I didn't know that you'd returned from the mountain of fire," Toko said.

"Nor I you." His grip on her arm tightened, yet his voice was soft. "Let me hear you explain what the girl from Himuka is doing tonight in the emperor's chambers."

THOUSANDS OF FIREFLIES flitted through the air, their tiny lights reflected on the surface of the water. Elegantly dressed revelers, laughing merrily, drifted in boats accompanied by strains of music. In the midst of the festivities, however, the emperor was already becoming bored. There was ever less in the world these days that could keep his interest for long. Even the fireflies had entertained him for no more than a moment, and once that moment had passed, the banquet was no different from the many others held throughout the year.

Worthless. There is too much in this world that is worthless. Nothing ever filled the emptiness within. It was this that made him willing to listen to a shadow that glided unobtrusively to his side. "Sukune bade me to inform you that he has caught a different kind of firefly—one that crept into the palace with the others." The emperor told the chancellor beside him and laughed deep in his throat. The chancellor, relieved to see the emperor finally smile, chose words that he hoped would win him favor. "How clever. I wonder what kind of firefly that might be."

"This sounds interesting. I think I'll go take a look." The emperor stood up abruptly. "You stay here and carry on with the banquet. I'll go back to my room for a while." Leaving the chancellor behind, he returned to his hall and climbed the stairs. Entering the throne room, he found Sukune and at his feet, the "firefly" dressed in the fine robes of a lady-in-waiting, her hands tied. She looked very young.

"Hmm. So this is it?" He gazed down at the girl, and perhaps due to her youth, she stared back up at him defiantly, her black eyes gleaming. She scrutinized him carefully as if weighing him. The emperor knew instantly that he had found something far more unusual than a firefly. "Who is she?"

"She can't have snuck in here without the aid of accomplices, but she won't talk yet. However, I can make a fairly accurate guess as to why she came to your room. She was after your magatama. I saw this same girl in the land of Himuka. She appeared right near the stone we were looking for and prevented us from obtaining it. I do not know where she comes from, but it is clear that she has some connection to the magatama."

The girl waited until he had finished his explanation and then announced boldly, "I'm not ashamed of who I am. If you really want to know, then let me tell you. I am Toko, daughter of Onetsuhiko of the Tachibana clan of Mino. I did not come here to steal anything. I came to take back what is rightfully ours. Lady Akaru's magatama belongs to us. It is worthless to you, so please give it back."

The emperor and Sukune stared at her in astonishment. She was an extraordinary thief, fearless even in the face of discovery. And her voice rang clear and free, as if she had nothing to hide. She was either extremely brave or very naive. But the emperor, to his own surprise, was enjoying this. It had been a long time since something had diverted him so completely.

Lady Akaru . . . Examining the girl closely, he now saw some resemblance. But Lady Akaru had never stared at him like this. She had regarded him timidly like all the other women. The only woman who had ever looked at him with such a penetrating gaze was his sister, Princess Momoso.

I want to hear what this girl has to say, he thought.

"Sukune," he said. "Wait outside the curtain. Let me question her." Sukune looked uneasy, but he left the room. When he had gone, the emperor drew his sword from its gold scabbard. Toko tensed for an instant but then realized that he was using it to cut her bonds. She did not know why, but from the moment she had first seen him, she had actually felt a faint liking for the man, and now that feeling increased. She could not understand it for she was convinced that he should be hated. Yet instead of inspiring fear, the emperor before her seemed sad and depressed, discouraged rather than ferocious. A sharp crease was carved between his eyebrows and only a shadow of his youth remained. Even so, he was still handsome. He reminded Toko of Prince Oh-usu.

"You said your name is Toko? Then, Toko, let me hear what you have to say. You came here to retrieve Lady Akaru's magatama. What do you plan to do with it? What do you need it for?"

"I need it to prove that I'm the bearer," she answered without bothering to explain any further. Rubbing her wrists to revive the circulation, Toko felt the blood returning to her brain as well. "The magatama is in that box," she continued. "The fact that I can tell is proof. The stone of power is calling me. Because I'm blood kin to Lady Akaru."

"The stone of power? But it has no power," the emperor said bitterly. "There's only a dead magatama in that box. When Lady Akaru first came to the palace, the stone glowed. But she never gave it to me, even though she said that she would. In the middle of the ritual, its light died never to return, even when she held it in her hand. Her deceitful heart tainted that vow and the light died."

"It wasn't her fault. It was yours," Toko said. The emperor glared at her, but Toko stared boldly back. "You did not love her as much as the prince. Akaru told me that when she met you, your heart was already occupied by someone else. Yet you still blamed it all on her."

The emperor remained silent for some time. Slowly, he reached out and picked up the box. He opened the lid and stared inside. Then he thrust it at Toko. "All right. Prove it. If you're capable of bringing life back to this cold stone, let me see you do it."

Now, at long last, Toko looked upon the magatama, semitranslucent, lying on a bed of folded silk. But it was only an ordinary stone. It could not compare with the two that Sugaru wore. Her confidence evaporated rapidly and was replaced by nervousness.

"You said you were the bearer. If so, then restore it to its original hue," the emperor pressed her.

She could not just stand there. She must pick it up. She thrust out her hand and grasped it. At first nothing happened. Then, just as she was about to despair, a point of light flickered in the depths of the stone. Clear and bright, it spread rapidly, until the stone in her hand shone brighter than the lamp and illumined the entire room. It was pure white, like a foaming waterfall or sun-bathed snow, with a sheen brighter than polished silver.

Thank the Goddess, Toko thought in silent gratitude. This white magatama, this clear stone, was hers. Tears filled her eyes.

"What's this?" the emperor whispered, stunned. "But the color . . ."

Toko wiped her eyes. "Now you know what I said is true. *I* am the bearer of this stone. Only I can make it shine. You must give it back."

The emperor stared at her—at this girl with her frank gaze who had made the stone radiate pure light, even though she was young enough to be his daughter. "It seems you've won," he said carefully. "All right then. You may have the magatama." Joy lit Toko's face. But the emperor had not finished. "However," he continued, "I will not permit you to leave. Serve me. Stay with me in place of Lady Akaru."

The flush that had rushed to Toko's cheeks drained slowly away. She stared at him, unable to digest what he had said. "What do you mean?"

"I'm asking you to be my wife," the emperor said, and for the first time since Toko had met him, he smiled. "If only I had met you first, instead of Lady Akaru. Then perhaps Mino would not have fallen. If it had been you, I could have loved. Use your magatama to fill the emptiness in my heart. You have the power to do that."

Stunned, Toko stood rooted to the spot.

IT BEGAN TO POUR as Sugaru neared the peak. A wind sprang up, whipping the leaves on the trees upside down and driving the rain against him. He was soaked through instantly, but he did not slacken his pace. It was as dark as night, and the heavily banked clouds flickered with an uneasy light. Holding his arms above his face, Sugaru looked up at the sky and realized how the god intended to punish him. *Ah, so that's what he's up to.* Swifter than thought, he drew Lady Kage's dagger from its red sheath and threw it down in front of him. A thick bolt of lightning split the sky and struck the blade with a deafening crack. The shock wave sent Sugaru flying. He flew head over heels, and then slowly rose to survey the damage. Looking at the smoldering ground around the blade, he muttered, "I certainly don't want to be hit by that." Trees rattled and creaked in the punishing wind and rain. Something borrowed that sound to speak.

Leave.

Sugaru pretended not to hear and tried to press onward.

You can only use the dagger once.

"I know that," Sugaru shouted to the treetops. "You're supposed to be a god. Why are you wasting my time repeating what I already know? Hurry up and show yourself."

Another bolt of lightning struck the ground. But this time, instead of aiming for Sugaru, it hit the tree beside him. Sugaru was thrown to the ground yet again by the explosion of light and sound. Gritting his teeth, he looked up at the tree. Its trunk was charred and flames crawled along the branches. That would have been enough to strike cold terror into any heart, but there was more. The flames licking the branches stretched and began to take shape. Under Sugaru's gaze, they formed a crimson serpent, its thick body coiled around the blackened tree trunk and its eyes made of burning flame.

He who sees me thus can never leave the mountain, the god said. *But it's unusual for anyone to demand that I reveal myself. Who are you? You're obviously no ordinary man.*

"You've got that right," Sugaru replied. "I'm Sugaru, bearer of the magatama of Izumo. I also have the stone of Himuka, and I've come to get yours."

The snake god merely flicked his tongue. Sugaru folded his arms. "Tell me what I need to do to get it. I need the Misumaru."

The snake god refused point-blank. *Never. It was given to me centuries ago by a shrine maiden. I vowed never to give it to anyone. That vow still holds.*

"The situation has changed . . . but even if I tell you that, I bet you won't listen," Sugaru said, half to himself. "Maybe there's no other way but to use force."

The fiery snake reared his head. *Surely you don't intend to fight me. Don't you know your place?*

"No, I don't." Sugaru's eyes gleamed and he seemed suddenly full of life. "You know, I haven't tested the limits of the magatama's power. And here you are, an opponent against whom I can use all I've got." Indeed, Sugaru had been dying for a fight all along. This was the perfect excuse to give full rein to the fighting urge that smoldered inside him. Nothing could have made him happier than to challenge the god, the greatest opponent he could have ever imagined. Placing his hands together in front of his chest, he took several deep breaths and drew the force of the two magatama into his body. Light and power filled his limbs, and the blazing fire in his eyes matched that of the snake god's.

"Now then, let's see who has the right to bear the magatama," he said, bracing himself to launch an attack.

The battle between Sugaru and the snake god was well matched. It raged over the rocky mountain peak beneath clouds so dark it was hard to tell if it was night or day. The only light was the flash of lightning, and the battlefield seemed like a world beyond time.

Your strength is an even match to mine, the god said finally. *But in the end, you will lose.*

"It's not over yet."

A god never tires. I can fight like this for a hundred years. But you, you're all too human.

Sugaru ignored him. Transformed into a ball of pure battlelust and speed, he had actually forgotten his own human body. While they fought, he had sustained an increasing number of minor injuries, mere scrapes and bruises so insignificant he did not even notice. In fact, with each injury, he felt spurred on to greater feats. At the same time, however, as the battle progressed, they gradually ate away at him.

Either way, the end will come, the god continued. *You cannot take the magatama. Know this. He who uses force will inevitably meet someone stronger. The Misumaru of the Goddess of Darkness will never pass into the hands of one like you. You have too much pride.*

Sugaru wiped his face with his arm, then licked the grazes where the sweat stung them. "Too much pride? As far as I'm concerned, you're the one who's arrogant." Sugaru launched himself yet again at his opponent. Whether he accepted defeat or not, death awaited him—but he had no intention of dying. It was not in his nature to back down from a gamble once he had cast his bet. He would fight to the bitter end.

A bolt of lightning hit the ground and Sugaru sprang back. Then he realized that the bolt had not been aimed at him but elsewhere. Surprised, he peered at the ground where it had struck and saw the sacred dagger. Someone else had picked it up and thrown it. He sucked in his breath when he saw who it was. Lady Kage, her face pale, stood holding the red scabbard. She was shaking visibly, but her face was filled with desperate determination, and she stared, unwavering, into the fiery eyes of the flaming snake.

"Please don't harm this man," she said. "There is no need to fight. Listen to what I have to say for I am descended from the one who worshipped you on this mountain peak long ago. There is no longer any need for you to guard the magatama. Please return the stone so that I may give it to this man."

Coiling his long body, the snake god sat flicking his tongue as he glared at the woman for several long moments. She was so close that not even Sugaru could have saved her. All he could do was watch, gripped by anxiety. Lady Kage too stood frozen, looking ready to faint.

Finally the god spoke. *Centuries ago I made a vow that I would not give this stone to anyone . . . not until a descendant of the shrine maiden should come to me and ask me to return it.* His tongue vanished and between his jaws there appeared a small, black stone. *Until today, no priest has ever dared to climb the mountain, to risk his life, to stand before me and look me in the face. Only you can rival the brave young maiden who drew me to her so long ago. I am released from my vow.*

He placed the stone in Lady Kage's palm. It looked like a sliver of clear night sky, its black darkness studded with specks of silver light, twinkling stars that shone in Lady Kage's hand as if their light came from an enormous distance.

My task is finished. I shall return to the lair that I left some time ago.

"Are you planning to leave the fight unfinished?" Sugaru asked, petulant.

You're lucky you escaped with your life, young man, the snake said. *But still, I haven't enjoyed myself so much in a long time. I will remember you.*

The snake dissolved before them, merging into the clouds with a flicker of lightning. The weather began to clear and the silence that follows a heavy rain enveloped the world. Rays of sunlight streamed through the cracks in the clouds. To Sugaru's surprise, the sun appeared to be in almost the same place as when he had first begun to climb the mountain.

So that's what it's like to battle the gods, he thought.

Lady Kage came toward him, her eyes brimming with tears. "Look at you, covered in blood. I should have come sooner."

For the first time, Sugaru noticed that he was bleeding. Open wounds lacerated his skin, and his clothes were in tatters. He tried to say that they were just shallow cuts and nothing to worry about, but then he felt the pain. He was so exhausted that his body seemed to be made of mud. He tried to smile. "To think that I had to be rescued by a woman. It's usually the other way around. How am I going to live this down?"

"That's not true," Lady Kage said, smiling through her tears. "You were the one who saved me. You told me that I wasn't defiled. It was you who gave me the courage to do this."

"Even so, I'm amazed you managed the climb up here." He looked at her with admiration. He had felt sorry for this woman with her pale, sad face, beaten by misfortune. Out of pity he had rescued her from the chancellor's hall. He had never guessed that she had such courage hidden inside.

"I could not stand by and let you die. I thought that the god would kill me there on the spot. But my faith in you won out. To be honest, it didn't matter to me anymore if I died."

"You outdid yourself, you know," Sugaru said. "You faced that god and with mere words you stilled him and sent him on his way. There's no greater shrine maiden in the world than you."

The tears Lady Kage wiped away were now tears of joy. "It was you who made me what I am. That makes me your shrine maiden . . . I think."

Sugaru sat down on a rock and winced. It was too much to even stand. "I'm not a god," he said. "I learned my lesson this time. And the meaning of pride. Although I don't like to admit it, that god was right."

Lady Kage tore her robe into thin strips and bandaged the wounds on Sugaru's arms and legs. Then she held out her hand. "This is yours," she said.

Sugaru stared at her in surprise. On her palm lay the black magatama, the night sky with twinkling stars. "Are you sure?"

She nodded. "It wouldn't be right if I didn't give it to you. You risked your life to get this stone and I risked my life to help you. That means it's yours. But . . ." She looked down. "If I give you this, you will leave me . . ."

Sugaru did not reach out to take the stone. Instead, he sat thinking for a long while. Finally he said, "If I could stay to help you, I would. But the task of gathering the magatama for the Misumaru isn't finished. I can't leave Toko on her own until we bring an end to the Sword and its master. And helping her won't be as simple as rescuing you from the chancellor's hall. You're free now. You've woken to your own power. Even without my help, you can live and be strong."

Lady Kage looked crestfallen, but she nodded. "I knew that it was not fated to be. I must be content with just having met you. But I will never forget. As long as I live, I will never forget you." She laid the magatama in his palm. The light of the stars within it did not fade even when it left her hand. "So please, remember me."

SUGARU NEEDED TO REST, and it was not until evening that he felt strong enough to climb down the mountain. Thus they had to walk the mountain trail by the glow cast by the stones. When they reached the familiar gate to the altar, they saw a light in the darkness beyond it. A man stood there holding a torch in his hand. Sugaru frowned, suspicious to see someone at the foot of the mountain so far from human habitation. "Who's there?"

The man's voice trembled, perhaps awed to see the strange light coming down the path. "Is that Sugaru? I was told by our leader to wait here for a man of that name. I bear a message."

"I'm Sugaru. You're Nanatsuka's man?"

The man answered with obvious relief. "I am to tell you to wait at Kazuragi. The leader and Lady Toko infiltrated the emperor's palace this evening. They'll send word once they're done."

"What?" Sugaru could not believe what he had just heard. "Toko too? How did that come about?"

"They said they were going to retrieve a keepsake belonging to Lady Akaru."

Sugaru groaned. "What's she trying to do? Make me pay for going? The idiot! I leave her on her own for a second and look what happens." He cursed to himself and then began questioning the messenger. "You said the palace, right? Tell me which part. How did Toko get in?"

"I haven't heard the details. If we wait, they'll send us information."

"How can I wait at a time like this?"

Lady Kage, who had been listening, looked anxious. "I think it might be better to wait. After all, your wounds are still bleeding." On the mountain,

Sugaru had insisted that with three magatama, his injuries ought to heal in no time, but he remained visibly hurt. "Please rest a little. Even if you leave for the palace now, you won't get there until morning. Surely even you can't help them right now."

"Oh yes, I can," Sugaru said. He felt the force of the three magatama welling inside him. Turning his attention inward, he realized that he was being summoned with a strength that he had never felt before. It was so strong that he felt if he but concentrated on that call, he would be whisked away, body and all, like a fish caught on a line.

"Sugaru!" Lady Kage screamed. To her eyes, it seemed as if his body was shimmering and growing fainter.

Sugaru started but then smiled at her. "It's all right. It's the power of the stones. I think there's a way to the palace. I'm going to try it." His eyes were merry. As Lady Kage stood watching silently, his body wavered and evaporated into the air.

He's gone. She stared at the empty space, devoid of any trace of Sugaru. He had gone like a whirlwind—the same way he had come.

6

"I MOST CERTAINLY will *not* become your wife," Toko said, furious. "Besides, I'm not even a woman yet!"

"Then I'll adopt you as my daughter," the emperor said. "I must have you by my side."

"Are you crazy? After what you've done to me and my people, I'd be totally justified if I murdered you in your sleep."

The emperor looked shocked. "You . . . wish to kill me?"

"If I were near you, I might," Toko answered, thinking of Nanatsuka.

"It wouldn't matter," the emperor said. "I'm tired. I've sent people to every corner of the land to search for the magatama that are supposed to give eternal life, but I don't care anymore. Even Momoso has gone. If the Tachibana who bear the magatama decree that I should die, maybe that's not so bad."

Toko could not believe what she was hearing from this man. He stood at the pinnacle of power in Mahoroba. What was he lacking that should make him so despondent? She could only stare at him incredulously.

"The people of Mino, I'm told, have served the emperor for generations," he continued. "If Oh-usu had not rebelled, I would never have been forced to act against your people. I did not wish to do that. And now, there is nothing that can fill the emptiness in my heart. Except perhaps you, who made the magatama shine pure white. When I saw you do that, I felt that for you it might be possible."

That's what the Keeper of the Shrine said. The mission of the Tachibana is to protect the emperor. But I came here to...

Toko shrank in horror at the thought that it might be within her power to heal him. Was that why she had been able to make Lady Akaru's stone glow? To Toko, the emperor's melancholy was starkly evident. Was that a sign that she should do something about it?

"Stay with me. Use the power of your magatama to cleanse me."

Toko felt as though she were caught in a spell. Fixed by his gaze, she could not move.

At that moment, a change came over the room. Toko cowered instinctively, struck by what seemed to be a sudden gust of wind. She shut her eyes, then opened them to find Sugaru standing in front of her. He looked ghastly, his hair tangled, his body bloodied and his clothes in filthy tatters. Cloth bandages patterned with purple wisteria stood out on his arms and legs. She stared, dumbfounded, and Sugaru grinned.

"You little tomboy! Can't you behave yourself for once?" he said.

"Where'd you come from?"

"Kazuragi." He pointed to his chest. Three magatama now hung around his neck. "I got the third one. It took a bit of effort, but I did it."

He radiated light. The emperor, momentarily dazzled, covered his face with his arms, but when he realized that Sugaru was human, he shouted, "Sukune! Sukune! To me! There's an intruder in my room!"

Sukune raced in, his sword drawn, followed by several other guards. They squinted against the light. An angry flush rose in Sukune's face when he recognized Sugaru. "You! You're the one who made fools of us on the mountain of fire!"

"It's been a while," Sugaru said. "As an old friend, though, let me warn you. Stay back. If you don't, you'll meet with far worse than you did in Himuka." Then he turned his dangerous, flashing eyes on the emperor. "So you're the ruler of this land, are you? Such a pleasure to meet you. A friend once told me that the world would be a far better place without you."

The emperor seemed to shrink in size before Sugaru's brilliance, the animation fading from his face. Even Toko felt Sugaru's tremendous power. He had transcended the human condition. She placed her hand on his arm. "Sugaru, don't," she said. "It's all right. Let's go. We have the magatama, so our job here is done. I got my own stone too. That's enough. We have a different job to do."

Sugaru looked at her strangely. "But wouldn't it take a load off your mind if the emperor were punished?"

"Let's go," Toko repeated firmly.

"Stay," the emperor said as if the word had slipped unbidden from his mouth.

Toko gazed at him, feeling only pity. Slowly, as if choosing her words, she said, "I won't kill you. The only person I care about, the only person I will kill with these hands is your son, Prince Ousu. No one else. I became the bearer of the magatama solely for that purpose—to lay the wielder of the Sword to rest. I will neither kill you nor let you live. That in itself may seem a punishment to you. But you brought it upon yourself."

Sukune and the guards leapt toward them, but Toko and Sugaru vanished from the spot. The guards blew their whistles and ran through the palace in their search for the pair, throwing the banquet into an uproar.

"I WONDER IF NANATSUKA and the others escaped," Toko said. "Knowing them, I don't think they will get caught, but still."

"I don't understand Nanatsuka. How could he have agreed to do something so reckless?" Sugaru said.

They were sitting on the hillside looking down over the palace. Although they could not see the fireflies from this distance, they watched the red lights of countless torches swimming along the palace streets. Doubtless it was total chaos below, but to Toko it seemed pretty. The night breeze toyed with their hair as they watched.

"Why are you crying?" Sugaru asked, hearing quiet sobs beside him.

"I don't know." Toko wiped her face with her sleeve. So much had happened to her that she could not tell exactly what had caused the lump in her throat.

"But . . . we've finally obtained the four magatama we need to make the Misumaru of Death."

"What did you mean by what you said to the emperor back there?" Sugaru asked.

"He wanted to keep me and the magatama," Toko said, striving to speak calmly. "He wanted me as his wife or daughter. He said I could fill the emptiness in his heart. I thought that maybe I could understand, just a little, how he had felt when Akaru rejected him. That's all."

"You're really weird, you know. You can pity even someone like the emperor. How can you possibly take revenge on anyone if you feel like that?"

"It's part of the nature of the Mino magatama. I'm not special or anything," Toko said. "And my only enemy is Prince Ousu. No one else matters. That makes it easier to overlook what others do to me."

"So you want revenge on Prince Ousu that badly." Sugaru sighed. He looked at Toko's magatama glowing in the dark. "If I asked you to give me that white stone, you probably wouldn't even consider it, would you?"

Toko raised her face and looked at him. She could see the pure white light reflected in his eyes. "You already know the answer. You know that it has to be me who takes the Misumaru, that I must be the one to do this task."

"But why?"

"Because you would be doing it for me. If it weren't for me, you wouldn't kill him, right?"

Sugaru looked flustered. "No, that's not true," he protested hastily.

"Sugaru, you're too nice. That's what gets you into so much trouble. But this is one thing that you can't do for me. I have to do it myself. Because I'm doing it to set him free." She spoke slowly and deliberately. Now that she had her own magatama, she seemed to shine. "I'm going to free him from the Sword, to cleanse him of its power. Only then will I be set free. Only then can I finally let these feelings go."

"With four magatama, you should be able to defeat the master of the Sword fairly easily. But once you bear those stones, you aren't human anymore," Sugaru said in a low voice. "Are you sure you want to do that? Don't imagine that you can kill him and return to being your old self."

"I know. But some sacrifice must be paid if I'm to become the bearer." There whatever happens."

Sugaru suddenly recalled the words of the god on the mountain. *He who uses force will inevitably meet someone stronger.* That was not Toko's style. Instead, she was behaving just like Lady Kage—just like a shrine maiden. Perhaps Toko was fit to be the bearer after all. Sugaru cleared his throat. He knew he had lost this battle. "I'll give you these, but you must hold to some promises in return," he said. "First, when you kill him, promise me you won't try to follow him in death. Second, when you're finished with the Misumaru, let them go. And third, when it's all over, return with me to Izumo. Kisako is there and it's not a bad place to live. And forget about Oguna forever. Can you promise me these things?"

"Yes, I promise." Toko nodded. "I'd be happy to promise that."

Sugaru untied the string of beads and handed it to Toko. "Thread your stone onto that string. That will make the Misumaru."

Green, yellow, black, and white; Midori, Ki, Kuro, and Shiro—now Toko possessed the string of beads, all four of them shimmering with color and light. It seemed far too beautiful to be called the Misumaru of Death. Yet this power was now hers. After searching for so long, it was finally in her grasp.

"How does it feel?" Sugaru asked.

"Not much different. It feels normal."

"I guess that's how it is."

Toko smiled. It was a smile of pure joy. Now there was nothing left between her and Oguna. There was nothing to stop her from joining him. "You'll have to teach me how to fly like that. Prince Ousu is already heading east. But with the Misumaru we should be able to close the distance instantly."

"You're going to start already?" Sugaru asked.

"I'm going straight to Prince Ousu," Toko said, her eyes shining and her face clear. "Now that I finally have the ability to do that, what else would I do?" She had sacrificed everything just for this moment. There was no reason to hesitate.

PART III

WHERE THE WHITE BIRD FLIES

Oh, thou who called my name
Standing in the midst of the flames
That burned through the field
Of Sagamu.

—Kojiki

chapter
eight

APPARITION

Apparition

IT WAS DAWN. Toko and Sugaru stood on the beach, watching the sky. The sun rose from the clouds, dappling the red sky with gold. Out in the sea, the islands lay like black shadows. Waves, pungent with the smell of the tide, rolled from the purple haze in the distance to wash against the shore. Not a boat or a person was in sight—just the day breaking quietly on the empty beach. The place looked as though nothing ever happened, as if each day slipped uneventfully into the next.

In reality, only one day earlier Prince Ousu and his men had launched a flotilla of warships to conquer the Emishi in the east. Despite the prince's fame and glory, it must have been a very subdued departure. No one appeared to have come from the capital to bid them farewell. The people of Mahoroba did not travel this way by choice, for the eastern lands were backward and primitive, home to a strange and foreign race.

However, none of this mattered to Toko. She stood for some time on the shore, inhaling the sea air and gazing at the mist on the horizon. Prince Ousu's warships must be out there in the distance. That was all that mattered. At last, she was close to her goal.

"We're a day too late," Sugaru said. "If we'd come a little more smoothly we could have settled everything before they sailed away."

Sugaru had given Toko the string of beads only to discover that she was not a very reliable navigator. She had no sense of direction, a deficit for which the Misumaru apparently could not compensate. That they had reached this beach at all was entirely thanks to Sugaru.

Toko, however, turned and smiled. "What's wrong with that? I've got the Misumaru, which controls wind and water. With this, I'm not even a day's distance away."

"You plan to pursue him even in the middle of the sea?"

"Actually, I think it's better that way. If by any chance he's still able to wield the Sword, no one else will get hurt."

"But traveling over water is risky, especially when you can't even stay on course over land."

"I'll use a boat. I'll make it fly like the wind."

"Hmm. A boat..."

Toko looked up at him. "Sugaru," she said earnestly, "please. Let me go by myself, all right? I know it was you who got us here, but I have to do the rest alone. I have to finish this by myself. That's why I set out on this journey in the first place. So please?"

Sugaru looked into her eyes and then nodded. "I know," he said. "You're the bearer of the Misumaru. I won't interfere. After all, I promised."

"I'm sorry, Sugaru."

"There's no need to apologize. As long as you keep your promise as well."

Tied on the shore they found an old weathered skiff, just big enough for one person. They decided to appropriate it, and Toko clambered in. Still dressed in the colorful silk robe she had worn at the palace, she looked quite odd in the little gray boat.

"How is it?"

"It feels fine."

Sugaru, his eyes cheerful and his manner easy, showed no sign of worry, but Toko knew that he would not budge from this spot until he saw her safely out to sea. She had always thought he was the most irresponsible person she had ever met. Yet, in the end, there had been no one more dependable.

"Thank you for everything," she said. "I'm sorry I caused you so much trouble. If it weren't for you, I would never have made it from Izumo to this point. I would never have become the bearer of the Misumaru."

Sugaru shrugged. "Stop talking as if it's all over. This is just the beginning, remember? Off you go and set things right."

"But I wanted to tell you now. I have no other way of thanking you." She hesitated for a moment and then asked, "Sugaru, why did you do it? Why did you come with me when you could have had Kisako? When, unlike Kisako, I have nothing to give you in return?"

"You've grown up suddenly, Shorty, to be so considerate."

Toko scowled. "You underestimate me. I've been wondering about that for a long time. I just didn't ask."

Sugaru looked down at her thoughtfully. "I go where I'm needed, that's all. Compared to Kisako, the load you carried seemed a bit heavier. After all, it's a big job—trying to fulfill the mission of your people. They're my people too, so I thought I should do something. Of course, rewards are important, but is that why you followed after Prince Ousu? Because you expected to get something in return?"

" . . . No."

"You see."

Toko beamed at him suddenly. She felt as though a weight had been lifted from her chest. "I guess I'll be off, then."

"Let him have it. No regrets, okay?"

Toko raised the string of beads in her right hand, bringing the water under her control. In Himuka, the Misumaru had raised the river to drown a village, but this was the sea. The current changed course and caught up her little skiff so that it shot across the waves—straight out into the bay, eastward, toward where the sun rose.

Standing on the shore, Sugaru stared after her, her figure a dark shadow backlit by the golden sun, until she dwindled to a speck on the horizon and vanished. "She's just a kid," he whispered. "Right to the very end."

When she could no longer see Sugaru or the cove, Toko turned and faced forward. Blue water spread out before her and the wind blew in her face, catching her hair. She was so elated she could hardly sit still. She did not forget the fear that lay cold across her mind, and her skin prickled with anxiety. Yet Toko sensed liberation ahead. Finally, she could bring it all to a close. By setting Oguna free, she would free herself from the task she had set. What lay beyond that, Toko could not begin to imagine, and so she did not even try. Her sole desire was to return everything to the beginning; that was all she had set out to do. It was for this purpose, and this purpose alone, that she bore the Misumaru and the sword from Mino.

It took so long to get this far . . .

She thought back on the journey since she had left home. Just as Oguna was no longer the Oguna she had once known, having come this far, she was no longer the same Toko. That was why she could be the bearer of the Misumaru and destroy the power of the Sword. Thinking about it, Toko realized that she had not embarked on this quest simply for her people. She had come here to keep a promise—a small, personal promise. Why otherwise would her heart be beating so fast even while her eyes sought the enemy she must defeat?

Shining waves. The little skiff skipped lightly over their crests like a flying fish. Toko recalled again the leaf boats she and Oguna had raced on the stream so long ago—*Oguna-maru* and *Toko-maru*.

In the end, we both reached the sea. Perhaps this is the best place to lay those memories to rest . . .

As SHE SPED ACROSS THE WATER, Toko saw a mist rising like a wall across the horizon. It seemed strange, for the weather was fair and not a single cloud lay over the land. Something must be there, and instinctively, she aimed the skiff straight into the middle of the fog. The sun above her head was abruptly extinguished, and a thick fog flew into her mouth and nose, choking her. Her field of vision turned white, and she could not even see the water in front of her.

A blue-white bolt of lightning split the haze, running across it with a thunderstroke that made Toko cower and throw her arms over her head. Another bolt landed even nearer. The roar split her ears and numbed her flesh. The malice emanating from the mist shocked her. *It's the Sword,* she thought. *I'm sure of it.* Sensing the power of the Misumaru, the Sword was acting against her—and the force of that threat was enough to dispel any foolish optimism. They were enemies and what lay before them was war. Sentimentality would be permitted only to the one who survived. And Toko must survive.

Biting her lip, she focused on the Misumaru. The four stones combined should have enough power to counterattack. Summoning the forces of wind and water, she centered their energy on dispelling the mist and binding the lightning. Huge waves swelled, rocking her boat so violently that her head reeled. As she gritted her teeth and fought to maintain control, she gradually began to see what she must do. She must find the source of the lightning—the Sword. The power of the stones could not temper the whole of the sea.

The sky had turned stormy, and a menacing blackness surrounded her. The waves rose as high as cliffs and flashes of lightning slid across their peaks. Gathering her courage, Toko steered the boat out of a trough to the top of a wave and then leapt from crest to crest in the surging sea, nearly capsizing more than once. Finally, luck turned in her favor. Between two great waves she glimpsed the prow of a warship.

There!

A wind sprang up and blew her close. Instantly, the sea began swirling about the warship, wrapping it in a great waterspout that climbed higher and higher. As the funnel of water neared the sky, the lightning weakened until finally Toko could not hear even a murmur of thunder. The Sword was sealed, locked inside with the ship so that its power could not stir. Bringing her little skiff to a halt, Toko gazed at the scene, her face flushed. She was drenched, but it did not bother her. The time had come. Sweeping back her dripping hair, she calmly drew her sword from her robe. It was with this that she must perform the mission before her. Placing the hilt against her forehead, she closed her eyes.

O Goddess who guards the Tachibana, protect me. Keeper of the Shrine, guide me. Mother, Akaru, be with me . . .

There was no turning back. Fixing her eyes on the vortex before her, she drove her boat into the whirling water and plunged through. Her boat was swept upwards in a spiral, as if it would be hurled to the top of the sky. Unable to keep her footing on the deck any longer, Toko fell into the maelstrom that whirled high above the sea. Within the center, however, a warm updraft blew—a fact that the Misumaru seemed to have known. The vertical wind caught Toko, buoying her light frame so that she descended slowly, almost swimming through the air. Forcing herself to remain calm, she watched the warship draw steadily closer and larger.

At last I am coming to meet you. Now is the time to make my wish come true...

2

THE SHIP SAT MOTIONLESS as if anchored at the center of the whirlpool. Toko noted with surprise that instead of pitch darkness, the bottom of the funnel glowed with a dim light. And it was unexpectedly quiet. The updraft must be sucking the thunderous roar of the water out the top of the waterspout. Toko glided down like a bird coming to roost—but she did not land like one. Slipping on the wet deck, she fell with a thump that she thought must have been heard over the entire ship. The vessel was large enough to carry at least twenty armed soldiers, but only one person was on deck.

Toko leapt to her feet. She knew at a glance that this was the man she sought. In one hand he gripped a naked blade that glowed with a faint bluish light—it was the Sword that lit the darkness. Seeing her, he froze, a startled expression on his face.

"Toko?" he said.

No words came from Toko's lips. She stared at him silently. Dressed all in white, Prince Ousu stood out clearly in the dim glow. He wore neither the armor nor the jewels that suited his rank. The Sword was the only thing that identified him as the prince. Yet even that he now tossed aside.

"Toko," he repeated. He seemed bewildered, as if he did not know what to do. "It *is* you. You really came. How did you get here?"

Barely a moment before they had been locked in deadly battle, but now, brought face to face, they could only stand like wooden statues, staring at one another. The prince's complete defenselessness threw Toko into confusion. The man who waited here should have been the prince of Mahoroba, vicious and brutal, surrounded by soldiers. And he should have forgotten who she was. But instead, he stood alone, his Sword discarded on the deck, calling her name—like Oguna would have. Toko pulled herself together. She must not be deceived.

"Your Sword can no longer summon the lightning. It's useless to resist. Where are your men?"

"I'm the only one on board. I ordered the others to a separate ship before I invoked the power of the Sword. But I never thought that you would be the one to come," he said, still looking stunned.

"And why shouldn't I?" Toko asked defiantly. "With that Sword you slew Prince Oh-usu, drove Lady Akaru to her death, and razed the land of Mino. Surely it shouldn't surprise you that I would come to seek revenge. This is the Misumaru, strung with the Tachibana stones. It took me all this time to gather them. I've waited so long for this day—the day I would destroy you."

"I see," Oguna said in a small voice. "Yes. It makes sense that you would want revenge."

"And you didn't stop there. You brought destruction to Izumo and to Himuka, too. I saw it with my own eyes. Your very existence brings ruin to Toyoashihara. You deserve my hatred, and more."

The prince looked resigned. "You're right. The only thing this Sword brings is hate and destruction. And there's no one who can stop it."

It was just as Toko had expected. His heart had been numbed by the ongoing slaughter. Probably nothing she could say would hurt or even anger him. Tears pricked her eyes and she blinked them away. If this was what Oguna had been reduced to, then she had been right. Now she felt she could kill him and bring it to an end. It should not be that difficult.

"I've been longing to see you for so long. I came here because I didn't want you to be slain by anyone else. I wanted to kill you myself so that I could see my Oguna once more."

Faster than thought, the Misumaru swept her straight to the prince. She held her dagger ready and closed her eyes. As long as she held it straight and true, as long as she didn't let go the moment the blade bit through flesh, she could do it. And she did. Her eyes still closed, she waited for the body her blade was in to wilt, to fall. It seemed like an eternity.

Then she heard a voice. It was Prince Ousu. "Toko," he said, slowly and deliberately. "That's not going to kill me. You mustn't close your eyes."

Shocked, her eyes flew open. The prince bent over her and she saw that her dagger, which should have pierced his heart, protruded instead from his midriff. He was far taller than she had expected—a whole head taller than she remembered. She had missed the mark completely. Panicked, Toko staggered away, her hand still grasping the dagger. Blood spurted from the prince's side, rapidly dyeing his white clothes crimson. He clasped a hand over the wound and grimaced with pain.

"Toko," he gasped. "What are you doing? You've got to finish it. You came to kill me, didn't you?"

"What're you saying?" Toko shouted. "You mean that's what you intended all along?"

Prince Ousu braced himself against the side of the ship. His face was pale, but he managed to school his features. "Toko, hurry."

Her hands shook. The blood that flowed from his wound pierced her eyes. Warm blood, from a living body. The color of pain. "But why?"

"An assassin shouldn't be asking that. Toko, you're taking too long. I didn't want to tell you . . . " His eyes clouded as he gazed at her. "I've been waiting the whole time. I knew. Lady Toyoao told me . . . but I couldn't believe it. I never thought I'd see you again. Yet you gathered the beads and came. All this way . . . " He groaned and his voice grew weaker. "I wanted someone . . . I didn't care who . . . to stop me. I wanted someone to do for me what I couldn't do myself. Yet it wasn't just anyone who came. It was you, Toko. Nothing could have made me happier."

This man could not be Oguna. So Toko had told herself. Yet she knew a boy who spoke like this. Who always ignored his own pain. Who had no shoulders to cry on so hid himself away instead. Who could sound like he didn't care at all when inside this was far from true . . .

"Come on, Toko. Finish it," Prince Ousu urged. "Then it will all be over. Finish what you came to do."

Toko raised her dagger. This is what she wanted, and he wanted it too. Yet even knowing this, she could not bring herself to deal the final blow.

I can't!

She felt a sudden sharp pain in her abdomen and bent over with a small cry. At first she did not know what it meant. But the change was clear. With a dull pain, something heavy rolled down inside her and fell as a drop of blood below the hem of her robe. Toko shrank back and stared at the red spot on the deck, paralyzed. Then she heard her own voice come back to her from long ago. *I won't become a woman until we see each other again. I promise. I'll be waiting for you the whole time, so please come back.*

Her shock and confusion manifested themselves instantly. The power of the Misumaru, which held the Sword in check, wavered. The whirlwind shook, and the warship, which had been held rigid, pitched violently. Taken by surprise, the two tumbled against the gunwales.

"Oguna!" Toko screamed, only realizing afterwards what she had called him. With an ominous creaking, the ship rolled in the opposite direction, and they rolled with it, unable to stand.

"The Sword," Oguna shouted. Raising his head, he noticed that Toko's face was as pale as bone. "Toko," he cried, "are you hurt?"

Her lips trembled but she said nothing.

"The Sword is waking. Once that happens, you won't be able to kill me." He reached out his hand, bewildered by the sudden change that had come over her. "If you can't do it, give me the dagger."

But she turned away. "No! I can't!" she cried in a strangled voice. "I can't."

She had believed that only she could free Oguna. She had come here totally convinced that she was chosen to be the bearer of the Misumaru. Yet at the last moment, she had been betrayed by her own self. She was not the one chosen to give Prince Ousu the release of death, even though he desired it. All she had been able to do was to keep her promise, and now that it had been fulfilled she had no power left at all.

The ship rocked precariously and waves splashed onto the deck. Seized by despair, Toko looked at Prince Ousu—at Oguna. "It's no good. I've lost."

"Why?"

But Toko did not even hear him. Shaking her head furiously, she cried, "What was the point? I don't even understand anymore why I did thi—"

Oguna reached out to grab her, but she had already vanished from the spot. The fierce wind and roaring waves snatched away even his voice as he called her name.

SUGARU OPENED his eyes, thinking that someone had called him, then sat up abruptly. He had been sitting on the beach gazing at the waves but must have fallen asleep. His hand touched something and he picked it up. It was the Misumaru.

What's this doing here? Why do I have it?

For a moment, his brain wouldn't function. *Toko must have left it behind.* But that was impossible. The four stones, green, yellow, black, and white, gave off a faint glow even in the sunlight. Sugaru had been chosen. He was the one invested with the power of the bearer. And the string joining the magatama was soaked with seawater.

He could not believe that the Misumaru would switch bearers easily. He had relinquished it to Toko, expecting never to hold it again, and Toko must have accepted it in the same spirit. That it had come back to him like this could only mean that something had happened to Toko. And that Toko, of her own free will, had let it go.

What happened? Is the Sword so powerful that it can defeat even the Misumaru?

"I need a boat," he said suddenly, but just as he was about to begin searching, he changed his mind. A boat would take too long. Impatient as always, he chose the most direct route. Gripping the Misumaru, he shot up as high as the clouds, as high above the sea as he could go, and let himself fall. He had plenty of time to examine the water below him before he hit the surface. This tactic proved successful. From his height, he could clearly discern the traces of power unleashed during the battle between the Misumaru and the Sword—they stood out like claw marks in the clear water. Following the disturbance in the sea current, he came across a warship on the verge of disintegration, caught in a whirling tide.

He nodded, his hair streaming in the wind. *That must be it.* From the sight, he could guess much of what had transpired. He was forced to admit that Toko had done a good job. The Sword remained sealed within the force that she had raised, trapped by the shining stones in Sugaru's hand. Sugaru stopped his fall and flew straight toward the warship.

Landing on deck, he saw that the vessel was crumbling. The keel was shattered, and the ship looked like it would break apart at any moment. Yet Sugaru knew that it would not sink. Because of the shining Sword. No matter how securely its power might be sealed, the Sword still protected its master. Sugaru looked down at the deck where the blade lay abandoned, glowing quietly with a blue light. When he touched it with the Misumaru, the light wavered for a moment and then went out. A mere ordinary sword remained. He picked it up with a sober expression, then, with a shrug of his shoulders, threw it into the sea.

"So long and good riddance."

The Sword's owner lay in the prow of the ship. Walking over to him, Sugaru saw that despite his wounds Oguna was still alive.

So Toko couldn't kill him after all... Sugaru was angry with himself for letting her convince him otherwise. He should have known all along that the girl couldn't do it. *Perhaps I should throw him into the sea too.* Being in a foul mood, he considered this thought seriously. The prince wasn't likely to wake up, and Sugaru would just be doing what Toko had left undone. But as he looked down at Prince Ousu, pity began to stir inside him. The cause of all this chaos now lay like a limp rag, totally defenseless. Close up, he looked as young and childish as Toko. And the only way to find out what had happened to Toko was to ask this youth.

The waves that had begun to lap at Sugaru's feet forced him to make up his mind. The warship, having lost the Sword, was sinking quickly. There was no time to waste. Picking Oguna up in his arms, Sugaru drew on the power of the stones and flew away.

3

SUGARU FLEW SOME distance along the coast until he found an abandoned hut on a point. Built on a small hill, it appeared to have been used by a lookout for lighting beacon fires, but there was no trace of any recent use. Taking this as a good sign, Sugaru carried his prisoner inside. He was not so foolish as to take him to a village.

Once inside, Sugaru began examining Oguna's blood-soaked wound. It was not as deep as he had thought, but neither was it shallow. Although it shouldn't prove fatal, it was the sort of injury that could become dangerous if it festered. He needed clean bandages and ointment. *I should be able to find some in a nearby village.* For a moment, he contemplated the situation. Oguna might wake while he was gone. It would be pointless to let him escape after having brought him all the way here. To be on the safe side,

Sugaru bound the prince's arms and legs securely, then left cheerfully on his errand.

SUGARU'S FRIENDLY nature usually worked to his advantage. Although he had a way with women, he enjoyed human company of all sorts and could converse quite happily with almost anyone. People were naturally drawn to his easygoing manner, which meant that he rarely lacked for anything when he traveled. As long as he smiled, people would stop to chat, and someone was bound to offer him what he needed. This time too it worked; Sugaru quickly obtained what he sought and returned with food and other supplies. Humming to himself, Sugaru ducked inside the door to see Oguna raise his head and glare at him.

"Ah, so you're awake," Sugaru said. "You look surprisingly fit."

Oguna was furious. Apparently, he did not like being tied up. Sugaru supposed that that was understandable. After all, his pride had been injured. But it made him appear quite different from when he had been unconscious.

"What's the meaning of this?" Oguna demanded in the tone of one used to wielding authority. "If you committed this outrage knowing who I am, you'll be sorry."

Sugaru bent over him. "Personally, I think it's pretty foolish to babble on like that when you've no idea where you stand," he said. "Of course I know who you are. You're Prince Ousu, heir to the emperor of Mahoroba, sent off to conquer the east. But you'd be better off considering why you're here."

"Who are you?"

"Sugaru."

Puzzled, Oguna stared up at the red-haired young man. "How did you capture me?"

"You were just lying there on the deck of that boat, weren't you? Oh, and by the way, your ship has sunk and your sword is just a piece of junk at the bottom of the sea."

Oguna's eyes widened as if in shock. For a brief moment, he lost his bold front and looked his age. Sugaru pressed the point home. "The Sword's power has been broken. The Misumaru has sealed it away forever. You have no power left. Whether you live or die is entirely up to me. And unlike Toko, I haven't the slightest compunction about killing you here and now." Although he fell silent, Oguna seemed less daunted by this threat than Sugaru had expected and glared straight back at him.

"There's only one reason I brought you back alive," Sugaru continued. "I want to know what happened to Toko. She returned the Misumaru. She subdued the Sword, yet she didn't kill you. What happened to her? Where did she go?"

Oguna turned his face away. "It's none of your business."

"You stupid idiot!" Grabbing Oguna by the collar, Sugaru yanked his head up. "It's far more my business than yours. I know her much better than you. She belongs to my people, and like me she bears the stones. We traveled together all the way to the western edge of this land to gather the Misumaru."

A faint groan escaped Oguna's lips, but Sugaru did not slacken his hold. Only when he saw the blood drain from Oguna's face did he remember that the man was wounded. Oguna was on the verge of fainting when Sugaru let him go.

He's so stubborn!

It had been foolish of him to forget that Oguna was wounded, yet how could Sugaru help it when Oguna behaved as if he felt no pain? "Fool," Sugaru muttered to himself. "What on earth does he expect to gain by such behavior?" He set about cleaning and rebandaging Oguna's wound. As Oguna recovered consciousness and realized what Sugaru was doing, however, his face turned white with fury.

"Get your hands off me! Leave me alone!"

"I'm just treating your wound. Hold still, will you?"

"Don't touch it."

Sugaru stared at him in exasperation. "Why can't you just accept a favor graciously instead of being so obstinate?"

"I don't need your help."

"Fine then. Go ahead. Let it fester and kill you."

"Do you think I care?"

"What's wrong with you?" Sugaru demanded. "Do you want to die that badly?"

"I won't let anyone touch it."

Sugaru was now determined to fix that wound no matter what, if only to annoy Oguna.

"I said leave it."

"Stop struggling. You'll just make it worse."

But Oguna continued to squirm and wriggle in his binds, though he had no hope of stopping Sugaru. In the end, he only succeeded in prolonging the whole process.

"Did you think I was going to smear it with poison or something?" Sugaru said. "I didn't know that princes were such ungrateful brats."

By this time, Oguna was limp with fatigue, but he looked up with tears in his eyes. "It was Toko's."

"What?"

"It was all she left me," Oguna whispered. He closed his eyes, utterly exhausted. Sugaru stared at him for some time. Then, realizing that Oguna had fainted again, he untied the ropes that bound him.

THIS IS CRAZY. Sugaru could not help but wonder what he was doing. Not only had he rescued the wielder of the Sword, he was actually nursing him. Toko was gone. That was what had thrown everything off-kilter.

Oguna would not be able to move for some time. His wound had made him feverish and he dozed both day and night. Under the circumstances, Sugaru did not feel he could abandon the prince to his fate. *He's just a kid, that's why.*

Had Oguna been a bold and seasoned warrior when Sugaru had found him on that ship, he would not have pitied him. The gap between the prince's reputation and the face of this boy was just too great. Sugaru scratched his head. *I've been cursed with yet another kid. Blast it. Why does this always happen to me?*

Judging from what little he had managed to glean from Oguna, Toko, unable to deal the deathblow, had left Oguna on the ship and used the Misumaru to spirit herself away. She might have come back to the shore, but then again, she might not have. Sugaru had never tested just how far the Misumaru could propel its bearer, but he felt it could probably bring its wielder to the very ends of the earth. Plus Toko had no sense of direction. Despite the immeasurable power of the four stones, they did not tell him where she had gone. Even Toko's white magatama was silent.

Still, Sugaru could not abandon the hope that she might suddenly reappear. Every day he visited the beach where he had last seen her, wandering from one end to the other, but he found no clues. Finally, on the seventh day, he saw something that had not been there before—a crimson comb lying in the sand. Picking it up he saw that it closely resembled the one Toko had worn in her hair. He gazed out into the bay. *Did the tide bring it here?* The sea seemed to be telling him that it had Toko in its keeping. Although Sugaru had refused to even think it, it seemed most likely that the ocean had swallowed her. *Are you planning to die, Toko, leaving only this as a memento?* How could he go back to Izumo and explain that to Kisako or his friends? He stood for a long time, scowling at the water.

When he returned to the hut, he found Oguna sitting up and looking much better. His fever had gone and the wound had closed. Sugaru held out some rice balls that he had brought back with him. "Here," he said.

Oguna hesitated but then, driven by hunger, reached out and took one. After all, he could not die yet. Although Oguna was still suspicious, he no longer showed open hostility.

Sugaru stared blankly into space while Oguna ate. "Did you learn something?" Oguna asked suddenly, appearing to sense a change.

Sugaru looked at him in surprise, for it was the first time that Oguna had addressed him of his own accord. "I don't know," he said. "I just found a comb washed up on the beach." His discouragement showed. "Maybe she drowned. It wouldn't be strange, I suppose. After all, she gave up the Misumaru."

Oguna looked down at the ground. "She's not dead. I know."

Startled, Sugaru demanded, "Do you have proof?"

Oguna looked a little forlorn. "No, I have no proof. But I did have a dream. I'd forgotten that we shared such a bond. I was afraid to even think of Toko. But now, it's Toko who refuses to turn to me. Still, I know what I know. She's not dead. She's alive somewhere."

What's with these two? Sugaru thought. They were joined by a bond that he could not even imagine, yet they remained almost totally oblivious of it and did not even ask themselves why they felt the way they did.

Oguna said stiffly, "I know I have no right to look for her. But . . . you could do it. I want you to find her."

"I don't need you to ask me." Sugaru looked at Oguna for a few moments and then said, "When I find her, if I learn that she no longer has any intention of killing you, the first thing I'm going to do is to come back and finish you off myself. The Misumaru isn't something that can be carried around forever without fulfilling its mission."

Oguna did not flinch. "I know," he said. "I will neither run nor hide. I will no longer turn my back on the fact that I'm the wielder of the Sword."

"Don't forget that the Sword is at the bottom of the sea," Sugaru pointed out, but Oguna looked back at him with a tormented expression.

"The Sword is just a tool, a medium for the god's power," he said. "If I could have rid myself of it so easily, no one would ever have had to suffer misfortune."

Sugaru walked out of the hut, leaving Oguna inside. *Misfortune... He's right. It brings even the wielder misfortune.* He had to admit that he had never even considered how the wielder of the Sword might feel. To wreak massive destruction, not just once but repeatedly, with no way to justify it—no wonder Oguna had wanted to die. If there were no way to thwart fate, then perhaps it would be kinder to kill him now. *I've really walked into a mess this time...* It would have been so much easier if Sugaru had never gotten to know Oguna as a human being. The illustrious commander of the eastern expedition and heir to the throne was just a lost and desperate boy. *Never mind that. The first thing I need to do is find Toko.*

Deciding to start once more from the beach, he flew to the end of the point. There, however, he found something entirely unexpected. Two warships, just like the one that had sunk, were preparing to moor in the bay. As Sugaru watched from behind a rock, he saw soldiers disembark. *They must be Prince Ousu's men, searching for their commander. They were pretty loyal to have remained behind rather than fleeing to the capital,* Sugaru thought. It took him a moment to make up his mind, but in the end he flew up behind the leader and hailed him. Startled, the man spun around.

"You'll find what you're looking for in the hut on top of that hill," Sugaru said.

"Who are you?"

Sugaru waved his hand. "I think you should hurry. It'll take you some time to get there on foot."

Frowning suspiciously, the leader gestured to his men. "Seize him!"

But Sugaru vanished before the soldiers had even swung their spears toward him. He reappeared on a rock ledge some distance away and stuck out his tongue. *I hope you have a happy reunion.* There was no need for him to keep Oguna captive. He had promised not to run or hide. And whether Oguna continued his journey to the east or not did not matter. He could never be far enough away to escape Sugaru's reach.

4

A MONTH PASSED and another was drawing to a close. Conscientiously following the emperor's orders, Oguna had led his troops safely as far east as the barbarous land of Sagamu. The people here were fiercely independent and protective of their freedom. Only a few powerful families paid tribute to Mahoroba, and the territory to the north belonged to the Emishi, a completely different race with their own language. Having no intention of ceding authority to Mahoroba, Emishi bands frequently harassed the borderlands.

The people of Sagamu welcomed the prince and his troops almost everywhere they went, but Oguna knew this reception could turn to betrayal at any moment. The people appraised him and his men with a blatancy he had not seen in the west, obviously curious to see what a prince who claimed direct descent from the God of Light could do. Although situated at the eastern edge of the country, Sagamu was still part of the same land mass as Mahoroba, and rumors of the prince who wielded the Sword had resounded even here, inspiring fear and awe. Oguna and his troops had learned how to take advantage of this, overwhelming whole cities without resorting to physical force, but even so they could not travel through the region entirely without incident.

The company from Mahoroba was riding north along a wide river that cut across the land. Rushes, fluffed with seeds, crowded at the water's edge, and the signs of autumn were everywhere. Once the colorful evening glow had faded from the sky, the insects would begin to buzz. The troop had to hurry if they were to reach the next village before dark, and heralds had already gone ahead to inform the chief and arrange sleeping quarters.

Other than the soldiers crossing the sunset field, there seemed to be not a soul in sight; there was only the wind rolling like waves through the grass into the distance. Looking ahead, however, the company noticed a man standing in the middle of the empty plain, as if he had been waiting for them all along. It was the moment just before the sun dyed the clouds crimson and everything stood out with a strange clarity. The youth's red hair blazed in the light. With his wild hair, towering height, and insolent expression, he was hard to forget.

As soon as Takehiko, the captain of the troop, caught sight of him, he exclaimed, "You again! What are you doing here?"

Sugaru grinned back wordlessly. Oguna and Takehiko came to a halt before him, bringing the entire company to a standstill. The captain opened his mouth again, but Oguna stopped him. "It's all right. His business is with me."

Takehiko turned to the prince with an expression of surprise. "But, sir, who is he?"

"I owe him," Oguna answered calmly. "He has something to tell me. Lead the men on. I'll catch up with you later."

"Do you intend to stay here on your own?" Takehiko looked doubtful, but Oguna did not let him protest any further.

"I promised. Please go on ahead. I'll come after you as soon as we finish. If you all wait here, you won't reach the village before nightfall."

Takehiko reluctantly obeyed the prince and urged his horse forward, casting a deeply suspicious glance at Sugaru. The soldiers passed by, one by one, until even the last packhorse had receded into the distance. After watching them depart, Oguna dismounted swiftly. The metal of his light marching armor rang faintly as he touched the ground.

"Well, you certainly look like a commander, don't you?" Sugaru said. "The way you sent your men off like that was impressive, particularly when you know why I'm here. I have to give you credit for remaining so composed."

Oguna gazed at Sugaru. "Where's Toko?"

"Nowhere. I can't find her."

Until that moment, Oguna had shown no sign of emotion, but now despair clouded his face. "You can't find her?"

"No, I can't. I went to every place I thought she might go. To Mino, to her village, even to the mountain where the shrine used to stand. Then I followed the same route she took to Izumo and searched through Izumo. She's not there. After that I flew to Himuka and met with Lady Iwa, to whom Ki, the Stone of Life, belongs. I went to Mahoroba, and searched the marketplace and Kazuragi. No one had seen her. She didn't turn up anywhere. There's nowhere left to look." The anger of one who has had all his efforts thwarted smoldered in his voice. "There's no proof anywhere that she's still alive. I don't give up easily, but that doesn't mean I don't know when it's time to call it quits. If she's dead, then she must be laid to rest, just like anyone else. You understand what I mean, right?"

"I can't believe it," Oguna whispered.

"If Toko's gone, I'm going back to Izumo. I have a home to return to and friends waiting for me. So . . . for her sake, I've come to finish this before I leave."

A gust of wind assailed them, tangling their hair. The sun had sunk below the horizon, and they faced each other in the rapidly falling dusk. Birds flying home to roost called to one another. "You told me you would not run or hide," Sugaru said calmly. "It seems you've kept that promise."

Oguna nodded. "Yes."

"Then you know it's time to die. As long as you live, Toko's mission will remain unfinished. Her wish will never be fulfilled. I expect that this isn't what you want, but it's not what I would have chosen either. I'd appreciate it if you'd go quietly when I kill you."

"No."

"What?" Sugaru took a deep breath. It had not occurred to him that Oguna would refuse. "Don't tell me you've suddenly decided your life is too dear to part with. Remember, you promised—"

But Oguna cut him off. "Toko's alive." Seeing that Sugaru had braced himself to attack, Oguna assumed a fighting stance. "I'm sure of it. I have to see her again. So I can't—I just can't die now."

"Enough!" Sugaru shouted, furious. "How can you change your mind so easily? I can't say I like people who want to die, but those who don't do what they say are even worse. Don't go pleading for your life in front of me. I can't bear to watch something so shameful."

"I've no intention of pleading for my life." Oguna placed a hand on the hilt of his sword—not the Sword but an ordinary blade. "But I can't give you my life. I didn't realize this before, but I do now. The only reason I could have died last time was because it was Toko. Only Toko could have killed me."

"Fine, then. Have it your way. But it's useless to resist. I'm offering to send you to Toko. It would have been nice if you could have recognized that as a kindness." Sugaru summoned the Misumaru's power—the power that gave birth to myriad lives and then extinguished them again. He would finish this with one blow.

A tremendous impact shook the world, and he was momentarily blinded by a burst of light. Something not only blocked his blow but threw him backwards. He landed on his back in the grass, stunned, feeling as if he had just slammed into an invisible wall. Bright spots floated in front of his eyes. Lifting his face, he saw Oguna less than half a pace away, looking down at him with his sword held at the ready.

"Please understand." Despite the fact that he had the upper hand, Oguna seemed to be imploring him. "Please don't make me use the power of the Sword. Toko's alive! I'm sure of it. Please look for her again."

"But I thought the power was sealed away," Sugaru said, surprised. "The power of the Misumaru was greater than yours. You weren't able to resist it at all. Were you just bluffing?"

"No. I was defenseless. I wasn't faking it." He looked somewhat sadly at Sugaru. "You probably can't understand, but until then I had never moved the Sword, never managed to suppress its power, even once. But when I saw Toko and realized why she had come, I was able to control it for the first time. That's why I could have died then—probably quite easily."

"You mean it wasn't the Misumaru that sealed the power of the Sword but you, because you wanted to?"

"Much of the Sword's power is still held in check. But its power now runs in my veins. The force that works to protect me moves faster than thought or will. And it grows stronger as my physical strength returns."

Sugaru clicked his tongue at his own folly. "What a laugh. I let you go thinking I could kill you any time only to find the tables reversed. I was a fool not to finish you off when you were weak."

"I'm sorry, but only Toko can slay me." Oguna did indeed look sorry. He sheathed his sword and then knelt before Sugaru on one knee. "I just can't understand why she would give up and vanish after coming so far. It's not like her. Do you know?"

Sugaru searched Oguna's face. He was very hard to understand—one moment he behaved like an adult and the next he was a child. "Is that why you can't die? Because you want to find out?"

Oguna's voice grew small. "It was Toko who taught me that the Sword was my problem. She made me realize that I had given up and was just running away . . . I have to see her again. I don't know why she left like that, but next time I want to do things differently."

"You're that convinced that she's alive, are you?"

"Yes, I'm sure she's alive somewhere."

Hearing this, Sugaru realized that somewhere inside he was actually relieved. Although he had come to kill Oguna and put an end to it all, in his heart he had not wanted to believe that Toko was dead. Perhaps he had really only come to test Oguna's conviction. *What a cowardly thing to do,* he thought as he looked at the youth in front of him. He had not expected Oguna to recover from his wounds so completely in just two months. Yet that was not necessarily a bad thing. Oguna was younger than Sugaru. He was at the age where sudden spurts of physical and mental growth were only to be expected, a thought that gave Sugaru hope.

"I think that if I decide to destroy the Sword myself, of my own free will, there might be a way . . . if I work with the magatama you wield. I didn't gain this power by choice. If it's possible to extinguish it, then that's what I want," Oguna said earnestly, watching Sugaru's face. "I'm asking this for Toko's sake also. Won't you help me try?"

Sugaru considered his request carefully, although he already knew the answer. Shrugging his shoulders, he finally said, "I don't know why I'm such a nice guy, but I take back what I just said about knowing when to call it quits."

DARKNESS HAD FALLEN, and Oguna spurred his horse after Takehiko and his men. Sugaru sat behind him. He had responded to Oguna's invitation not just to test his idea but because he was tired of traveling alone. Although fearless in the face of demons and gods, Sugaru yearned for human companionship.

It was a weakness known to few and one he never even admitted to himself. Roaming the land alone went against his nature. He needed friends; it was his loyal companions who made him the man he was. Unable to find even Toko, he found the loneliness much harder to bear, and this had put him in a bad temper. Although Sugaru remained unaware of it, it was this part of him that Oguna had touched. He found himself drawn to this boy who was struggling so desperately to find his way on his own.

In the darkness they saw the red light of torches up ahead. They finally caught up with Oguna's men at the entrance to the village where they were waiting. Together they hurried into the stockade. The chief, head of one of the most powerful families in Sagamu, had come out to welcome them. Following behind, Sugaru was impressed by the large man. Despite his graying hair, he was obviously still hale and strong and, judging by the scar on his forehead, was a seasoned warrior.

Returning the chief's greeting, Oguna betrayed no sign of his youth. He drained the cup of sake given to him and smiled with easy confidence, bearing himself with a dignity that was no less than that of the chief.

I see. So that's how a prince behaves, Sugaru thought as he watched the chief usher Oguna inside the main room of his hall. Takehiko, Sugaru, and the others were led into a courtyard where a lavish feast had been prepared. Someone clapped a hand on Sugaru's shoulder and he turned around to face Takehiko.

"What did you say to the prince?" Takehiko demanded. "Just because our lord is generous, don't make the mistake of thinking you'll get away with anything. If something happens to him, it will be disastrous for everyone. We'll make sure you pay for it." Several other soldiers closed in around Sugaru, who gazed calmly back at Takehiko. The man looked to be about thirty. Lean and sinewy, he was no longer young but was not yet experienced enough to keep his feelings from showing. Right now, his expression betrayed both suspicion and a touch of envy. One glance had told Sugaru where his value lay as a soldier—honesty and loyalty. He was the type of man who, once he had pledged fealty, would remain steadfast even if it cost him his life.

Sugaru shrugged. "We weren't talking about anything important. Your prince asked me to come with him, so I came. That's all."

"I don't believe you," Takehiko said, pressing Sugaru. "Who are you? You appeared out of nowhere once before, didn't you? You were the one who told us where to find the prince. What relation are you to him?"

"No relation in particular," Sugaru answered coolly. "I merely tried to kill him twice, that's all. Who knows what will happen next time?"

"What?" Color suffused Takehiko's face, but at that moment a young soldier came running up and called out to him.

"Captain, the prince bade me convey a message. His lordship begs you to entertain personally the man who joined us today, as he is greatly in the man's debt. Twice he has saved the prince's life."

Silenced, Takehiko stared at Sugaru for a long moment, and Sugaru watched with interest to see how he would react. The man's expression cleared suddenly. "You really like a joke, don't you? Why didn't you just say so in the first place? I would never hesitate to welcome someone who had saved the prince himself."

Sugaru grinned broadly, highly amused, and Takehiko, taking this as a sign that they had overcome their differences, thumped him repeatedly on the shoulder. "Come. Let's drink the night away."

5

FISH AND FOWL on skewers roasted over a bright fire in the center of the courtyard. The chief plied the men from Mahoroba so generously with sake that they grew merry and broke into song and dance. It was impossible for Sugaru not to join in, and soon the men were treating him as if he had been a member of their party all along.

"Where're you from?" Takehiko asked.

"Izumo. How about you?"

"I'm from Kibi. We're practically neighbors. Drink up, drink up." Takehiko seemed to have concluded that Sugaru was a good man. "We're both a long way from home here in the remotest corner of the nation, aren't we? I couldn't believe at first that the emperor would send the crown prince to such a dangerous place as this virgin land."

"Why did he choose Prince Ousu to lead the expedition?" Sugaru asked, drawing him on.

"The prince volunteered to go. He has suffered so much." Takehiko fell silent for a moment and then continued. "After his aunt, the Itsuki no Miya, passed away, he lost his only ally. The emperor is heartless. I can't understand why he would hate someone as kind and good as the prince."

"I heard about the prince when I was in the capital," Sugaru said after draining his cup. "People were saying that you might as well serve the thunder god, that the men under him risk being struck by lightning. Yet you say he's kind."

"As long as we serve under him, we'll never be subjected to such a fate," Takehiko stated flatly. "I learned that soon after we set off on these expeditions. No matter what the rumors say, he's the model of a true leader, someone who deserves our respect."

THE NIGHT was far advanced, and the fire had died down to embers. Although Takehiko had insisted that he would stand guard the first night in this new place, Sugaru had volunteered to take his place. He had never been drunk in his life. In fact, sake only made him more alert, whereas Takehiko, unable to keep pace, had been left staggering.

Once the men had all retired to their sleeping quarters, the starlit garden sank into sudden silence. A sliver of moon, thin as the tip of a fingernail, perched at the top of a huge zelkova tree, and the chirping of the crickets grew louder. Sugaru did not find watchman duty difficult. Since he had begun to carry the Misumaru, sleep had become less essential. He could also go without food for several days before feeling the effects. But he saw no reason to rejoice in a life without the pleasures of food and sleep. He particularly found the long nights hard. Tonight, he felt content for he had shared food, drink, and laughter with others for the first time in a while. The memories of company lingered after the others had gone to bed.

He was not sure how long he had been there. He was just looking up at the stars, trying to judge the time, when he heard a faint noise behind him—the sound of someone walking stealthily. He swung the spear from his shoulder, glad to have something to relieve the boredom. *I wonder if it's an assassin. From what Takehiko said, that wouldn't be unusual.* He crept to the corner of the hall and, waiting for the right moment, stepped out suddenly. A shadowy figure jumped back as if startled.

"Who goes there?" Sugaru demanded. To his surprise, the figure responded with a question of his own.

"Is that you, Sugaru?"

Sugaru lowered his spear incredulously. "And just what is the prince of Mahoroba doing wandering about alone at night?"

It was Oguna. He peered intently at Sugaru as if surprised to see him there. "Did they make you serve the night watch?"

"Not really. I volunteered."

"I thought you must be Takehiko."

"He had too much to drink. What about you? Did something happen to make you leave?"

"Well, yeah." Oguna was dressed only in a thin robe, as if he had come straight from his bed. "I'd rather do without nighttime hospitality."

"Were you visited by an assassin?"

"I would have preferred an assassin," Oguna responded reluctantly. "It was the chief's daughter."

Sugaru burst out laughing but smothered it quickly with his hand. "You didn't? You mean you ran away?"

Oguna said nothing, but from the scowl on his face Sugaru guessed that he had hit the mark. "But the chief must have sent her as a gesture of goodwill. If you run away, you'll just stir up trouble."

"But why would he do that? I don't understand it. It's so unfair to the girl." He sounded angry.

Sugaru struggled not to laugh aloud. He could not believe this was the same person who had accepted the chief's welcome as if he were accustomed to such treatment. "I'm amazed you've managed to get away with that so far. There must be many men who would offer their daughters to the crown prince as a form of hospitality. Yet you've never accepted? Not even once?"

"I don't want to. It's too dangerous."

"So you're afraid," Sugaru said bluntly. "Surely you've been with a woman at least once, haven't you?"

Oguna thought about making some excuse but instead kept his mouth shut, which only amused Sugaru more. "You mean you've run out of the room every time?"

"I often spend half the night outside anyway," Oguna answered finally. "I usually wait with the night watch until the sky lightens and then scout around the area."

"But think of the poor girl. She'll be humiliated."

Oguna seemed taken aback at this thought but then said gravely, "If we became lovers, she would only suffer greater misfortune. I know that. My older brother loved a woman and that love drove him to his destruction. How can I repeat the same mistake after seeing that?"

"Personally, I think it wouldn't be bad to find a woman you could love so much you didn't care if she brought you to ruin," Sugaru said, reflecting on his own behavior. "I suppose the imperial family must be rather large, but what happened to that brother?"

Oguna gave Sugaru a sour look. "You mean you haven't heard? I killed him. It was my older brother who found me in Mino and trained me. Yet, in the end, it was I who slew him. I hear that Lady Akaru followed him in death. So how could I lead a woman to the same fate?"

They sat on the ground under the starry sky and talked in hushed voices. Oguna seemed to have no intention of returning to his room and every intention of staying outside until daybreak. Bit by bit, he related his story. "It was my older brother who taught me the ways of command, and those lessons as his shadow have been drilled into me. Having killed him with my own hand, I can never be free from his influence. That's really why I took on the expedition to vanquish the Kumaso in Himuka. And this one to the east as well as."

"You mean you're trying to be Oh-usu, the warrior?"

Oguna paused for a long while and then said, "I'm still his shadow. No matter how much I try to prove to the emperor that I have no intention of rebelling, he is suspicious. No matter what he tells me to do, I have no choice but to obey. Even though I know these campaigns are just excuses to keep me away from the capital."

"I can understand why he'd want to do that," Sugaru agreed, a bit unkindly. "After all, Prince Oh-usu was just a man, whereas you actually wield the Sword."

"I'm used to being feared and hated," Oguna said in a low voice. "Yet I still hoped that the emperor would at least understand that I wouldn't rebel. I don't want anything for myself. Yet he never even tried to understand me, or my mother."

His mother? Sugaru thought for a moment and then prompted Oguna. "I've never heard anything about your mother from anyone. Takehiko told me that your sole ally was the Itsuki no Miya, although he said she had passed away."

"He was talking about my mother," Oguna said.

"You mean your aunt."

"No, my mother." Oguna turned his face away. "If you think about why I'm the only one who can wield the Sword, you'll understand. The blood of the God of Light runs far too thickly in my veins. That's why."

Sugaru caught his breath at the enormity of the taboo that had been broken.

"Let's change the subject," Oguna said abruptly. "I shouldn't have talked about this here."

"Wait a minute," Sugaru began, but then he forgot what he had been going to say, his attention caught by the appearance of a strange creature in the shadow of a tree. Its slender form resembled a doe, but it cast a faint white light, almost as if it were burning in the darkness. Its riveting beauty held Sugaru's eyes, yet he was alarmed by the way it stood motionless, staring intently as though studying them.

"What is that?" Sugaru hissed, jerking his chin toward it. Oguna turned to stare at him rather than at the creature.

"You mean you can see it? I thought I was the only one who could."

"Don't underestimate the bearer of the Misumaru. That thing doesn't appeal to me. I'm going to find out what it is."

Oguna grabbed his arm hastily. "No, don't. When it's time to find out, I'll be the one to do it. It appears wherever I go."

"What?"

"Just pretend you don't see it. As long as we stay on our guard, it'll leave before morning."

Sugaru realized that there was still much that Oguna hadn't told him. Was this creature one of the reasons he spent so many nights outside?

"Have you always seen it?"

"No." He looked at Sugaru hesitantly. "The first time I saw it was after my mother died—on the night I received news of her death when we were on our way west."

Sugaru turned to look at the creature once more. Even its eyes glowed white, like two moons. Sugaru felt a chill, as if death were looking him in the eyes. Oguna grabbed him and turned him around. "You mustn't look at it. If you do, it will come to you. I knew that it would appear tonight."

"Why?"

"Today, when I faced you, I used the power of the Sword. That's why—" But he did not have a chance to finish. The doelike creature suddenly broke into a run. Even Sugaru recoiled. It sped light-footed from the shadows straight toward them. Nothing, it seemed, could stop its flight as it raced like flame across the ground. Oguna pushed Sugaru aside and stood to face the charging beast. Sugaru could only blink—frozen and helpless for first time in his life.

The creature soared through the air and plunged into Oguna's chest, fusing with his body. But, to Sugaru's amazement, in the next instant it leapt out the other side and ran off, vanishing from sight.

After some time, Oguna sighed. "It's all right now," he said. "It won't come back tonight."

"What was that thing?" Sugaru was practically shouting.

"The power of the Sword," Oguna said listlessly. "The power you sealed with your Misumaru has left me and taken shape. It wanders about seeking to return to its master. Right now, I'm able to keep that from happening."

"What? That thing is no sword. What is the Sword's power anyway? The Misumaru doesn't act on its own like that."

Oguna looked as if he wanted to weep. Struggling for self-control, he said, "I have wondered what that power is for a long time, about why it tries to protect me even against my will. My mother, the shrine priestess, gave me the Sword. Yet sometimes I think that she is really the true owner."

Sugaru frowned. "But I thought your mother died?"

"She killed herself. In order to protect me. Before I left for Himuka, we had a fight. I told her that I wouldn't take the Sword, that I would never wield it again. She told me that she would willingly sacrifice her own life to protect mine. When I left . . . she put her words into action. How can I justify hating her when she loved me so much? That creature is my mother's soul incarnate. My mother." Oguna clutched his arms to his chest as he spoke.

A chill crept over Sugaru. "That's crazy," he said, his anger rising. "If you think that's a mother's love, you're out of your mind. That's not love, that's delusion. My mother died when I was little, but even I can tell you that much."

"Maybe we're both crazy—mother and child," Oguna said sadly. "But right now, I don't want that power back. When I encountered Toko again, I realized that."

6

WHEN MORNING CAME, Oguna walked among his soldiers, talking to each one as though nothing had happened. He wore a very different face in the daytime. He appeared cheerful, speaking easily to his men and exuding confidence and energy. Even his faint hint of arrogance became his station as crown prince. *No wonder that ardent admirers like Takehiko exist in his ranks,* Sugaru thought. No one knew the Oguna who faced the dead alone at night.

Surely he can't keep this up for very long, though. No one can last on just an outward display of bravado . . . But within a few days Sugaru had changed his mind. Oguna, it seemed, could. At the very least, he had grown so accustomed to pushing himself that it no longer felt like a strain.

Oguna was trying to organize the local men into an army under the emperor's banner to subdue the northern Emishi. Oshiba, the chief, had gathered warriors from all over Sagamu. A mixed assortment, they numbered over five hundred. Oguna and his men spent a month equipping them for battle and training them to work together under a commander. Sugaru, who had no desire to affiliate himself with Mahoroba, stayed aloof and instead spent his time wandering the area in search of any signs of Toko.

Finally, the day came when the soldiers marched off amidst a fanfare of conch shells and a flutter of colorful banners. Everyone gathered to bid them farewell. Sugaru too watched them leave, recalling as he did so how Oguna had come to him at dawn that very day. "I intend to win this battle without resorting to the Sword," he had declared. "I've tried many times before. I think it can be done."

If he had to come specially to tell me, it probably means he isn't totally convinced...

That same Oguna was now riding past him, sitting high in the saddle. His burnished gold helmet, fastened with a crimson cord, sparkled in the sun. All eyes were on him. He appeared more than worthy to be the descendant of the God of Light.

Sugaru stood on the path outside where they had been staying. Once Oguna had passed by, he had a clear view of the people from the chief's hall gathered in the courtyard. The women were now spilling from the building, which instantly drew Sugaru's attention. He had long been curious about the caliber of the chief's daughter whom Oguna had jilted. If she was a beauty, Sugaru just might approach her himself. It was with this ulterior motive that he tried to peer through the hedge to get a better look. But at that moment a voice called out to him from behind.

"What are you doing there?"

Hastily schooling his features, Sugaru turned to find a man with a scar across his forehead glaring at him. His interrogator was, of all people, the chief himself.

"You're one of the prince's men. Why aren't you going off to battle with the others? You're still young."

Sugaru, who never changed his attitude for anyone, responded in his usual off-handed manner. "I don't belong to the prince. I'm my own man."

The chief raised his eyebrows. "If you're not his man then what are you?"

"A guest perhaps. At any rate, I didn't come here to fight."

"If I were your age, I'd be eager to go to war whether I was a guest or not," the chief said, his beard wagging. "This is the first time I haven't led my men to battle." He looked disappointed. "I'm still strong enough to fight, but it's unavoidable considering my position. Don't your arms weep to see the troops marching boldly off without you?"

"It suits me better to be the commander rather than a follower."

"You're pretty blunt." The chief fixed Sugaru with a keen, appraising look and, apparently, rather than being insulted, liked what he saw. "I doubt we'll see a commander who surpasses the prince for a long time. He's a natural. I'd heard plenty of rumors, but I could tell he was far from ordinary as soon as I laid eyes on him. He's so young, yet he already has tremendous leadership capacity without a trace of ambition or desire."

Thinking of the chief's daughter, Sugaru almost burst out laughing. "Yes. Right. No desire."

"He told me he has no intention of demanding new territory in Sagamu. Whatever land is reclaimed he plans to return to the people. He's admirable, truly noble. Although the fact that someone so young should be so selfless and detached is troubling. He may not live long."

Actually . . . he could be right. The chief's words pinpointed something that had been bothering Sugaru for some time, although it was only now that he identified it. Despite Oguna's passion for the task at hand, an ill-omened shadow seemed to cling to him. *Oguna said that he doesn't want anything for himself. And he really doesn't.*

The elderly chief of Sagamu continued. "Once in a while a man like him comes along—someone with innate ability who excels in everything yet who has no desire nor any attachment to the world. Such people die young, almost as if the gods can't wait to have them back in heaven. They're impatient to leave this world, like a bird taking flight, never looking back. Even while they live, there's an air about them that suggests their lives will be fleeting. The prince has that same look, though to someone who has lived as long as me, that's also what makes him so compelling."

If Oguna dies, Sugaru thought, *our mission would be fulfilled without even using the Misumaru.* Strangely, the feeling this stirred in his breast bore no resemblance to joy. "You know," Sugaru said abruptly, "I think I'll go catch up with that army after all. Sometimes it pays to listen to our elders."

A SENSE OF FOREBODING had driven Sugaru to travel north with Oguna's troops, but the events that transpired came as a surprise. No battle broke out. Instead, the foreign tribes the large army confronted engaged in only a few short skirmishes before scattering and retreating back to their final outpost. There Oguna and his officers merely negotiated a settlement, and as the leader quickly capitulated, the Emishi were conquered without a fight. Oguna ordered his men to make camp without even setting foot in the village.

When Sugaru stopped by the commander's tent, he found Oguna in an unusually cheerful mood. "Well, that was a letdown," Sugaru said. "You lead such an impressive army. I didn't expect someone from Mahoroba to keep all that strength in check."

"It went exactly as planned," Oguna said, almost boasting. He must have been very pleased to have his scheme succeed for he was unusually lighthearted. "But I know that the real test starts now. We've managed to quench the enemy's battle fever, but the problem now is that we must check that same passion in our allies. Many of my men are still burning to fight. Just because we succeeded in settling things peacefully doesn't mean those feelings can be easily subdued. They need an outlet or they'll explode. A large-scale project that can take the place of war." He smiled suddenly. "Besides it would be a waste to disperse such a large force without putting them to good use. I've been thinking about this for some time. Did you see the huge wetlands surrounding the swamp on the way here? I noticed when I was surveying the land for this expedition. That swamp was formed when the river changed course, damming up a tributary."

Oguna took a stick and quickly drew a simple map on the ground. "If we build a canal here at the shortest point, we can drain the swamp. With over five hundred men, we should be able to finish the work in half a month. The land there will be very good for growing rice. And it'll provide an outlet for the water, as well as for the bottled-up energy of the men."

Sugaru looked at Oguna as if he were seeing him for the first time. "Is that what you were thinking about as you marched your army to battle?"

"I can't help it—it's just my nature. I'm actually better at building than fighting . . . " He suddenly looked embarrassed and erased the map with the toe of his boot. "I like engineering better than commanding an army. It's useful. Although no one sees me as anything but a conqueror."

IN THE MIDDLE OF THE NIGHT, however, everything changed. Oguna's troops, lulled into a sense of security by their bloodless victory, were attacked under cover of the dark. The assault was aimed with deadly accuracy at the army's nerve center—Oguna's tent. Arrows rained down and the guards were felled one after the other by the wild invaders. The plot was so cleverly executed that not even Sugaru, who had remained awake, was aware of it until the arrows flew.

Oguna was too trusting after all! Sugaru could only conclude that they should have subdued the village rather than believing the Emishi. He grabbed the spear beside him, forced now to fight. The Misumaru shone brightly, illuminating the darkness in place of the extinguished torches. He saw at a glance that their attackers were few in number but highly skilled. Joining the fray, Sugaru searched the crowd for Oguna. Although the area around him was now a confused melee, the situation was still manageable. Other soldiers, realizing that something was wrong, were already running over from other parts of the camp, and the attackers ebbed away like the tide, seeming to take this as the cue to retreat.

"After them. Don't let any escape!" Takehiko bellowed. The darkness, however, aggravated the confusion, and Sugaru could hear Oguna's men colliding with one another. *They can't hope to compete with the invaders' expertise,* Sugaru thought.

Where is Oguna? If the prince had been hit, this would end in much worse than the chaos of the attack. Sugaru, however, quickly found him. He was being forced back into his tent, surrounded by his men with whom he was arguing heatedly.

"We must treat your wound first, sir. Please don't move."

Sugaru peered inside the tent. "Are you hurt?"

Oguna looked up at Sugaru, his eyes blazing. "It's nothing. Just a scratch. We've got to catch them."

He was right. It was only a superficial wound. Yet the fact that his attackers had succeeded even in grazing him in the midst of a well-equipped army demonstrated that they were no common adversaries.

"There's no way we can catch them," Sugaru said. "I never expected the Emishi to be capable of something so sophisticated."

"They aren't Emishi," Oguna said bitterly. "That was just a disguise. This isn't the first time I've been attacked by opportunists in the midst of another conflict. I'm guessing they were from Mahoroba."

"You mean they were men from your troop?" Sugaru asked in surprise.

"No . . . I think they were assassins. Probably sent by the emperor."

"What? The emperor sent you off to fight the Emishi because he wants you to be killed in battle?"

"My own men understand. But the soldiers from Sagamu won't. They'll believe it was the Emishi and descend upon their village. I have to show them who the real murderers are."

But Oguna's fear was soon realized. Receiving a report from one of the soldiers sent after the assassins, Oguna flew out of his tent to see flames rising from the direction of the Emishi village.

"Yet another crime will be added to my name," he whispered as he stared at the fire.

Sugaru noticed that Oguna was shaking with anger. Then he blinked in surprise. Less then ten steps away from Oguna stood the creature—like a graceful, white doe. Oguna had buried his face in his hands, but he did not weep. Then slowly he raised his head and looked at the creature. He did not seem surprised to see it standing there. He gazed straight into its burning, blue-white eyes.

Sugaru strode over and grabbed him by the shoulders. He thought he could guess what Oguna was thinking. "Don't," he said. "Don't use the power of the Sword."

"There's no other way left."

Sugaru shook him, trying to distract him from the creature. "Don't ruin everything over something like this," he shouted. "You said you wouldn't use it, remember? If you want to stop your army, I'll do it for you. Don't take that creature back into yourself." He finally managed to jerk Oguna around so that he was facing away from the thing. "Don't look at that thing. I know what it is. It's madness. If you don't keep it out, you'll go mad too."

"But . . . it's my mother," Oguna said.

Sugaru was forced to acknowledge just how difficult it was going to be to sever the Sword from its master. While despising the Sword's power, Oguna could not help craving it. For him, it represented something he could not completely reject—something that comforted him even as he tried to turn away, something to which his heart returned when wounded.

His mother . . . Sugaru could understand, but he must not sympathize. He hardened his voice. "You're too old to yearn for your mother. You'll never grow up until you vanquish that thing."

Oguna's eyes wavered. "Vanquish it?"

"Break with it. If you don't, I'll kill it. That's what I came here to do in the first place."

Sugaru was focused so intently on Oguna that he failed to watch the creature. But it recognized what he was trying to do. Kicking off the ground, it launched itself at Sugaru. By the time he noticed, the flaming white body was already upon him, its jaws opened wide to reveal sharp, wolflike fangs. The impact of its forepaws knocked Sugaru to the ground just as the Misumaru whisked him out of reach. His chest burned where the creature's paws had touched him. He shuddered to think what would have happened if it had sunk its teeth into his throat. Its doelike appearance was just that—appearance only.

What a monster! Sugaru was on his feet instantly, his spear at the ready, but the creature had vanished. Only Oguna stood there, staring vacantly at Sugaru—his body glowing like blue flame.

"You fool!" Sugaru yelled. Although Oguna and the creature had their own separate wills, in the end they were one. They could not be challenged separately.

"Don't get in my way," Oguna said in a low voice. "I'm going to the Emishi village to stop my soldiers. That's all."

"You're out of your mind. You'll destroy your allies as well as your foes. Your own men will die."

"Stay out of this."

Nothing Sugaru could say was going to stop him. It was his emotions that ruled Oguna now—deep, raging feelings that suppressed every other part of him. There was no choice left but to fight. Sugaru focused on the Misumaru. The four stones shone with a blinding light and began drawing the wind. The Misumaru centered this force on the Sword, compressing its lightning will into a single point and striving to seal it away. The Misumaru could create space. It was this that enabled the bearer to move instantly from one place to another. And it was this that eliminated the Sword's power, channeling it into a different dimension. Concentrated on a human being, this force could erase someone from the face of the earth. It took four stones to raise this power to the extreme of death itself. Having been the bearer now for some time, Sugaru understood this instinctively. But he had never tapped that power to its limit.

I guess it can't be helped . . .

The two powers slammed together with a force that ripped the leaves off the nearby trees. Sugaru thought he had steeled himself for this battle, but it was far harder to seal the Sword than he had anticipated. He knew it would be fatal to underestimate Oguna, yet his power surpassed even Sugaru's expectations. Sugaru was hampered by the fact that his usual style of scoffing at his opponent was useless. Worse still, he was plagued by doubt. He could not rid himself of the fear that if he killed Oguna, who believed that Toko still lived, he would be killing Toko as well. Moreover, Oguna had found his way too far into his heart for Sugaru to utterly reject and destroy him. For some reason, Sugaru actually liked the young prince. It was at this weakness, so brief that it could not even have been called an unguarded moment, that the Sword struck. It sundered the net of power woven to bind it and sent Sugaru flying.

He's so strong . . . Unable to withstand that force, the string joining the stones together snapped. *Perhaps his power surpasses even the Misumaru,* Sugaru thought. After all, Oguna drew strength not only from the Sword but also from his mother, who had transcended death to possess her son. Sugaru watched the stones fall to the ground. Anger washed through him, not for himself, but for Toko.

"Wake up!" he yelled at Oguna. "How do you think Toko will feel? I thought you said you wanted to see her again!"

The blue-white flame launching itself at Sugaru vanished, replaced by Oguna. He stood staring at Sugaru, as if he had been shaken from a dream and only now realized who Sugaru was. Sugaru waited a little longer, preparing himself for another attack, but Oguna did not slip away again. He appeared to have escaped the creature's control. Sugaru chose his words with care. "As long as you continue to wield that Sword, as long as you harbor that creature, we're enemies. Even if Toko is alive, even if you do meet her again, we're still enemies. Take a look around. See what you've done. You lose yourself."

Oguna did as he was told and surveyed the scene. The earth itself had been gouged open and the trees torn out by their roots and burnt black. Wisps of smoke still rose from their charred remains. That the damage did not extend into the distance was only because Sugaru had consciously fought to contain it.

"You've tried to extinguish that power before, right?"

"I've tried many times," Oguna answered, despondent. Completely returned to his senses, he seemed overcome with shame.

"You've got to sever yourself from that thing."

"I know . . . "

The blue-white flame had left him. The only light was cast by the magatama, which Sugaru had gathered together again. In their glow, Oguna looked like neither a glorious prince nor a daring commander. In fact, he appeared so forlorn that Sugaru couldn't help berating him. "How can you act like such a great leader before your men and be so utterly useless when it comes to yourself? It's your lack of will, of belief in yourself, that lets that creature get inside you."

"The man you see in the daytime isn't me. It's my older brother. I know what he would think, how he would act. I learned it all from him, and that's the role I played. I'm still doing that."

"Oh, come on. Are you trying to excuse yourself by saying he never taught you how to deal with your mother? What are you? Just a puppet?"

Despite this scolding, however, Oguna only looked at Sugaru. His eyes were full of sorrow. "I don't understand myself very well . . . " he whispered. Then, he said more defiantly, "I should never have been born. I know that. I should not be here. But that's not what my mother wants. She sacrificed her own life for mine, to protect me. That's what that creature wants. That I'm alive at all is because of my mother. Without her, I would have been snuffed out by the emperor's hand long ago. In Himuka and in Izumo, my father's shadow came for me. Each time, the Sword intervened and saved my life. I know it's not right. But as long as I'm alive, how can I justify rejecting my mother?" His shoulders drooped. "If I really wanted to, I think I could probably sever myself from that creature. But if I do that, what would I have left? I'd be all alone—isolated among people who hate and kill their own kin."

"What do *you* want?" Sugaru asked. "Surely you aren't living just because of what your brother or your mother want? You must have desires of your own. Why don't you try to fulfill them? Why don't you recognize what you really want?"

"I'm not in a position to—"

Sugaru cut him off. "Worry about your position later. It's because you've got nothing inside where it counts that strong-willed people can push you around so easily. You can't even decide between right and wrong. Why don't you try choosing something for yourself and sticking to it, without worrying about other people? If you choose something evil, then at least people like me could do something about it. The way it stands now, you've got no way out. Make up your mind. What do you want to do?"

Oguna bit his lip. "I want to meet Toko again," he said finally. "I want to live so that I might see Toko."

"Then work toward that and don't get distracted. Show me that you can find her yourself. That's what Toko did. She told everyone she was going to get the magatama and she lived up to her word."

"Toko was always stronger than me." Oguna's face softened. Sugaru felt for a second as if he were seeing the old Oguna. "I don't expect that there's any way to make up for breaking my promise, but if she's alive somewhere, I want to find her."

In the end, I guess Toko really is the only one who can help him change. Who else but Toko, Sugaru thought, could stand a chance against the power of the Sword when it was augmented by the spirit of Oguna's dead mother? Even with four magatama, Sugaru had not been able to destroy Oguna's power or sever him from it. Staring at the broken cord of the Misumaru, Sugaru suddenly remembered that there ought to be another stone. *Toko said there were five magatama in Toyoashihara guarded by five Tachibana clans. I wonder what would happen if we added the other one . . .* But he could not remember whether she had told him where that other land was. He wished he had listened more carefully, but it was too late now. *It all comes down to the same thing,* he thought irritably. *We won't get anywhere without Toko . . .*

*chapter
nine*

REUNION

Reunion

WITH THE CRUSHING DEFEAT of the Emishi tribes by the prince's army, Oguna's fame spread rapidly, albeit against his wishes. In the end, he had no choice but to act like the leader he was acclaimed to be. Having won the people's awe and also gained their fear, he launched his canal-building project. This selfless dedication to the betterment of Sagamu astonished the inhabitants of that land. Only Sugaru realized that Oguna was motivated by the desire to atone for what he had done.

The project was even more successful than Oguna had anticipated. His hardworking men finished far ahead of schedule. Oguna then handed over the entire project to the chief and prepared to depart. "Are you sure you want to give it all to us?" the chief asked incredulously. "This was really your achievement. Surely the emperor of Mahoroba will be displeased. Allow me to keep this territory in your name as it was you who won it back from the Emishi."

"I already told you," Oguna responded. "Land belongs to those who cultivate it. I won't allow Mahoroba to interfere. Let me write you a deed to the land as proof."

The chief looked at him searchingly for a moment but finally said with deep reverence, "Wherever you may go, our hearts belong to you. If you but send us word, I will provide men, supplies, whatever you need."

"I thank you for the offer," Oguna said. He smiled suddenly. "But don't even bother thinking that. Concentrate instead on cultivating these fields. My men and I were never meant to settle down in one spot, and I doubt we ever will."

The warships were launched and stood ready in the bay. Waving farewell to a crowd that was loath to see him go, Oguna boarded his ship and breathed a sigh of relief.

"You're quite the object of worship, aren't you?" Sugaru teased him as he climbed aboard Oguna's ship as if he belonged there. Oguna's face lit up at the sight of him.

"I can't understand why people are so impressed just because I didn't ask for anything."

"I expect because most people in your position would do just the opposite," Sugaru said dryly. "Greed and power generally go together, you know. That old man told me you were going to die young because you don't have enough attachment to the world."

Oguna looked uncomfortable. "He's wrong. What I desire is just different, that's all. Look at you, Sugaru. If anyone's going to die young, it would be you."

"What're you talking about?" Sugaru frowned.

"You stayed with me all this time, even though you have absolutely nothing to gain by it. You've been kind to me even though you aren't related to me in any way. You're the one who doesn't seem to have any desire."

"Ha! Fat chance," Sugaru said. "I never do anything that doesn't have something in it for me. I'm just a bundle of desire. I guarantee it. And besides, I come from a long-lived family. My father was unlucky, but most of us are tough like my grandpa. It's my dream to get to his age and bully my grandchildren."

"Bully your grandchildren?" Oguna burst out laughing. When he laughed, he looked so carefree he seemed a different person. Sugaru realized suddenly that Oguna was opening up to him. It had happened so gradually that he hadn't noticed until now.

"I wish I were you," Oguna said. "It must be good to have a home to go back to."

"Well, I can't go back with the Misumaru. Not until I've finished this. Once it's over, I'll go home in a flash."

"It won't be long now," Oguna said with a conviction Sugaru found puzzling.

"How do you know that?"

"We're on our way from Sagamu to Hidakami. That's our last destination, the eastern edge of this country where it borders on Emishi territory. The success or failure of this mission will most likely be determined there. That's what the emperor expects. And I can't help but think that Toko is there somewhere in Hidakami."

"Hidakami?" Sugaru's voice rose sharply. "I've heard that name before. Hidakami! That's it! The other place where there's a magatama. It's Hidakami, the land where the sun rises." He looked at Oguna. "Why would Toko be in Hidakami? You don't think she's looking for the other magatama, do you?"

"I don't know," Oguna said quietly. "But last night I dreamt of her. She was standing with the rising sun behind her. So we're heading east. I've heard that Hidakami is a vast country, but I'm sure that's where I'll find her. I just know it."

THE THREE WARSHIPS carrying Oguna and his men pushed east night and day, until they reached the mouth of a river so wide it looked like a bay. They sailed straight up it. The low-lying tideland along the edges made it difficult for the ships to approach the banks, but the river's breadth meant that they could sail far inland quite easily. Before them, as far as the eye could see, spread fields of dry, withered reeds interrupted by the occasional glittering marsh. There were no mountains in sight.

"It certainly *is* vast," Oguna said, straining to discern the horizon that separated the land from the shimmering white sky. "I remember what Nanatsuka once told me. That the plains spread on forever and the antlers of the deer look like trees in the distance. I thought he was exaggerating, but now that I've seen it for myself I can understand what he was talking about."

Sugaru gave him a quick glance. "You sound quite fond of him."

"He gave me so much . . ." Oguna paused. "But he'll never forgive me for killing my older brother."

"That's not the impression I got."

Oguna's eyes grew round. "You know him? Where did you meet him? Is he alive?"

"He certainly looked alive and well to me. And he has a whole troop of men under him. He's the leader a gang of highwaymen near the capital. He's planning to overthrow the emperor."

"That sounds like him all right." Oguna laughed faintly, but then his face darkened and he fell silent. Sugaru gazed off across the plains. He had no idea of where to start looking in a land so wide and empty. *Is Toko really here somewhere?*

A soldier came back from the prow of the ship. "We've sighted people. I believe we must be approaching Karuno, the village the chief of Sagamu told us about."

Oguna quickly pulled himself together. "Good. Let's send a messenger. Prepare to land."

ONCE THE BOATS were moored along the shore they settled down to await the return of the messenger. They could not afford to begin traveling in a strange and unfamiliar place without a guide.

"I wouldn't be surprised at anything that happened here," Takehiko confided to Sugaru. "Why, even the rivers flow toward land instead of to the sea."

"You're joking."

"Didn't you notice?" Takehiko broke off a reed and flung it into the water. The current caught it and began carrying it upstream. Sugaru stared at it in disbelief. Oguna, who was standing beside him, began to chuckle.

"That's not so strange. The river is just influenced by the tides. I bet it flows so gently that the full tide pushes its way upstream."

Sugaru looked at him, impressed. "You're pretty smart."

"I'm guessing there must be a large marsh or lake farther up. Maybe even an inland sea. This is the first time I've seen this kind of topography." Stroking his chin thoughtfully, he said, "We need to make a survey. We don't have any maps of this territory."

"But we'll have to travel for days to get to high enough ground to view the land," Takehiko said.

Oguna suddenly turned to stare at Sugaru.

"What're you looking at?"

"Nothing. I just envy you. You could survey the area in no time, couldn't you?"

"Yeah, well," Sugaru said, conspicuously failing to get Oguna's hint.

"You're lucky. The power you wield helps others. Even though I wish it were otherwise, the Sword's doesn't."

"I never said I was going to help anyone."

"But you're always helping others."

Sugaru glared at Oguna. "Don't go thinking that I'll succumb to flattery. I've no intention of helping the emperor in his conquests." He was, in fact, highly susceptible to flattery.

"I wouldn't think of using you as a scout," Oguna said. "I just thought how great it would be if I could fly like you."

Sugaru's mischievous streak raised its head. "Well, if it's only once, I suppose I could take you up high enough to see the land."

"Really?" Oguna looked up quickly, and Sugaru grinned at his expression.

"You're rejoicing too soon. Don't blame me if you get the fright of your life. The Misumaru is capable of things you've never even dreamed of."

"It won't scare me."

"Remember you said that."

Sugaru shot up into the air with Oguna—straight up, higher than when he had looked for Oguna at sea, far higher than he had ever been. When he had reached his limit, the air was thin and as cold as ice, and the speed of their fall was such that he thought his flesh would be sliced to shreds. Oguna, it seemed, did not know what was happening or even where he was. Sugaru yelled into his ear. "What you want to see is below you. And don't you dare faint. Take a good look at it while you can."

Through the cracks in the clouds the earth looked like a gray blanket. Peering down at the earth, Oguna finally understood what it was and let out a yell. Dropping through the clouds, he saw an immense landscape spread out below—the whole country surrounded by a jagged coastline, a sight that only birds had ever seen before. The river along which he had been standing was quite short, a silver ribbon stretching to the bay of an inland sea. The plain, dotted by the occasional forest, stretched on beyond the marshes as far as the hills that bound it to the north and west. Oguna could see houses in some of the low-lying areas. Everything looked small enough to grasp in his hand. He held his breath and stared. From this height, where even the colors faded, humans seemed completely insignificant, and their frantic scramble to acquire land, meaningless.

Oguna was so quiet that Sugaru glanced over at the boy, wondering if he had indeed fainted. But Sugaru was disappointed. Oguna was simply gazing saucer-eyed at the scene below, forgetting even fear.

"All right. You've seen enough. We're going back."

"Wait—can't we stay just a little longer?"

"You want to smash into the ground?"

Just as Sugaru was about to return to their original spot, he felt something familiar . . . a faint jingling that seemed to call him.

What's that?

But the next instant their feet had touched the ground and the sensation was gone. Recollecting himself, Sugaru was startled to hear Oguna laughing excitedly.

"Sugaru, you're amazing!" Oguna said between gasps. "I never imagined it would be like that. It's just as you said. I can't believe it. Simply amazing."

Sugaru was reminded of how babies squeal with delight when held high in the air, fearing no danger. "I'm not doing it again," he said brusquely. "The Misumaru isn't for entertainment."

"Do you often do that?"

"Fairly often, yes."

"I always wished that I could fly like a bird," Oguna said wistfully. "I'd love to wing through the sky, free from the limitations imposed on mortal men. The more I know about myself, the more I feel like I can't move, like I'm stuck. That's my fate, I guess. Sometimes I feel so trapped I can't breathe."

Sugaru suddenly recalled how Toko had spoken many times of *freeing* Oguna. Perhaps through the strange bond that joined them she had sensed his deep despair. Perhaps, even while they were apart, she had somehow known that the blood of the God of Light, flowing so thickly in his veins, prevented him from finding a place where he belonged.

I think I'm beginning to understand why I no longer want to kill him.

"I'm leaving," Sugaru said, almost to himself. Oguna looked at him in surprise. "I'm going to use the Misumaru to travel around Hidakami. I may find Toko or I may find the fifth magatama. I felt something just now."

Oguna did not protest. "You're free to do as you like," he said.

Sugaru looked at him, disgruntled. "You could at least say that you want to go look for Toko yourself. Are you really sure you want to see her again?"

Oguna returned his gaze with an anguished look. "If I were in a position to say that, I wouldn't bother envying you."

A YOUNG FISHERMAN walked along a beach. His steps across the white sand were light as he headed for home. His name was Matachi, and his tanned arms and legs moved with a vigor born of the rolling waves and the sea breeze. Having just heard the most extraordinary news from his friends, he was full of excitement and his steps quickened. As he passed through a windbreak of black pines, his house came into view. He lived in a small village with his elderly mother—and a guest who had joined them only three months ago.

"Hey, Ma! I'm home!" Matachi called out in a strong voice tempered by the sea. He glanced around the room hastily. "Where's the girl?"

"If you mean Miya, she's out back." His gray-haired mother raised her head from her needle and thread and frowned up at her son. "You never used to hang around the house during the day. Not before Miya came."

Matachi pretended not to hear. "I brought you some *kinme*." He held out a fish and then said in a rush. "I heard the most amazing thing. They're saying that a warship full of soldiers came up the river to the bay. The commander is a prince dressed in shining armor. Nothing like this has ever happened to us. I've got to tell Miya."

"A prince in shining armor? What on earth is he doing here?"

"I wish I knew." Matachi headed for the door.

"Matachi," his mother said sharply. "Don't get too involved with that girl. We're only taking care of her for the time being. Remember. She comes from the palace of the Dragon King under the sea."

Matachi cast her a sullen look and left. Walking behind their house, he came upon a young woman crouching in a small field. She was brushing the dirt from the vegetables that they would pickle for the winter. It moved him just to see her perform such an ordinary task. The girl he and his mother called Miya was slimmer and fairer than the village girls. When they had found her lying on the beach she had looked like a wilted flower.

The girl, sensing someone there, turned and smiled at him. "Welcome home, Matachi."

This simple greeting also made the youth happy. Until a month ago, the girl had hardly been able to speak. "Aren't you cold?" he said. "The sun's going down."

"No, I'm fine." She held up a turnip. "Look how big it is. This was one of the first things we planted after I came here."

Matachi wished he had more things like this to share with her, more ways for them to understand one another. He did not care where she came from. All that mattered was that she was here now. "A prince is coming to Tsuno-ore north of here. He'll be splendidly dressed. Would you like to go and see? All the young people from the village are going."

Miya's eyes widened. "A prince?"

"A prince from the capital far to the west. A descendant of the God of Light."

The girl's face tensed, the relaxed expression suddenly wiped from her face. Matachi feared that she would revert to the way she had been when they had first found her—totally unresponsive. Hastily he retracted his statement. "It's okay, Miya. If you don't want to, we don't have to go. Forget what I said. Please don't be angry."

Miya smiled weakly. "Why would I be angry? I was just surprised, that's all."

Her smile restored his confidence for he assumed it meant she agreed with him. "Miya, you should get out more. You're looking much better. You need to have some fun. You don't know anything about this place yet." Recalling his mother's words, he hesitated for a moment but then said, "I want you to like my village. I want you to get to know my friends. If it's all right with you, I'd like you to stay here with us forever. To me, you're just a regular girl, and like regular girls, I'm sure you don't like being alone, right?"

Miya remained silent for a long time, her eyes downcast. Finally, she looked at him and said, "You're right. I'm just an ordinary girl like any other."

"Then let's go together tomorrow," Matachi said, his voice lively. "You'll come, won't you?"

"To see the prince?"

"Or to do anything else. It doesn't really matter to me."

"I'd like to see that prince," Miya said, as if deep in thought. "I want to do what everyone else does."

"Great! And Ma won't be able to get in the way then, either."

"Is that so?" His mother was standing right behind him, her hands on her hips. "Even on my old legs, I can walk as far as Tsuno-ore. If he's that marvelous, I want to see him too."

2

"MOTHER," MIYA SAID. She was putting wood on the fire, getting ready to make breakfast. Matachi's mother turned toward her, thinking that the girl must have made yet another mistake. Miya was not a very accomplished cook. But that was not why. "Would it . . ." Miya said hesitantly. "Would it be all right for me to stay here? As a daughter of this house?"

Matachi's mother was not surprised. She had been vaguely aware that Miya had lain awake all night. "Are you sure you mean that?" she asked.

"If—if you'd be willing to let me stay."

"Are you saying that you're in love with Matachi?"

Miya blushed. "He's a good person. And I'm indebted to him for rescuing me."

"Well, I'm sorry, but the answer is no." Like most fisherwomen, Matachi's mother was blunt. "You're a good girl, but that's quite different from marrying my son. I don't know what kind of difficulty you're in, but I don't see how you could ever fit in as the wife of a fisherman in our little village. I saw what happened—the Dragon King himself carried you to shore during that storm. How could a girl who has been touched by the sea god possibly be content living here? Why would you even think of it?"

Miya looked down and twisted her fingers together. "Because I want to forget what happened. I've lost my power. I'm nothing but an ordinary girl. If I can, I want to start over, here, where you found me . . ." Her voice trembled. "There's no place left for me to go."

Matachi's mother's expression softened. "Don't be so hard on yourself. You'll only get sick again. There's no rush. Take your time and think about it. I'll forget that I even heard what you just said. And don't even suggest it to Matachi, all right? You know he'd just go bouncing all over the place like a puppy dog."

Miya nodded silently, but something about her had changed. She looked troubled, as if annoyed at being unable to suppress her anxiety. On impulse, Matachi's mother asked, "Do you know something about this prince who's coming?"

Miya took a deep breath and then let it out slowly. "No," she answered in a strange voice. "I don't. That's why I want to go and see him."

SEVERAL DAYS HAD PASSED when Sugaru suddenly materialized in front of Oguna and his men on the path to Tsuno-ore. There was no need to ask how his search had gone. Oguna could tell at a glance that it had been unsuccessful.

Sugaru scowled. "I'm ready to give up." He vented his frustration on Oguna, who had dismounted and ordered his men to take a short break. "The only time I sensed something calling me was when I flew with you that first day. Since then I haven't felt a thing, no matter where I went. Why?"

"How should I know?" Oguna answered. "If you only heard it that one time, then you should think about how it differed from the other times. Can't you recreate those same conditions?"

Sugaru grabbed Oguna by the collar. "Come with me then."

"What?" Oguna said, frowning.

"It'll only take a minute," Sugaru said, not waiting for an answer. "I just want to test something. The only difference I can think of is that you were with me that time."

Thus it was that they rose high above the earth for a second time. And Sugaru found out for certain. Something was calling him, and it was because he was with Oguna.

"I just don't get it," Sugaru said when they had landed. "Why you? You're not even a Tachibana. Why are you able to make the magatama respond?"

"How should I know? And besides, I can't even hear it," Oguna said, understandably confused to be the brunt of Sugaru's exasperation.

"Then why did you choose to go north? You said you were going to Tsuno-ore, right? Why did you decide to do that?"

Oguna looked at him blankly. "I just felt it was the right thing to do. There was no special reason."

The sound of the summons had come from the north. Sugaru groaned. "Oh, never mind. I can guess." *It must be Toko. The Misumaru is responding to Oguna's subconscious knowledge.*

"What can you guess?" Oguna asked, intrigued.

"That it works better when I'm with you. I'm coming to Tsuno-ore."

THE BEACH was jammed with people. Everyone from children to the elderly had gathered to see the prince and his procession. Even for those friendly toward Mahoroba, the capital was so far away it seemed like a dream world and its inhabitants imaginary. Matachi and his mother believed Miya to have come from under the sea; to them the emperor in the capital seemed just as distant as the Dragon King. Just as they had unquestioningly welcomed the girl from another world, so too they welcomed the prince.

"Ma, shall I carry you on my back?" Matachi asked. The crowd was so large that they were standing some distance away on a dike lined with pine trees. The procession from Mahoroba looked very small, their heads half hidden.

"I can see properly," his mother answered. "I saw his face shining."

"That was his helmet, not his face."

Miya stood silently beside them. They were on the dike because she had not wanted to go any farther into the crowd.

"Perhaps we're a little too far away," Matachi said, glancing at her. Miya had been staring intently at the procession, but she turned her eyes toward him and her face relaxed.

"No, this is fine," she said, and then whispered almost to herself, "It's perfect because it's far away. From this distance, I can see how separate we are. A peaceful life would never suit those people. They're different."

"I guess you're right."

Miya continued quietly, "I can tell. They're beautiful . . . and sad."

Matachi looked around the pine grove and then tapped his mother on the shoulder. "Look, over there. Isn't that Toneh from the next village? You haven't seen her for a while, have you?"

As soon as his mother had gone off to talk with her friend, Matachi grabbed Miya by the hand. "You must be bored. Let's go over there." The waves washing the shore left trails of white foam on the sand. Plovers ran about on their tiny feet, pecking for food. Matachi led her to a place where they could overlook the sea. There he stopped and looked into her face, his eyes dazzled. If Miya knew what he intended, she gave no sign as her eyes followed the plovers.

"Miya," Matachi said earnestly. "Stay with me. I'll work hard. I won't let anything make you sad. It doesn't matter to me where you came from. Ma says that you'll leave someday, but I don't believe her. You want to stay here, don't you, Miya? You want to be part of our village, right?"

Miya said nothing, but when she turned her face to him she looked as though she were about to cry.

"I'll help you. If you feel the same way, I'll take care of you all my life. Say yes, Miya. Don't you like me?"

Miya hesitated for a long time before she opened her mouth. Then finally she began. "I—" But what she had been about to say, Matachi would never know. She gasped suddenly and froze, looking as though she had seen a ghost. Sensing something behind him, Matachi turned around and saw a young man who seemed to have appeared out of nowhere. He was tall and lanky and his hair, tied in a ponytail, was a startling red. Around his neck he wore a necklace of many colored stones.

"So there you are." His voice was low. "I've been searching all over for you. In fact, the word *search* doesn't even do it justice."

The girl's face turned so pale her veins could be seen under the skin. She was too stunned to even cringe, but when the young man reached out to grab her, she pushed his hand away and ran behind Matachi.

"No!"

"Miya, who is that?" Matachi demanded.

"I don't know."

"What the hell are you talking about?" the young man fumed. "What's wrong with you, Toko?"

"I don't know you. And I'm not Toko."

Extending his arms to shield her, Matachi said fiercely, "Leave her alone. Didn't you hear her? She says she doesn't know you. So hurry up and get lost."

Sugaru fixed him with a stony glare. "Stay out of this."

The fishermen of Matachi's village were tough and always eager for a fight, and Matachi was as hot tempered as the best of them. He flew into a rage. "No!" Toko screamed, but he had already swung a hefty punch. Sugaru calmly caught his fist in his own and held it so tightly that Matachi could not move. Looking into his surprised face, Sugaru said, "Don't interfere. Toko still has a job left to do."

"You're the one who's interfering," Matachi yelled, his breath coming in gasps. "There's no way I'll let you have Miya. She's staying with me. She's my wife."

"She's what?" For the first time, Sugaru hesitated. He looked at the girl in disbelief. She stood there clenching her sleeves.

"I'm not the girl you're looking for," she stammered. "I'm sorry . . ."

"Damn you!" Sugaru yelled, rounding furiously on Matachi and punching him in the face. "You've ruined everything."

Shocked, Miya ran in front of him. "Sugaru, stop it! Matachi didn't do anything wrong. It's not his fault."

"Oh, so you know my name after all," Sugaru said, glowering. "Why did you say you didn't? Did you think that things would just work out fine if you forgot everything?"

The words stuck in Miya's throat, and her hands froze as she tried to help Matachi sit up.

"Did you think that you could throw everything away and go on living as someone else? I never thought you were like that. Do you have any idea how much trouble it was to find you?"

"But . . ." the girl finally managed to whisper. Tears began to flow and her face twisted. "What else could I do? How could I face you or anybody else again?"

Sugaru watched her cry, somewhat perplexed.

"Why did you have to find me?" she sobbed. "I wanted you to forget me, to think I was dead."

Sugaru stood silently for some time, his arms crossed. Finally, he said, "All right then, at least let me hear your side of the story. Tell me how you wound up like this."

"Miya!" Matachi finally found his voice and grabbed her by the arm. "Don't go. I couldn't bear it if you went off with him."

The girl from the Dragon King's palace looked at him with red-rimmed eyes. "Don't worry. There's nowhere for me to go. But I need to set things straight."

SUGARU TOOK TOKO to a deserted end of the beach. Once they were alone he asked, "Are you seriously thinking of marrying that guy?"

"I don't know . . ." Toko said miserably. "I'm not yet one of them. I don't even know if I ever can be."

"Getting married is for women. Since when have you been able to do that?" Toko hung her head and pushed a shell around in the sand with her toe.

"So you mean nothing matters anymore? You've suddenly changed your mind despite the single-minded passion with which you pursued Oguna? Then I guess you're right. Toko's not here."

"Who wouldn't blame me for what I've done?" Toko said softly. "Especially you. There's no way I can defend my actions to you. But until now I was just racing ahead blindly. I didn't know anything about myself or anyone else."

"And what do you claim to know now?"

"How insignificant I am. I didn't have it in me to kill Oguna. I was a fool to think that I'd been chosen for such a mission. To think that I could rise to the same level as him. I'm just an ordinary girl like any other."

Sugaru stared at her in astonishment. "You? Who invaded the emperor's own palace to retrieve the magatama?"

"I was pushing myself, that's all." Toko sighed. "I could do it because I'd convinced myself that I was the only one who could defeat Oguna. But I was wrong. Once I realized that, everything came tumbling down."

Sugaru frowned. "But why didn't you come to me then? We were in this together, right? I waited there for you, regardless of the outcome. How could you leave me with just the Misumaru and disappear? That's what really makes me mad."

"I'm sorry. I just couldn't think. I wanted to run away from everything—and more than anything, from myself."

Sugaru sat down on a rock and gazed out to sea. "How did you get here? And why here?"

"It wouldn't have been strange if I had died, you know. I was drowning and thought that was the end. It seems like a dream now, but in the sea I met a god who looked like a huge snake." Toko spoke slowly as she remembered. "He saw the Misumaru and told me that he recognized it. He said that he had guarded one of its stones for a long time and was now on his way home, having given the stone to someone else. He asked me why I had it."

Sugaru had been sitting with his chin in his hand, but at this he raised his head. "That's the god on the mountain. So his home was in the sea, was it?"

"I had no desire to live anymore, but somehow I couldn't let myself sink to the bottom of the sea with the Misumaru. I asked the god to return it to a man called Sugaru on the beach. He told me he would."

"Ah, I see."

"Then he asked me what I wanted to do. I told him that I wanted to go far away and forget everything. That was all I could think of at the time. He told me that he was on his way to visit an old friend who lived in a lake to the east and that he'd take me there. He let me ride on the back of his neck. When I came to, I was lying on this beach." She looked at the surf as if she might see herself still lying there. "It was Matachi and his mother who found me and brought me back to their house. They were very kind to me, though I was a complete stranger. I'd gone a little funny when I first got here. I couldn't speak. But they still took care of me and I eventually recovered. I thought that if I stayed here I could forget . . . Oguna."

"Is that really what you want? To forget Oguna? Can you really do that? Just turn your back and forget about him despite the situation he's in?" Toko did not respond. "If so, then why did you come to the beach at Tsuno-ore today? If you were going to forget him, you didn't need to bother coming all the way to see him."

"That's different. I came as one of the villagers," Toko said. " I didn't realize that he was going to come here. But it gave me the chance to see him as a prince from a far and distant world. I'm ready to forget Mino. There's no point in clinging to what I've already lost . . . "

"So you've given up on avenging your people. You won't take revenge and you won't fulfill the mission of the magatama, which was passed down by the Tachibana from generation to generation. You no longer care what evil the blood of the emperor's line may perpetrate, is that it?"

Toko clutched her chest, hunching over as though each word stabbed her to the heart. "That's right. That's the kind of girl I am. It's unforgivable, isn't it? I can't do anything right. I'm not strong like you. The Tachibana have you, Sugaru. So please, just let me forget."

"Of all the—" Sugaru sighed. "Did you know that Oguna came almost straight here? He wanted so badly to meet you one more time that he instinctively sensed where you were, something not even I was able to do. But if this is the Toko that he's going to find, I can't help but pity him."

Toko stared at Sugaru, stunned. Noticing her surprise, Sugaru shrugged. "I've spent quite a bit of time with him since you disappeared. Right now, I probably understand him better than I understand you. I guess it's because you're a woman now . . . You've changed, Toko. You're boring in fact."

Toko blushed. "Well, that's just fine with me. But I can't believe it. Oguna was with *you*? What were you doing?"

"I was going to finish what you had set out to do, and then things just kind of happened," Sugaru explained. "Besides, Oguna was the only one who believed you were still alive, so I ended up staying with him while I looked for you." He stopped and then he added, "I've never met anyone as strange as him before. For one thing, he doesn't have any sense of self."

Toko couldn't help joining in. "It's not that he doesn't have a sense of self. He just can't express it easily."

"But that's no good. The will of the Sword is far greater than his, and so it manipulates him. There's nothing strong enough inside him, nothing he can lean on to help him withstand that power. The only thing that keeps him from using the Sword right now is his desire to see you again. Such a thin reed and yet he's clinging to it desperately to keep his balance in a very precarious place. Toko," Sugaru said forcefully, "he has nothing but you. If you could see him now, you'd be amazed by the desolation in his eyes. He's surrounded by people who worship him, yet nothing touches his heart. There's no one who can understand and lighten the load he bears. Not even I can ease his burden. The power of the Sword is far too entrenched. The only person who might be able to do it is you. Because you're the only person he really wants."

Toko looked down. She did not speak for a long time. Sugaru finally rose and walked over to her. "It's about time you admitted it, Toko," he said, without any trace of reproach. "Neither of you seems to have any idea of how firmly you're joined together, even though you have no thought for anything but each other. Stop trying to run away from the fact that you couldn't kill Oguna. You love him so much that you're willing to forego revenge and abandon your mission altogether. Right, Toko?"

Toko tensed but did not look at Sugaru when she finally spoke. "To you, I'm probably still a silly child. But I've been thinking a lot. In fact, that's all I've been doing since that day . . . the day I met Oguna on that ship, the day

I realized that I could never kill him." She turned her back on Sugaru and looked at the sea. "Oguna had not changed a bit, and yet he had. Even so, there was nothing in him, whether changed or unchanged, that I could hate. He was so familiar, so dear. Yes, I love him. I love him more than anyone else in the world. For as long as I can remember and even now, I've loved Oguna and no one else. But that's not enough, Sugaru." She spoke clearly, without hesitation. Sugaru could only stare at her. "Even though I love him, I can't help him. By loving him, I will only repeat Lady Akaru's mistake, heading straight into misery and finally following him into death. I've known this all along, ever since the high priestess of Mino told me that Oguna is a Takeru... She told me that just like Prince Oh-usu, he would not live long. And he really is. He's just like Prince Oh-usu... Even if I love him, all I can do is let him break my heart. If I can't kill him with my own hands, then I want to get as far away as possible. I can't bear to see him die before my eyes. Not if all I can do for him, even though I stand by him, is to die alongside him."

Well that's a surprise. Sugaru groaned inwardly. *You can never take women lightly. They grow up so suddenly, as if shedding a skin.*

"Please don't tell Oguna about me. Don't tell him you met me here."

"You're not going to meet him ever again?" Sugaru asked quietly. "Even though you know how he feels?"

Toko bit her lip. "Lady Akaru was one of the greatest women I've ever known. If even she could not prevent that from happening, then how can I? Please, Sugaru, please leave me be."

"You won't regret this decision, even if Oguna dies without finding any relief?"

"What can I possibly do about it?" Toko snapped, turning on him in a flash of anger. "I'm just a girl. That's all. How can you be so mean? Do you really want to kill me that badly? Is it that wrong to want to live an ordinary, happy life?"

"Oguna needs someone to support him."

"Since when did you become Oguna's ally? That's weird, Sugaru. You're supposed to be the bearer of the Misumaru."

It is weird, Sugaru thought. *This isn't how it's supposed to be...*

"I just don't believe you can forget him, Toko. And I don't know what you mean by ordinary happiness. Still, it doesn't matter. I can't force this on you. That's not my place." He ran his hand through his hair and then said in a resigned tone, "Do you remember that the fifth magatama is supposed to be in Hidakami—the land of the rising sun? I wasn't planning to carry on as the bearer, but I guess it can't be helped. I'll go look for the fifth magatama. If I manage to gather all five stones, then maybe I can do something about Oguna myself. I'll leave you alone, if that's what you want."

A flicker of disappointment crossed Toko's face, but she stood up without saying anything. After a moment, she whispered, "I guess you can never forgive me."

"There's nothing to forgive." He looked at her for a long moment before he left. "We must each choose our own path in life. We can't tell others what to do, so there's no point in criticizing their choices."

3

AFTER SUGARU DISAPPEARED, Toko lingered on the shore. She felt as if he had left a great hole in her heart through which a desolate wind blew. *This is the end of everything... I've said goodbye to my past. Now it's time to begin a different life as a different me.* Somehow she wished that Sugaru had rebuked her more sharply. Perhaps if they had parted in anger, it would have been easier to forget. But instead, he had been strangely perceptive, and now she was left feeling deserted. She never intended to see him again, yet she could not help grieving. Her guilt would last as long as memory remained. She had dragged him from Izumo only to run away and leave him to shoulder everything.

But what else could I do? There was no other way... She wept a little, feeling sorry for herself, before heading back to where she had left Matachi. Although she did not want to meet anyone right now, she needed to make sure that he was all right after being struck by Sugaru. The sun was already sinking in the sky. She must have stood on the beach much longer than she had thought. She walked quickly through the long shadows of the trees, searching for Matachi. The crowd was beginning to disperse, and this made it harder to find anyone.

Feeling slightly uncomfortable, Toko began asking passersby if they had seen Matachi from Yata. She ignored their curious glances, but as soon as she turned her back, she could hear them talk.

"That's her. The one from Matachi's place."

"You mean the one they said the Dragon King brought?"

"But she looks so ordinary."

"Still, there's something about her . . . "

This was the first time Toko had left the house and mingled with others. She had known she would be the focus of gossip, but it still made her keenly aware of the distance between her and the villagers. She was not sure that she could ever close that gap.

Just as she was beginning to think that Matachi and his mother must have gone home without her, she finally saw them. The sight of their familiar faces almost made her cry. Matachi ran toward her as soon as he saw her.

"Miya! Where'd you get to? I looked all over for you."

His eye was slightly swollen, but his souvenir from Sugaru did not look that serious. Relieved, Toko struggled to smile. "I was looking for you. I thought you must have been angry with me and gone home."

"Where's that guy?"

"He left. You won't see him again. Let me apologize for him. I'm really sorry. Does it hurt?"

"Never mind about that," Matachi said in a rush. "Does that mean you've decided to stay, Miya? I know that I was no match for him, but you aren't planning to go back with him, are you?" Toko shook her head silently. "I couldn't bear it if you left," Matachi continued. "I love you."

"Even though I'm a complete stranger from the Dragon King's palace?" Toko whispered. "Can you still love me, now and forever?"

"Of course! Forever," Matachi said, his spirits suddenly high. He grabbed her hand. "Come with me. I'll introduce you to the chief. I was just talking to him. With his blessing, we could even get married."

Led by Matachi, Toko soon found herself standing before the chief. Like most men of the sea, his voice was rough and he spoke so forcefully that Toko at first thought he must be angry. He smiled, however, and his leathered skin creased with wrinkles. "Ah," he said. "So you're the girl who came from the sea."

"My name is Miya. The villagers of Yata have taken care of me."

The elderly chief looked her over from head to toe. "You're quite an attractive young woman. I heard that Matachi had discovered a treasure, but now that I see you in person, I'm not surprised that people made so much fuss." He looked at Matachi. "You must be the envy of your friends. But make sure you behave yourself."

Matachi laughed happily, relieved that the chief, instead of reprimanding him, appeared to approve. As it turned out, however, the chief's intentions differed drastically from Matachi's, a fact they only learned the next day after they had returned to Yata.

"MIYA! Where are you?"

The sun was still high in the sky when Matachi came home. Sensing a change in his voice, Toko knew instantly that something was wrong. She ran out to greet him, still clutching a bowl in her hands.

"What is it?"

Gasping for breath, Matachi said, "Miya, we've got to get out of here. Let's run away together."

"What on earth happened?"

"We should never have gone to Tsuno-ore. It was a mistake to take you there. Someone told the prince from Mahoroba about you. And apparently he was very interested. He's bringing his men to Yata. The chief intends to give you to the prince as a token of hospitality."

Toko felt the blood drain from her face. Matachi put his hands on her shoulders and shook her. "I know. It's awful. You must be furious. Just because you come from the sea is no reason that you should be offered like tribute to the prince."

The bowl Toko was holding slipped from her grasp and fell to the floor, splitting in two and spilling flour into the dirt. But neither of them had eyes for that.

Oguna is coming. He's coming to me...

"I won't let this happen. Let's run away. Or let's get married right now. I won't let them take you away," Matachi said, his voice fierce. He pulled Toko into a tight embrace. Coming to her senses, she hastily pushed him away.

"Wait. Please."

"Let her go!" Matachi's mother stood in the doorway. "How could you behave so shamefully?" she snapped. "You need to cool off."

"It's your fault!" Matachi yelled. "Why did you agree to this?"

"Because I thought it was the right thing to do," his mother replied. "I need to talk to Miya. It's women's talk, so you go wait outside. And don't wander off either. You're already the laughingstock of the village. Honestly."

"Miya, don't listen to a word she says, all right?" Matachi was upset, but his mother ruled their home.

After she had shut him outside, his mother changed her tone. "I hear that you met an old friend yesterday," she said quietly. "What did he call you?"

"Toko..."

"That's a nice name. Let me call you Toko from now on. For that's who you really are."

"But I intended to forget that name. There's no one who would come to meet me," Toko said somewhat defensively. *Oguna is coming. He's coming to me...*

"Matachi needs to wake up. But you at least must be aware that your destiny isn't here. Just as with the prince, you were born for a different purpose."

"No, that's not true. I'm not like him. I'm just an ordinary girl who can't do anything special. Please tell the chief that I can't do it. There's no way I can go out there to meet the prince."

Matachi's mother did not speak for a few moments. Finally she said, "This is a quiet and peaceful village, Toko. Nothing extraordinary has happened here since the day I was born. True, my husband died young, but that's not unusual. Such things happen in every village. But then you arrived in the most extraordinary fashion. And now, less than three months later, the emperor's son and crown prince has appeared. Surely it's not strange for me to think that these two events are somehow related." Toko could say nothing. "When the chief told me, I felt that this was meant to be. You're the one most suited to fulfill the prince's desire. That, I thought, must be why you left the Dragon King's palace under the sea."

"No, that's not true," Toko interrupted, frightened by this line of thought. Matachi's mother walked past her and over to a wooden chest in the far corner of the room. Kneeling in front of it, she opened the lid and took out a silk robe, neatly folded.

"This is what you were wearing when we found you." She laid it in front of Toko. "The seawater has stained it a little, but it's still beautiful. An angel's robe. There's an old folktale about a maid from heaven who flies away when her celestial robe is returned. Still, let me return this to you." She looked Toko in the eyes. "It's your choice. You could choose Matachi instead. But if you do, we will all suffer. If we shame the chief, Matachi will no longer be able to stay here. A different woman will be offered in your stead, but most likely that won't satisfy the prince, and the young woman may already have given her heart to another."

Toko took the robe in her hands and stared at it, then suddenly turned her face away. The sight of Oguna standing on the deck of the ship rose in her mind. His face, his voice, the blood he had shed—and finally she realized that she could no longer turn and run away. Here she was, back at the same place she had been on the day that she had fled from that ship.

"I'm not saying these things out of spite," Matachi's mother said quietly. "I'm not saying them because I want to be rid of you. Please understand that. When we find a seabird with a broken wing, we might take it home and nurse it. But when that bird recovers, we set it free. Because that's best for all of us."

"Yes," Toko said, taking a deep breath. "I think I probably knew all along that I was clinging to this place out of fear. I was afraid. And I'm still afraid. But it can't be helped, can it?"

"Afraid? Of the prince?"

"No. Of myself," Toko answered. "But at the very least I don't want to stay here and cause you all trouble. If it's best for me to go to the prince, then I'll do it."

Matachi's mother sighed. "I thought you would say that. I feel a little bad about it, but it still doesn't change the fact that this is for the best. Would you like to wear this? I'll help you dress."

Toko nodded. She did not particularly want to adorn herself. But if she was not going to go as Miya, then it seemed most fitting for her to go as she had first come. Helping her into the robe, Matachi's mother said, "You've grown more beautiful every day over these last three months. I can understand how my son feels. He's going to miss you for a while."

I'm going to meet the prince . . . I'm just like Akaru. Even in the way that I can't resist this fate. Toko suddenly recalled the white bird she had seen one evening so many years before—the omen from Lady Akaru's New Year's dream. Now she thought she understood its meaning. The white bird represented the imperial family, tainted with the pure yet cursed blood of the God of Light. Those who came close could lose their very lives. Lady Akaru must have realized that. And the high priestess as well. But still they acquiesced.

I don't know what's right. I was never trained as a shrine maiden. We've lost the prophecies and everything. There's only one thing that I'm sure of . . . the prince is Oguna.

She could hear a commotion outside. Perhaps the prince's procession had already arrived or perhaps it was just a sign that he was approaching. Toko, however, could not bear to wait any longer.

"Wait until he's here," Matachi's mother admonished her. "A messenger will surely come to tell us when he arrives."

"I can't stand to wait passively for something bad to happen. I'd rather believe that I plunged into it of my own accord." *Lady Akaru had probably felt the same way,* Toko thought. "Thank you so much for everything. When I'm in a position to thank you properly, I will. I'll never forget your kindness. Farewell."

Toko slipped through the door. Raising her head, she saw a huge crowd of people lining the road. The prince had almost reached the house. He wore no armor and was accompanied by only a few men. Nor did he sit astride a horse. He had come on foot. The entire village appeared to be there, creating a wall of people, yet none of this registered in Toko's mind anymore. Not even the prince's companions entered her sight. She saw only Oguna.

Oguna showed no surprise when he saw the girl who came out of the house. He appeared to have come convinced that it would be Toko. "I thought it must be you," he said, his voice filled with deep relief. "I just had to make sure. How I've longed to meet you again. Even though I knew that it would only cause you misfortune, I just couldn't help myself. I was sure you were alive."

Toko stared at Oguna's face, holding her breath. She knew far too well that to love Oguna could only bring sorrow and pain. Yet she could not resist the look on his face. What more could she ever hope for? How could she ever break this bond? In that moment, Oguna had fulfilled the promise he had made so long ago. He had come to meet her.

Before she knew it she had wrapped her arms around him—just as she had so often done in Mino. But Oguna was so tall, his arms so long, that it was she who was enveloped in his embrace. The chief and Oguna's men stared transfixed at the couple, clasped together, their shadows merged into one.

"I just had to find you. Even though I knew I had no right, I just had to. You're all I have."

"How can you say you have no right?" Toko asked with her face buried in his chest. "It's I who have nothing to offer. I can neither protect you nor kill you. I don't even have the Misumaru anymore. All I can do is love you."

"I will make you grieve," Oguna said. "I came even though I knew that. I wanted to meet you. And now, I want you by my side . . . as before. I know it's selfish. I have no right to want that."

So I'm not the only one touched by foreboding. "I too know there's no future," Toko said. "But it doesn't matter anymore. Despite my knowing, I can't stop my feelings. I love you. Now and forever, no matter what happens, I love you. So I'll stay by your side." She smiled through her tears. "I'll stay by your side, to the very end."

Matachi's mother, who had been watching from the doorway, walked over to her son where he stood with his back turned. "I thought this would happen. And I was right, wasn't I?"

"Leave me alone," Matachi groaned.

"Don't be angry. Just consider it to have been a good dream. You've lost nothing, whereas that girl has lost everything. She has given up all she could have had to go to a much harder place—the place where she belongs."

4

THE FACT that Oguna had returned with a woman caused quite a stir among his men. Such behavior was unthinkable to those who had grown to know him amidst his many military campaigns. They looked at one another in consternation.

"What's gotten into him?"

"Why would he pick a girl from a fishing village?"

"Did you see her? Was she that attractive?"

"She's nothing compared to the women in the capital. I can't understand what he's thinking."

"But I heard she came from the Dragon King's palace."

"Really? Tell us about it."

Takehiko suddenly appeared. "Shut up and get back to work!" he barked.

The company was staying in Tsuno-ore. As there were not enough buildings to house them all, only the officers slept under a roof, while the rest made do with a temporary bivouac. But they were used to such things, so no one complained. They often had to make camp in the middle of nowhere, and compared to that, being able to pitch their tents near human habitation was far more pleasant. The soldiers were quite popular wherever they went thanks to the prince's fame, and consequently each had his own particular view of the women from the various lands they had traveled through. Oguna was the only one who had until now stayed aloof.

"How dare they criticize the prince? That's going too far," Takehiko grumbled, yet he too was puzzled. He crossed his arms, lost in thought. It was true that the prince had undergone a sudden and drastic change. The light in his eyes made it clear that this girl was special. *He's still young. I forget that sometimes . . .* The thought made him anxious. *I just hope that this doesn't take a turn for the worse. Especially as in his situation he must be on his guard at all times.*

Toko, on the other hand, had no time to worry about what the troops thought. The life of Oguna as prince was totally new to her, and everything he said or did made her heart race. Each time she looked at him she marveled to be so close. Constantly surrounded by people, he barely had time to speak to her. But there was no rush. She was content just to watch him and to smile when their eyes occasionally met. Her euphoria lasted until the end of the day. When it came time to draw the curtains for the night, she was forced to consider her own position. After supper, the chief had come to inform the prince that his sleeping quarters were ready.

I guess there're no sleeping quarters for me. I suppose that's only natural, Toko realized. *I've been given to the prince, haven't I . . .* Suddenly she was thrown into a panic. While she had committed herself to staying by Oguna's side, that was not at all the same as spending the night with him. His attendants, with whom Oguna had been discussing the schedule for the following day, paid their respects and left one by one. Finally Oguna said, "We should go to our room too. I bet you were surprised that there's so little time to relax. But this is what it's always like."

Toko followed him into a room half the size of the one they had just been in. It was dimly lit by a single oil lamp. She had been looking forward eagerly to talking with him alone, but now she found herself unbelievably tense. She had thought of so many things she wanted to tell him, but she couldn't remember even one. Compared to her, Oguna appeared quite calm.

"I'm so glad you came, Toko," he said easily. "I thought we would never spend time like this together again. The people of Mino would be justified in hating me for what I did. When I think about that, I can hardly stand it. Yet I can't stop thinking about life in Mino. I was ignorant then, and life seemed so happy. And you were there."

"We fought a lot too though," Toko said, her voice hesitant. "I realize now how selfish I was. I took my frustration out on you a lot, and it was always me that punched you first."

"That's true." Oguna laughed. "Yet if anyone else hit me you'd come running over to hit them back. You were such a tomboy, I never got a turn."

"But you're the leader now," Toko said, wondering why her heart beat so loudly. She thought that even Oguna must hear it. "You have the power. What a difference between then and now."

"Does it really seem that way to you?" Oguna sighed. "That's not true, you know. I wish you'd give me some of your strength. Someone who's truly strong is able to think of others—like you do for me. But it's all I can manage just to take care of myself. I've always been like that." He walked over and gazed into her eyes. "I never kept my promise to you. You must have thought I was terrible. I haven't done anything for which I can hold my head up in front of you. In fact, I can hardly believe you're here. Why do you even like me? You ought to hate me."

"You want to know why?" Toko took a deep breath and suddenly felt more at ease. Her heart was still racing, but something had changed. "I think it's because I'm the only one."

"I—" Oguna began, but then stopped abruptly. To Toko, it seemed as if something had come between them and hidden him from her sight. She did not know what it was she had seen in his eyes; she only knew that it was not good. The expression on his face, however, remained gentle. "You should rest here tonight. You must be tired. It would be good for you to get some sleep." He made to leave the room.

Caught off guard, Toko called out, "Wait. If I stay here, where will you sleep?"

"Don't worry about me. I often spend nights outside."

When he had gone, Toko suddenly felt deflated. It had been a waste of energy to feel nervous. And how like Oguna to go out and leave her the room. *I guess I'm not really ready for that yet, am I . . .*

She felt herself blushing as she pulled up the covers. Looking back on it, she realized that with all the fuss over whether she would become a shrine maiden or not, she had neglected to learn anything from her mother about the facts of life.

I wonder if Kisako knew? Of course she did. She was so confident . . .

As it turned out, Toko did not need to worry. The next night Oguna left the room again. And the next night and the next. She finally realized that he did not intend to ever spend the night with her in his room.

TAKEHIKO, who had been discussing the route they would travel with Oguna, glanced around and, confirming that there was hardly anyone about, asked bluntly, "Pardon me sir, but what do you plan to do with the girl?"

"What do you mean 'plan to do with' her?" Oguna asked, looking surprised.

"Are you planning to bring her along?"

"Of course," Oguna said. "Why do you ask? Is there anything wrong with that?"

"No, nothing."

Oguna cocked his head. "Does it seem strange? To bring her along?"

Takehiko stammered uncomfortably but finally blurted out what was on his mind. "It's just that I wondered why you want to keep her with you. You seem to be pleased with her, yet you do not seem to, er, spend time together, if you know what I mean."

"Is that what you meant?" Oguna laughed. "It's all right. That doesn't change the fact that she's very special to me. I've no intention of leaving her behind. Just think of us as a brother and sister reunited after years of separation."

Takehiko thought they had discussed this out of earshot of anyone else, but Toko had overheard. She hurried away and feigned ignorance even when Takehiko, leaving the prince, passed her and cast her a suspicious glance. After he had gone, however, she thought about what he had said. *Everybody thinks it's strange. And they're right. It is strange. They must all wonder what on earth I've come here for . . .*

Even she herself was beginning to wonder why she had come. Her position was highly ambiguous. Oguna's men seemed perplexed over how to treat her. While they paid her the respect due to the prince's lover, she could tell from their eyes that they were not convinced she deserved it. To Oguna, Toko was simply Toko, but to her, Oguna was more than just Oguna. He was worshipped by all the men he led—men who had placed their lives in his hands and followed him to the remotest frontiers. If she were to stay with Oguna, it was not enough that he accept her. His men must accept her as well.

Judged by their standards, however, she was not likely to garner much respect. First of all, there was nothing for her to do. Oguna was busy all day long and had almost no time to talk to her. He only came to her at night, but as he left almost immediately, they had had very little time for conversation. She could not help but brood about it.

Oguna said we were like siblings . . . It seemed quite likely to her that he might want to innocently reconstruct the past. Perhaps he wanted no more than that. But for Toko, the distance between a brother and a sister was nowhere near close enough. No matter how fond they might have been of each other while growing up, it was not a strong enough bond for her to stand by him even in death.

He's so dense, Toko thought indignantly. *He doesn't have a clue how momentous a decision it was for me to come with him.* She uncrossed her arms. If he didn't understand, then she would just have to make him.

Oguna failed to notice any change in Toko's demeanor. It probably did not even occur to him that she might have heard his conversation with Takehiko, and even had he known, he would not have wondered what she thought about it. That night, as usual, he talked about old times for a while and then bade her goodnight.

"Just a minute," Toko said in a stern voice. "There's something I need to say to you."

Oguna turned back, noticing with surprise that she was angry. "What's wrong?"

"I want to ask you something. Where do you go every night? Is there some reason you have to go out? You're a prince. I hope this isn't the case, but do you have a woman you go to, like Sugaru did?"

Oguna looked even more surprised. "What are you talking about?"

"Answer me."

"I spend the night with the watchmen or scout around the camp. I'm not doing anything in particular."

Toko looked up at him. It was clear from her expression that she didn't believe him. "Every night? You expect me to believe that? When do you sleep? And why do you leave me behind?"

"It's not safe for girls to walk around at night," Oguna said, floundering.

"Then why don't you stay here with me? You could at least stay with me once. I came here intending to stay by your side, but we never have any time to talk. I can't help but wonder what I came here for." If she wavered at all, she wouldn't be able to continue, so she plowed on. "Why can't you stay here with me? There's a bed. What's wrong with spending more time together?"

In the past, Oguna had had the unfortunate habit of missing the point entirely, incurring Toko's wrath. This time proved to be no different. He said, with what he thought was the utmost consideration, "But if I stayed with you at night, it would dishonor your name."

Toko's anger exploded. "Just what do you think I am? Your men are already wondering what's going on. Why did you ask me to come with you in the first place? If you can't be clear, then I'm leaving."

"No!" Oguna hastily blocked the doorway. "Please don't go."

"You've never once said you love me. It was all one-sided on my part, I guess."

"I love you."

"You're too late."

"Then what can I do?" Oguna wailed. "I love you, Toko. I want you to stay with me. Just having you near me gives me courage. If you're here I feel that I can face anything. I don't want to lose you. Not again."

Toko looked at him, then said in a slightly calmer tone, "If that's the case, if you really think that, then show me. It's not the same as when we used to live together so long ago. There's so much that we don't know about each other."

"What do you want to know?" Oguna asked in a small voice. "It's true. So much has happened since we were separated. The only thing about me that hasn't changed is my feelings for you."

"Your feelings haven't changed? Not at all?" Toko asked carefully. "If so, then those feelings are not for me. Because I *have* changed. I'm not the same person I used to be. But you don't even try to learn about that. If you wanted to, you could find out easily. But you don't."

Oguna fell silent, seemingly at a loss for words. "Show me why I'm here," Toko pressed him. "Instead of talking about your memories of the past. We can't change our memories, but there are many ways to change the present and the future."

"Ways? You mean . . . " Oguna suddenly reached out and cupped her face in his hands. Before she had time to think, she felt his lips on hers. "Like this?" Without waiting for an answer, he pulled her into his embrace and kissed her again. Toko could not have been more shocked if the whole world had turned upside down. While appearing not to understand, Oguna had known even better than Toko what she was trying to say. Perhaps he understood things that she did not even know about. Having suddenly lost the advantage, Toko panicked. She felt almost afraid of him. His arms were far stronger than she had imagined, and if he wanted, he could have his way with her whether she liked it or not.

"Let me go." She could not show him her temerity now, yet she was already thoroughly frightened. She pushed him away. "Okay. I understand. Please . . . "

Oguna released her instantly. Pulling away from her, he looked into her eyes. "I won't do it again. I know that this is one way to show you, but if I do that, I'll lose you. You're more precious to me than that. I can't expose you to the power of the Sword." And with that, he turned and left. Thrown into confusion, Toko had no words with which to stop him, and by the time she ran after him to the door, he had disappeared into the night. She stayed there for a while staring blankly into the darkness outside and thought, *How stupid of me to forget. Oguna has changed too.* He was no longer a little boy who would not do anything without her urging. He was not the weak child who used to follow her around everywhere. Perhaps it was her eyes, not his, that had been fixed on the shadows of the past. *But what does the power of the Sword have to do with this?* She stepped outside, intending to find Oguna and ask him, when a dark shape moved in the night and she heard a familiar voice.

"I wouldn't advise you to leave your room, unless you wish to get the guards in trouble."

It was Takehiko. He did not sound friendly. Annoyed, Toko glared at his shadowy figure. "And is it your custom to allow the prince to walk alone at night despite the danger? Why don't you stop him?"

"He's special. He has divine protection," Takehiko said. Then, as if he had decided this was a good opportunity, he added frankly, "I must ask you not to tempt him. Surely you must understand by now."

"Tempt him? Me?"

"Like you did tonight."

Toko practically choked with anger. "You were eavesdropping? How could you?"

"I found it strange, that's why. I understand very well that you're a childhood friend. But that's all. You should accept the fact that you're very different from the prince, who is of noble birth."

"And just what do you think you know about Oguna? You know nothing."

"It's true that His Highness doesn't speak about himself to his men," Takehiko said slowly. "But you can learn much about a man when you serve him night and day on a long journey like this. Every night, His Highness meets with a god."

Toko suppressed her indignation. "Who did you say he meets?"

"You know that the prince bears a special Sword. It was given to him by his noble aunt, the Itsuki no Miya. The power of the God of Light, which is not of this world, resides inside our prince. Perhaps that's why he has never attempted to approach a woman, as though he has taken over the sacred role of his aunt."

Feeling a rush of relief, Toko chided herself for rejoicing at a time like this. "You mean he spends the night not with a woman but with a god?"

"Those chosen by the gods must pay a price. At least that's how I see it. I must beg you not to upset his peace of mind. I beg you for the sake of all of us and for the sake of Toyoashihara. It's not something that should be disturbed just to satisfy one individual."

Toko almost felt herself agreeing with him, but he was really saying that she wasn't needed. "Are you asking me to leave?"

"You're attractive. There must be many men other than the prince who would willingly court you. Surely it's better for you to live a peaceful life."

Toko took a deep breath and let it out slowly. She found that she actually liked this blunt-spoken man, and not just because he had said she was pretty. She changed her approach. "Well, if that's what you think, then tell me this. Why did you choose to follow Prince Ousu when you knew full well that your life would be far from peaceful? Surely it's because you saw something in him that was worth it. You couldn't serve him if you valued your own life. I know that much. And let me tell you something. If you worship him because he wields the power of the Sword, then you're gravely mistaken. If you've been with him night and day, then you must know that he's suffering. The Sword only brings destruction. And it's destroying him. Do you intend to just stand by and watch? We don't need the Sword in Toyoashihara. And the one who understands that best of all is your prince."

Takehiko fell silent, apparently dumbfounded. After some time, he muttered, "I thought you were just an ordinary girl, but you speak like a shrine maiden . . ."

Toko broke into a smile. "I am just a girl. But I'm a girl who came here ready to sacrifice her life for your prince. My commitment is just as strong as your own or that of anyone else."

Takehiko hesitated and then said somewhat uncomfortably, "I'll have to think about this. I seem to have been mistaken in my judgment of you."

Toko was still smiling as she watched him stride away. Takehiko too was worried about Oguna. That in itself was enough to make her like him. *He's the same as me. He loves Oguna for the person he is, not because he's a prince or the master of the Sword.* It gave her courage to know that people like that surrounded Oguna. As she thought things over, she realized something else. Although she had told Takehiko that she had come prepared to sacrifice her life, she no longer felt that way. *I'm thinking of something even harder than laying down my life. I want to live. And I want Oguna to live too. Now and in the future. I know that it's defying destiny. I know that there's not even a chance in a million when it comes to the wielder of the Sword. Yet I can't help it. I love him. And I want him to live . . .*

5

"WE SHOULD DIG A WELL," Oguna said simply.

The plains of Hidakami were far broader than any the company from Mahoroba had ever seen, and the villages were much smaller and more widely scattered, with large empty tracts of land between them. This trend had become even more pronounced the further inland they traveled. There was just not enough water. Even though they were camped near a village, the supply was too limited to quench the thirst of the troops.

"It makes more sense to dig a well than to haul water all the way from the river. We have the manpower to do it. And, in the end, it will benefit the village too."

Thus it was that the villagers were called upon to investigate groundwater veins. A diviner was brought in to help, and all the locals gathered to watch the soldiers work. The activity livened up the quiet village. And at the center of it all was Oguna.

Toko watched in fascination. It amused her that Oguna's love for engineering had remained intact. Sometimes she looked at him and his men through the eyes of the villagers. Understandably, from their perspective, the company from Mahoroba appeared dazzling. The prince in particular seemed to have descended from the heavens.

So this is what it means to belong to the lineage of the God of Light. Wherever he goes, people are drawn to him. She watched Oguna fondly as he pitched right in, his legs soon becoming splattered with mud. The old Oguna had never stood out like this, perhaps because he had been a foundling. *He looks so cheerful and confident. This must be one side of him too. When he was in Mino, he wasn't where he belonged. He wasn't as happy then as he thinks he was...*

The man she saw in the light of day was closer to the real Oguna. His eyes shone as he rallied others around him and threw himself into work he loved. But something caused him so much pain that he longed for the old days in Mino. *And that something, whatever it is, appears at night,* Toko thought. *Even without the power of the Sword, Oguna would be a leader. But instead of fearing him, people would love him.* She clenched her fists. *If only he wasn't the master of the Sword, he could make others so happy. And by doing that, he himself would be happy. I can imagine what that would be like . . .*

The well was a success. To the cheers of the crowd, pure water suddenly gushed into the hole they had dug. The soldiers began horsing around, throwing mud at one another, and the children laughed and ran about excitedly. Although war might be imminent, everyone shared in the joy of this moment, moved by gratitude for the bounties of nature and by the wonder of water springing from the earth.

Catching sight of Oguna's mud-smeared face and clothes, Toko burst out laughing. "You dig a well and the first thing you do is make a mountain of laundry. You'd better wash that off quickly or no one will know you're a prince."

Wiping his face with the palm of his hand, Oguna said, "If that well dries up before we've washed, we'll be in trouble. We'll all have to go around naked."

"It won't," Toko responded, looking at the water. "I don't have the Misumaru anymore, but I can tell that much. Too bad I didn't have it though, because I could've found that water vein in no time."

Oguna looked at her, intrigued. "Is that what your magatama are like?"

"Yes. With the Misumaru, the power of the wind and the water flows through me and I become one with it. I think it's probably the power of the Goddess of Darkness herself. She loved the earth."

"When you've wielded so much power once, don't you want to do it again?"

Toko considered this for a moment. "Not really. It's not like being possessed or anything. When I'm actually wielding it, it's even a little frightening because I'm no longer totally human." She brushed back her hair. "When you wield the Misumaru, you feel, almost to a painful extent, the exquisiteness of the power that runs through nature. You understand that wind, water, and life are constantly flowing through the world. I'm glad that I experienced it. Even now, I feel things more deeply than before. The world is more beautiful. Everything on this earth is beautiful. Because everything we see here is the coming together of an unbelievable exquisiteness. This well is just one example."

"You're lucky," Oguna said. "It's very different from the power that I know. Maybe that's why Sugaru always looked so cool and composed. It's not like that for me."

"Can't you let go of the power of the Sword?" Toko asked sadly.

"The Sword is part of me," Oguna said in a low voice. "To throw it away, I'd have to cut away part of myself. But . . . when that time comes, I'd be willing to, I think."

"You mean you'd be willing to die?"

"Yes, probably."

He says that so calmly. The thought hurt her. "In that case, don't bother."

Oguna reached out a hand and touched her lightly on the cheek. "Let's not talk about that now. There, look at your face. Everyone will wonder what happened to you."

Toko put a hand to her cheek and looked at it. "Oguna! You've got mud on me!"

He chuckled and walked off toward Takehiko. The village women roared with laughter when they saw Toko and she made herself smile for their sakes. She and Oguna looked quite the pair.

I KNEW THIS would happen, Toko thought when she was alone in her tent. From the very beginning, she had known that the more time she spent with Oguna the more she would fear losing him. Each day they shared together was a day full of undiminished laughter, life, and goodwill. Yet the air of a man with no future still clung to Oguna. Even when he laughed he appeared ephemeral, almost transparent. Many times she wanted to reach out her hand to grasp him and keep him from vanishing.

Is there really nothing I can do but wait, paralyzed by fear and grief, for the day when Oguna will disappear? She did not have any power to match the one that bound him. But it had never been her nature to sit idly by. It was the god he met at night that tore him from her. *I've got to learn more about what that Sword is.*

SENSING THAT IT was past midnight, Oguna left their room as usual and went off alone into the trees. The moon was bright and the light it cast created patterns on the carpet of fallen leaves. Although Oguna stepped softly, the leaves whispered underfoot. Gazing up at the full moon that hung in the treetops, he told himself to be on his guard. The silver creature seemed to increase in strength as the moon waxed, almost as if it were part of that heavenly body.

Stopping suddenly, he heard a faint sound behind him. No matter how light-footed one might be, it was hard to hush one's footsteps when walking on dry leaves. *Another assassin. He would have been smarter to come on a dark night,* Oguna thought. He had long ago given up being surprised at how far the emperor's shadow reached. Feeling annoyed rather than angry, he turned and called out, "Show yourself."

A slight figure appeared from behind the shadow of a tree a little ways away. Peering at it, Oguna realized that it was not an assassin. The sight, however, struck terror in his heart.

"Toko! What are you doing here? And how did you get out in the first place?"

"Don't you remember? We were always good at sneaking out." She smiled as she approached him. "It's cold, isn't it?"

"Such a foolish thing to do, especially when you always fell."

"That's not true. I only fell once. Or maybe two or three times."

But Oguna could not laugh. "This isn't a game, Toko. You've got to go back immediately. It's not . . . safe here." He put his hand on her shoulder but then hesitated. Was there still enough time to take her back? Perhaps it would be better to send her on her own.

Toko looked up at him earnestly. "I know it's not safe. But I want to be by your side. I want to know how you spend your nights."

"You won't get away with just knowing," Oguna said, panic in his voice. "You don't know just how different I've become. There's a creature coming, a creature that is Power and Death. It used to be a part of me and it wants to be reunited. It's dangerous for me but even more dangerous for those who are with me."

"A creature?"

"Sugaru saw it once, but he had the magatama. I don't have anything to protect you with. Why did you follow me here?"

But Toko remained unflustered. She said firmly, "You face this thing every night on your own. Can't anyone share that with you? To know means to share. Even if I can't do anything to help you, won't it make a difference to at least have someone who knows?"

Oguna had never thought of that, and it made him pause. "But who would even consider sharing something as hideous as this?"

"Someone who loves you," Toko said. "To love someone means not to leave them on their own. You have to learn that you aren't alone. I'm here."

"Toko, I'm glad you feel that way, but—" He hesitated and then said helplessly, "I don't know if you can understand, but that's exactly why you are in the most danger. The creature wants to eliminate you. Its rage feeds its power. It knows that the part of my heart you occupy is growing larger."

"You mean it wants to possess you?" At last, Toko realized what relation the creature had to her. She remembered what Takehiko had said about the prince never approaching a woman. What he had said now took on a new meaning.

"Tonight the moon is full," Oguna continued, "and the creature's power is at its height. If I'm not careful, I may lose. You're more important to me than anyone else. But it's all I can do just to confront my own self. I need to concentrate all my energy on that."

The thought occurred to her that by her very existence she distracted Oguna and placed him in danger. "You make that creature sound like a jealous wife," Toko said.

"Not a wife, a mother," Oguna said quietly. "She loved me more than anyone. And she died for me, leaving that creature behind on earth. To her, I was everything. Even in death, that's still true."

Toko felt a cold shiver run down her spine. "That's not what a mother is like."

"My mother was no ordinary person. Nor was my birth normal."

Toko could think of nothing to say. She could only stare at Oguna.

"You know, don't you?" he said sadly. "Yes, I found my parents. And I cannot escape those shackles."

"What difference does that make?" Toko was practically yelling. "Yes, I knew. Don't you see? Even though I knew, I still chose to be with you."

Oguna's fingers gripped her shoulders so hard it hurt. "She's coming," he whispered desperately. "We're too late." He yanked Toko toward him and pressed her face against his chest so firmly that she thought she would suffocate. "No matter what happens, you mustn't move away from me. You understand? There's nowhere else that you can hide. And close your eyes. If you look at it, it will take your soul."

Toko's knees shook, making her feel like a coward. But she had to admit she was afraid. And closing her eyes magnified her fear. Oguna's breathing sounded harsh, and she could feel his heart pounding. She clung to him tightly, her own heart racing, and the beating of their hearts fused into one. Something was coming. She felt it with complete certainty. Its presence transformed the quality of the very air around her. The hairs on the nape of her neck stood on end.

I chose to do the stupidest thing in the stupidest possible way. But it was too late now. She was as helpless as the time when she had fallen into the pond so long ago. And this time, everything depended upon whether or not Oguna could save her. She could feel him staring at something even as he held her in his arms. The creature must be very close. Toko heard a low female voice, haughty and domineering.

Release her.

"No, I won't. I won't let you harm her."

She is not worthy of you, the woman said coldly. *You need concern yourself with only one woman—me. Of all men on earth, you are closest to the gods. You do not need a woman from this world. I will protect you. You need look only upon me.*

"Mother, I cannot fulfill your expectations. I'm not a god. I grew up in Mino with Toko. It's impossible to erase the days we spent together."

Is that why you have been resisting me? For such a foolish reason as that? It does not matter where you were raised. You cannot erase the bond of blood that joins us. Such thoughts are nothing but memories, whereas the bond that joins us runs in your very veins. You are mine.

"Even so, I want—" Oguna began but the woman cut him off.

Stay with me. You need not fret. Surely you know that there has never been a time when I did not think of you.

Toko gripped Oguna harder. She could feel that he was struggling to remain detached.

Let the girl go. The voice suddenly sounded harsh.

"No."

She'll be the ruin of you. She's detestable.

Which one of us is really detestable, Toko thought. Despite her terror, she felt anger swelling inside her.

Kill her.

"If you kill Toko, then I will kill you and sever this tie," Oguna suddenly said aloud. His voice was low and hard.

If you kill me, you too will die.

"Even so, I will kill you."

You cannot kill me. I am your mother, the creature said gently. *I know how you suffered when you killed your brother Oh-usu. Would you also turn your hand against the mother who bore you? For a mere girl?*

Toko felt Oguna's pain as if it were her own. Why did the woman press him so relentlessly? Toko could not bear it. She had not come here to make Oguna suffer like this. But Oguna spoke again. "Even so, I will kill you. You and I were not meant to be together on this earth. I was never meant to be born. I should never have existed in Toyoashihara."

If that is how you feel, then I accept, the creature agreed abruptly. *I would rather choose that than have you taken by another. Kill me and rejoin me. If we return our souls to the state prior to our worldly births, perhaps we can rise to the heavens together.*

Toko prayed desperately from the depths of her heart. *Somebody, help! Please!* But there was no one who could change this situation. There was only Toko.

"Stop," she said to Oguna. "Please don't."

"Toko."

"I don't want you to go to that extreme for my sake." She opened her eyes, which had been shut tight, and looked toward the creature. Something white seemed to flash before her eyes. She blinked in surprise for instead of the creature she had been expecting, she saw a woman—a tall, slender woman, wearing a gown with trailing sleeves. Her black hair flowed down her back like the night. Although terrified by this apparition, Toko could still see that the woman's face was noble and even beautiful. She must have been an unsurpassed beauty when she was alive. Toko could also see the resemblance to Oguna. So this was his mother—the person Toko had wished for many years that she could meet.

I must at least give you credit for your courage, the woman said. *You're an impudent girl to look at my true form.*

"I won't let you kill Oguna," Toko said. "You don't want him to die either, right? For it was you who protected his life with the power of the Sword."

Yes, it was. And I can continue to protect him. But it goes against my will to have his heart taken by another. I will not have him sever his bond to me when I have sacrificed so much for him. She pointed a pale finger at Toko. *Everything will be fine once you are gone. We don't need you. This child belongs to me, and to me alone.*

Toko cringed as the phantom reached out to grab her. Would the woman steal her soul so that she could never return to the living again? The thought froze Toko's heart. At that moment, a light shone. Caught in its beam, Oguna's mother hesitated. Frowning, she shielded her eyes with her hand. *What is this?*

Toko turned to see its source. A yawning distance stretched behind her, and through it, the light shone like an arrow. Somehow it seemed familiar. An even more familiar voice spoke in her ear.

"Toko, this way. Come back."

But I haven't moved, she thought. *Where's Oguna? I thought he was right here.* Instantly, she understood, and understanding, she opened her eyes. Although she had thought they were already open, they had still been shut tight.

There was Oguna. She was lying in his arms, as if she had fainted.

Toko started to speak and then saw the Misumaru shining on her chest and Sugaru's face peering into hers. So this had been the familiar light, and it was Sugaru's voice that had called her.

He smiled smugly. "Honestly. You're always getting into trouble, Toko. I came to your rescue, didn't I? You owe me one now."

chapter
ten

THE LAST
MAGATAMA

The Last Magatama

N O ONE WAS surprised to see Sugaru appear out of nowhere. It had happened too many times before. But Oguna's men were astounded to learn that he knew Toko. Takehiko stared at the two of them and groaned. "I'll never figure either of you out. Obviously, you're both good friends of the prince. I just pray that it turns out for the best."

"I can't vouch for myself, but you don't need to worry about Toko at least," Sugaru said. "She'd do anything for the prince, no matter how crazy." Toko felt like kicking him, but she had to acknowledge that this statement improved her status yet again in Takehiko's eyes. After he had gone, she turned to Sugaru. It was a little easier to talk about last night's hair-raising experience in the light of day.

"If you hadn't come, I would have died, stripped of my soul. I put on such a brave front the last time I saw you, but now I owe you my life."

"You were in a pretty tight spot," Sugaru agreed, looking pleased that Toko seemed so penitent. "But I can't criticize. After all, you were the one who said that being with Oguna could cost you your life."

"I did say that, didn't I?" Toko recalled the day on the beach when she had parted from Sugaru. "I knew exactly what I would be getting into. I vowed that I'd stay as far away from Oguna as possible because I hold my life just as dear as anyone else does. Yet as soon as I saw him, my resolve disintegrated. I had no choice but to follow him, no matter what might happen. I guess that's our fate."

Oguna had wept when Toko had regained consciousness, something she had not seen him do since he was five or six years old. She had been forced to shove her own needs aside and focus on comforting him. His sense of responsibility toward others was far greater than that of anyone else, and he had been deeply affected by what had happened. Toko was very glad that she had survived, of course, but for Oguna's sake as well as her own. She knew now that if she really cared about Oguna, she had better not die before him.

"I want to live," Toko said slowly, watching the sunlight on the camellia leaves. "Last night brought that home to me. What I did was really stupid, but I learned a lot from it. I even found out a little more about the nature of the Sword's power. Not to mention the fact that I've seen how that creature of death keeps Oguna in its clutches and won't let go. I don't know if I have a chance against it, but I'm not going to run away anymore. I'm going to stand my ground to the bitter end and try to survive."

"That sounds more like you, Toko. You've really pulled yourself together."

"You think so?" Toko hadn't noticed any change herself. Things had just happened.

"You know, I've been thinking," Sugaru began, but then said abruptly, "Actually, first there's something I've been wanting to ask you. It's about the Misumaru. We've got four magatama—what's the fifth one supposed to be?"

Taken by surprise, Toko thought for a moment. "Let me see. I'm trying to remember what Lady Toyoao said . . . There were eight stones in the necklace worn by the Goddess of Darkness. They were called Aka, Kuro, Ao, Shiro, Ki, Midori, Kagu, and Kura. The Goddess took Kura for herself and gave Kagu to the God of Light. Of the stones that were left, Ao belonged to the Water Maiden who gave it to the Wind Child. That leaves five."

Sugaru touched the necklace around his neck. "The stones here are Midori, Ki, Kuro, and Shiro—green, yellow, midnight blue, and white."

"That leaves Aka. The stone in Hidakami must be Aka!" Toko said, excited at finding the answer.

To her surprise, however, Sugaru said, "But Aka was supposed to be the one guarded in Mino."

"What?" Toko's voice rose. "But I retrieved the stone of Mino from the emperor's palace. It's Shiro, the white one, not Aka."

"Even so, the stone of Mino was originally Aka, meaning bright, and it was supposed to shine pale pink. Lady Akaru was *named* for the beauty of that magatama."

Toko looked shocked. "I never heard such a thing before. Where did you learn of this?" Sugaru did not answer. "Kisako's the only one who would know," Toko realized suddenly. She frowned. "Since when have you been talking to Kisako?"

Sugaru grunted noncommittally. Toko looked indignant. "So you *did* go to see her, did you? And here I thought you were going all over Hidakami in search of the magatama."

"What difference does it make?" Sugaru said, feigning indifference, but he looked unusually flustered. "With the Misumaru, it's just a short flight away. I went back to Izumo when I was looking for you before, you know. Anyway, don't change the subject. What I was trying to say is this: I can't figure out what kind of magatama we're supposed to be looking for—the one that's in Hidakami."

Confused, Toko said nothing. The magatama of Mino was Aka, yet the one she had found and brought to life was Shiro. One stone had some of the attributes of another—what could that mean? "I don't get it either," she said.

"Well, I've been thinking about it, and I think it's because these stones belong to the gods. They aren't real stones. Their color, their light, and their power are manifestations of something else," Sugaru said. "What we see here, these stones that we call magatama, maybe they don't actually exist in this world. If so, then the fact that one changed color might be insignificant."

This thought made Toko uneasy, and she stared intently at Sugaru. "What have you figured out? What are you trying to say?"

"Well, actually . . ." He took a deep breath and then said, "I arrived with impeccable timing last night, didn't I? But it wasn't because I knew what was going on. It never even occurred to me that you would be with Oguna. But I heard you. I knew that you were calling for help."

Toko started and then blushed. "But . . . I didn't call you. How could I? After what I had said to you."

"Yet I still heard you. Clearly. Like the jingling of a bell. The four magatama that I bear don't seem to respond to the fifth stone, the one that should be here in Hidakami. Instead they're drawn to you, just as if you *were* the magatama."

Toko looked baffled. "But . . . that's so weird . . . "

"Maybe not. If you consider the possibility that a magatama doesn't have to be a stone. Think about their purpose. I went back to Izumo to ask about that. The magatama were a gift to quell the evil power left on this earth. Right now, that power is what we call the Sword, the force that flows through Oguna's body. But you no longer wish to destroy the master of the Sword. You now want to help him. Right? I don't know why, but it seems that the Misumaru is in agreement with that desire."

"But why?" Toko asked, her face troubled. "That desire comes from pure selfishness. Even though I knew what my mission was, I abandoned it simply because I couldn't stop myself from loving Oguna. There's no way that the Misumaru could be on my side."

"Perhaps you're right . . . Maybe it's me, not the Misumaru, that's in agreement." He grinned. "At any rate, there's no one else in the world who so willingly lays their life on the line to confront the Sword the way you do. That at least is certain. Personally, I think the force of that love could easily rival the power of a magatama. Either that, or the true bearer of the Misumaru is you. Just as you once believed."

"I don't believe that at all now," Toko said. Sugaru's words embarrassed her. She was painfully aware of just how ordinary she was.

"Well, never mind. I'll hang on to the Misumaru for now. Who knows? The magatama of Hidakami may exist after all." Sugaru waved and walked off to renew old friendships.

Left behind, Toko was bewildered. Why would he compare her to a magatama? And what a shock to learn that the one from Mino was Aka, not Shiro. *If that's true, then what happened to Akaru's magatama? Does the original one vanish when the bearer changes? Perhaps we'll find a stone in Hidakami as beautiful as Akaru.* Suddenly she wondered what the color could mean. The Tachibana of Mino had never hidden their magatama away. Nor had the high priestess hesitated to give hers to the emperor when she read the omens. It was a treasure but one that was meant to be used. The Keeper of the Shrine had known that well.

If the magatama she had entrusted to Lady Akaru was the original stone of Mino, then why did it change color? *She told me that the mission of our people was to protect the emperor's line...*

Toko had been standing there for some time, lost in thought, when Oguna approached through the camellia grove. It was clear from his expression that he was despondent. Toko was not surprised. Last night's encounter had been so traumatic it had made him weep. She could guess how hard it would be for him to recover after that.

"It's a lovely day, isn't it?" she said, overly cheerful. "I slept fine. I'm better now."

Oguna sighed. "I'm sorry," he said. "I can't bear to think what would have happened if Sugaru hadn't come."

"Why are you apologizing? You have every right to be mad at me. It was my own fault. I followed after you even though you warned me not to."

"I'm apologizing for taking you from that little fishing village in the first place. I should never have done that. It was a mistake to keep you here just because I wanted to." He stared at her with anguished eyes. "I never want to go through that again. I'd rather have my arms and legs chopped off. The more I love someone, the more I hurt them. I thought that with you, it would be different. I thought that I could protect you. But I was wrong. You too will—no. I just can't let that happen."

"Are you planning to send me away?" Toko asked in a small voice.

"You have Sugaru," Oguna said dully. "He can take you somewhere safe. And his power will never cause you grief. He's better than I am, in every way. As a person, as a man—"

But Toko did not let him finish. Before she even registered what she was doing, she had slapped his face so soundly that the noise of it echoed in the clearing. "You coward!"

"What do you mean?" Now Oguna was angry too. No one had dared to slap him for years, and Toko's accusation seemed totally unjustified.

But Toko stood her ground. "Just what I said. You're a coward. I'm the one who nearly died, but did you hear *me* say anything about leaving you? So why are you the one to run away? At the very least you could try to comfort me."

"Are you saying that I should make you stay? How could I possibly do that?

I'm not that stupid. Surely you don't want to stay here after what happened, so what's wrong with my saying so?"

"Because I do want to stay, that's what. How can you be so stupid?" Toko yelled. "Sugaru is better than you? Instead of wasting your time telling me what I already know, why don't you try to become stronger? I don't want to die either. But I made a commitment to stay right here with you even if it meant death. I don't care what you say, I'm not leaving you."

"I don't want you to stay," Oguna insisted, just as cross as Toko. "I'd rather you were far away than to have to watch you die in front of me."

"Why don't you try cheering me up instead? Why don't you tell me you're going to try to live, with me, together?"

"Because that would be a lie. You know that, Toko."

They stood staring at one another. After a tense pause, Toko said quietly, "There are times when I'd rather be lied to."

"If you were the same Toko as the girl from my childhood," Oguna said hesitantly, "then maybe I could ask you to stay here with me. And you'd probably be safe. But that's not what you mean, is it? And I can't see you as a little girl anymore. Now that you're here in front of me, I know that."

"That's why you won't tell me what I want to hear?" Toko felt her cheeks burn and was annoyed with herself. "You're saying you don't want me near you because I'm not the same girl I was in the past?"

"I can't keep you here without exposing you to the power of the Sword," Oguna protested. "Being angry with me isn't going to change that. Because you're a woman. How can I stop myself from loving you as a woman? If we're together . . . then there are things that I would want. And I don't think anyone could blame me for that."

Sugaru suddenly poked his head out of the bushes. "Well, I wondered what you were quarreling about, but now I see it's just a domestic spat."

Oguna started and turned bright red, even to the tips of his ears. Toko thought her own face must be on fire. "How could you!" she spluttered. "How long have you been eavesdropping?"

"Since you landed him that nice fat wallop," Sugaru responded calmly. He looked at Oguna and chuckled. Finger marks still showed on Oguna's cheek. "You hit the crown prince. It ought to do him good."

"You're one to talk," Oguna said sullenly.

"I've no intention of interfering. There's no point. But there's something I wanted to tell you. If you've come this far, there's only one thing you can do. Accept it. Acknowledge the fact that you're gambling against the odds. Personally, I think this could be an interesting match. Count me in."

"Just because it's not your problem doesn't mean it's okay to poke fun at us," Toko snapped.

"I meant that I'm willing to help you. To the extent possible, anyway."

"How?" Oguna asked him uneasily.

Seeing his expression, Sugaru answered merrily, "I'll be Toko's shield. I'll protect her from your scary mother. That should make it a more even contest. Just remember that I'm not the one who can vanquish that beast. Even if I wanted to, I couldn't do it. It's you who will be tested."

2

TOKO FOUND THAT the addition of Sugaru made her relationship with Oguna that much more complicated. Just as she had been acutely conscious of Oguna's mother coming between her and Oguna, now Oguna seemed keenly sensitive to the close bond between Toko and Sugaru. As it was not rational, no amount of explanation would change anything. *This is really quite difficult,* she kept thinking.

Having confessed their love for one another, Toko and Oguna felt even more awkward than before. Toko realized that Oguna seemed somehow aloof, but she hesitated to pursue him. With Sugaru constantly there, she kept losing her nerve. At night, Oguna went out as usual, but she did not know how he dealt with the power of the Sword.

Their private problems, however, were superseded abruptly by the demands of daily life. War had begun. Though it would be Toko's first battle with Oguna's troops, war for soldiers was inevitable. Hidakami was situated far deeper into Emishi territory than Sagamu. Power struggles among the Emishi had already escalated, and the arrival of soldiers from Mahoroba naturally aggravated the conflicts. Word reached Oguna's company that the Emishi were mustering several hundred warriors, and the situation grew tense. It would be impossible to pressure such a large group into submission. They would have to use force in what was likely to be a fairly evenly matched battle.

"The time has come to test our strength," Oguna told his men. "The emperor has sent us here for this very purpose—to overcome this obstacle. Victory won here will bring you great honor and distinction."

As Toko watched Oguna, the seasoned military commander, she thought, *This is the world as he sees it—conflict within and without*...

Toko's life since the war in Mino had not been exactly tranquil either. She was much more accustomed to war than many women. Thus, it never occurred to her to sit idly by as the troops began their feverish preparations.

"What's gotten into you?" Sugaru asked, surprised to see Toko garbed once again in men's hakama and with her hair tied in a ponytail.

"I should be asking you that question. Why aren't you helping?" Toko asked.

"I have no intention of helping the emperor subjugate other people."

"That's rather ungrateful considering that Oguna's troops are feeding you."

"I don't hold any grudge against the Emishi."

"Neither do I. But I can't stand by and watch Oguna's men be killed," Toko insisted.

"Do you intend to stay here even during the battle?" Sugaru said in disbelief. "No one else is expecting you to do that. In fact, I plan to remove you to safety until things settle down."

"Well, I'm not going," Toko said. "In my opinion, the more helping hands there are, the fewer people will die. You should help too, Sugaru."

When Takehiko saw Sugaru helping his men prepare for this decisive battle, he looked skeptical. "Since when have you been on our side in a war? You're going against your word."

"Toko won't take no for an answer," Sugaru said grumpily. "She's so stubborn."

"You stayed because of Lady Toko?"

"What excuse could I give to seek safety all by myself when I promised to protect her? Mind you, I wasn't talking about war when I promised."

"What's going on here?" Takehiko exclaimed. "Are you the one who's really in love with Lady Toko?"

"Nope."

"Hmm." Takehiko pondered this for a moment. "Oh well, forget it. I'll never understand the three of you. And we can certainly use your help. With the prince on our side, I don't expect to lose, but still, you never know what could happen in a place like this."

AFTER ANNOUNCING that they would attack at daybreak, Oguna donned his armor though it was not yet dusk. This time he would not be alone in his vigil—the entire company would be up all night. *He probably has no time to even think about that creature,* Toko thought. *And no time to spend with me either . . .* She had not spoken with him for the last few days. Even though he was the only reason she had stayed. She was ashamed at herself for wishing it could be otherwise, but she had to accept that that was how she felt. She did not understand Oguna, and the more she loved him, the more anxious she became. *Things were so much simpler before. I was satisfied just to love him. Why can't it be the same now?*

Though they longed for each other, the littlest things kept the pair from expressing their true feelings. It would have been no comfort to Toko to know that all lovers go through such trials. Death stalked the love between her and Oguna far too closely. It was impossible to be patient when they had so little time to accomplish so much.

There would be no moonrise that evening for it was the time of the new moon. Instead, the winter stars shone brightly. Toko, shivering with cold, was counting them when she heard a faint clanking of metal. Oguna appeared before her, his armor gleaming faintly in the starlight like a river in the dark. "My men laud your courage in staying even though we stand on the brink of battle. They call you a brave woman." Oguna spoke in the regal tone of a prince. After a slight pause, he added, "But I know something they don't. I know the terrible memories that war must bring back for you. Yet still you chose to stay. You're braver than any of us."

"If I had just sat down and cried when we lost Mino, I would not be who I am today." Toko spoke slowly, but inside her heart raced at the thought that Oguna had come here just to speak with her. "Instead of hiding myself away, I went out and learned. The tests I faced made me stronger. I still hate war. But I won't let it overwhelm me with terror."

Because I have faced something far more terrifying, she thought. *It's all relative.*

"You give me courage. I have so much to learn from you."

"What could you, the commander of an army, possibly learn from me?"

Oguna looked at her. With his armor glinting, he seemed somehow unapproachable, and Toko felt uncomfortable under his gaze.

"I'm going to sever myself from the Sword." He spoke very quietly. "I have to find it in me to do that. No one can take the place of my mother, yet it was my own weakness that made her into what she has become. I must lay that creature to rest. You are more important, and in order to be with you, I must seal away the Sword."

Toko started. Her voice rose. "No. If you kill her, you'll die too. If that's the case, then what's the point?"

"I didn't say I was going to kill her," Oguna said gently. "I'm going to lock her away inside of me, as part of myself. To even attempt it will mean laying my life on the line, but pain is unavoidable. I never had the courage to try before. I didn't know if I could really live with the Sword as part of myself . . . I didn't know if it was even permissible." The intensity of his gaze told Toko how heavily this question had weighed on him. Tears welled in her eyes at the burden he bore just by wanting to live.

"Promise me that you'll do your very best to survive—so that we can be together. That's all I'm going to think about."

"It means so much to me that you're here, Toko. Do you know that?"

"I stayed purely for my own sake, though. To satisfy my own need," Toko said humbly. She had never felt so happy in her life. The gloom that had weighed upon her only a moment ago seemed to have evaporated as if it had never been.

"I'm not going to use the Sword in this battle," Oguna said. "I'm going to fight to the end without it. And when the battle is over, I will come to you. If you don't mind." Toko knew immediately what he meant, but just to be sure, he added, "I'll stay with you until morning if that's all right."

Toko meant to answer boldly, but she barely managed a whisper. "That would make me very happy."

Oguna's armor made it too awkward to embrace, so he contented himself with a light kiss after which Toko ran away, embarrassed not by his kiss but rather by the fact that she wanted more.

THAT NIGHT TOKO learned that hope multiplies fear many times over. Oguna had declared that he would not use the Sword, no matter what. But that meant he would be as vulnerable as any other man. He could be slain by a single arrow. The tense atmosphere in the camp and the sound of people moving about kept her awake most of the night. She lay down in her tent but left the oil lamp burning. She must have dozed off for a second, however, for when she looked up she saw a woman standing in the lamplight, tall, beautiful, dressed in white with long black hair—Princess Momoso, Oguna's mother.

"What do you want with me?" Toko said sharply. "You must begone. That's what Oguna said."

I know. That child is trying to cut me out of his heart. He is making a grave mistake.

"How can you say it's a mistake? You're dead already. It's wrong to cling to that form for so long."

Why do you think I sacrificed my life for that child? The woman asked only to answer her own question. *Because his life is short. As a priestess, I can foresee what will happen. If I do nothing, his father will kill him. But with my power I can protect him. From his father, the emperor.*

Toko was at a loss for words. "His own father would kill him?" she asked finally.

The emperor fears him. He fears the godly power he sees in the one who can wield the Sword.

"But that's . . . Then there's all the more reason that Oguna should not wield the Sword."

Once I'm gone, his father will kill him. Princess Momoso's voice was cold. *I cannot be cut out or sealed away so easily. If that child still insists on trying, I will aid the emperor in his attempts to kill him. I will kill my son so that we can be reunited. We can be one again, like we were before he was born.*

Toko shivered. "Do you want to cling to Oguna that badly?"

Of course. He is mine. *I will not let him choose another.* She reached out and grasped Toko's chin between her icy fingers. Toko froze and stared up at her, unable to move. *How dare he neglect me for someone as lowly as you?*

Where's Sugaru? Toko wondered desperately. He was supposed to be her shield. Where was he now that she needed him?

Princess Momoso smiled slightly. *But I can see that you are not an ordinary girl. Your heart does not cease beating even when I touch you. And I suppose on closer inspection you are pretty enough.* Toko sensed a shift inside the woman, like a shadow falling on the water's surface. She held her breath, waiting to see what Oguna's mother would say.

Give me your body. If that boy fancies you, then I will be you. We're the same, you and I. We both want him to live. We want to be by his side. We want him to love us. You see? We're the same.

"No! We're not the same at all," Toko shouted. "You're his mother. That's your son you're talking about."

I want to be with him now and forever, the woman continued. *To always gaze upon his face. I could not bear it if he turned away or forgot me. I would rather use my power to kill him. If you would but relinquish your place to me, however, there would be no need for him to die. I could possess your body and live with him for eternity. You do not want him to die either, do you? We're the same.*

Toko felt ill. Logic made no impact on this apparition. The only thing this woman had was her will. "No, I won't. I can't let you do that."

How narrow-minded you are. You wish to control him and keep him to yourself. Will you force me to kill him because of your selfishness?

"No!" Toko shook her head. "You can't. That's not love. It doesn't matter what you say, that's just plain wrong. What possible good can it do you to cling to Oguna like that?"

You don't understand anything, do you? Princess Momoso said. *He exists only because I protect him. Make me your enemy and you will see just how helpless he is without me.*

A shiver ran down Toko's spine. "What are you planning to do to him?" she cried. "Why won't you rest in peace and leave him alone?" The apparition cast her a cold look. Toko thought she saw a black shadow spread its wings behind the woman.

The choice is yours: you or the boy. That is all that you can do—choose.

Drenched in a cold sweat, Toko opened her eyes. The apparition melted into the shadow cast by the oil lamp. Leaping to her feet, Toko flew out of the tent to look for Sugaru. He was right outside, warming himself by the fire.

"Sugaru! You didn't even come!"

Sugaru looked up at the fuming Toko with a puzzled frown. "What do you mean? I looked in a minute ago, but you were sleeping so soundly I didn't bother to wake you."

"Well, you should have! That evil creature came to me in my sleep. Instead of appearing before Oguna, tonight she came to me."

Once again Toko felt the woman's fingers on her face and she began to shake violently. Sugaru held out a bamboo flask. "Here. Drink some of this. It'll help you relax."

Although she knew it was sake, she drank it and then choked.

"How does that feel?" Sugaru asked.

"It burns."

"It's too strong for you. It's *yashio-ori,* quite a potent brew."

More than the sake, it was Sugaru's behavior that helped Toko calm down. She told him what had happened.

"That's good news," Sugaru said, ever the optimist. "It means that Oguna has distanced himself from the power—far enough that the creature panicked and threatened you. And don't you dare give in to that threat, either. Just let her be."

"But I can't help worrying about Oguna." Toko found it hard to believe it was an empty threat. The woman's words had seemed to imply a hidden meaning. "Why now, when we're on the verge of war? Anything could happen. Sugaru, please, protect Oguna. Don't worry about me."

Sugaru shrugged and rolled his eyes. "I knew you'd say that. I'm not here to carry love letters for you two, you know. Don't expect me to go just because you asked."

But Toko ignored him. Love made her strong. Yet even as she sought desperately to ensure Oguna's safety, doubt crossed her mind. Princess Momoso's words echoed in her head. *We're the same, you and I.*

Is there a difference? Between my feeling and hers? Toko thought. *Is there really any difference between us?*

3

THE WAR was not going well. Faced with their first real setback, the soldiers were frustrated and tense. Even Toko could see that. Being at the rear, she had no way of grasping the whole picture, but she could sense the tide of events in her very skin. The feeling of defeat—like loose soil swept away by a surging torrent—was something she already knew well from Mino. At times, her heart beat so wildly she thought it must break.

Oguna's mother is planning to beat him down. She's pushing him into a corner so that he'll have no choice but to use the Sword. He's bound to give in. Who wouldn't in the face of such pressure? But whether she liked it or not, there was nothing she could do. Even if she could use the Misumaru to fly to Oguna's side, it would not help to either scold or encourage him. Oguna's will was his own. And if, in the end, he failed to sever the bond with his mother, Toko could not complain, for she did indeed want the same thing as his mother. While Toko might hate the way Oguna's mother protected him, as long as she did so, Oguna would survive. He would live.

Ever since Princess Momoso had appeared in her dream, Toko had been plagued by a terrifying thought. Was she responsible for shortening Oguna's life? After all, he had placed himself in grave danger for her sake so that he could divorce himself from the Sword. Though she loved him and desperately wanted Oguna to live, perhaps she was actually fated to destroy him against her will, thereby fulfilling the mission of the Tachibana. *If so, then what should I do? Would it be better to let his mother have my body to protect Oguna? But I don't want to. I can't.*

While one battle raged around her, another raged within—and the odds were not in her favor. Unable to spare any emotion for the external world, she buried herself in her chores. It was a shout announcing retreat that finally jolted her back to reality.

"Did we lose?" she asked the commander of the supply troop.

"We can't lose," he responded with a grim expression. "Our orders are to withdraw temporarily."

They were located several days' march inland where the flat plain that had seemed to stretch on forever finally gave way to rolling hills. Choosing one of these hills as their rallying point, they moved their camp to elevated ground. The retreat was more like a rout, and the soldiers from the battlefront arrived in considerable disarray. Toko's eyes widened when she saw their wretched state. How could they have suffered so much damage in just a single day of fighting? Not one among them had remained unscathed. And far fewer had returned than had set out that morning.

Where's Oguna? And Sugaru? Toko thought. *Sugaru has the Misumaru,* she reminded herself, trying to remain calm. If anything had happened to Oguna, he would have come and told her. Surely even the easygoing Sugaru would do that much. But in her fear, she found herself doubting him nonetheless. He might have become so involved in the fray that he had forgotten to keep her informed.

At that moment, Sugaru appeared in front of her. "Sorry," he said. "I was too busy fighting. I didn't have a chance to come back."

Toko clenched her fists. "Sugaru!"

"Oguna's still there," Sugaru said in a rush. "He cut off the attackers to allow the soldiers to retreat to the last man. That's why I was so busy."

Toko decided there was no point in being angry. "So Oguna didn't use his power then?" she said.

"Didn't you see the light?" Sugaru asked with a frown.

"No," Toko said, shocked. "The hills cut off any view."

"I don't think it was Oguna, but the power of the Sword was definitely invoked at some point. I don't understand what's going on. Nothing about this battle makes any sense. But there's no time to talk. I came because Oguna's wounded and won't let us treat him. Can you come?"

For a moment, Toko could not breathe. "Yes," she gasped. "Please take me to him."

As they flew, Sugaru gave her some details. "It was a terrible battle. Takehiko's unit was decimated and the main force completely scattered. Some of them will probably never make it back. Oguna's trying to rally them and bring them back safely, but he's been wounded fairly badly."

When they reached the site, Toko felt she was walking into a nightmare. The men had felled some trees to form a barricade far too simple to call a rampart. Those too wounded to stand had been carried to this makeshift shelter while the clamor of battle echoed nearby.

Just like Mino. But there was no time for Toko to dwell on the situation. Urged on by Sugaru, she walked into a grove of trees behind the barricade and found Oguna lying in a tent with two attendants. One supported his

head. Oguna's face was deathly pale, and it seemed to take all his strength just
to remain conscious. He was still clad in armor, but the burnished surface
was now soiled with blood and dirt and the shirt beneath was stained dark
with blood.

"Here. I've brought Toko," Sugaru said.

Oguna turned toward Sugaru with an accusing look, but when he saw Toko,
all his strength seemed to drain away.

"You take care of that wound now and leave the battle to us," Sugaru
continued. "Don't worry. I'm here. I won't let them get any closer."

"But this is my fault. I have to take responsibility."

"Tell me that when you're well enough to stand."

Oguna cast Toko a pleading look. "I'm not the only one who's injured."

"As far as I can see," Toko said bluntly, "of those who aren't already dead,
you're the most badly wounded. Stop stalling. Let's get that armor off."

It took Toko and Oguna's two attendants to remove his armguards and
breastplate. Oguna cried out, unable to bear the pain. Although Toko had
prepared herself for the worst, even so, the sight of his injury made her gasp.
"It's awful . . . "

It was his right arm that was injured. Rather than a gash from a blade, a
hideous burn spread as far as his shoulder, as if fire had raced along the inside
of his gauntlet. "How did you get such a wound?"

"It's our fault," one of his men said, his face anguished. "Even though we
were with him, we failed to protect him."

"What happened?" Toko asked him. She could not ask Oguna, for it was
all he could do to fight the pain.

"He crossed swords with the enemy commander . . . When we saw their
army, we couldn't believe our eyes. We couldn't understand it. We came here
to stamp out the Emishi, who ravage the land. But the Emishi army looked
just like us. They wore the same armor, used the same formation so that we
could not tell ourselves apart from them. Even the commander who led them
looked exactly like the prince."

"What?"

"I know it seems impossible, but it's the truth. Their armor, their helmets,
everything about them was the same. It was like looking into a mirror. Of

course, we were furious. The prince as well. We launched straight into battle. The prince joined Takehiko's unit, made up of the best warriors, and they scattered the enemy until they came face to face with their commander. But when he and the prince crossed swords, a bolt of lightning struck."

"The Sword..." Toko whispered, shocked. She looked down at Oguna's wound.

"It served the enemy, not the prince. We were dumbstruck. You can't begin to imagine what we felt. At that moment, it seemed to be us, not them, who were merely a reflection on the water."

"That's impossible!" Toko was practically shouting. "I don't understand."

At that moment, Oguna spoke, his voice as quiet as a breath. "I do... I was able to sever myself from the Sword, but not to seal its power within me."

Toko squeezed his sound hand. "So you didn't use it? Just like you promised."

Oguna seemed to nod with his eyes, but his face twisted in agony. "I know him..." he said, but she learned no more for with that he fainted.

TRUE TO HIS WORD, Sugaru kept the enemy troops from coming any closer, and though it took him a day and a night, in the end the attackers retreated. While this gave Oguna's troops breathing space, it did not disperse the dark cloud that hung over them. Oguna was tormented by a high fever and his condition worsened. It was clear to everyone that the situation was grave.

Sugaru called Toko aside and, after some hesitation, finally shared what was on his mind. "I've seen that kind of wound before. In Izumo. If we want to save his life, it would be better to amputate his arm as soon as possible. Once it festers, the poison will spread through his system and he'll never have another chance."

Toko was exhausted. She had not slept at all, and she found that she could not stop the tears flowing down her face. "Cut it off? It's his arm, Sugaru. His right arm."

"He may lose an arm, but at least he'll live. Although I suppose that some people would rather die." Sugaru was being strangely fair. "He'll have to decide which is better."

"Oguna's delirious," Toko sobbed. "He can't make that kind of decision."

"Then you do it, Toko. You decide for him."

Toko wept, and as she wept she remembered that Princess Momoso had also told her to choose—between herself and Oguna, one or the other. But as Toko had no intention of relinquishing her place to that woman, she had in effect chosen herself. And was this the result? *Was it my selfishness that caused Oguna to suffer like this?*

Suddenly, she felt angry. It was so unreasonable. *It's not fair to force a choice on someone like that. She's the one in the wrong. I will not accept either choice. I don't want to lose . . .*

Perhaps she did not want to lose to fate. She did not want to lose to anything that tried to wrest Oguna from her grasp. She would not accept that on any terms. She stopped crying and looked at Sugaru.

"What?" he asked, looking startled. Her eyes burned with a strange intensity.

"Sugaru, do you think I can wield the Misumaru once more?" Even her voice sounded strange.

"What are you planning to do?" Sugaru asked cautiously.

"I don't know . . . but I think it's possible. I beg of you, by that white stone, Shiro, to let me bear the Misumaru one more time."

Toko held out her hand, suddenly firm and sure, like a shrine maiden possessed. Compelled by something in her voice, Sugaru undid the string around his neck. He did not know where the force inside her came from, but when he handed her the Misumaru, he was not surprised to see that it continued to glow.

Toko felt herself reunited with the power of the Goddess who loved this land. The wild, unruly force of the earth and its tranquility; the clear, rising power of purification and the stagnating power of decay; the power of creation and of elimination—all these she felt, and within them she found what she had known intuitively must be a part of the power of the beads. The power to heal—to cure those who lived and to release those who were dying. The path of that force was very narrow. Only with the fifth stone would the collection of magatama be free to transcend the Misumaru of Death. But despite only being the thinnest of threads, it was still there.

She fastened the Misumaru around her neck and returned to Oguna's side. The Misumaru filled the dimness inside the tent with multi-colored light and shone upon Oguna's face where he lay unconscious.

If Oguna wishes to live, if he has the will to do so, the power of the Misumaru should work.... If he wishes to return to me... Goddess of Darkness, please, help me... Filling her thoughts with this prayer, Toko gently placed her hand on the cloth that covered Oguna's wound.

She felt the power expand inside her, and although she strove to remain aware, she lost track of how long she stayed like that. It seemed like forever and, at the same time, like a mere instant, but only because her consciousness faded when her strength was spent. It was not until she woke the next morning that she learned what had happened. It was the noise of Sugaru rushing loudly into the tent that woke her.

"Toko!" he cried. "What have you done?" He looked surprised to see Toko just sitting up and rubbing her eyes.

"What are you talking about?"

"You mean you don't know? Every soldier who was wounded, down to the very last man, has recovered. And so completely you would never have known they were injured. Was it the Misumaru?"

Coming to her senses, Toko hastily removed the cloth from Oguna's arm. His wound was healed. There was some scarring, but the limb no longer held any fever and the skin had regained its healthy tone.

"I can move it. It doesn't hurt anymore," Oguna said. "You fixed it for me, didn't you, Toko? I could feel your power flowing into me. That's a noble force you wield."

"Well, I could never have managed a stunt like that," Sugaru said. "It never even occurred to me that the Misumaru could be used that way."

"Me neither," Toko said. Gingerly, she reached out and touched Oguna's wounded arm. "This scar will remain." She seemed sincerely disappointed.

"Who cares?" Oguna laughed.

"But I wanted to cure you so that there would be no trace left at all." It made her sad to think that his perfect form would be marred in any way. Though she did not think about it often, she was aware that he had the unclouded splendor and grace that belonged to those descended from the God of Light.

"Nothing can ever go back to what it was before. A wound is a wound. You can't erase that fact," Oguna said without a trace of regret. "I have many scars. Every time I was wounded and healed, I could feel myself change. I have one here, too..."

Seeing him place his hand against his midriff, Toko was unable to speak.

Oguna looked at her earnestly. "I can never erase the fact that I was burned by the Sword, even if no scar remains. I have bidden farewell to that power. I did so from the bottom of my heart. The creature told me that if I parted with it, it would align itself with those forces that want to destroy me. And it did so." Toko nodded. Oguna sighed slightly. "Without you, Toko, I would have died. The Sword is still stronger than I. It has left me, but now it is beginning to move of its own accord. The result may be much worse than we could imagine."

"Even so, you have taken the first step. You have made the decision to live," Toko said earnestly. "And it was your own choice. So don't you dare regret it."

"Mmm," Oguna nodded, but he did not sound totally convinced.

WHEN OGUNA finally returned to the camp, his men greeted him with great relief. His first task, however, was to bury the dead. Even Oguna, who had been confronted with death all along, had never lost so many comrades in a single battle. Among the missing was his loyal captain, Takehiko. It would have been too much to expect Oguna to be cheerful.

"I didn't bring my men here to die so far from home," he confided to Toko. She was the only one to whom he showed his utter discouragement. "In the past, many men deserted my army because they recognized that they had nothing to gain by serving under me. Those who have followed me this far are truly loyal. They chose me as their leader to the bitter end. But I failed to fulfill that trust. I brought them to the remotest part of the country to die. They probably wished they had never come with me."

Toko was beginning to realize that being a leader was not easy for Oguna. He bore responsibility for every life entrusted to him, a weight that at times threatened to crush him. Though Toko did not want Oguna to suffer any more grief, she could not change what had happened. Oguna had chosen to live and had parted with the Sword for that purpose. As a result, he had lost his invincible power and with it, many of his men. As their commander, he could not help but feel remorse.

It's his mother's doing. She intends to make him suffer, to shake his resolve so that he's forced to return to the way things were before. Toko could not stand it. If Oguna had been selfish and egotistical, he might have been safe. But he had far too much integrity even toward those who served under him, and this put his life at risk.

Later, Sugaru said, "You've got to do more to comfort him, Toko. He looks like he's in the depths of despair despite the fact that you cured him."

"He can't be happy just for himself," Toko answered. "He's not that type of person, and nothing I could say will change that." Although Oguna had not hidden himself away like he had as a child, his mien was at the moment very similar. His despair affected his men, who were also beginning to lose hope. Some, realizing that the Sword had turned its back on Oguna, even left ranks and disappeared into the countryside.

"If he's not going to get over this now, then when will he? We don't have much time left," Sugaru said.

Toko was fully aware that time was pressing. "I want that fifth magatama," she said abruptly. "I think it's our only hope for eliminating the power that makes him suffer. Without a power stronger than the Misumaru of Death, we can't confront it. Lady Toyoao told me that five stones would give the Misumaru the power of rebirth. If we're to tear Oguna from that phantom's grasp, we need something as strong as that. You told me you couldn't find it, but it must be somewhere."

"You go look," Sugaru urged her. She still wore the Misumaru around her neck, and Sugaru had not asked her to return it. He had relinquished the role of bearer to her. "I don't know what happened to the last one, Aka, but you just might be able to find it. Your yearning for it is much stronger than mine." He added brightly, "Go find it and win this woman's war over Oguna."

Toko glared at him, but Sugaru ignored her. She had to acknowledge that what he said was true. She had indeed resolved to confront Oguna's mother in a gamble for his life.

4

TOKO had no sooner decided to search for the fifth magatama than three armor-clad messengers rode up to their camp. They made no move to dismount. Instead one of them announced in a loud voice, "We, the army of Mahoroba, led by the prince who bears the Sword as proof of his descent from the God of Light, have justly punished you, the followers of an impostor who falsely calls himself 'prince.' You have been rendered defenseless, incapable of resistance. Yet our prince, in his mercy, has refrained from slaying the remnants of your army and has sent us instead to parley. Have your leader come forth."

Enraged at the enemy's claim to be the legitimate army, Oguna's men swung their spears to the ready and fitted arrows to their bows, their faces white with fury. Oguna, however, raised his hand. "Wait," he said. "There's no need to be hasty."

The messenger continued. "We have captured many of your comrades. Among them is your captain, Takehiko. If you kill us, the prisoners will all die. Is that your wish?"

"Let's talk," Oguna said. He stepped forward and walked through the entrance of the stockade to approach the enemy soldiers. He wore only a leather breast guard over his clothes and appeared very young. Yet there was something in his manner that unnerved the messengers, despite the fact that they had the upper hand.

"You..."

"I am Ousu, crown prince and heir to the imperial throne of Mahoroba," he said. "Why do you lie?"

The messengers stared at him intently while he spoke, but when he had finished, their leader responded, "Our commander is the true prince. You are nothing but bandits who exploit the prince's name for your own selfish ends. Do you still claim legitimacy in the face of your abject defeat by the Sword?"

"It is true that your leader wielded the Sword," Oguna said, his voice measured and controlled. "What do you want? What are you trying to gain by branding us as renegades?"

"The penalty for impersonating a prince is very grave," the messenger said, ignoring his question. "You must be punished. But if you desist from this fruitless war and surrender yourself as the leader, we will spare the lives of the prisoners. If, however, you refuse, we'll turn not only the prisoners but also you and every one of your men into corpses. Which do you want?"

Oguna smiled faintly. "I see. You want my life. That's all, right?"

"Choose."

"All right. If you promise not only to spare the lives of the prisoners but to set them free and guarantee that you will never bother any of my men again, I will accept the terms of your bargain."

"Our prince is merciful. He will surely do as you ask." The man turned and pointed toward a hill to the north. "You must come alone to the cedar wood on that hill tomorrow at dawn. If you are not alone, or if you fail to come at the appointed time, we will kill the prisoners. Remember that."

"I understand," Oguna said. The messengers turned their horses and galloped off, checking over their shoulders frequently. Oguna, however, merely watched them recede into the distance without issuing any orders.

Toko was the first to reach him. She had been listening to this altercation from some distance away, but the content had been so shocking that she unwittingly tapped the power of the Misumaru and appeared in front of him. "What on earth were they talking about?" she shouted. "How dare they say that to you? Why did they call you an impostor?"

"I know who their leader is," Oguna said, with a dark scowl. "There's only one person who could come up with a scheme like this. Someone who knows everything I've done . . . including what I did to my brother; someone who saw it all. And now he's sneering at me, gloating over the fact that I've been caught in the same web that once ensnared my brother." Toko was startled at the extent of Oguna's rage. She had never heard him speak with such venom before. "Sukune. The emperor's shadow. The emperor ordered him to follow me everywhere. I knew that. It was he, and those who served under him, who made all those attempts on my life. But he was just a tool. He only acted under the emperor's orders. So I thought there was no point in hating him. But this is going too far. I'll never forgive him for this. Or the emperor who's behind it all."

"Oguna," Toko said fearfully.

"He used the power of the Sword. How he managed that, I don't know. I don't know, but I can't let him continue," Oguna said, an edge in his voice. "I can't allow someone like him to wield that Sword. It's not right."

"No, Oguna. That's the same as saying that you want the Sword back."

"I can't let Sukune use it."

"If you confront him when you feel like this, it'll be disastrous." Toko was at her wits' end. It was dangerous for Oguna to become so enraged at the thought of someone else wielding the Sword. Toko could see that, but Oguna couldn't. Because he rarely expressed any anger, the fury he felt now was too explosive for him to fully control.

"You don't understand, Toko. I can't back down. I'll go and defeat Sukune alone. I have to show him who the true master of the Sword is."

"But you were supposed to have severed yourself from it," Toko shouted.

"What's the point in severing myself if it's only going to start acting with a mind of its own? I have to finish it. By myself."

"Don't you see? It's the Sword that's doing this. It's trying to draw you to your death. If you do what it wants, you'll die."

"I can't help it. In the end, this is the only way to stop its power."

"You're so stupid!" Toko yelled. This was too much. She felt betrayed. Oguna had not chosen her after all. It had only looked like he had. When it came to a crisis, his resolve had easily crumbled.

At the sight of her tears, Oguna started, as if coming to his senses, but Toko had had enough. It would only make her more miserable to let him see her tear-streaked face. As she still bore the Misumaru, that thought alone was enough to spirit her away.

Materializing in a forest on some unknown mountain, Toko paused to weep. *What am I going to do? I can't possibly find the fifth magatama in time. Oguna will leave at dawn tomorrow. And his mother will take him.*

There were no leads to guide her, and even if it were possible to find the last stone, she could not hope to do it in just one day. Time was far too short. She wracked her brain for an answer but found none. Just as she was about to despair, she suddenly remembered someone who could help—in Himuka at the western edge of the country. Lady Iwa, the greatest priestess in the land.

Lady Iwa was not yet a year old. But she might know something about the fifth stone. After all, she had been born with the stone called Ki in her fist. Once the thought had occurred to Toko, she could not put it out of her mind. Clinging to this slim chance, she rose to her feet. The distance between Himuka and Hidakami was immense. The entire country of Toyoashihara lay between them. But she had the Misumaru, and Sugaru had already proven that it could take her there. It was too soon to give up. She must try every option.

THE MOUNTAIN OF FIRE was no longer smoking. It was already late in the day and the sky was turning a pale, hazy purple, but the air was not yet cold on her skin. Whereas the camellia trees in Hidakami were still barren of buds, here in Himuka they were already heavy with flowers. Exhausted, Toko stumbled through the slanting rays of the sun until she caught sight of the infant's mother, Lady Hayakitsu. The lady had just left the gate of what looked to be a newly constructed building. In fact, all the houses appeared new, having no doubt been built after the flood. Lady Hayakitsu joined a group of women and chatted with them as they moved off down the street together. Toko debated calling out to the women but decided against it. Lady Hayakitsu would welcome her with surprise and delight—there was much that Toko wanted to tell her, but there was no time. She wanted to meet with Lady Iwa and return as quickly as possible.

Toko flew a short distance and found herself in the courtyard of a house. Lady Iwa lay in a cradle in the middle of a large room, the doors of which were flung open onto an inner garden. Bathed in the late afternoon sun, the baby girl gazed at the ceiling and stretched her hands up toward it. Colorful toys hung from a beam and stirred faintly in the breeze.

Lady Iwa had grown much bigger. Her skin was fair and her face was very cute. But the sight of her robbed Toko of confidence. She had been a fool to waste all that energy traveling to the far western edge of the land. This girl was probably nothing more than what she seemed—a baby. What deep questions could she possibly expect her to answer? But when she looked anxiously into the cradle, Lady Iwa turned her large eyes toward her, and they were the eyes of a wise old woman. Fortunately, the magatama allowed Toko to hear the infant's thoughts and to translate them into the language of the land.

What's wrong, my child? What is troubling you that you should come so far?

Toko almost choked with emotion just to be asked this question. Having been on her own for so long without any guide, her relief was so intense that she could have cried. "I have to find the stone of Hidakami," she said. "The last magatama. I just have to have it. By tomorrow morning. Please, Lady Iwa, help me. There's no one else I can turn to."

You already wear four magatama around your neck. That is enough to give you powers no ordinary person could dream of. Why do you want more?

"To destroy the Sword and save its master. The Misumaru of Death is not enough to stop the Sword from drawing Oguna to his doom. I need all five. Why can't we find the magatama of Hidakami? Is it because the stone from Mino has disappeared?"

The magatama of Hidakami exists, Lady Iwa said. She closed her eyes in thought and then looked again at Toko. *But it is beyond your reach. Neither you nor Sugaru can obtain it. It cannot be found by the bearer of the Misumaru.*

"But why?" Toko cried.

Because it is no longer possible to obtain any power greater than death in this world. In the past, when the gods walked the earth, perhaps, but now it exceeds our capacity. Or so the Goddess of Darkness thinks. A power so great that it does not belong in this world can only bring calamity—just as the Sword has.

"Then is it impossible to save him? Is there no way for us to resist the evil power of his mother?" Toko clasped her hands together and pleaded. "Please. Give me the power. I will show you that I can turn misfortune to fortune. I love Oguna. I would not use that power for any other purpose."

Another woman once thought the same thing—the mother of the one who wields the Sword, Lady Iwa said quietly. Toko felt as if she had been slapped. *She once thought 'Nothing evil can be born of love.' Do you intend to obtain this power so that you can vie with her over that youth and determine which of you is the greater evil? Is that really what is best for him?*

Shocked, Toko fell silent. After a long moment, she whispered, "But . . . I . . . what should I . . . Do you mean that I should quit defying her?"

I cannot tell you what you should do. You have walked your own path thus far. No path will satisfy you except the one you find for yourself. But there is one thing I can tell you, you who will likely be the last Tachibana woman to bear the Misumaru. The magatama do not draw their power solely from the stones. Your Misumaru is missing Aka, the stone from Mino. You must think about what that magatama means.

TOKO HAD NO CHOICE but to return empty-handed. Fortunately, her flight had left a trail that she could follow, making it even easier to return to camp than it had been to find Lady Iwa. Before she knew it, she found herself once again beneath the trees on the mountainside. Despondent, she stayed there, motionless, for some time. Curled up in a ball, she thought about what Lady Iwa had told her. *Aka, the stone from Mino. The magatama that vanished with Akaru. How does Lady Iwa expect me to understand the meaning of that? Akaru loved the prince so much that she gave up her life for him. Must I do the same . . . ?*

Toko thought back on what Akaru had done, feeling the pain of those memories all over again. Was it selfish to hold out for what she desired? Was it an unforgivable sin to want to live—and to want Oguna to live as well? Would fate deny her this?

Night fell and a curtain of blackness spread beneath the dark trees. Toko pondered her situation until she felt her head must burst but came to no conclusion. On impulse she decided to return to the camp. It was cold and lonely here by herself. There was no reason to stay. She materialized beside the stockade on the spot from which she had first vanished. The torches had been lit. To her surprise, Oguna was still there, standing alone, as if he had never moved.

"Toko!" He grabbed her in his arms as if to keep her from disappearing again. "I thought you'd never come back."

Toko was sorry. She should never have left his side. She should have stayed with him, particularly now, when he had prepared himself to die tomorrow. "I'm sorry," she whispered, clinging to him. "I was such a coward."

Oguna peered into her face, trying to see it in the torchlight. "I'm the one who wanted to apologize. All I ever did was make you grieve. You've done so much for me, and I was never able to do anything for you. But—I have to go tomorrow. I just have to."

Toko said nothing.

"I'm not asking you to understand. That would be too unfair. But no one else can do this for me. I have to do it myself. As the commander of this army, I cannot let Takehiko and my men die. I have to save them. And it has to be me who takes back the Sword." He took a deep breath. "Because the Sword is not only my mother, it's also a part of me. It is only right that I should take responsibility and bring it to an end. I want to live—with you. I still want that. But if I do not go tomorrow, I will no longer be me. Please forgive me . . . if you can. I mean it when I say that I love you. Now and forever, more than anyone else."

Oguna has already chosen, Toko thought. He was no longer speaking from anger but from the depths of his heart, after long and careful thought. She could feel that. And she could feel his love for her. She knew that this choice was the best answer that he had been able to find.

There's nothing I can do. Never had she felt so utterly powerless. Up until now, Toko had risen to the occasion whenever faced with a challenge, convinced that she could change the course of events by the force of her will. But now she understood for the first time that she must let go. Because Oguna had a will of his own. Even if he walked forth into death, if that was what he decided he must do, she would not bend his will to hers just to make him stay. *I am not like his mother,* Toko thought, surprised at this discovery. Unlike his mother, she could understand Oguna. She could recognize what he desired and abide by his will.

"I won't stop you," she said, smiling through her tears. "If you insist that this is what you must do, I won't interfere. Don't worry. I'm not angry. Perhaps I should do everything in my power to stop you from going tomorrow. And because I choose not to do that, perhaps it is really me who is driving you to an early death—"

"No, that's not true," Oguna said hastily. "Are you sure you're not angry with me?"

"I love you. Therefore I can trust you. I believe in what you choose to do. If you believe it is the right thing and go of your own free will, then I will not try to stop you."

That was what Lady Akaru had done. She had believed. She had not acted on the basis of what she thought would happen. She had simply believed in the one she loved. Her beauty came from her ability to trust completely, regardless of the outcome. *I too can believe,* Toko thought. *No matter what Oguna does. Even if he vanishes from this world.*

"I would ask of you one more thing." Oguna's voice was almost a whisper. "If I do not come back, I want you to live. Even without me by your side, I want you to live, for me, just as strongly as if I had lived."

Toko realized that Oguna must also be thinking of Lady Akaru. Akaru's death had been hard on Toko, but she knew that it must have been even harder for Oguna.

"All right," she said. "I promise."

Oguna stayed with Toko until just before dawn. Then he left alone for the hill to the north. Toko, who had dozed off just for a moment, dreamt of a white swan flying. When she woke, Oguna had already gone.

The swan had come to her for but a moment, only to fly away. And she had neither pursued him nor tried to stop him. She had let him follow his heart. Those with wings are drawn to the heavens. That was his nature, and she had accepted Oguna completely, including that. She had loved him on the basis of that acceptance, without trying to change him or make him her own. If his mother was also a part of Oguna, there was no point in vying with her. Toko chose instead to accept, to relinquish the fight entirely and with it, any attachment to either victory or defeat.

I will have no regrets. After all, Oguna came to me. I will not cry...

But the tears spilled from her eyes. She had accepted everything only to lose it all.

OGUNA CROSSED THE FIELD of withered grasses under the dark sky, flushing out a herd of deer. Watching them race away, he remembered what Nanatsuka had told him and realized that he had not yet hunted the deer of Hidakami. He had not been able to enjoy even one leisurely day tracking game. He wished that he could have done that before ... before all this. His men would have been so happy. If he had lit a fire on the spot and roasted the meat, just as he and Nanatsuka had once done, Toko would have enjoyed it too.

The lively image floated before his eyes like a mirage and evaporated just as quickly. All that was left was the broad, dark field and the frosty cold. Oguna patted the drooping head of his steed and urged it forward. He could not turn back. He could no longer turn his eyes away from the task he had set himself.

Oguna dismounted at the bottom of the hill and started up on foot. Dawn was beginning to tinge the sky. A crimson stain spread through the darkness as though pushing the night away and bringing the world into sharp relief. He reached the top of the hill just as the sun's first golden ray shone forth from the east. There was a clearing in the grove of trees at the top, and there, Sukune waited, his armor gleaming. Oguna saw no one else, although he suspected that Sukune's underlings must be nearby, most likely concealed behind the trees. Oguna strode straight across the clearing. He wore no armor and was clad only in the white that he always wore.

"You cannot know how long I have waited for this day," Sukune said.

It was the same soft voice that Oguna remembered, but now its very gentleness sounded cruel. "You won't have to chase me from one end of the country to the other anymore, will you? You must be very grateful," Oguna said. He realized that he had learned to speak with this quiet control from Sukune.

"I am the emperor's shadow. I go wherever the emperor wills. I do whatever he bids me. But it was not for him that I waited for this day, but for myself." A smile touched his almost feminine features. "You have no idea how I felt when you appeared in Mahoroba bearing the Sword, O son of Princess Momoso. Nor can you ever guess how I felt as I watched you use that Sword to kill Prince Oh-usu and usurp his place as crown prince."

"What are you trying to say? That you despise me?"

"You're not the legitimate heir to the emperor. You were abandoned and buried. Yet you used your power to rise to the height of glory as crown prince. You are the epitome of all that is most despicable."

"But it was through your scheming and that of the emperor that I was forced to kill my own brother, Oh-usu. My brother had become an obstacle, and now, so have I. That's all, isn't it?" Oguna could almost see his father behind Sukune and he barely managed to keep his composure. "You exploited my power and then when you found me in your way, you sent me as far away as possible. Yet still I did not turn my hand against you. Because I myself accepted that my very existence was unforgivable. Why do you hate me so much? Even though I've volunteered to remove myself from your sight, regardless of whether you hate me or not?"

"Because I am far more suited to be the crown prince than you. Didn't you think it strange that the power of the Sword should have transferred itself to me? I have the right to wield it. The blood of the God of Light runs in my veins too. I too am a son of the emperor. And I am the eldest, born before Oh-usu, born when the emperor himself was still the crown prince."

Oguna drew in a sharp breath and stared at Sukune. He supposed he should have guessed, but it had not even occurred to him. *My brother—Sukune is also my brother.*

"My mother was too lowly to become the emperor's wife. Thus, I became his servant and was promoted to the position of his shadow. No doubt the emperor has never guessed. I have served him like a loyal slave for years. I watched without protest as Oh-usu, my younger brother, rose to the position for which he was born. But then you appeared, bearing the Sword. It became clear that you had been concealed and trained as Oh-usu's shadow. From that moment, I began to think."

Oguna thought he could guess how Sukune felt. There were some things that only someone who had served as a shadow could understand—like how it felt to be invisible with no one giving you a moment's thought; to be relegated to the darkness that lay behind the glory of another. Oguna could empathize with Sukune, something he was sure that Prince Oh-usu had never been able to do. He also understood why Sukune had succeeded in transforming himself into Oguna so masterfully that he could absorb the power of the Sword. They were very similar. Much more so than Oguna and Oh-usu had ever been, despite the fact that they looked almost identical.

"I shall do to you what you did to Oh-usu. I will return to the capital as the commander who triumphantly vanquished the Emishi. The people will welcome me with great rejoicing as the crown prince. And I will at last stand in the light of day, as the son of the emperor."

Two conflicting emotions—anger and pity—warred in Oguna's heart. If he gave in to his anger, he could easily wrest the power of the Sword from Sukune's grasp and destroy him. Just as he had done to Oh-usu. But he had already been through that once. And in Sukune, he could sense the same misery he himself bore—the pain of brothers who would never be loved by their father. Oguna had at least become a prince, albeit from no desire of his own, but Sukune had been forced to watch from the wings. He had dwelled in the darkness much longer than Oguna.

"I cannot kill you," Oguna said. "If you wish to return in victory, then do so. Princedom was, after all, a station I acquired only through deception. I will give you the name of crown prince and all that goes with it. But I cannot let you take the power of the Sword. That I will destroy here. I will not let you wield it again."

"The Sword chose me. You have no claim to it."

"You're wrong," Oguna said bluntly. "Even now, the Sword seeks me, not you. Your intentions just happened to be in alignment with those of my mother."

"Let's find out who's right then." Sukune placed his hand on the hilt of the Sword.

I do this of my own accord, regardless of my mother's wishes, Oguna thought. In order to seal his mother's will inside him, he must offer himself freely. At that moment in time, Oguna felt no hate, not for anyone. That at least was a comfort.

Light, so brilliant it looked like the rising sun, burst up from the hill and pierced the sky.

5

THE MISUMARU lost its light. It did not glow even when Toko gave it to Sugaru. This could only mean one thing—its mission had been fulfilled. The power of the Sword had been extinguished from the world.

"Why did you let him go?" Sugaru demanded. "You knew full well what he would do." When Sugaru had seen the light flash from the hill at dawn, he had been so upset he was beside himself. If he had had the Misumaru, he would never have let Oguna go without doing something. "I knew Oguna wanted to die, but I never imagined that you would agree to that."

"There was nothing else I could do . . . " Toko said, feeling numb.

"There must have been something."

"No." Toko shook her head. "Not something *I* could do at any rate. No matter what I might have tried, it would only have tied him down. He chose to go of his own free will, you know."

"And you just accept that?" Sugaru asked. "Frankly, I'm just a little devastated. You know, I quite liked that kid. I would have found a way to keep him alive, no matter what he said."

Toko glared at him. "You've got some nerve, Sugaru. Do I just accept this? How can you even ask? Of course, I don't!" Tears welled rapidly in her eyes. "I wish that I could die too. But I can't, because I promised." The tears began to fall and she could not stop them. She tried not to hiccup but without success.

"I'm sorry," Sugaru said, suddenly repentant. "Why do you always have to act so tough?"

He's right. I always pretend that I'm all right when I'm not. Maybe she had wanted to put on a brave face for Oguna until the very end. She had promised him that she would live. But now, all she saw ahead was an empty horizon, stretching on forever like a withered field that would never bloom again. She stood here, alone, not knowing what to live for.

SUKUNE did not go back on his word. He released Takehiko and the other prisoners and they reached the camp on the evening of the following day. Just the sight of them, all at least able to walk despite their wounds, brought Toko some comfort in her grief. Takehiko told them that as soon as they had been freed, the enemy forces had struck camp and hastened away as if pursued. Having achieved their purpose, they would probably head straight for the capital.

"They told us that we could serve under their 'prince' if we wished, but there wasn't a single one among us who was willing. How could we ever serve an impostor? We gave our lives to only one man, and now that he's gone, there's no need for us to return to the capital." Takehiko turned to Toko. "I've had enough of serving under the emperor. The prince should never have had to throw his life away. I'm going to build a tomb in his honor and spend the rest of my days here."

"But surely you have a home," Toko said. "You must have some place to return to."

Takehiko shook his head. "The prince traded his life for all of ours. He will always be our commander, now and forever. Even if Mahoroba forgets who the true prince is, we never will. I speak for all of us. We'll remain here to guard his tomb and stand by him."

Oguna's men were true to him. They follow him even now that he's dead. If he should never have lived, then why was he so well loved? Toko turned her face away. Every thought hurt, a reminder of the gaping wound in her heart.

"Toko, what do you plan to do?" Sugaru asked her, his voice cautious. "We talked about this before, remember? I told you that if Oguna died you could come back to Izumo with me. That offer still stands, you know."

"Things are so different now," Toko said quietly. "Everything has changed. Everything . . . including me . . . " She hesitated but only for a moment. "I think that I will stay here too. I don't want to forget Oguna either. I'll make this my home and live in this land. I think that I can do that. After all, I won't be alone."

"You plan to stay here forever? To live with the dead?" Sugaru asked. "You make it so much harder for me to leave."

"Don't feel sorry for me." She paused for a while. "Give me a little more time," she said finally. "I'll come up with a better reason. It's just that I can't think at all right now. I can't quite believe Oguna's gone. It feels like he might turn up at any moment."

THEY CLIMBED THE HILL to the north but found nothing—no body or any other trace of Oguna. They would have to bury his armor and belongings instead. Takehiko and his men threw themselves into their work just the same, and within a few days they had made a large mound. Toko thought it was huge, but Takehiko considered it far too small.

"This is not a fitting mausoleum. I'm going to keep building."

Toko gazed up at the mound of earth. Though she could understand Takehiko's feelings, regardless of the mound's height, it was just a pile of dirt, a tomb that stirred in her no memories of Oguna—not a single gesture or facial expression, not even the sound of his breathing. No matter how long she might gaze at it, it would never convey to her his presence.

The day was overcast and the cold air bit her to the bone. Gray clouds hung low and not a ray of light peeped through. Desolate branches, bereft of leaves, pierced the sky. The company stood a while longer in that spot, numbed with cold, then finally turned away, their hearts as frigid as the scenery. Long before they had reached the camp, snow began to fall. At first the flakes were few, swirling lightly in the air, but soon they fell so thickly they blocked out the sky.

"It looks like it's going to stick," Sugaru said, gazing up at the snow. Sitting behind him on his horse, Toko looked up too. One flake, then another and another, drifting in the air. *Like white feathers.* Something familiar and dear suddenly filled her heart, a feeling so powerful it almost overwhelmed her. Silver snow dappled her vision, shutting out the broad expanse of plain that should stretch before her. For some reason, the snow falling from the heavens seemed much closer to Oguna than his burial mound. Toko drew in a deep breath and savored the sensation. The warm feeling that filled her contrasted starkly with the icy cold of the white crystals.

"What is it?" Sugaru must have noticed the change. At first, Toko could not put it into words. There was no rational explanation, but somehow she felt certain that Oguna was nearby, here, on this earth.

"I just can't help feeling that Oguna is back," she said finally. She could feel a hot flush suffuse her cheeks. Sugaru's look of concern deepened.

"Maybe you're coming down with a fever."

"No, I'm not," Toko protested. Still, it was odd, she thought. How could she feel any joy at a time like this? But that was exactly what filled her heart. As if Oguna were alive, standing just over there. Suddenly she was afraid, and her heart began to pound. "Do you really think it's strange?"

"You bet I do. You've been in the cold too long, that's the problem."

Sugaru told Takehiko that he was riding on ahead and urged his horse to a gallop. The wind whipped their faces and the snow flowed past. Even the flakes that caught in her face and hair seemed like part of a dream. She half believed this premonition, but at the same time, she was afraid to. *Who wouldn't be afraid,* she thought. How could she be sure that she hadn't lost her mind? That would be terrible, when she had promised Oguna that she would be strong. *But I feel him. Just like I used to feel him in my dreams. As if he's still here . . .*

The horse raced up the gentle slope, and the camp at the top came into view. Toko was afraid to open her eyes. She did not want to confront her own despair. But Sugaru, his hands on the reins, suddenly let out a cry of surprise. "Hey! I must be seeing things. Who is that standing there?"

There should have been no one at the fort. Everyone down to the last man had gone to the mound for the funeral. But there up ahead in the falling snow stood a figure dressed in white, as if he had come from the heavens with the snow.

Toko thought she would faint. Perhaps she had. For she had no memory of how she managed to leap to the ground and run to him. But when she came to her senses she was clinging to Oguna. To Oguna. And he was warm.

"Well, you don't appear to be a ghost," Sugaru said in astonishment. "You know, we've already built your tomb. It's so big you have to crane your neck to look up at it. So what're you doing here?"

"That's right," Toko said. "We thought you were dead." She was still so afraid that her voice trembled.

"I died. But I came back," Oguna said.

Toko shivered. "Does that mean you're going to leave again?"

"No, I'm staying. If it's all right with you. I'll stay by your side until my hair turns gray. But the prince Ousu is dead. Or rather, Sukune took him away. So I actually no longer exist."

"What about the Sword?"

"It's gone. I'm no longer its wielder. My mother took that part of me with her when she left. She's now at rest, forever."

"Really?"

Oguna smiled and tightened his arms around her. "That tomb won't go to waste. After all, the person I was up until now has really died. But the man who wanted to live, the man who wanted to be with you, has come back. Guided by the Misumaru."

"By the Misumaru?" Shocked, Toko pulled back from his embrace to stare at him. "But I didn't do anything. I decided to abide by your wishes and do nothing."

"The light of the Misumaru reached me," Oguna said gently. "When I lost my body in the radiance of the Sword, I felt myself separate from this world. My mother beckoned to me. But I saw the magatama, with its beautiful multicolored stones, shining far in the distance, just like that time you healed the burn on my arm. And that's when I realized that if I wanted to come back, I could."

Sugaru sucked in his breath. "But that's resurrection. So you've truly come back to life."

Toko felt as if she had been bewitched. That which she had not even attempted, that which should have been impossible, had actually been done. "But how could that be? There were only four magatama in the Misumaru. Lady Iwa told me that it was beyond our capacity to gather five stones."

"There were five stones shining," Oguna said casually. "You had four and I had one. Just like when you healed my wound."

Toko cast an astonished look at Sugaru and then turned back to Oguna, asking breathlessly, "What color was your magatama?"

"Light blue."

"Light blue?" Toko gaped at him.

Sugaru poked her. "What's this all about?"

"Ao, the light blue magatama, was the first stone to be lost. Long ago, in the time of the gods. It's part of the legend. You know, the Water Maiden and the Wind Child—" Toko broke off abruptly. The Water Maiden and the Wind Child were the founders of the emperor's line. The blood of the Water Maiden, who belonged to the people of Darkness, had merged with the blood of the last child of the God of Light through the magatama. If there were truth in the old legend, the emperor and his kin carried within them not only the power of the Sword, but also the power of the Water Maiden's stone. Toko reasoned that far and then looked at Oguna with renewed wonder.

"You used the Misumaru yourself then, didn't you?"

Oguna looked at her blankly. Clearly, he had not done so knowingly. But he must have. Though he himself was not a god, he had been able to wield the Sword because of his lineage with the God of Light. And though he was human, he also carried within him a magatama of the Goddess of Darkness. During his struggle to defy the Sword, he must have found the power of the stone inside him. The stone had resonated with Toko, and his will to live had brought him back to her. It was not Toko who had brought him back. He had opened the path himself in order to respond to what was in her heart.

"My mother intended to take me with her. But at the last moment, I relinquished the part of myself that wielded the Sword, the prince, to Sukune. That is what saved me. The man I am now is not the one my mother desired, the one who wielded the god's power. It's the other part of me." Oguna looked earnestly at Toko. "Sukune will return to the capital as the crown prince and heir, as the hero who bears the Sword. That person is no longer me. And I don't mind. It was only fair. Because it turned out that he too was my brother. Just like Oh-usu."

Toko smiled, finally reassured that even if she took a deep breath, Oguna would not disappear. "So only *my* Oguna came back to me, is that it? You're no longer a Takeru. Sukune took that with him as well."

"Takeru?"

"A hero destined to die young."

"Mmm." He hugged her silently for a while and then said, "When I walked toward the light of the Misumaru, I knew that Sukune did not have long to live. But in return he will gain a fame that will never fade. His name will live on as a legend long after he has died. I . . . will remain unknown and nameless."

"That's just fine by me," Toko said emphatically. "Now we can settle down and till the earth. We can live quietly and surely. And only we will know just how wonderful that really is."

Toko and Oguna had given up everything, even hope and desire, trusting in the outcome. And in the end, everything they had really wanted had been returned to them. This realization rendered Toko speechless. Fate had sent them off into the world only to free them from its violent grip—urging them to live.

They heard shouts behind them. The others had arrived, and realizing that it was Oguna, they came pounding up with a noise that made the earth shake.

"It's the prince!"

"The prince is standing! Am I dreaming?"

"He's alive!"

In their astonishment, they threw decorum to the wind and began grabbing at the young man to make sure he was real. Oguna was mobbed and Toko and Sugaru along with him. Some cried, others laughed, and all of them so loudly that it sounded like a great celebration. The weight of their grief lifted and dissolved into the sky. Even the snow, falling like a blizzard of flower petals, added joyful gaiety to their gathering.

THE DEEP LAYERS of snow finally melted and the wind changed. Grass shoots erupted from the moist black earth and the dormant meadows began to breathe with life. Storm clouds gathered and then dissipated, and each time the blue sky peeking through appeared softer and milder. Looking up at the clear sky, Toko saw a large white bird flap slowly across it. She stared at it, startled, but then smiled. Far from being an evil omen, this was a perfectly normal sight. Flocks of swans, recognizing the signs of spring, were preparing to migrate north. The season was changing.

Toko watched the bird fly away and then turned and waited for Sugaru. Like the swans, he too was preparing to leave. Sugaru had spent the winter with them in Hidakami, but now that the weather was changing he had decided to return to Izumo. Carrying a large bag over his shoulder, he grumbled, "It's so far when you have to walk. How I wish that I'd gone back when I could still use the Misumaru."

"You're perfectly welcome to stay here with us, you know," Toko said. Oguna, who was no longer the commander of a conquering army, and Takehiko and his men, who were no longer soldiers of Mahoroba, had thrown themselves into developing this land, where they planned to stay.

"It's not a bad place," Sugaru said. "But there're people waiting for me. I need to go back."

"To Kisako, right?" Toko said.

Sugaru grinned. "Not necessarily. There are countless women waiting for me."

"No, to Kisako. Admit it. How many times did you visit her?"

Only Midori hung around Sugaru's neck now. It no longer glowed, but he did not mind. It still retained its meaning as a charm for safe childbirth, an heirloom to be passed down through his family. Sugaru laughed. "Kisako's actually quite worth courting now. She's resumed her training as a shrine maiden. Next to Lady Toyoao, she's gathered quite a bit of respect in Izumo."

Sugaru liked a challenge, Toko knew. Still, she was impressed by Kisako's efforts to adjust to life in a new land. Just like Toko, she was no longer the girl she had been before. "The women of Mino don't change their minds easily once they've made a decision," she said. "I expect that Kisako will become a great shrine maiden."

"I'm betting she'll waver," Sugaru said happily. "If she still insists on becoming a shrine maiden even when I tell her that I've traveled the length and breadth of Toyoashihara but failed to find anyone to rival her, *then* she's the real thing."

"You're so evil," Toko laughed. Being Sugaru, he was bound to stir up trouble, but in the end, the odds were high that Midori would become Kisako's. *Kisako's in Izumo. I'm in Hidakami. The Tachibana of Mino have been lost, but we'll set down roots elsewhere. And our blood will carry on...*

Something suddenly occurred to her. "Sugaru, do you think the last magatama that was supposed to be in Hidakami still exists? The one we could never recover?"

"Maybe. Someday it might suddenly turn up."

"Lady Iwa told me that it was beyond our reach."

Sugaru ran a hand through his hair and said simply, "Then it will probably be kept for your children or your grandchildren or your descendants. You and Oguna's descendants, that is."

"Children?" Toko stammered.

"Honestly. What are you going to do if you blush even at the mention of children?"

At that moment Oguna approached leading Sugaru's steed. Takehiko and the others had also gathered to say farewell. They surrounded Sugaru, who said goodbye to each one in turn. When he finally mounted his horse, Oguna said, "You'll pass the capital on your way back to Izumo, won't you? Do you think that you'll see Nanatsuka again?"

"Yeah, I'd like to. We've got a lot to talk about," Sugaru said.

"If you do, could you give him a message from me? Tell him that I hunted deer in his homeland. And that, if possible, I'd like to hunt deer with him."

Toko's eyes shone. "Of course! It would be wonderful if Nanatsuka came back to Hidakami. I'm sure he'll find much of what he has lost right here. And I want to tell him about us. We've really gained so much here."

"Tell him from me that Hidakami is just as wonderful as he told me," Oguna added. "It's just like he said." He turned to Toko suddenly and said in a whisper, "But there're so many snakes. I just found out this spring. That's going to be a problem."

"Oguna," Toko exclaimed. "Don't tell me you're still afraid of snakes? Even though you've grown up?"

"I'll be sure to tell Nanatsuka," Sugaru promised. He laughed merrily.

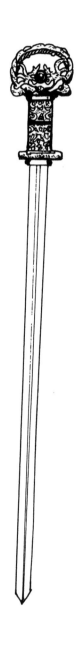

Afterword

Yамато Takeru is by far the most celebrated hero in Japanese mythology. Even in grade school when I first read a children's version of the *Kojiki,* an eighth century record of legends about the origins of Japan, I remember thinking that he was clearly special. In the latter half of the *Kojiki,* which deals with the world of men, no other character receives such passionate attention from the narrator, who extols his origins, achievements, and premature death.

The more carefully one reads this legend, however, the more confusing Yamato Takeru seems. Violent and unruly, he rips his elder brother to pieces with his bare hands, yet by merely donning women's clothing, he is transformed into an attractive maiden. He weeps before his aunt yet is so arrogant he taunts a god. Despite such contradictions, no Japanese can remain unmoved by the tragic tale of this warrior, forced to travel the land from one end to the other in obedience to a father who has rejected him and to die far from home, an ode to the beauty of his homeland on his lips. That Yamato Takeru is the archetypal Japanese hero is amply demonstrated by the enduring popularity of Minamoto Yoshitsune.

To me, Yamato Takeru's image as a tragic hero has always seemed too firmly rooted in the Japanese psyche to be used as subject matter for a novel. But then I discovered something quite unexpected. While reading the *Fudoki,* ancient records on Japan's provinces and the mythical origins of geographical names, for a seminar on ancient literature in my third year at university, I came across the legend of the naming of Hitachi. This story presents a completely different side to Yamato Takeru's character. (The following is an abridged translation by the author.)

441

> . . . *Long ago, the heavenly sovereign Yamato Takeru stayed on the hill of Kuwahara, and when he was given food, he made the people dig a new well. The water gushed forth, pure and sweet, and as it was very good to drink, he said, "Much water pools here." Thereafter this place was called Tamari [from the verb* tamaru *"to pool"].*
>
> . . . *According to the elders, when the heavenly sovereign Yamato Takeru was staying in the palace before Auka Hill, he set up a great cookhouse on the shore, and so this place was named Oh [from the word* oh *meaning "great"]. Furthermore, when his consort Princess Ototachibana came from Yamato, it was here that they met, and thus this place was named Auka no Mura [from the word* au *"to meet"].*
>
> . . . *According to the elders, when the heavenly sovereign Yamato Takeru bivouacked in this field, the locals told him that the fields were full of deer and the sea was full of abalone, so Yamato Takeru went to hunt in the fields and sent his consort, the Tachibana princess, to fish in the sea, and they vied to see who could catch the most. The heavenly sovereign caught nothing, but the princess's harvest was very great. The heavenly sovereign remarked to his companions, "I have tasted enough of the sea to grow tired of it," and so this village was named Akita no Mura [from the word* akita, *past tense of "to grow tired of"].*

These passages caused me to search through the *Kojiki* and the *Nihon Shoki,* an eighth century chronicle of legends concerning the rulers of Japan. Had Princess Ototachibana traveled through the eastern lands with Yamato Takeru before casting herself into the waters of the Hashirimizu Sea to appease the god? According to these records, however, she did not. Both place her death en route, before they reach the eastern lands, although the route taken differs slightly in each of these chronicles. The *Kojiki* and the *Nihon Shoki,* however, are not necessarily the only truth. The deeds of both Princess Ototachibana and Prince Yamato Takeru are, after all, a fusion of many different myths and legends.

At any rate, I found this story very amusing. Here we have the prince and his princess, usually painted in such a tragic light, competing to see who can catch the most food. And the princess wins. It suddenly dawned on me that I did not have to let Yamato Takeru's conventional image as a tragic hero limit me. Rather, I could let my imagination run free.

When I finished writing *Dragon Sword and Wind Child,* I had no plans to write another novel. In fact, it was a wonder that I finished the first one at all. I felt drained and had no idea whether the first book would even meet with a positive response or make it possible for me to write another. It was the success of the Super Kabuki theatrical performance of *Yamato Takeru* that inspired me to tackle this story. I finally realized that many people have used, and will doubtless continue to use, the Japanese archetypal hero Yamato Takeru in their creative work. Suddenly I felt an urgent need to write, anxious not to lose this opportunity.

Even so, *Mirror Sword and Shadow Prince* was a long time in the writing. Able to pour into it all the dreams I had nurtured over the years, I was much less reserved than with the first book. Toko is still the character that I found the easiest to develop.

— NORIKO OGIWARA
August 2005

HAIKASORU
THE FUTURE IS JAPANESE

MARDOCK SCRAMBLE BY TOW UBUKATA

Why me? It was to be the last thought a young prostitute, Rune-Balot, would ever have . . . as a human anyway. Taken in by a devious gambler named Shell, she became a slave to his cruel desires and would have been killed by his hand if not for the self-aware Universal Tool (and little yellow mouse) known as Oeufcoque. Now a cyborg, Balot is not only nigh-invulnerable, but has the ability to disrupt electrical systems of all sorts. But even these powers may not be enough for Balot to deal with Shell, who offloads his memories to remain above the law, the immense assassin Dimsdale-Boiled, or the neon-noir streets of Mardock City itself.

ROCKET GIRLS: THE LAST PLANET BY HOUSUKE NOJIRI

When the Rocket Girls accidentally splash down in the pond of Yukari Morita's old school, it looks as though their experiment is ruined. Luckily, the geeky Akane is there to save the day. Fitting the profile—she's intelligent, enthusiastic, and petite—Akane is soon recruited by the Solomon Space Association. Yukari and Akane are then given the biggest Rocket Girl mission yet: to do what NASA astronauts cannot and save a probe headed to the minor planet Pluto and the very edge of the solar system.

ALSO BY NORIKO OGIWARA—DRAGON SWORD AND WIND CHILD

The God of Light and the Goddess of Darkness have waged a ruthless war across the land of Toyoashihara for generations. But for fifteen-year-old Saya, the war is far away—until the day she discovers that she is the reincarnation of the Water Maiden and a princess of the Children of the Dark.

Raised to love the Light and detest the Dark, Saya must come to terms with her heritage even as the Light and Dark both seek to claim her, for she is the only mortal who can awaken the legendary Dragon Sword, the weapon destined to bring an end to the war. Can Saya make the choice between the Light and Dark, or is she doomed—like all the Water Maidens who came before her?

WWW.HAIKASORU.COM